A Tincture of Madness

A Novel

by

Terence Donnellan

A Tincture of Madness

First edition: 2012

Copyright © 2012 by Terence Donnellan

All characters are the product of the author's imagination and are not based on people living or dead.

Book design by Terence Donnellan. Cover image extracted from an iron pour photo of the sculptor Michael Dominick.

Printed in the U.S.A.

TerenceDonnellan.com

978-0-9856774-1-1

For the Donnellan Seven

There was never a genius without a tincture of madness.

~ Aristotle

People who dance are considered insane by those who can't hear the music.

~ George Carlin

Madness is terrific I can assure you, and not to be sniffed at; and in its lava I still find most of the things I write about. It shoots out of one everything shaped, final, not in mere driblets, as sanity does.

~ Virginia Woolf

Introduction
(Part One)

I only took a few steps outside the Hotel Du Cap's grounds when I knew it would be futile to try to go anywhere, as there were hundreds of bloodsucking paparazzi waiting for me like vultures after a slaughter. I went back inside, asked for the morning papers, and caught a glimpse of the catastrophe I had caused. Every tabloid, and almost every non-tabloid, had somehow found out about the previous evening's incident with President Napolitano and made me the cover story. *The International Herald Tribune* had "Blasket McManus out of control! Attacks celebrities and calls Italian President a c***sucker at star-studded dinner at Lake Como!" This wasn't true at all. My words were nasty and hurtful, but if they're going to quote me, they could at least quote me correctly. Even though my mind was simultaneously drowning in an ocean of liquor and flying through space like an astronaut because of the crystal methadrine, I won't make excuses for my behavior. It was wrong and I deeply regret what I said and did.

After returning to my suite chagrined and embarrassed, I went to the mini bar, opened a bottle of Jameson, and did another line of methadrine. At noon, I received a phone call from my agent, Kyle. He was beyond furious at me. Everything would have been forgotten and perhaps forgiven if I hadn't spoken to the press. Now, President Napolitano wanted my blood; he had also banned me from Italy for life. Kyle was speeding in a Porsche from Lake Como to Cannes. Before he hung up, he told me he needed to see me as soon as he arrived. I realized I had really screwed up this time. Nervous and scared, I decided to do a few more snorts of meth in the hope that this would straighten me out. A half hour later, an apoplectic Kyle called again saying President Napolitano called President Sarkozy of France telling him I better not be allowed on the festival jury. Kyle said I needed to resign immediately. I hung up without replying. There was no way I was going to resign. If I did I would never be able to live it down, and I would never again be invited to Cannes. This was my last opportunity to explain myself. But what could I say?

I thought about everything that happened in the last year, everything that had happened since I finished *The Promised Land* and began winning prizes and accolades. I thought about my sadly beautiful wife, Gwendolyn, and our precious baby, Bartholomew. I couldn't get their deaths, which were really murders, out of my mind. To combat my drunkenness I snorted another fat line of methadrine and suddenly I saw it all! I saw how everything fit together.

I realized giving an artist an award was the worst thing you could do to him or her. And the worst thing an artist could do was accept the award, because an award was nothing more than a bullseye, telling the media where to aim their poisoned darts. For a few hours, for a night, the creators of award ceremonies give the world the illusion they care deeply for art and artists, but when the award show ends, that's when their work begins. From that point forward, the award givers' and the media's job is to destroy those who have just won the awards. Your best friend at the award ceremony hires the hit-man the following morning.

As I looked back on the scores of artists who had been destroyed by fortune and fame, and the jealousy of others, none stood out more than Orson Welles whose first film, *Citizen Kane*, was the greatest of its day, and still is the greatest film ever made. In the eyes of the untalented and jealous, he had too much genius for one man. Anyone who knows his long and disruptive history knows he was the only man in the last century who could conceivably be compared with Michelangelo or Leonardo da Vinci as a creative genius. He did not paint or sculpt like they did, because those were the mediums of the Middle Ages. Orson used the tools of his time: theater and radio, and then film. He showed the world the greatness of film, the possibility of what film could do and be, and powerful producers destroyed him for this.

I knew what I had to do. I called room service and had my butler bring me up pens and paper. I also had him bring up two more bottles of wine. I would resign but not before giving an explanatory speech. I knew I had to say something that would make sense of all that had happened. I knew it was my duty to warn the other award winners, and those who would soon find themselves in the position I was in. My mistake was not just accepting the award for the Golden Palm, and the various other awards. My mistake was believing I needed the confirmation awards are supposed to bring. Before the awards I had everything I had always wanted—I had Gwendolyn and our beautiful baby boy, Bartholomew. They brought me more happiness than any man had a right to. Once I became famous the media wanted to destroy me. My vanity for acceptance and public recognition killed Gwendolyn and Bartholomew. My stupidity pained me more than I could endure.

When the butler came with my notebook, pens and wine, I tipped him lavishly. After closing the door, I took a good long guzzle directly from the bottle, laid out a thick line of methadrine to steel me for the evening's ceremony, and began to write my speech. My room phone rang a number of times, but I refused to answer it.

A few moments after the phone stopped ringing, I heard a discreet knock on the door. When I peeked through the eyehole, I saw my butler dressed in the required formal uniform of black jacket and pants, crisp white shirt and black bow tie. I opened the door a crack. The butler apologized for intruding and informed me President Sarkozy had phoned several times with the desire of speaking with me. I told him if Sarkozy wanted to talk with me, I would be at the Palais des Festival at 7 PM for the screening of Emir Kusterica's film. I closed the door and finished writing the most important speech of my life.

At 6 PM, I showered, put on my tuxedo, and did another line of methadrine. At 6:30, I left my hotel and had my driver drive me to the Croisette so I could walk up the red stairs of the Palais des Festival. At 6:50, I did one more quick snort and stepped out of my limousine. Paparazzi were everywhere. Every step I took was met with the flash of hundreds of camera light bulbs.

At the top of the red stairs were the other jury members— Theodoros Angelopoulos, Claire Denis, Peter Greenaway, Paul Auster, Sophie Marceau, Gong Li, Julian Schnabel, Aki Kaurismaki, Catherine Keener, Alegandro Gonzalez Inarritu, Harvey Keitel, and next to them, President Sarkozy. After I said hello to my peers, President Sarkozy asked to speak to me privately. We stepped a few feet away from the others, but still in full view of the hundreds, maybe thousands, of press people. President Sarkozy said he could not allow me to be part of the jury after what I had done at Lake Como. He apologized but said he didn't want to make this an international issue and cause problems with Italy. I looked at him and tried to say something, but words would not come. I had been up for three days straight, drinking, and snorting methadrine, and my body had finally run out of energy. President Sarkozy bent toward me trying to hear my words. Unable to utter a single syllable, an uncontrollable force seized me! I opened my mouth and chomped down on Sarkozy's ear. The president shrieked and pulled away from me. When he did, a piece of his ear was ripped from his head. I couldn't believe his ear was in my mouth. I spat out his bloodied flesh on the red carpet as he continued his high-pitch ululations, blood dripping down his neck. Security men tackled me to the floor and shackled my wrists behind my back with metal handcuffs. Even though my arms were held and my wrists bound, I tried kicking and even biting, but there were five officers holding me. Before I knew it, I was in a police van. All the while flashbulbs were popping and the crowd was stunned to silence. I was taken to the Cannes jail and put into a dank and cold solitary cell. Moments later, four big brutal looking guards came in and held me down. A doctor stepped in the cell, had them turn me over, pulled my pants down and stuck a big needle full of tranquilizing drugs into the flesh of my skinny white ass.

Kyle was my first visitor. After telling me I slept like a coma victim for twenty-six hours, he introduced me to a French diplomat and the United States Ambassador to France. I was told the crime of attacking the President of France was punishable by a minimum of twenty years in prison. Beyond that, it was an embarrassment to Cannes, the film community, and most of all to France. Since the torn piece of ear was surgically reattached, and since President Sarkozy didn't want to embitter the film world, jeopardize relations with filmmakers or the United States, they said I would be returned to America, if I signed the document they placed in front of me. It was a long and detailed twenty-seven page legal paper. Without reading it, I scribbled my name in the blank space above a line with my name typed neatly below it. Within hours, I was on my way back home.

Or so I thought.

The legal document I endorsed banned me from France for life and gave the United States government legal authority over me. The document allowed the U.S. government to commit me to Bellevue Psychiatric Ward for indefinite evaluation. If I had known, I would have never put pen to paper.

I do not know how long I have been imprisoned in this beige-walled mental asylum, a year? Two years? Five? There are scores of white-smock-wearing doctors here. The psychiatrist who has been treating me forces me to take Thorazine and other mind-numbing drugs every morning. He wants me to say I never made *The Promised Land.* He says, it's all in my mind. He says, I have a long history of mental illness and have never made any films. He also says I am a danger to society. He is lying! They are simply trying to silence me! The psychiatrist has told me if I do not admit I am not a filmmaker he will be forced to do what hasn't been done in thirty or forty years: he will give me a lobotomy.

If you are able to read this manuscript, it is because of the kindness of Cassandra, my devoted night nurse, who I told my story to, and who urged me to write it down. She allowed me to use her laptop computer late at night when no one else was around. Cassandra told me she would smuggle the manuscript out to an understanding publisher because she believes in me. She knows I am telling the truth.

Let me give you the facts, not as the worthless press has reported them, but as they actually happened. Subtracting the lost years since I've been in here, on a February 2nd (I remember the exact date as it was a day I always celebrate, James Joyce's birthday), I was invited to a

4

private film screening at the Director's Guild on Fifty-Seventh Street in Manhattan. The film we saw was a hideous piece of drivel with a tremendous amount of explosions, car chases, men shooting all varieties of firearms, and women dressed almost exclusively in bikinis. (It was a Jerry Bruckheimer production, which should tell you enough.) When the lights came up we rose from our seats and were forced into the usual small talk where complimenting the director, producers, and actors was obligatory. Behind the director's back, three friends and I spoke about how awful the film was, and what a wretched state the film industry was in. I should mention that since my colleagues and I are all older than fifty—I was at the time fifty-six—and not of the digital generation, we are not the type of directors currently hot or highly regarded in Hollywood.

My colleagues and I were there not because we were eager to see the film. We were there because we needed to say hello to the various purse holders of our industry. I have never lived in Los Angeles and travel as infrequently as possible to that smog-filled and culturally-eviscerated land. Consequently, when studio heads and powerful producers come to New York it is often necessary to mingle, smile, and shake hands when I would prefer to be anywhere else.

After greeting and saying hello to a number of industry people, the other three directors and I went to a bar to commiserate about our plights. Earlier that day, I had received news from Kyle that my last hope of receiving financing for the project that I had spent the last three years trying to cobble together had fallen through. That was the reason for my attendance—I had anticipated pitching my movie to…well, to anyone I thought would fund it. That didn't happen. The combination of not being able to get my project set up through my agent, and hearing a twenty-six-year-old hack director lauded got to me, and I just couldn't bring myself to beg people I did not respect for funding.

After four hours of drinking Jameson Irish whiskey at Druids in Hell's Kitchen, I bid my companions adieu and weaved my way down Tenth Avenue back to my apartment in the Piano Factory on Forty-Sixth Street, a few blocks from the bar. My wife, the artist Gwendolyn Sangeeny, wasn't home; she was attending Art Basel/Miami Beach, an annual gathering of art dealers, art collectors, con men, transvestites, pickpockets, thieves, bored socialites, and the occasional artist. Although I was extremely drunk, I couldn't fall asleep and decided to take some sleeping pills. Perhaps it was a mistake mixing sleeping pills with heavy alcohol intake, but I wasn't a neophyte in this. I have always had trouble sleeping. I have often drunk to excess, and I have often taken sleeping pills after a night of drinking. Apparently, this time I overdid the intake. The police report, and subsequent media accounts, say I swallowed an entire bottle of Seconals. That is false.

Not that I remember the events precisely. What I recall and what I recount is based on a spotty memory and details Gwendolyn supplied. According to her, she returned home earlier than expected from her trip to Miami and found me passed out on the floor of the bathroom. My mouth was open and a foul pool of yellowish-brown regurgitation had stained the white tiles. Gwendolyn immediately dialed 911. Though she tried to keep the matter hushed up, one of the doctors or nurses at St. Luke's-Roosevelt Hospital let the press know the film director Blasket McManus had been admitted for an overdose. The *New York Post* got a hold of this and, in order to sell more newspapers, termed it a suicide attempt. Other leeching tabloids followed suit. Apparently, when the attending physician asked my wife how many pills I had taken, Gwendolyn, wanting to be on the safe side, overestimated and told him the full bottle of fifty pills. Gwendolyn had refilled my prescription at Esco pharmacy on Ninth Avenue before leaving on her trip, so she knew how many pills were in the bottle. There may have been fifty pills when she gave it to me, but that doesn't necessarily mean that I swallowed the entire bottle. I think, in my inebriated state, I spilled most of the pills into the toilet. Of course, I can't be sure. But I *am* sure that I would never intentionally try to kill myself. I do not wish, however, to debate about these minor details. I'll just say that after two days in the hospital—where, after a day of recovery, I was forced to meet with a snot-nosed, young psychiatrist and answer a battery of questions to determine whether, in his opinion, I was still suicidal or not—I was allowed to sign myself out and return home. After a day there, with the phone ringing relentlessly, Gwendolyn suggested we leave the city to avoid prying reporters and other fabricating press people. Knowing the Vineyard was rather empty in February, we went to our place up in West Tisbury.

For the first few days, I was rather depressed and though I didn't drink any Jameson, much against Gwendolyn's wishes, I drank copious amounts of red wine. When my drinking at home was too much for my young, beautiful, third wife, (she was thirty-one at the time), I called a taxi and had the driver take me into Oak Bluffs. At the Lampost on Circuit Avenue, I spent a number of evenings sitting on a stool, drinking beer, talking to one of the barmaids and to some of the locals I had gotten to know over the years.

Unfortunately, this joyous state couldn't last forever. Eventually, I had to eliminate alcohol intake from my daily activities and get back to work. Gwendolyn wasn't the type of woman who was going to dote on me. She was serious about her painting and spent her time productively. Shortly after we were married, I built her a crude twenty by fifteen foot studio a short distance from the main house. With Gwendolyn busy attacking canvases, I usually spent the early part of the day walking in the woods that surround our house gathering kindling for our fireplace. Gwendolyn's studio was built as a summer studio, so it is unheated. Since we were there in the chilliest winter month, she purchased a kerosene space heater and used it to warm the place, but it was still drafty and cold. Nonetheless, every morning by nine or perhaps ten she was out there working. Sometimes it was so frigid she wore two or three pairs of wool pants, two or three sweaters, fingerless gloves and a thick Russian hat. After a short lunch around one, she would return to the studio and work until seven or eight o'clock at night. With her working so diligently, I felt that I should be doing more than brooding during the days and using liquor to self-medicate during the evenings.

The urge to write a new screenplay had returned, but as I sat in front of the computer, gazing at the blank Word document, nothing came. Instead of writing, I surfed the internet, or answered the numerous e-mails sent from various colleagues and friends. One friend asked what I thought of the *Entertainment Weekly* article written on my alleged suicide attempt. When I got a copy and read it, I realized the article was little more than an obituary. It said all my better films were at least a dozen years old, or older, and even the best among them seemed dated. The gist was that I had had a good run, and if I had died it wouldn't have been a great loss to the film world. Perhaps true. I was, however, not quite ready to write myself off.

It would be easy to say my near-death experience and my age forced me to think of death, but that's not accurate. I have thought about death my entire adult life, so contemplating my ultimate demise wasn't new. What I did think about, and this may sound egotistical, was my legacy. I didn't want to admit it but the *Entertainment Weekly* article stung. After all the toil and sweat I had put into my films, I amounted to little more than a footnote in the history of cinema. As a young man, I had grand ambitions of wanting to, if not change the world through film, at least give a good kick in the teeth. It seemed to me I had failed on all accounts.

In ruminating upon my legacy, I realized that after nine low-budget independent films, one more indie would change nothing. Financially, I had few alternatives. After being stymied for days, I decided to write the script I wanted to write and disregarded all budgetary concerns. After three labor-intensive winter months, I had a tremendously moving and important screenplay entitled *The Promised Land*. There was only one problem: it was five hundred and seventeen pages long. Nonetheless, I sent the screenplay to Kyle's office.

I didn't expect him to phone me the next day, or even three days later, but I did expect to hear something within a week or ten days. Finally, on the third week, Kyle called. He said he liked the script and felt it was extremely relevant, but thought it was financially unfeasible due to its length. (The average screenplay is between ninety and one hundred twenty double-spaced pages, with a page equaling a minute of screen time. Therefore, my film would run in excess of eight hours.) Kyle wanted to give me some positive news, so he told me he liked the script enough to send it to some producers we both knew. At that point, he wouldn't tell me which producers because he didn't want me to call them.

To my great embarrassment, the script became one of the bigger jokes going around Hollywood. At the Ivy, and elsewhere, instead of saying "Hello" at lunch, it was now customary to say "Have you read Blasket's script?" whereupon both parties would laugh. One of the wittier retorts making the rounds was, "No, but it fell on my big toe and I had to be rushed to the hospital."

Regarding the length, I wasn't completely crazy. Werner Fassbinder's great film *Berlin Alexanderplatz* is fifteen and a half hours long. Bela Tarr's film *Satantango* is seven hours. Ingmar Bergman's *Fanny and Alexander* is four. Dennis Potter's *The Singing Detective* is six. Bernardo Bertolucci's uncut version of *1900* is also six hours. Erich von Stroheim's original version of *Greed* is ten hours long.

Many of the better producers in Hollywood, in my opinion at least, still believe cinema is capable of producing art, not just box-office bonanzas. Some of these producers hate what has become of the film industry as much as I and so, after weeks of being the butt of jokes, one of them said, "This script is so unmakeable we have to make it."

Steven Soderbergh, who uttered the words that changed my life, has tasted both success and failure. After winning the Grand Prize at Cannes in 1989 for *Sex, Lies, and Videotape*, Soderberg's next four films were critical and commercial failures, and it looked like the boy wonder was all washed up. During this period, a critic writing for the *Los Angeles Times* asked Soderbergh what he was going to do now that his film career was over. Steven said that the box-office failures didn't bother him too much, or they only bothered him in that he disappointed his investors. He went on to say many of the directors whom he admired most never were great box-office successes. If he was lucky, he said, he might be able to have a career like Blasket McManus. He went on to say that as a teenager and young man, he had watched all of my films and his desire had always been to do what I had done: make small, but interesting and relevant films outside the studio system.

After his early stumbles, Soderbergh has gotten himself back on track, and has become one of Hollywood's most influential and powerful players, as a writer, director, and producer. Kyle knew of Steven's admiration for me, so he was one of the producers who received a copy of my screenplay. After reading it, Steven was quite excited, but like everyone else, he felt it would never be made because of the length. Nonetheless, something inside him wouldn't let him pass on it. Wanting to get the opinion of someone he trusted, he had a copy of the script sent to his actor friend, George, who had heard the rumors and jokes about *The Promised Land* and was eager to see what all the fuss was about. After reading, his opinion was the same as countless others: it was good, in a dark and twisted way, but it would never be green lit.

In theory, that should have been the end of it, but Steven reread it, and when he finished he called George again and told him, "One way or another, I'm gonna get this made, and I think you'd be perfect for the Connor Gazelle role." George replied, "If you can get it financed, I'm in."

That was all Steven needed. After getting my number on the Vineyard from Kyle, he called and said me he was interested in producing my movie, but an eight-hour film was impossible; a five-hour film he could probably produce. We spent about a week meeting and talking on the Vineyard before he had to return to L.A. Over the next six weeks, I e-mailed him pages, he reviewed them, e-mailed them back, and we talked on the phone. On the seventh week, we had a workable script.

As I am eager to get to the film, I won't waste time recounting the casting of every role, or discuss how the financing was set up. I'll only say that I was extremely grateful we were able to get the talented cast and crew we got, and I was exceptionally pleased with all of their performances. *The Promised Land* did, after all, go on to win seven Academy Awards and top honor at the Cannes Film Festival.

Winning the Golden Palm at Cannes was one of the crowning achievements of my career. Being invited back the following year to head the jury should have been the diamond on the diadem. Unfortunately, it was a disaster. As inexcusable as my actions were, I do not believe they were sufficient reason to ban me for life from two of the most beautiful and glorious countries in the history of the world, Italy and France. And I certainly do not believe I should be locked away in this insane asylum.

It is my hope that by writing a novelization of the film, and by showing how seminal events in my life shaped me into being a filmmaker and artist, that the Italian, French, and United States governments will come to understand that I was simply a victim of my own passionate and artistic temperament, that I deserve a pardon, and should be set free. Artists, who by striving to create great works of art, court almost certain failure (and more often than not end up as alcoholics, or drug addicts, or suicides, or homeless, or in the madhouse, or some combination of these) and cannot be expected to display the same dispassionate behavior as those who work traditional jobs, endeavor to raise respectable children, and contribute weekly to retirement accounts. If countries and governments wish to celebrate artists' creations they must be willing to put up with a certain amount of aberrant behavior—as long as that behavior does not cause permanent damage or death. Because it is this behavior, this willingness to go where others dare not go, to risk what others dare not risk, that is the fuel that produces the art. Without it there is no art, there is only shopping and television.

Introduction
(Part Two)

It has occurred to me that there may be a few readers who do not know who I am. Therefore, before I get to the film, I think I should say a little more about my past. I would also like to say a few words about Gwendolyn, the love of my life, and the woman to whom I dedicated *The Promised Land.*

I met Gwendolyn on Martha's Vineyard where she summered while in college and after. The first time I saw her was at the Lampost. I was down at the far end of the bar, talking with some of the year-rounders who liked to be away from the center of the action. She came in with friends, sexy young women full of energy and laughter. Over time, I saw her more and more and I started buying her beers, and an occasional shot. That's how I got women to talk to me, by buying them beers. At my age, I probably should have been in a classy restaurant in Edgartown: me and my wife and another couple. We'd talk about our kids, mortgages, health care, and the stock market. But I didn't want to talk about any of those things, least of all my kids. I was ashamed of what a lousy father I was, and I hated to think about how I screwed up my relationship with them, so it was a subject I avoided.

Gwendolyn worked up-island as a gardener, a cook, and all-around handywoman for a wealthy couple who lived off Tea Lane in Chilmark. She lived in Oak Bluffs in a house up by the graveyard on Pacific Street. Because there were ten people who lived there—a mix of young men and young women—there were parties almost every night. With the additional friends who stopped by to talk, drink, smoke dope, and listen to music, sometimes it got too much for her, so Gwendolyn came to see me. I was the old guy with the salt and pepper beard—that's how her friends referred to me. At that time, she was twenty-four and I was forty-nine. We'd sit and talk, and share a bottle of wine or two as we discussed painting, which is what she studied in school.

It didn't take too long for our talks to move beyond art to more personal areas. Gwendolyn told me about all the guys who were chasing her. She'd laugh and tell me what lines they'd used on her and the various ways they had tried to impress her. But she wasn't a tease, she'd let some of the guys catch her, and it wasn't always the best looking ones. Pretty boys bored her. She wanted ones who had scars or maybe a crooked tooth. In her freshman year, she had fallen in love with Tom Waits' music and tried to exist in the milieu he created. She searched for a guy who she felt could be the doomed hero from his song *Romeo is Bleeding*. When she had found him, she kept him for three years. When he started talking about marriage and settling down, she dumped him. On the Vineyard, she had a few relationships, but none of them lasted long. She wanted to be free again and have fun.

Gwendolyn had countless questions for me. She wanted to know about my first wife and other women in my life. She wanted to know what it was like living in New York City all those years ago. Like a lot of college kids, she read about New York in the big old, bad old days of the late sixties and early seventies, and I guess she liked hearing about it firsthand. She also wanted to know what it was like for me growing up as a kid and how I got into making movies. She was convinced that everyone who had become famous had a certain amount of luck, but more importantly, she felt that some event had driven them to want to succeed so badly that nothing would stop them. She wanted to know what event had driven me. I hadn't really thought about this. When I did, I realized she was right. I told Gwendolyn it was my desire to kill a man that had changed everything for me.

Even though the event happened decades ago, I can still remember the man and the night as clearly as the evening it actually happened. It was on the Upper East Side of Manhattan, outside of Maxwell Plum, which at the time was a well-known and fashionably hip bar. I was standing in a darkened doorway, a few doors down the block. In my hand was a ten-pound metal barbell, the type used to hold round metal weights on each side. The weights had been taken off. The man was about forty years old. What hair he had left was light brown and receding. He wore a dark blazer and an open-neck, button-down yellow shirt. His gait was unsteady, as I knew it would be, as I was waiting for a drunk, a well-dressed and wealthy drunk. Clearly intoxicated, and seemingly happy, he was muddling his way through Petula Clark's *Downtown*, "*When you're alone and life is making you lonely, you can always go downtown…*" I held the bar so tightly that my hand hurt. I wanted to hit this well-dressed stranger with such force that I split his head open. This was my Raskolnikov moment. I wanted him to look me in the eyes. I wanted him to know what I was going to do, not just take his money but take his life. When he was about three feet from me, I jumped out from the shadows and raised the bar as high above my head as I could. I took two steps toward him and swung the bar with all the strength I had...

*   *   *

Both my parents were alcoholics. They owned a rundown bar not far from where we lived in Brooklyn. My father bartended and my mother cooked the hamburgers and the rest of the limited menu. Because they spent most of their off-hours there, they were rarely home. My brother, Declan, is nine years older than I. As a kid, six seven eight years old, he was supposed to watch over me. But at seventeen, eighteen, nineteen, the last thing Declan wanted to do was be a babysitter. He often took off to hang out with his friends or girlfriend. He told me if Mom and Dad asked, I was to tell them he was at home with me. When he was eighteen, Declan left home for good, so I ended up raising myself.

I hated to be alone in the dark and lonely house, so I went down to my parents' bar. The only time I was able to speak with them was the hours between when I got out of school, around 3 PM, and before the men and the occasional woman came in after work, around 5 PM. They made me anything I wanted to eat. When the patrons came in they had to be attended to, and I was left alone at one of the tables. I knew the regulars and I often heard them say "Is Blasket all right by himself over there in the corner?" My mother always answered, "He's fine. Don't worry about him." Many nights I fell asleep at the corner table, and was discovered by my parents after everyone had left, and my parents were ready to go home. After a few years of this, I stopped going to the bar with any consistency. My parents told me to study and get to bed early. I studied, but my studies were easy, and I never went to bed early. As soon as I finished my homework, I went to one of the local movie theaters. Often I saw the same double-feature day after day because it was better to sit by myself in the dark watching the figures on the screen than being home alone.

One afternoon when I was nine, I came home from school and was startled to hear noises coming from my bedroom. There was never anyone home so I went up to investigate. I opened the door and found a naked man on top of my naked mother. My mother was moaning and her legs were wrapped around his waist. I screamed at the top of my lungs. My mother yelled at me to get out of the room. A few moments later, she came out of the bedroom dressed. She made me promise not to tell my father. "If you do," she said, "your father will throw us both out on the street." I thought that my mother would immediately end the affair. She didn't. My mother and the man, Mr. Puffington, continued to see each other for a few more years, until he just stopped showing up at the bar. My mother screwed him once or twice a week in our house, in my bed. I thought she had sex in my bed so my father wouldn't notice the sheets or messy bed. She didn't seem to care what I thought about it.

After first discovering my mother in my bed, whenever I came home from school, I entered the house quietly. If there were sounds coming from my bedroom, I took the subway into the city. I was probably about ten years old when I started going into Manhattan by myself. Almost always I went to the movies. I had money from my mother and Mr. Puffington. I hated to take their bribes, but I needed the money for the movies and for the candy I used to buy. Often when I went down to the bar, I saw Mr. Puffington talking to my father about sports teams or boxers. On the surface, it appeared they were the best friends. My hatred was exacerbated because Mr. Puffington always called me "sport." "Hey sport, how's school?" On the days he was screwing my mother, when he knew I knew what he had done, he winked and gave me a dollar or two. "Here, Sport, buy yourself some candy." My mother also gave me money as a way to buy my silence. I couldn't even tell my older brother, who was rarely home anyway. I felt if I told him somehow my father would find out and my mother's warning of being thrown out on the street would come true.

During the week, I never had a babysitter as my mother usually came home by eleven or maybe midnight. On the weekends, however, my parents didn't return until after three or four in the morning, so I had a babysitter—a daughter of one of the bar regulars. Siobhan was eighteen, cute and fun with strawberry blonde hair and baby fat still on her rosy cheeks. We played board games or she read me stories. Well, we started out by her reading me stories, by the time I was twelve I had read more books than she had, so she had me read her stories.

One Saturday when I was about to turn thirteen, Siobhan told me to get into bed as she had a birthday surprise for me. I went upstairs, put on my pajamas and got under the covers. She came up smelling of whiskey. My parents had plenty of booze around the house and often she would treat herself to it. I felt this was quite natural and normal. For my parents, Irish whiskey was the cure-all for every ailment. From as young as I can remember my father or mother would give me a shot of whiskey if I scraped my knee or if I had a cough or if I had a tummy ache or a cold. When I got a little older, seven or eight, if I couldn't fall asleep at night, my father would give me half a glass of Jameson or Powers. Alcohol was as present in my house as milk or orange juice was in most others' houses. My mother always started the day with a vodka and orange juice. My father started his day with Schlitz beer. He never failed to remind me, "Schlitz is a good morning beer because it's light and goes well with toast, but Guinness is a good afternoon or evening beer because it's fuller and better than most meals."

Siobhan stood over my bed and said, "I'm going to make you feel better than you've ever felt before." Siobhan bent and gave me a kiss and pulled down my blankets. Back then, I only had the vaguest

14

understanding of sex. Consequently, I was quite embarrassed when Siobhan pulled down my underwear and laughed when she saw my thin, erect pecker, saying "Oh, how cute, you barely have any hair." Her mouth began to work on me before she got up in the bed. Before she took me in her mouth again, she said, "I want you to pull my ears." So, as she sucked me off, I held onto her earlobes and pulled. The better it felt, the harder and quicker I pulled. It was only a minute or two before I "felt better than I'd ever felt before." I felt better than ever five times that night.

Unfortunately, right after Siobhan's birthday present, I was told by my father that a thirteen-year-old boy didn't need a babysitter. This was the worst news of my young life. I couldn't stop thinking about pulling her ears and pulling other girls' ears. When I returned to school on Monday, I was convinced I could tell if a girl was a virgin or not by the size of her earlobes. The bigger the earlobe, the more sex she had had. This also made me think about my mother's ears. I wondered if Mr. Puffington was pulling my mother's ears. I thought they would get bigger and bigger and my father would know what was going on, and we would be thrown out on the street. Of course, her ears didn't grow and my father never grew wiser—or at least he pretended not to. Maybe he just didn't care.

When I was thirteen, I started washing dishes one or two nights a week at the bar. When I was fourteen, my father asked me to walk home one of the drunken bar patrons, a woman named Beatrice. Beatrice was at least thirty, and not particularly pretty because she was missing one of her front teeth. She lost the tooth by passing out at my parents' previous New Year's Eve party. She was, like all the other patrons, completely drunk and fell face first toward one of the wooden tables. He mouth hit first. In the process she lost her tooth, loosened a few others, and was a bloody mess. I was in the back washing dishes and had to come out with ice wrapped in a clean white dishtowel to put on her mouth.

A few weeks later, she was drunk again and came into the bar's kitchen to personally thank me for helping her out. My father came in and asked me to walk her home because he didn't want her passing out again and hurting herself.

When we started home, Beatrice seemed to sober up, and said, "Let's go to your house." Like a lot of my father's customers, she had been at our house because, after closing time, my parents often invited friends and bar patrons back to our house to continue their drinking. This was to avoid problems with the law and to not jeopardize their liquor license. When we got inside she pulled me into my bedroom and stripped off her clothes. She lay on the bed, spread her legs wide and

15

told me what to do. When I was inside her I leaned down and started pulling on her ears. She slapped my hands away and asked me what I was doing. I thought I was showing her how sophisticated and experienced I was; instead I came across as some nutjob. When we were done, I was afraid she was going to tell my father what we did, so when I was at the bar I pretended I didn't see her. I wouldn't even look in her direction.

But Beatrice was a determined woman. After being ignored for a few weeks, she came into the kitchen again drunk and asked me to walk her home. I told her to walk herself home, but my father made me take her. We went back to my house and did it again. Soon after this, my father started asking me to walk other drunken women home. This always happened as soon as I finished my shift as a dishwasher. My father gave me a dollar or two and pointed to the woman who needed to be walked home. Somehow, we always ended up in my bed.

Being asked to "walk" women home continued for five or six more months, until Beatrice said to me, "You know, we don't have to go through your father to do this. This could be just between us." I didn't quite understand what she was referring to at first before it hit me: my father was pimping me out to his bar patrons. Even though this was what my mind told me, I still couldn't believe it. I didn't think he knew I was even having sex. Before I jumped to conclusions, I asked Beatrice what my father was charging these days. She told me at first he wanted fifteen dollars, but she had bargained him down to ten—a decent amount of money back then. As soon as we were done and Beatrice left, I got dressed and ran down to the bar.

My father, as usual, was bending over the bar talking to one of his customers. My father was a skinny six-foot-five, with a shock of red hair that had traces of gray around the edges. He was so tall that constantly leaning over the bar had bent him like a palm tree arching toward the sun. I went behind the bar. My father turned to me. I called him a "fucking pimp" and I swung at him. He caught my hand and, as the patrons were watching, twisted it and marched me into the kitchen so that we were alone. He threw me against the counter. I fell to the ground and he booted me as hard as he could in my side. The wind was knocked out of me and my ribs felt like they were broken. My mother screamed. But before she could ask what was going on my father said, "This is the goddamn thanks I get for getting you laid?" That was it. He walked back to the bar and resumed his conversation. My mother didn't say a word, so I suspected she knew what was going on as well.

When they came home that night, I waited until I knew they were asleep. When they were, I found my father's key to the bar and went back. One at a time, I started smashing liquor bottles against the walls, against the chairs, and against the tables. I had probably smashed thirty or forty bottles by the time the police showed up. My parents had to come pick me up at the police station, but charges were never filed against me. After that, we really never talked much, not that we talked much in the first place. My parents were really just strangers who allowed me to live in their house.

When they died, (my father died first and my mother died seven months later) I was only seventeen. My father was fifty-nine and my mother was forty-eight, but they both had cirrhosis of the liver. When we got around to reading the will at my father's lawyer's office, which wasn't until after my mother died, I just naturally assumed that the bar would be left to Declan and me. But that's not how it turned out. Neither of my parents kept the best of books and the bar's financial records were in complete disarray. On top of this, my father's will hadn't been updated since I was thirteen years old. As I was a minor at the time, everything was left to Declan, and I was to be under his care. I tried to explain to Declan and the lawyer that my father would have changed the will if he had thought about it, and that since I was going to be of legal age in less than a year, the bar should be both of ours. But Declan wouldn't have that. He was twenty-six, married with two young children, and he had been working full time at the bar for a number of years. Not only did my brother take over the bar, he also moved his wife and young kids into my parents' house. Declan told me when I turned eighteen, the legal drinking age, he would allow me to bartend. I was so furious at his greed that I told him to fuckoff and that I would never work for him. I stormed out of the office and, later that day, moved out of my parents' house.

The death of my parents, and Declan cutting me off from what was rightfully mine, led me into alcoholism, drug abuse, bar-room fights, nights in a drunk tank, sporadic employment, broken romances, car crashes, and petty thefts until I found myself standing in the shadowed doorway with the steel bar in my hand with a hunger and desire to commit murder.

Three days earlier, my boyhood friend Hector had asked me to be the best man at his wedding. Hector had gotten his girlfriend pregnant and after months of debate about what to do, he decided to marry her before the baby was born. The wedding was going to be in two weeks. I didn't have any money, as any money I made went to feeding my desire for drink, for movies, for jazz clubs, or for books, pretty much in that order. Normally, I didn't care about my appearance, but there was a woman, Pilar, who I was in love with when I was in high school, who

17

was going to be at the wedding. She was from a Spanish family that had come from outside of Barcelona. She had dark exotic eyes, hair as black as licorice, and olive-hued skin. Although we had never dated, she was aware of my feelings towards her. I had asked her out at least a dozen times, but she said she wouldn't date me unless I gave up my notorious love affair with the bottle, which I couldn't do. I hadn't seen her in more than two years and wanted to impress her. To do so, I needed a good suit and a good pair of shoes. The only way to get enough money for those items was by mugging someone.

*   *   *

When the man from Maxwell Plum saw me step out from the shadows he stopped, as if he were quite aware something dreadful was about to happen. I ran up to him and swung the metal bar at his forehead. But at the last second, I pulled my hand away. I missed his head and caught the edge of his left shoulder. The strength of the blow knocked him to the ground. I stood over him looking down into his eyes. I thought he was waiting for me to hit him again or demand his wallet and money. Since I didn't, we just stared at each other for what seemed like an eternity, but what was probably only four or five seconds. I dropped the bar. It clanked against the cement sidewalk and rolled into the gutter. I turned on my heels, but I didn't run and he didn't call out or scream. I walked along Third Avenue down to Fourteenth Street where I caught a train back to Brooklyn.

When I got back to my room, I sat on the edge of the bed and broke down crying. I realized that I had been living in a fantasy world for years. In order to block out the pain I was feeling, I got blindly drunk, smoked dope, dropped acid, or took any other drug available. When straight, I lost myself in movies, in jazz, or books. The world of movies was much more real to me than my actual physical life. At that point, I realized I had to change my life, or I would end up killing someone or in jail.

Sobering up, going straight, quitting drinking and drugs, whatever you want to call it, is a boring story. Countless variations have been told so there is no need to go into the lackluster details here. I'll just tell you my sobriety allowed me to eventually marry Pilar, and to write and direct my first film, *A Brooklyn Love Story,* which was loosely based on the failed mugging.

After relating all this to Gwendolyn, and glossing over the next two decades of my life, how my marriage ended, how I walked out on my young kids, and how I started drinking again, Gwendolyn filled me in on her plans for the future. She was a big fan of the abstract expressionists: Pollock, Kline, de Kooning, etc. She wanted to paint like these guys; globs of colors and slashing lines, but she felt she couldn't create anything that wasn't just a bad reiteration. And she was right. Her work wasn't very good, just typical college pastiches of famous works of art.

Her idol was Joan Mitchell, the great abstract expressionist. One summer when I was on the Vineyard, the Museum of Modern Art was having a Joan Mitchell retrospective. Gwendolyn wanted to go but couldn't afford to do so. I bought her a plane ticket and told her she could stay at my apartment in New York. She wanted to know if I was going to go with her. I said no, she could go by herself. One of her friends told her she shouldn't go because I was just buying her a ticket and letting her stay at my place because I wanted to sleep with her. She asked me if this was true. I said of course it was true. She laughed and took the ticket and keys to my apartment. When she returned three days later, she gave me a hardcover copy of the Joan Mitchell book MoMA had put together.

When I saw her the following summer, she was working at an art gallery in Edgartown. It was one of those places that sell watercolors of sailboats on the sea and other seascapes. She was all excited to see me, gave me a big kiss and a hug, and told me she was going to bring some wine by that night. She also congratulated me because my film, *The Man Who Cried Wolf,* had gotten some press at the Sundance Film Festival over the winter. I told her she was more than welcome to stop by, but I had a new girlfriend, Alexia. The look on her face showed me how surprised she was at this. I guess she just expected that if she wanted me, I would be sitting home alone waiting. She brought the wine by but the scene was a bit awkward, or worse. Alexia was very condescending and cold. Even though Gwendolyn was only about five years younger than Alexia, Alexia treated her like a child or a teenager.

The next year, Gwendolyn went to graduate school at Yale. After graduation, she moved to Williamsburg, Brooklyn and took part in her first show in New York. It was a group show but she had three abstract paintings in it. At the opening in Chelsea, everyone told her how great her paintings were. Excitedly she asked me what I thought. I gave her a kiss on the cheek and told her to enjoy the night and that we'd talk soon. Because there were other people around she just smiled, but I could tell she was annoyed with me. A few days later, she came over to my apartment. When she asked my opinion, I told her she was just like hundreds of other young artists. They would graduate from a prestigious university and a gallery would put them in a group show because the galleries know they come from wealthy families, have wealthy friends, and these people will buy their art, so there's little risk involved.

This annoyed her. I didn't really care. I asked her what she knew or had to say about life. Here she was a young woman who, after four cushy years in the Ivy League, took a break before going to graduate school at one of the most expensive universities in the world. Because of this, she felt she had something profound to say? I told her she needed to do something to separate herself from the thousands of college-kid artists who did exactly what she did. She was pissed and said, "You know if you told me you really liked my work I was going to let you fuck me." *Let me?* Who did she think she was? Certainly I desired her, but that didn't mean I wanted just a quick fling, a one-time thing. I told her to get the hell out of my apartment and to come back when she had some dirt on her soul, and wasn't just some pretty little rich girl.

As soon as she left my apartment I regretted what I said because I didn't see her for a number of years. I probably wouldn't have said it if I hadn't been drinking and wasn't jealous of her. I did believe in what I said—she *was* a spoiled rich kid in many ways, but there was talent there, and what she had—the life on the Vineyard, graduate school, rich parents, and no financial worries—was everything I wanted when I was young and never had. I was also still with Alexia, who would eventually become my second wife.

Introduction
(Part Three)

Alexia came into my life after I received some notoriety from the Sundance Film Festival. I didn't win the Grand Prize, but *The Man Who Cried Wolf* won the Audience Award. Because my name had been in the press, people started looking at me and treating me a little differently. It seemed like they wanted me to acknowledge them. It didn't matter if they had seen the film or not, or if the film was good or bad. What mattered was *The New York Times* had given me a good review. Other films of mine had been reviewed before, but this one was on the front page in the Sunday Arts & Leisure section. Suddenly people wanted to meet me. Not a lot of people, but some—those who were impressed by names in print. For most, I was still quite unknown and remained so until *The Promised Land*.

Prior to Sundance, I had screened the film for a number of people. Some liked it, some didn't, which is standard; you're never going to please everyone. But some of those who didn't like it now purported to be great admirers. The others, who had previously praised it, became even more enthusiastic. Not everyone changed, but enough did to make me notice. During this period, I was invited out to fancy soirées, private art openings, and dinner parties.

One of the producers of the film was contacted by a woman editor from *New York* magazine; she wanted to meet me. The woman threw a dinner party in a fabulous apartment overlooking Gramercy Park, which is where I met Alexia. She was seated to my right; the editor was to my left. It was a rather sober affair on my part. I barely drank at all, maybe four or five glasses of red wine. Alexia and I talked a little, but mostly I talked with the editor. Just as the dinner was ending—servants in uniforms were picking up the coffee cups—a hand under the table caressed my inner right thigh. I turned to Alexia. She smiled and asked me when we were going to see each other again. Even though I felt our backgrounds were too different for us to have any deep or lasting connection, she was so pleasing to my eyes that I dismissed my own instincts, which told me not to pursue her.

Alexia lived down in the Village on Fifth Avenue just north of Washington Square Park, in one of those beautiful limestone buildings built in the early nineteen-hundreds. Not everyone in her building was descended from wealthy families, but many were. The doorman, in a dark green uniform and cap, wasn't there just to open doors; he was there to make everyone feel as if he or she came from the most rarefied class. He touched his cap when the women came and went. With the

21

men, he nodded solemnly, as if he was keeping their secrets. For many he was.

Alexia worked at Christie's Auction House in the Post-War and Contemporary Art Department. When we became a couple, she started to invite me to Christie's for the evening receptions, which were given to generate interest for the current exhibit. Invited guests were served cocktails or champagne as they wandered through the galleries looking at the various objects on display. After an hour or so, one of the department's experts gave a little talk and we'd all learn something. Initially, I was only interested in contemporary and post-war art, and Impressionism and Modern art. But the more I saw, the more I liked what I saw. Christie's, like its counterpart Sotheby's, was designed to service those who consider themselves to be the upper crust of society. Knowing nothing of this world, I made myself a student.

I started going to Christie's once or twice a week. I learned about Old Master paintings, South Asian and Indian art, photography, American paintings, and to my great delight, Irish paintings. Seeing paintings by Ireland's greatest painter, Jack Yeats, was of the highlights. After viewing exhibits, I bought the painting catalogues of upcoming sales. At home, I carefully read through the textual essays as I looked at the art and evaluated the prices while listening to jazz and sipping Irish whiskey. Later, I got to attend some of their prestigious night auctions where some paintings sold for millions of dollars. I never really liked going to these events because I was uncomfortable sitting in a room with men and women raising bidding paddles for million dollar lots as casually as someone in the street would raise his or her hand for a taxi. As much as I loved art, with all the poverty and misery in the world, I thought it was sinful, even criminal, to spend a million, or five, or ten, or fifty, or one hundred million dollars on a painting or a sculpture.

I was even more baffled by the applause that came after a work sold well above its high estimate. I never understood why the audience clapped. It certainly wasn't for the artist; the artist had been long removed from the equation. Did they clap because of the price? Did they clap for the auction house? For the buyer or seller? Or for themselves because they were part of this privileged world? I didn't know. I did know that my relatively impoverished childhood had made me feel a lot of anger toward the buyers. I didn't have to think of the suffering and poverty in the Middle East or Africa, or some land far enough away to be abstract. A few blocks away from Christie's location at Rockefeller Center there were men and women living in cardboard boxes wrapped up in filthy blankets.

At the end of the auctions, buyers were congratulated by their colleagues and friends for their winning bids. On many of these evenings it took a good deal of resolve for me not to go over and violently punch one of the well-dressed millionaires squarely in his face with enough force to break his nose. I envisioned the blood splattering across his face as he hit the carpeted floor, and I envisioned kicking him in the face with my black boots until security came and pulled me away. In my mind, injustice wasn't a vague or inconsequential issue; some men and women were responsible for the injustices, for the poverty and misery, in America and around the world. One of the gains from acting unjustly is financial rewards—financial rewards that allow for the purchases of outrageously priced art. I knew that not all wealthy people who purchased art helped to perpetuate injustices; nonetheless, there were enough violent feelings inside of me toward the moneyed-class that I stopped attending auctions.

A few months into our relationship, Alexia asked me to have dinner with her parents. I wasn't wild about the idea, because meeting parents usually means declaring your intentions. But I figured I could at least spend a few hours eating with them, so I agreed. I didn't realize what Alexia meant was for me to go upstate with her to spend the night in Harrison in Westchester where her parents lived.

I rented a car and drove us north. The house was something out of *The Lifestyles of the Rich and Famous*: an aged red brick edifice with stately white columns out front, a well-manicured lawn, and flower gardens in the back part of the estate. This surprised me because Alexia had told me her father was a professor of Medieval Literature at Purchase College, hardly the kind of job to pay for a spread like that. I later learned her mother was born into an enormously wealthy family. She had inherited somewhere in the range of thirty million dollars and invested it wisely. Looking back, I realize what they were doing was seeing if I was after their only daughter's eventual inheritance.

Alexia's father, Roderick, looked just like me. We both had beards, but I had more hair on my head. He was probably twenty pounds heavier, and probably at least ten years older. He could have been mistaken as my older brother. I almost laughed when I saw him. But I could tell by Roderick's demeanor, as well as his wife's, this wasn't the type of family that would laugh at all of the obvious Freudian implications. Her mother, Elizabeth, was a thin blonde woman who was active in the charity circuit. She spent many evenings in New York where, like the fictitious Wellingtons from my film, *The Promised Land*, they had an apartment on Sutton Place.

We had a drink before the meal in the wood-paneled library. It was something right out of a Merchant-Ivory film. Her father asked me what

I was doing for work. I knew Alexia had filled him in about me, just as she had filled me in about him. But people like to hear directly from the source. I told Roderick a little about my films. He wasn't too impressed. He told me, "I don't go to the cinema. Don't really see the point." This was meant to put me in my place; it was his house after all, and Alexia was his daughter, so I took this in stride. He was the type of professor who dealt almost exclusively with fawning students and was used to having his authority go unquestioned. His specialties were Chaucer, Milton, and Spenser, those fun boys.

By the time we sat down to dinner, I had gotten tired of Roderick's jabs at the film industry. Although I agreed with a number of his comments about the shallowness of most of the current films playing, I didn't want to admit it to him. Instead of having to defend my own profession, I wanted him to defend his. I asked him if he was reading anyone who had been alive in the last hundred years. He said he didn't feel there was any need to do so. I told him that was about the stupidest thing I had ever heard anyone say. Both women looked at me as if I were crazy. Apparently no one, at least no one at the dinner table, had ever confronted or contradicted the old man. I said, we're living in the twenty-first century, not the seventeenth, don't you think you should find out what the creative minds of your day are thinking? He asked me who I thought was worth reading. I was going to say Dan Brown just for laughs. But I knew I wouldn't get even a chuckle. Instead, I rattled off some of the older writers I liked, William Gaddis, David Markson, and Thomas Bernhard, and some of the newer, Willy Vlautin, David Mitchell, and Brian Evenson. Both women—their reactions were almost identical—turned to him as if we were playing tennis and our comments were like tennis balls hit back to the other's court. He said, almost sheepishly, he was reading a science fiction novel where clones take over the world. The statement, as innocuous as it was, was what got me thinking of cloning, which was the initial impetus for *The Promised Land*. The idea of cloning stayed with me for years. And, as is often the case, cloning, while interesting, turned out to be only a minor theme as more important issues came into play.

After Alexia's father told me about the sci-fi story, he asked, almost in an English accent, where I "schooled." "Where did you school?" I hadn't "schooled" anywhere. I didn't want to tell him this. I had also never discussed my schooling, or lack thereof, with Alexia, and I didn't want this night to be the first time we discussed it. I knew it would have reflected poorly on her if she discovered in front of her parents the man she was dating had never attended college. Her parents were not the type who knew or associated with people who had not "schooled." It was inconceivable for them to envision their daughter dating a man who did not have an office where his various diplomas were hung on the wall. Nonetheless, I told Roderick I went to Columbia University, which was true in a sense. When I was nineteen, I heard about Columbia's Great Books courses, so I went up to the university and got a syllabus. On it was a listing of books called the Western Canon. At the time, I knew nothing about the Western Canon, or any other canon. All I knew was these books supposedly shaped the history of thought in the Western world for the past two thousand years. There were probably a hundred or two hundred books you were supposed to know. Although I didn't have the money for a formal education, I did have an immense desire to learn. Whenever I had a chance, I bought a used copy of one of those books and read it. Alexia and her parents accepted what I said about going to Columbia at face value, and that ended the questions about my past. After the meal, we had another drink and it was time for bed.

When we went upstairs to the bedrooms, the house was deadly quiet. Alexia and I were given a bedroom down the hall from her parents. I figured we'd just go to sleep and get out of there early in the morning, but Alexia wanted to have sex. This was surprising because she was far from being sexually aggressive; in fact, I practically had to make an appointment if I wanted to have intercourse with her. When we did have sex, Alexia showered immediately after—as if she were afraid to contaminate her perfect body with semen and sweat, and wanted to pretend the things we did never happened. Here, with her parents just down the hall, certainly within hearing distance, Alexia wanted to make love like a pornstar. She got on top of me and moaned loudly as she rocked the bed back and forth. I tried to keep her quiet by putting my hand over her mouth. She had other ways of getting attention. She moved with such passion that the headboard banged up against the wall again and again. I put a pillow between the headboard and wall, but you could still hear the bed scraping the floor.

Did Alexia want her mother to know she was having sex with a man who looked like her father? Did she want her father to know she was having sex with a man who looked like him? I didn't ask. I was afraid to open any of the metaphorical closet doors, afraid of all of the skeletons that would spill out.

A few days later, Alexia's father told her I wasn't quite as dumb as he had expected. This was a ringing endorsement, as he had never had anything but condescension for Alexia's suitors. With this somewhat tacit approval, I started getting invited to Alexia's dinner parties. Prior to this, I had been excluded because I was told they were all work related.

Alexia's apartment was beautiful and large enough for dinner parties for twelve. This was important because the way you rise in Christie's, or anywhere else in the art world, was by getting collectors to spend money. Alexia used her parties to recruit new collectors. Art collecting is a social game as much as anything else. You needed to talk about your purchases if you wanted to be part of the in-crowd. When Alexia invited new collectors to her dinner parties there were always more seasoned collectors there to impress the newbies. Everyone talked of which galleries had good shows, what was worth seeing, and what was overrated. Inevitably, I was asked who I collected. On rare occasions I was asked what I collected (not everyone collected paintings, some collected photographs, a few collected sculptures, and the very brave purchased installations or video art.) No one assumed for a moment that I didn't collect. Why would I be there, after all? Sometimes I said I collected debts. This usually got a couple of phony chuckles. Unfortunately, it was true. I'd racked up plenty of credit card debts on films that were never made. The dinner parties happened without fail every Tuesday night. Wednesday and Thursday there were often art openings to attend in Chelsea. On Friday, many collectors left town for their country homes.

Alexia got a reputation of having the best dinner parties and to be invited was a high honor. If a person or couple didn't get invited back and asked why, Alexia always replied "Oh, we were just having some of my bigger collectors." The implication was obvious: if you wanted to get invited back, you'd better start buying more art. Many of Alexia's clients were from the financial sector: hedge fund managers, leverage buyout experts, merger and acquisition specialists, or just your average over-priced lawyer. These were the people who drove the art market.

Quite often, I left the dinner parties before any of the other guests. Alexia wanted to know why I never wanted to stay over on dinner-party nights. I made various excuses. The truth was her kind of people took a lot to get used to. Faulkner said, "The past isn't dead, it's not even past." Although my social stock may have been rising and threatening to catapult me into an association with a different class of people than I was used to, inside of me my past of bars and marginal characters was very much alive. Alexia's people were the swells, those who did the so-called right thing: not just going to college, but going to the best universities, getting advanced degrees, and prestigious jobs. These were the kind of people featured in network television shows to exemplify virtue. After a few hours with these people, I had to get away. I had to wipe all the virtue off of me.

I left Alexia and usually went to one of the bars in my neighborhood, Café Andulcia or the Holland Bar. Once her guests left, Alexia called to talk. When she didn't find me at home, she wondered where I was. (The only time I carried a cell phone was during film shoots when I needed to have one.) I told her where I went, and she said she wanted to come with me, to see what I saw in the bars.

A few nights later, I took her to the Holland Bar, which used to be just south of the Port Authority on Ninth Avenue, one of the few blocks that was still filled with denizens and derelicts from what Jack Kerouac's patron saint, Herbert Huncke, used to call the Deuce, Forty-Second Street. The Holland was the kind of bar you used to see along the Bowery so many years ago. The place was small with a rickety bar counter, stools to sit on and some dated beer advertising placards affixed to the tobacco-stained walls. Inside here, no one talked about art or work because many didn't have steady work. Drinking, when done correctly, is a full-time job. Many of the characters in here were direct descendants of the bar-flies in Harry Hopes bar in Eugene O'Neill's *The Iceman Cometh*. I didn't go to the Holland because I thought the patrons were better or worse than those from the outside world. Such thoughts didn't concern me. I went there because no one high-fived friends about their latest deal or talked about "meeting next quarter's numbers." Those of us who went to the Holland went there to get away from the world. We went there to drink until the liquor began to dance inside of us. Or maybe I simply went there because the drunken patrons reminded me of my parents and their bar, my home away from my non-home.

Alexia wanted to leave before her second leg passed through the doorway, but I made her stay. I made her see part of my world, just as she made me see part of hers. Normally, she didn't drink beer, but that's what she had here because she was afraid to drink out of any of the glasses. She hadn't asked me much about my past when we met. Apparently, the fact that I had been written about in *The Times* was good enough for her. That was a story she could sell to her friends: she was dating a director from Sundance. At the Holland, she began to ask questions. She wanted to know why I had only made two films in the last six years. Alexia wanted to know what I was doing during that time. She didn't know anything about films. She saw movies, of course, but didn't know anything about how they are put together and how difficult it can be to get one made. She was like so many other people who only saw movies with the big stars. She thought they represented what movie making was really like. She had no knowledge of all of the people who aren't big stars, or known writers and directors, those who often spent years trying to get a single film made.

After making *A Brooklyn Love Story,* it took me four more years before I made my first feature, *The Mute.* This was about a young boy who witnesses all kinds of tragedies and moral failures in the adults around him. Because he cannot speak, the boy creates his own world through writing stories. When he grows up, he hopes his first novel will impress his parents. He wants them to understand and love him more. When they read what he's written, which is mostly about their drinking, they are outraged to the extent they never want to see or talk to him again. As you can imagine, Disney didn't rush to hire me, nor did any other Hollywood studio.

Even though I wasn't "in demand" as they say, I wasn't idle either. I wrote dozens of scripts. Once I finished a script, I was on the phone trying to set up a lunch or some other type of meeting. When I wasn't, I was at my desk drawing storyboards or creating the scene breakdowns and budgets. A lot of writers just write. When a script is finished, the writer hands it off to a producer or director and their job is done. A lot of directors just hire writers. I didn't do that. The only films I made were the ones I wrote myself. Even though I didn't have money to produce my own films, I did what a producer does. I broke the scenes down, figured out a shooting schedule, came up with a budget. I went over the numbers again and again, trying to find ways to do it as cheaply as possible. I storyboarded every shot so when I got together with the cinematographers and editors they knew what I wanted. I spent years on different scripts this way, only to have no one want to make them. It was incredibly frustrating and because of that frustration, I began to rely more and more on the Jameson.

When I told Alexia these things, I could see the disappointment in her eyes. She wanted to know why the films were so important that I had spent years on them when they ended up amounting to nothing. She asked why I didn't just get a regular job before backtracking and saying she understood. Like Gwendolyn, Alexia studied art in school, but not to be a painter, she studied art history and knew the difficulty of many artists' lives.

I gave Alexia some details about my painful childhood. But I didn't want to dwell on that unpleasant chapter in my life. Her father was a scholar, so I wanted to impress her with my learning. I told Alexia, as a teenager and young adult besides seeing hundreds and hundreds of movies, I read many philosophical books about the meaning of life: not just western religious texts but also books on Buddhism and Hinduism and other aspects of Eastern thought. I didn't read these books like most college students—in order to glean enough information to pass a test—I read them because I wanted to know what the great thinkers down through the ages had thought.

I drank some more Jameson and told Alexia how there may or may not be an afterlife, but I knew we have only one physical life, and that life had to have meaning and purpose for me. I felt my purpose was to make movies. By creating something out of my experiences and thoughts, I might be lucky enough to produce something called art. If so, this would benefit others and help them in their lives, just as art had helped me in mine. Without movies, books, and music, I don't know how I would have gotten through life.

Alexia was quiet for a while before kissing me on the cheek and saying "Let's go home." We went back to my apartment at the Piano Factory. When we went into the bedroom, she lit candles. We took our clothes off and got into bed, but Alexia didn't want to make love. She wanted to talk. She asked me about her father. Did I think he was smart or a good person? I hedged. I told her he seemed nice enough. She said he was, but he also wasn't. She both loved and hated him. To the outside world, Alexia always presented a confident and self-assured façade, as if she never had a single problem or difficulty in life. Since she came from money, almost everyone she met assumed she breezed through life like a spring bird in June as it moved from flower to flower. In her youngest days, it was like that, but in her teenage years things changed.

Growing up, Alexia's mother was often too busy to be with her, so much of the parenting duties fell to her father who had a somewhat leisurely schedule because he only had to teach three classes per week. As a young girl, they were incredibly close. Alexia confided in him just as other young girls confided in their mother. When she was in eighth grade, she started to develop physically. With her silky black hair, coffee-bean-colored eyes, and tender demeanor, her father said she reminded him of a young Ali McGraw. Instead of calling her Alexia, he started calling her Ali. Alexia felt this was very sweet and didn't let anyone else call her Ali, not even her mother. In ninth grade, Alexia went to school dances with her friends. Naturally, there were boys there, and naturally Alexia was attracted to some of them. She told her father about one of them, a boy named Spencer. Roderick told Alexia that eventually she would go on dates with boys, so she needed to know how they would act.

On a Saturday evening, when her mother was at a charity event in Manhattan and planning to stay overnight at their Sutton Place pied-à-terre, Roderick cooked dinner and made himself a few drinks. Later in the evening, he joined Alexia in the living room where she was watching *Saturday Night Live*. He sat down next to her and told Alexia to pretend they were on a date. Shortly later, Roderick put his arm around Alexia. He told her this is what a boy will do. Alexia was rather uncomfortable with this but said nothing. Roderick slipped his other hand inside Alexia's shirt and unhitched her bra at the back. Alexia was shocked when her father started fondling her breasts with his big hands, but still she said and did nothing. Roderick slipped his hand down her pants, inside her panties; with his middle finger, he started fingering his daughter. As horrified as Alexia was, she was so afraid of offending her father that she did nothing. Unable to say something, or directly confront him, Alexia finally said she had to use the bathroom.

She stayed in the bathroom for a long time. When her father knocked on the door, asking if she was all right, Alexia came out and said she wasn't feeling well. She went straight to her bedroom. She said she didn't cry because it felt so unreal. It was beyond what she could ever imagine. The incident was never spoken of, and Roderick never again tried to assault her. Nonetheless, she couldn't get the incident out of her head. She never told anyone about it until she went to college, fell in love for the first time, and told her boyfriend about it. She told me that sometimes she wasn't even sure if she was imagining the whole thing or if it actually happened. She would go back to her diary and reread the words she had written when she was a girl, the words that described what her father had done to her. She said by putting it down on paper it made her feel like it happened to someone else. She kept the diary all these years to remind herself that it wasn't an illusion, that her father had sexually molested her.

A few weeks later, Alexia brought up the idea of marriage. We had been together less than six months, so this kind of talk was much more serious than I wanted. I was also unsure if she really loved me. I thought Alexia wanted me because I had been damaged by my parents just as she had been damaged by hers. I didn't really know if this was enough to base a relationship or a marriage on. Nonetheless, I was old enough to know no marriage is perfect. I also wanted to give my system a break from the booze, cut down on the drugs. I didn't want to turn into one of those bitter old men in my father's bar, the old men who would have made the world a more perfect place, if only they were given the opportunity. As a boy and teenager I saw them too often, sitting alone in the corner, or at one of the battered wooden tables, saying nothing for hours until the liquor finally summoned up the spirit of a dead insurgent inside of them. They ranted and raved about how horrible the world was. They fell silent again when they realized no one was listening or cared. A few more years alone in the bars, I would have become one of them.

Instead of marrying Alexia right away, I moved in with her. I figured this would give us time to see if we were really meant to be together. A year later we were still together, relatively happy, so I asked Alexia to marry me. As soon as she said yes, I told her I wanted to sign a prenuptial agreement. She laughed saying I had no money to take. I told her it wasn't my money: it was hers, her parents. I knew they had doubts about me, so I wanted to show them I didn't care about their money, and I didn't. My need for money was minimal as I spent most of my time watching the movie projector in my head. Like Hamlet, or almost, I could be bounded in a nutshell and count myself king of infinite space.

After a lavish ceremony at her parents' house, we went on our honeymoon. Kyle had given me a pre-wedding present: the use of his condominium in the town of Rapallo on the Italian Riviera, home of Ezra Pound during the Second World War. It's a luxury one-bedroom with a patio and small lawn that overlooks the Mediterranean Sea. During our week there, we visited the pleasantly picturesque neighboring towns of Santa Margarita and Portofino, and slightly further south the cliff-side towns of Cinque Terre.

For our second week, we went to Rome where Alexia picked out one of the most beautiful hotels in all of Italy, the Westin Excelsior on Via Veneto. I was stunned by its lavishness. We didn't have just a room; we had a plush and magnificently expansive suite, one seemingly made for visiting royalty, or perhaps for weekend getaways for the Pope. I complimented Alexia on her fine taste, but inside I was . . . well, not unhappy, but uncertain or even afraid of what this extravagance portended. When Alexia was in the shower I went online and found out it cost—converted to American dollars—almost four thousand dollars a night. When we got married her parents gave Alexia ten million dollars as a wedding present. This was part of her eventual inheritance. At this point I should have realized there was a gap between Alexia and me as wide as the Grand Canyon.

When we were at his condo, Kyle phoned to tell me a top executive at Paramount was excited about a new script of mine. Months earlier, I started writing a commercial comedy I titled *A Hollywood Love Story*. I wrote this because I was concerned about the upcoming cost of our honeymoon, and because I wanted to show Alexia I could make money if I needed to. I also wrote it to show the studios I could write and direct a film with wide appeal. I thought by playing the game I would be allowed to make a smaller, more personal film. Kyle said the executive wanted to meet me as soon as we returned to New York. This gave me some comfort and I told myself that one day I would make a lot of money, and one day Alexia's tastes would be less extravagant.

After spending like a king and queen in Rome, we drove up to Florence. The lodging I picked was just off the Ponte Vecchio, the historic bridge over the Arno River. At a cost of—converted again—less than one hundred dollars per night, it was a good bargain. Besides our cozy room, there was a rooftop garden where we had breakfast and where we had cocktails in the evening with other travelers. It was rather bohemian, but clean and more in line with how I liked to travel.

On our second afternoon, we pleasured our visual senses by viewing the masterpieces of Renaissance art at the Uffizi Museum. Afterwards, we walked past the Grand Hotel and decided to have a drink. Plush and magnificent, with a past that reeked of old money and a clientele that flaunted its new, it was such a beautiful architectural structure that it was impossible not to be impressed. Alexia said there was a much better class of people staying here than in the fleabag pensione I had selected. She said we should move immediately. I told her I wasn't going to take a suite at the Grand Hotel just to bask in the glow of strangers. Alexia shook her head back and forth and looked at me disdainfully. After that, everything we did became a battle.

By the time we got back to the States, things had cooled considerably between us. Three days later, I was on a plane to L.A. It turns out that the film producer from Paramount who "liked" my *Hollywood Love Story* script, wanted it so his much younger, and very untalented girlfriend could star in it. She had seen an earlier comedy of mine, *Patron Wanted,* where a young, struggling artist is saved by the patronage of an older woman (sort of a *Harold and Maude* story). She helps him get an art exhibit at a major gallery and he becomes a big success with half a dozen women fighting with each other for his love. But it's all an illusion. There is no wealthy woman who saves him. He has to continue struggle along with his modest successes. The "actress" liked this and wanted me to direct her. (This was one of the few films where I actually made some money. It also allowed me to buy my house on the Vineyard back in the late 1980s before the prices went skyward.) The producer and his gal pal wanted all kinds of script changes which made no logical or coherent sense, but which showed off her spectacular body. She certainly had a body worthy of viewing, but she lost all her appeal when she spoke in a high-pitched babyish voice. Things only got worse when she tried to "act." Later, I found out from a friend that the producer had been trying to get her work through just about every director in town, but no one was willing to ruin their reputation for his girlfriend.

32

When I returned to New York without a film to shoot, Alexia was annoyed. Instead of verbally displaying her annoyance, she said nothing. Shortly after this, I received a phone call from Kyle regarding a Hollywood star who wanted to buy the rights to an older film of mine, *Prodigal Son,* which also made a little money. He wanted to remake it with himself playing the father—he had issues growing up with his father, and now as a father he had problems with his own son.

I never liked remakes. It's what Hollywood does because Hollywood is now run by marketing people. The remake is marketed on the greatness of the previous film. This requires little work for the marketing people. What it shows is a lack of imagination and the lack of willingness to support original voices. Take a look at some great films: *A Bout De Souffle (Breathless), Wings of Desire, Psycho, Planet of the Apes, The Stepford Wives, Les Diaboliques, Le Femme Nikita, Alfie,* and see how Hollywood ruined the remakes.

I had no interested in selling the rights, but I wanted to impress Alexia, so I told Kyle the star could call me at home. Like most women, Alexia thought the "Star" was incredibly sexy and manly. He called a few days later and Alexia picked up. When he told her who he was, Alexia thought it was one of my friends playing a joke. Short story short, I took the phone and we set up a dinner meeting.

We met for dinner at Babbo in the West Village. After some casual chit-chat, the Star said that by buying the rights and starring in the movie himself, he was going to make sure I got the recognition I deserved. His first offer was fifty thousand dollars. I said, "No." (The average price of a screenplay for a mainstream Hollywood film was between three hundred thousand dollars and six hundred thousand dollars. The highest price paid for a produced screenplay when the writer does not direct is currently five million dollars.) He made a few more offers, upping it each time. I refused these as well. He changed his tactics. He said, "You did a great job, but I'm gonna take it to the next level. We'll put some money into it, get some real good production value. I know some top-notch screenwriters in L.A. who will punch it up—nothing too drastic, a little tweak here and there, something to get asses in seats. You know what I mean, right? This your first film?" When I continued to decline his small price increases, he finally said, "Fuck it, I'll produce and direct it myself. I'll save some money that way. I'll give you two hundred thousand dollars for the rights. We'll do a good job. You come out and stay at my house in Malibu. We'll hang."

When I turned down his two hundred thousand, he looked around the restaurant, as if for a director who would yell, "Cut" because I wasn't saying my lines correctly. After a few moments of silence

33

between us, he finally took off his sunglasses and said, "You're fucking with me, aren't you? I know you are. And I respect that, I do. Me and you, we're not money men, are we? So why should we talk about dollars and cents? Let the suits handle it." Theatrically he raised his hand for our waiter and ordered a bottle of Cristal champagne. This was to celebrate our working together.

When I returned to Alexia she was like a kid on Christmas Eve waiting up for Santa Claus. "How'd it go? Did you sell it!? How much!? What was he like?" I joked around with her for a while. I said we were going to have our agents handle it. That wasn't good enough for her; she wanted to know dollar figures. "Didn't he make you an offer? I thought he said he was going to buy it." When I told her I had turned down two hundred thousand dollars, she thought I was joking. When she finally realized I wasn't, she became furious. She cursed me and said, "What do you expect? Just to live off my money?"

What Alexia didn't understand was the star wasn't just trying to buy my story, he was trying to buy me, and I wasn't for sale. Alexia couldn't understand this because she had never had anything that wasn't for sale. She never created anything out of the smithy of her soul. So many in the film community talk about the erosion of culture, the demise of film as an art form, but when it comes to them standing up for their beliefs they end up taking the money. I had created something and put my name to it. I wasn't going to allow anyone else to claim my creation as his own. The Star could have offered me ten million dollars and I would still say no. This has nothing to do with the quality of the script or the film. You are either for sale or you're not. The price is just a footnote. Once you sell your integrity you can never buy it back. I didn't care if Alexia understood this or not. I didn't care if anyone else understood it. I understood it. If your beliefs are subject to change because of financial persuasion or any other kind of persuasions, those beliefs have no value or validity.

We went through the motions of being a couple for a few more months until the week before Thanksgiving. I came home one afternoon to find Alexia's father, Roderick, sitting on our couch waiting for me. He stood up and told me Alexia wanted to end the marriage, but she didn't just want a divorce; she wanted an annulment. I took a seat on the couch.

After a few moments of silence, Roderick told me he would give me a million dollars if I did not contest the annulment or file for a proper divorce. I was so dazed by Roderick's offer I got up from the couch, put on my jacket and walked out the door without saying a word. I walked to the Hudson River Greenway next to the West Side Highway and sat on a bench looking out into the water. I couldn't just go back to my apartment in the Piano Factory. I had tenants there. Although they were renting month-to-month, I just couldn't kick them out. I had some friends I could stay with, but I didn't want to see anyone and explain that my wife wanted to erase my existence from her life. I sat alone on the bench long after the sun had set. Eventually, I walked north. I walked the entire length of the Bike Path, all the way up to One Hundred Twenty-Fifth Street. From there, I cut across town to St. Nick's Pub on One Hundred Forty-Seventh Street.

It was midnight when I arrived and there was a jazz band playing. I ordered a club soda but I didn't even hear the music. I wasn't thinking of Alexia any longer. I was thinking of my first wife, Pilar. I had abandoned her when our children were small. Parnell was three and Lily was two. At the time, I didn't want to be burdened with a wife and two young kids, so I went out at night with friends. I met a sexy blonde named Vivian and before long I moved in with her. We stayed together for about nine months, until I could no longer live with a woman who wanted nothing more out of life than getting stoned and going dancing. Renting apartments was relatively cheap back then, so I found a place in the Village. I never offered Pilar financial support, and didn't even think about emotional support. Pilar moved back in with her parents, and I didn't see my kids again until Parnell's ninth birthday.

After the band at St. Nick's finished up it was after three. I knew Alexia was staying with her parents up in Westchester or in their Sutton Place apartment, so I went back to our Fifth Avenue place. I sat up all night trying to understand how the cruel and self-centered young man I was had turned into someone so self-righteous and seemingly principled. It was almost like I was looking at someone else's life, not my own. I fell asleep without any insight into who I was.

The next day, Roderick showed up and again offered the million dollars to me. If Alexia had simply said it was over, had spoken to me maturely, I wouldn't have even listened to Roderick's talk about money. I had told her in the beginning that I didn't care about her money. But since Roderick was so persistent, I listened. I wanted to know if the money was his idea or Alexia's. I also wanted to know why Alexia suddenly wouldn't talk to me. I don't know if I believed him or not, but he said the money was his wife's idea. It was his idea to not have Alexia talk to me. Roderick told me we were different classes of people and it would be best to end things as quickly and professionally as possible. I told him that legally, I was entitled to half her assets including the ten million dollars we were given as a wedding present. I didn't know if this was true or not, but I said it. I could have also brought up Roderick's sexual molestation of his daughter, but I didn't. Roderick said I would never get anywhere near ten million. I told him if he could make it so that I walked away with a million dollars after taxes and lawyer fees, I would agree. He agreed immediately and asked if Kyle would be the lawyer to contact. Since he knew about Kyle, it was obvious Alexia had been consulted about buying me off. It pained me to think Alexia would believe that I had my price just like everyone else. But I wasn't keeping the money for myself. I didn't want a dime of her or her family's money. I called up Kyle and told him what had happened. I knew divorce law wasn't his field, but by asking him to find a divorce lawyer for me he would be guaranteed a fee.

After I gave the details to my divorce lawyer, I took a train up to New Bedford, Massachusetts. From there I took the ferry across to Martha's Vineyard. I knew getting the lawyers to finalize the annulment and cut me a check would take time, especially around the holidays. I called my renters and told them they could stay through January. I spent Christmas and New Year's Eve in the Vineyard bars, mostly the Lampost, but also at the Wharf and David Ryan's in Edgartown. For transportation to my liquor oases, I hired a pretty, post-college woman named Leslie. I have a beat-up 1975 Land Rover on the Vineyard. It's dented and rusty, but it runs perfectly and is great for the many bumpy dirt roads on the island. Leslie had her own car, but I told her if she drove mine and something happened to it, I wasn't going to be too worried. And I only drank at the bars four or five nights a week. This also gave me someone to sit and bullshit with when I drank—not that I didn't have people to talk with, but I always liked showing up with pretty young women. It gives an older guy an air of mystery.

Often before I went into town for the night, I had a drink or two. Even though I hired Leslie to be my sober driver, I still invited her to join me for a pre-night-out cocktail or two, or three. She was reluctant at first before she took to it like a fisherman. After a few weeks of going to the empty winter bars, I grew bored. Instead of going out, I stayed home and snorted heroin, which was pretty common on the island, at least in certain circles. Leslie didn't do any, but many of her friends did and she was able to get me what I wanted. At the end of January, I realized I was in no shape to go back to the New York. I gave my renters a call and told them they could stay another month.

When I wasn't drowning myself in drink or drugs, or sleeping, or nursing a hangover, I thought about my younger years. I thought about my brother, Declan. Those thoughts led to my next script *Brotherly Love,* which was a cross between the biblical Cain and Abel story and Sam Shepard's *True West.* In order to write it, I had to leave the desolate

36

Vineyard. Leslie drove me to the ferry landing and gave me a big kiss at the dock.

When I got back to Manhattan, I picked up the million-dollar check Kyle was holding for me. All the while when I was away, I was thinking about my kids and my ex-wife, what I would say to them. Although I had sporadically kept in touch with Parnell and Lily over the years, our relationship was never that close or intimate. I wanted to write a letter to explain myself but, really, what could I say that would justify my actions over the last twenty or twenty-five years? Unable to come up with anything, I went to a drugstore and purchased three of those phony sentimental Hallmark Cards that said "Thinking of you." Inside each card, I inserted a check for three-hundred-thousand dollars and wrote, *Love, Dad* to my kids, and *Love, Blasket* to my ex-wife.

About ten days later, at a little after nine in the morning, I heard persistent knocking on my apartment door. The banging continued for some minutes. I didn't want to answer it because I had been up all night partying with two women I hired and I thought it was my one of my neighbors annoyed at the noise. After realizing it was futile to ignore the banging, I opened the door. Standing there was my ex-wife and my two children. My hair was disheveled, I was in need of a shave, and I stunk of booze. All I had on was my boxer shorts and a white t-shirt. From the trio's vantage point they could see my two women, Ling and Keisha sitting on the couch. Both were naked save for their panties. Ling's were red. Keisha's were black. A silver wine bucket was next to the coffee table that had a mirror with some lines of cocaine on it.

After a long pause worthy of Beckett or Pinter, I invited my long lost family in. Quickly, Ling put a magazine over the mirror and picked it up and walked into the bedroom with Keisha. I followed them in, put some pants on and came back out.

I had enough respect for my family that I didn't try to lie to them about who they girls were. I had already paid them, so after dressing they left. I told my ex-wife and kids I needed to shower, and that I would meet them in forty-five minutes down at the Galaxy Diner on Ninth Avenue. After showering and shaving, for some reason I put on my best suit. I must say I felt slightly ridiculous showing up at a diner in a suit and tie on a Saturday morning.

Pilar lives in Brooklyn with her second husband. Parnell lives out in Boulder, Colorado, and Lily lives upstate, outside Syracuse where she teaches high school Social Studies. When Parnell was young, I used to allow him to stay with me during the summer when I was up on the Vineyard. As soon as he graduated high school, he moved there and became a carpenter. Parnell fell in with a group of guys who spent summers on the Vineyard building houses and winters out at Vail, Colorado where they skied and worked in the restaurants and bars. Eventually, he got tired of going back and forth each year. He met a girl and moved to Boulder, Colorado, which is close enough to the ski slopes for both of them. Lily got married young, moved to Syracuse where he was from and got divorced three years later. She stayed in the area because she had a good job.

When Pilar received her check, she thought I was playing some kind of cruel joke. Knowing me all too well, she wasn't even going to try to cash it. But her husband, my children's stepfather, convinced her it was worth a try. When the check didn't bounce, Pilar thought I had sent the money because I was dying. When she learned Parnell and Lily also received checks she was more convinced I was dying and asked them to come to New York. Parnell and Lily were reluctant, but Pilar told them they should see me before I was buried.

Over black coffee and scrambled eggs, I filled them in about Alexia and where the money came from. Although they were sympathetic to my romantic failures, they didn't quite understand why I was giving them the money. I told them no amount of money could make up for the failure of not loving them when I should have. It had taken me a long, long time but I had finally realized what a terrible father and husband I had been. It was too late to change the past but I wanted to make their futures a little easier, if I could.

After a long silence at the table, Pilar said I should keep more than one hundred thousand dollars for myself. I explained the other hundred thousand wasn't for me. I had already allocated the money on a homeless Vietnam veteran I had seen for years in various locations in Hell's Kitchen quietly begging for money. His name was Willy. I'm not sure where he slept.

When I decided I was going to help Willy, I went to the Skyline Motel on Tenth Avenue to talk with David, the manager, who I got to know because I went to the motel bar to watch the NBA playoffs—they have the biggest screen in the neighborhood. I worked out a deal with him where Willy would be given a room for a year. I also arranged groceries to be delivered twice a week from the Amish Market on Ninth Avenue. When the details had been worked out, I found Willy. I took him back to my apartment, made him take a long shower and shave off his beard. When he came out, I gave him some of my old clothes to wear. I took him downtown to Century 21 and bought him a new wardrobe, nothing too fancy, but better clothes than the rags he'd been wearing for years. During this time, he didn't say much. He looked at me as if he didn't quite comprehend what was happening. Once I settled him into his room, I went down to the New School for Social Research to talk with a professor I knew there. I asked him to have a few graduate students in Social Work act as interns and look in on him a few days a week. The professor wanted to know what would happen after a year was up. I didn't have an answer. Sometimes you just have to take a chance with people.

Since I had given away the money I received from Alexia, Lily wanted to know what I was doing for income. When I returned from the Vineyard, I knew I needed a real job so I talked to the people at the New York Film Academy where I had done some teaching in the past. Once I started teaching again, a few of the young women developed the student-teacher infatuations that were common at most colleges. They hung around the room after the class had concluded and invited me out for coffee or a drink. They were so young and innocent that I didn't bother to pursue any of them. I didn't care about innocence. I wanted experience. I wanted a woman who had dove to the depth of her being and scouted around for the shards of her life, came up panting for breath, but was still eager to reveal what she had unearthed in that dark and sunless world. I discovered that was Gwendolyn, but it would be a few more years before she reentered my life.

Introduction
(Part Four)

After Alexia dropped-kicked me from her life, I avoided relationships and spent most of my time concentrating on teaching. This solitude allowed me to finish my film *Brotherly Love* within the next year. It has a two week run at the Quad Theater on Thirteenth Street, got decent reviews, and it disappeared. Financially it broke even, which didn't please my investors. This made me think about giving up making films altogether. It just didn't seem worth all the effort and struggle. Nonetheless, fourteen months later, I was again directing another film. This one didn't do too well, so I won't speak of it.

About a year later, I was sitting home on a late autumn afternoon when my doorman buzzed me and told me a Ms. Sangeeny was here to see me. It took me a few beats to recognize the name. After telling him to send her up, I held my apartment door open as I awaited her entrance from the elevator in the hallway. When the elevator doors pulled wide, it seemed like time-lapse photography: I was waiting for the pretty girl who had left me five years earlier and instead what walked toward me was a fully-formed woman. Gwendolyn was less girlishly pretty than when we first met, but her maturity had made her more beautiful. Her hair, which fell to past her shoulders, had always been dirty-blonde. Now it was darker with less of the summer yellow that had always been there. Her green eyes seemed somber and a little sadder. It was as if something inside her had been damaged or lost.

When we hugged, she held the embrace longer than I expected. We sat on the sofa across from the fireplace. Gwendolyn told me she had been back in New York for a few months but couldn't decide whether to see me or not. That day walking in Hell's Kitchen she just decided to stop by and say hello. She brought a bottle of 18-year-old Jameson with her. I got glasses and ice. Gwendolyn filled both of our glasses with the golden liquid and began telling me about her last few years. On the Vineyard, she met a Croatian man named Milos who was on vacation. Milos was only there for three weeks but that was enough time for them to dip their toes into the ocean of love. Not wanting to write letters or e-mails or talk long distant on the telephone, he asked her to go with him back to Dubrovnik where his family owned a seaside restaurant. She accepted and became part of his family. She worked as a waitress or a barmaid or a hostess or whatever they needed. She learned to speak Croatian and French, and they travel regularly to Italy and France and Spain and Portugal and Greece, and many of the other European countries. She said that for three years their love was as blissful as the love school-girl poets write about.

But she got pregnant. Milos told her to get an abortion and she refused. He started to hit her in the stomach, to beat her when she was sleeping, to do anything he could to cause a miscarriage. She was so in love she decided to do what he wanted. She felt it was better to give up the baby than to lose the man. But during the procedure something went wrong. There was a tremendous amount of bleeding, and later she learned she would no longer be able to have children. Gwendolyn had always dreamed of having a daughter who she could raise and love as her parents raised and loved her. She wanted to have this child with Milos. Now, unable to have children, she began to hate Milos. She also hated herself for being so stupid to listen to him. She didn't have the courage to leave right away, so she stayed but would not have sex with him. He stopped beating her, but he would bring other women home and have sex in their bed, making no effort to conceal his infidelities. Two months after the abortion, she left Dubrovnik and went to Paris where she rented a desolate room on the outskirts of town. She did little besides paint and drink. After relating all this to me, Gwendolyn was silent. She stared into her glass of Jameson for a while and wiped away a few tears. She asked me about Alexia and what I was working on. We had another drink as I filled her in on the details.

The next day I took the L Train out to Williamsburg where she had her studio. Hanging on the walls or stacked against the walls were close to seventy-five oil paintings of various sizes, all of them of babies. But these weren't cute innocent babies. They were babies that were dead or had been killed; they were scattered around gravesites and they were dumped in garbage bins or landfills. It was rather gruesome and I didn't know what to say. Gwendolyn said let's go get some coffee. Although it was only eleven in the morning, instead of going to a coffee shop we ended up going to an empty Polish bar where we both ordered beers.

Gwendolyn asked me if I remembered her telling me about her college boyfriend. The story of their breakup wasn't as lighthearted as she had originally told me. She had gotten pregnant and felt she was much too young to have a child. The boyfriend loved her dearly and wanted to keep the child, but she said it was her choice and she had an abortion. The boyfriend was crushed by her decision. He dropped out of school for a year and never spoke to her again. The ordeal caused her a lot of suffering and partly explained why she was so wild in her younger days on the Vineyard. She said it was also the reason why she avoided relationship and love; she was too afraid of being hurt or hurting someone else. With Milos, she had decided it was time to try to love again. Consequently, she put everything she had into the relationship

41

and tried to do everything she could for him. It was also why, when it ended, it ended so horribly. Afterwards, when she started thinking about everything that had happened, Gwendolyn felt God was punishing her for having an abortion. She felt that she had no right to be allowed to have a child. I sympathized with her but told her God had nothing to do with it.

I invited her back to my apartment for dinner that night. Afterwards, we went to bed for the first time. It wasn't as magical as I once imagined it would be. When we took our clothes off and got into bed she told me I should have just raped her when she was young and pretty and forced her to be my girlfriend. It hurt me to hear this because I knew it wasn't true. She would have never wanted that and I would have never done it. What it told me was how much pain she was in. I think she understood this by the way I was looking at her. She tried to dilute the brutality of her words by saying she wanted me for a long time. She said the real reason she didn't come see me was because she was afraid I wouldn't be here or that I would be married, and if I were married or no longer living here there would be no one in whose eyes she could find her younger self. I didn't know how you could find your younger self in anyone's eyes but I let it go.

Before I turned out the light, I saw there was great sadness in her eyes. When we started to make love she began to cry. I stopped, but she didn't want me to. She said, please just fuck me and don't ask me anything. So I did. When we were done, she lay with her head on my chest silently sobbing, her tears wetting my skin. I held her and caressed her soft hair with my hand until she fell asleep. She stayed for the next few days. A few days after that she moved in.

At this time, Gwendolyn worked two days a week in an art gallery manning the front desk. She also taught painting two days a week to a college friend's mother. The woman took up painting late in life, wasn't very talented, but she was a wealthy Upper East Side woman with lots of money, so the pay was good. Gwendolyn didn't want to do either job because it cut down on her painting time, but she couldn't survive on the few paintings she sold on her own. I told her I would pay the rent on her studio and I would pay for all her paintings supplies for a full year, after which if she wasn't able to sell them, she would have to get a full-time job. This allowed her to quit the gallery job and reduce her teaching to one day per week. Nonetheless, she still felt guilty for my financial input. I didn't think I was being foolish in what I was doing. I saw her talent and knew she needed to paint to find any semblance of happiness. If she wasn't happy with herself, she wouldn't be happy with me. But she wasn't happy for a long time. Her paintings weren't coming together with any resolution. This depressed her. To combat her depression, she drank. Sometimes the first thing she did in the morning was open a cold beer. She'd sit at the breakfast table and have two or three beers before she was ready to talk or face the day. I was surprised that she never seemed that drunk. Maybe that had something to do with the drugs she was on. After the abortion doctors gave her a variety of anti-depressants. Sometimes they worked; sometimes she just didn't want to take them, hating how they made her feel. She told me all they did was numb her brain and stop her from thinking. She said she needed to get to her deepest darkest thoughts no matter how horrible they made her feel. It was only when she got into these dark places that she felt she found something inside herself she wanted to express.

Eventually Gwendolyn had her "moment of clarity." She was working on another one of her death paintings when she felt she could no longer go on. She looked at it for a long while before picking up a pair of scissors and plunging them through the canvas. She said this felt so good she started slashing and breaking up her other paintings. She called me a little later and asked me to bring a change of clothing to her studios: socks, shoes, underwear—the whole bit. When I arrived, there were forty or fifty ripped up, shredded, and broken canvases on her floor. There was practically no more room to move.

Gwendolyn's building and the one next to it were former warehouses that had been converted into artists-lofts years ago. They were now being renovated and converted into upscale housing for non-artists. Like many of her friends, it wasn't long before Gwendolyn was forced out of her loft. Out front was one of those big industrial-size dumpsters. It took us two hours of riding up and down an old freight elevator to get rid of all her death-scene paintings.

When we came back into her empty studio, Gwendolyn took off her clothes and rolled out a long swatch of canvas on the floor. She told me she wanted to christen her new beginning by having sex. The hard floor and rough canvas didn't make for an ideal bed, but I didn't complain. Afterwards, she put on the new clothing and we went to dinner in Williamsburg.

Her next painting phase was self-portraits. Sometimes Gwendolyn would use a mirror to paint herself. Other times she projected images of herself on the wall by using a video projector. To get the images for this Gwendolyn had me come to the studio and take nude photographs of her with her digital camera. Although she was loosely painting figuratively she wasn't trying to accurately portray herself like a photorealist painter or even like some better known figurative painters, John Currin, Lucien Freud, or Jenny Saville. If there were any influence, it might have been

Jack Yeats. I had some books on his work that I picked up at the National Gallery of Ireland in Dublin. She liked the looseness of his brushstrokes and how he used figures to capture or express emotions. What Gwendolyn was trying to do was find some essence of herself and somehow have this come out in the paint. The female figure was just something to drape paint on. By globbing it on thick and dark or just adding light touches here and there she was able to evoke echoes of the abstract expressionist painters she loved so much. At the same time there was still a recognized figure visible.

After the spring semester, the New York Film Academy told me they were making "curriculum changes," and I wasn't needed any more. They couldn't come right out and say it but what they were doing was bringing in someone younger, someone who wasn't so caught up on filmmakers from the fifties and sixties and seventies. This was a blow not only to my ego, but also to my wallet. In order to have at least some income, I contacted a real estate broker on the Vineyard and rented out my place up there. This kept us away from the Vineyard for more than two years. But even that money wasn't enough to live on because my income from teaching was just enough to make ends meet. Now, with nothing coming in, we were broke.

Except for her college days, Gwendolyn had never been broke before. I was a little ashamed of having a good deal of experience in this area. In my Knut Hamsumesque younger days, when money was tight, I would cut down on luxuries. Luxury for me is eating. Drinking was an essential, something I couldn't do without. The worst period of not eating is the first few days. That's when the hunger pangs are almost non-stop. When you don't give your stomach food it eventually starts eating itself, eating any excessive fat, thereby shrinking itself. After a week of only one meal a day or so, your body adapts to having very little food and the hunger pangs are less severe—at least during the day. At night in my semi-starving days, I would often be awakened by a stomach crying out like a newborn baby. When this happened, if I had it, I would eat a piece of Pepperidge Farm Bread. It's a good and nutritious bread, and it's a relatively cheap food source. I'd wash it down with water and go back to bed. Sometimes you can fool your stomach this way and fall back to sleep. When I awoke in the morning, I would have coffee. At noon, I would allow myself a bowl of soup or a salad. Without those morsels, I wouldn't be able to concentrate at all. Being constantly hungry bothered me but I wanted my physical hunger to match my intellectual or artistic hunger. I told myself eating like a normal person would mean living like a normal person with a normal job, something I refused to do. Since that's how I felt when I was

Gwendolyn's age, I wanted to see if she had the same burning desire. If she said, let's get jobs, I would have gotten a job, but I would have thought less of her. But she didn't. She didn't even consider getting another job. And that's one of the reasons I loved her so much, she had the same needs and desires I had. Of course, I could have sold my home on the Vineyard, but that was never really a consideration because I knew if I sold it I would never be able to afford another one.

During those long months we drank coffee and drank alcohol but ate very little. Despite our impoverished finances, we had time, which is what we both valued more than money. Time allowed us both to complete a good deal of work. Eventually, I finished another screenplay, *Damaged People*, and Gwendolyn signed with a new art gallery. It was a small space in Bushwick, Brooklyn.

To celebrate our brightening future, we decided the time was right to get married. Neither of us wanted a big ceremony and the money was rather tight, so we decided to have the ceremony at our house on the Vineyard. Since we had a young couple as tenants, we made a deal with them. I allowed them to come to New York to stay in my apartment for a week in exchange for allowing us to use the Vineyard property for the same time period. They were happy to do this because New York was normally too expensive for them. Once this was settled, it was only a month before we were exchanging vows. Gwendolyn invited her family and some close friends. The only people I invited were my kids, Parnell and Lily. Although I had twice before made a vow "to have and to hold, for better or for worse, for richer, for poorer" etc., I knew this would be the last time I would ever say those words. After the vows, we had some sandwiches and beers and a few bottles of Irish whiskey. Her parents were a little disappointed. They expected something bigger and more bountiful, but Gwendolyn looked dazzling and was fabulously happy, so in the end they were pleased. After a week back on our beloved island, we returned to that other island, Manhattan.

I was soon on pre-production for *Damaged People*. The logline for this is: an innocent young man is arrested for his father's crime of armed bank robbery. He now must decide whether to rat out his father, sending him to prison for a mandatory life sentence, or plead guilty and condemn himself to five to ten years in prison. It wasn't really about the crime; it was about family relationships, love, and sacrifice. When it was released, the film received decent reviews but only made a small profit. In this age of blockbusters, small profits and good reviews are seen as failures. Consequently, I entered another long stretch where I couldn't get a film going. Gwendolyn was still drinking a lot, well, more than me, which is a lot in anyone's book. But the sun was starting to shine in her direction. She moved on to a better gallery, this one was on Rivington Street in Manhattan. Her solo show got a rave review by a well-known critic in *Art Forum*. This got her a lot of attention.

Gwendolyn was desirous of great reviews and strong reaction to her work, but she also hated it when it came. She hated that her success or failure depended on a handful of individuals. She didn't shoot to the top tier—that takes a few years—but she was plucked from her small gallery to one of the better Chelsea galleries, where she was given another solo show.

At her opening, I was introduced by one of the gallery assistance as Mr. Sangeeny. I *was* her husband, obviously, but this made it look like I was just an accessory, that I had no life or career of my own. We started going to more and more art openings because Gwendolyn wanted and needed to meet more collectors. When Gwendolyn and her new admirers were talking about art, I was left to wander the gallery on my own. I don't care how much you like art, there are only so many times you can circle a gallery and look at the work. Consequently, I spent most of my time talking to whoever was serving the wine, usually some actress who was doing catering between acting gigs. I got the hint that I was unwanted at art openings when Gwendolyn asked me not to attend a private opening at the Gagosian Gallery. There were going to be a number of big-name collectors there and Gwendolyn didn't want me to embarrass her with my drinking. It was about this time that Gwendolyn stopped her excessive drinking. She still drank, but only a glass of wine here and there.

While Gwendolyn was at the Gagosian opening being wooed by collectors and other admirers, I stayed home and fondled a bottle of Irish whiskey. I was about half way through the Jameson when I grabbed my jacket and ran out into the street. I thrust my hand into the air and shouted for a taxi. I think my cabbie was a little surprised at how intoxicated I was, but I suppose those who drive the pubic for a living get used to people like me. I told him to take me to Second Street and Avenue B—I wanted to go to Save-the-Robots. When we got there I was surprised to discover the old tenement building that housed the after-hours club was no longer there. It had been torn down, as had the abandoned gas station across the street, and replaced by newer structures. The gas station was an oasis for artists and musicians. The perimeter of the property had an overgrown and ever-growing sculpture with pieces of tin or steel, or any other kind of object, welded together to form a fence. Inside bands played and cans of dollar beer were sold out of an ice-filled garbage can. Years ago, the corner was a real drug bazaar with coke, heroin, or any other drug, readily available. No one really cared about the neighborhood, so you could do what you wanted, relatively speaking. This made for some wild times. You could cop your drug of choice before descending the stairs of Save-the-Robots. Often I wouldn't emerge from the after-hour club until the sun had been up for hours. But that scene was long gone. If I hadn't been so drunk, I would have remembered Save-the-Robots had been closed for many, many years. But in my inebriation, I fell into some fantasy of a world that was. I was trying to enter or reclaim a past that no longer existed. The city was different now; the moneyed crowd and trust-fund hipsters had taken over. Gone were the dark and dangerous streets that gave the city a unique sense of vitality. This was all part of the Disneyization of Manhattan. The effort to make the city safe and bland for suburbanites and tourists ruined it for those of us who wanted nothing to do with that other America.

My world, the one I used to live in, the one I thought I lived in, had all but been eradicated. This sobered me, but I still wanted another drink. I walked over to Avenue D and talked with a Puerto Rican bartender who grew up a block away. A little while later, a friend of his came by and I asked him if he could get me some coke. He made a phone call and I got what I wanted. I thought it would be uncool if I stayed there and snorted it so I walked down to a bar on the Lower East Side. Before entering, I stepped into a darkened doorway, took my house key, dug it into the gram of white powder and did a few snorts. Inside, I had a drink while I waited for the rush to hit me. When it didn't, I went into a bathroom stall and snorted a few more key-tips of the coke. This time, I felt something but not enough, so I took bigger and bigger snorts hoping to feel something, anything. Very quickly, I realized I had been ripped off. But I didn't want to give up on the drugs so I snorted about half of what was left. I figured I would get at least a little bit of a buzz. I did, but it wasn't what I expected.

I woke up on a stretcher. I had been having alcoholic blackouts on and off for years, so being unable to piece together the previous evening wasn't entirely new to me. There were a few other people in the room but this wasn't enough information to tell me what had happened. I figured out I was in a hospital but didn't know which one. After a few minutes, a nurse walked in and I saw her New York Medical Center nametag. I was in too much pain to just get up and leave so I closed my eyes. I don't know how much time passed before I reawoke, maybe ten minutes, maybe two hours. But by this time I was ready to go. When I signed myself out, my hand was shaking like Ray Milland's when he has his first drink at the bar in *The Lost Weekend.*

On the street I tried to piece together the details from the previous evening. I still had the small plastic bag of white powder with me, so I tasted a bit with my tongue. I realized I had copped heroin thinking I was buying cocaine. How or why I did this I'm not sure. In my desire to get a high from what I thought was cocaine, I was doing just the opposite—falling into a deeper and deeper narcotic haze until I passed out. Apparently, when I passed out at the bar patrons got scared, called 911, and an ambulance took me away.

I'll spare you the details of facing Gwendolyn when I came home. She understood my frustration, and not being a moralist she didn't try to lecture me. Nonetheless, it was almost three days before I had another drink.

The following year, Gwendolyn was invited to be in a show at P.S.1 over in Long Island City. This eventually pushed Gwendolyn to the forefront of up-and-coming artists and she was able to support herself entirely from her art. Actually, she practically supported both of us, as I had nothing coming in. Our Vineyard tenants had also moved out. Like many transient Vineyard couples, they found the island too expensive and were moving to Maui, Hawaii, which was also expensive but the winters weren't as bleak or barren.

Two weeks after the P.S.1 exhibit opened, Gwendolyn got a phone call from her dealer who told her it would be a good idea to strike while the metaphorical iron was hot and go to Art Basel/Miami Beach to ingratiate herself with a wider audience of art collectors. She was torn between going because she didn't really like all of the phony socializing and because she was a little worried about my mental state. Although I was working on my next script, *The Ceremony of Innocence,* about a war correspondence, I found myself unable to write without a drink or two as a kickstarter. After a few hours I was too drunk to write coherently and didn't seem to really care. I told Gwendolyn to go because we needed some time to be apart, and that maybe that would help us both. She packed her bags.

The Ceremony of Innocence came about because I had been reading a great deal about the Bosnian War and also about the Rwandan Genocide, and I envisioned a story about a journalist or photographer, like James Nachtwey, who had spent his life following and writing about wars. His aim from when he was a young man was to write about the injustices in the world. But after thirty years of being a correspondent he realizes that he has accomplished very little, perhaps nothing. Anyway, the journalist comes back to the States and tries to live in a world where good intentions and good deeds do not make a happy ending inevitable—more often than not they go ignored or forgotten. There's more to it than that, but we'll leave it there.

While she was in Miami, Gwendolyn called a few times but I didn't always answer the phone and when I did I didn't have much to say. I suspect her history of depression made her understand what I was going through, and probably it is what gave her the impetus to return sooner than expected. Bob Dylan sings, "Strange how people who have suffered together have stronger connections than those who are most content." I think that's sums up Gwendolyn and me.

Her love and suggestion that we go to the Vineyard after my "overdose incident" allowed me time to write the script for *The Promised Land,* which, sadly, and perhaps ironically, allowed me to create the film that brought me the fame and recognition I had always desired and, in doing so, killed Gwendolyn, our son Bartholomew, and destroyed my life.

But enough melancholy. Let's get to the film.

The Promised Land

A Blasket McManus Film

CAST

Senator Richard Wellington......................................Brian Dennehy
Claudia Potter...Catherine Zeta-Jones
Connor Gazelle..George Clooney
Bridget Wellington...Abbie Cornish
Gabriel Patrick..Edward Norton
Asher Mitchell. ....Michael Douglas
Peter Morgan..Peter Gallagher
Roger Zales...John Goodman
Kimberly Galway...Rebecca Hall
Keno Crawford...Terence Howard
David Diamond..Stanley Tucci
Candace Wellington.......................................Blythe Danner
Seisko Upendo...Samuel Jackson
President Mobley.....................................Denzel Washington
Will O'Reilly.......................................Philip Seymour Hoffman
Dick Lofton..John C. Reilly
Steve Lowell...Jeffrey Wright
Bob Hevens...Robert Downey Jr.
General Msambee......................................Lawrence Fishburne
Zack Taylor..Chris Cooper
Robert Jackson..........................Chris "Ludracris" Bridges
Sarah..Ziyi Zhang
Manlea......................................Djimon Hounsou
Richie Wellington.......................................Woody Harrelson
Pamela..Kirstie Alley
President Swinemore.....................................Robert Duvall
Yvette...Beyoncé Knowles
Johnny Gobo...Edward Furlong
Billy Tyler...Jaden Smith
Mr. Tyler...Forest Whitaker
Professor Samuelson.......... ....Sandrine Bonnaire
Harrison Silver..Steve Carell
Suzy Kasmir...Parker Posey
Perky Perkins...Anna Faris
Cassidy Canyons...Salma Hayek

As many of you will recall, the film opens with a symbolic Edenic sequence: amid a small clearing on a tree-filled mountainside a young couple frolics nakedly on a blanket. Next to their opened bottle of wine is a picnic basket, out of which an apple has spilled. As they start to make love, rain clouds form above them and a soft spring rain begins to fall. The couple disengages and run toward the shelter of their tent, pitched not far from a trickling brook. The woman brushes against a tree, causing the limbs to vibrate; the leaves shake and a few rain droplets fall from a green leaf into the brook. The water rushes down the small tributary, down the mountainside, and eventually into the Hudson River.

We follow the Hudson River from far upstate until we begin to see houses along its banks. Further south, we see a small village. Continuing down the Hudson, we pass the Bear Mountain Bridge, the Tappan Zee Bridge, the George Washington Bridge, and we come upon the grand metropolis that is Manhattan. After viewing the city's west side, we circle the Statue of Liberty and head north up the East River. We pass the canyonous buildings of Wall Street and lower Manhattan, pass the Brooklyn Bridge, the Manhattan Bridge, and the Williamsburg Bridge, slowly rising higher and higher, until we reach Midtown where we have a God-shot of the entire city.

From the east of Manhattan looking west, we slowly zoom in on a building on Third Avenue and Forty-Ninth Street. From the long shot of the building, the film cuts to a closer and tighter shot of Senator Richard Wellington in his office. Wellington's assistant, Keno Crawford, enters the office and speaks. (From this point on, I will relate the story through an omniscient narrator.)

—He said it was a film project for NYU. His name's Johnny Gobo.
—Film project, my ass. This is harassment.

Senator Wellington turned away from Keno and went to the window to press his forehead against the glass in order to look downward. Fifty-seven stories directly below, a student with a video camera sat sipping a latte in the cool, early-spring air. Over his shoulder, Wellington called out,
—Get me Asher Mitchell.
—Yes, sir.

Keno's desk was posted outside Wellington's office like a sentry box. Slipping behind it, Keno pressed the speed dial button for Wellington's lawyer. The senator opened his private bathroom door so

he could inspect himself against the inside door mirror. His hair was thinning, but not all of it was gray. After sucking in his gut, he turned to look at himself in profile. If he was more than a few pounds overweight, Wellington told himself, it was only because he had a hearty and lusty appetite. A voice called through the still-opened door.
—Senator?
—I got it.

Wellington walked to the round, wooden worktable in the center of the room and hit the speaker button on the Polycon video-conferencing device.
—Asher?
—Hello Senator.
—I have a kid who's been following me for weeks with a video camera. Wants to portray me as some kind of killer just because I hunt. Can you find some way to prevent him from following me?
—How do you know that's what he wants?
—Has me strapping a deer to the roof of my car after our last hunting trip upstate. It was rather bloody and I don't want that image of me in the press. Is that so hard to understand? I was bringing it to the butcher. I wanted the venison.
—There it is; simple explanation. You were hunting for the meat. Who wouldn't understand that?
—Liberals, pacifists, non-hunters. There are plenty of people who wouldn't understand, and the Democrats and Gazelle will find a way to use it against me.

Knowing Wellington, Asher Mitchell felt there might be more to the story.
—Anything else he might have seen or filmed that you don't want in the press?

Wellington hesitated a moment, wondering how much he wanted to reveal. Reluctantly, he began to unburden himself.
—Well...I think he got me coming out of a restaurant in Washington when I was over-served.
—*Over-served?* How over-served were you?
—I might have been wobbling a bit. When I got into my car and pulled away, I sort of bumped into a parked car or two. But I don't know if he caught that.
—So he got you driving drunk. That's not good. What else?

Wellington got up, closed the door to his office, and sat on the coffee table in front of the twin toffee-colored couches.
—There is this friend of mine. I think he filmed her coming out of my apartment in Washington. She left the restaurant with me, and he was

there in the morning when she left. What the hell does he want? I'm human.

—Is this an ongoing thing or...

—No, it was a one-night thing. We're friendly, that's all. She's married.

—So besides killing deer, driving drunk, hit and run, and committing adultery, you have nothing to hide, correct?

—He got me taking a big bag of money from this guy Vito from Brooklyn.

—Vito from Brooklyn?

—I'm kidding. That was a joke. No bag of money. That's it, what you mentioned.

—Well, I think we'd better find out who this kid is. And, if he's serious about broadcasting it, I think you're going to have to find a way of beating him at his game. I'd prepare Candace. Sooner or later it may come up and better she hears it from you than from the press.

—Maybe we could dig up some dirt on him. Keno found out he's a student at NYU. He wants to do an interview with me.

—Then do the interview. It's much better to get these things out of the way now instead of when we're closer to the election.

—I'm not doing an interview with a college kid, especially one who secretly films me.

—Doesn't your daughter, Bridget, go there? Maybe she knows him. Can you get Bridget to talk to him, tell him to lay off?...Senator?

—I don't know. Our relationship has been strained lately. I get the feeling sometimes she doesn't trust me.

—Call her. It's better to try the friendly approach first.

☐☐☐ 2 ☐☐☐

After ascending the pair of entrance steps to Gotham Bar and Grill on East Twelfth Street, Wellington hesitated for a moment. Seeing him, the Maître d's hung up the phone, stepped briskly from behind the reservation podium, and extended his hand.

—Senator, what a pleasant surprise.

Wellington allowed his left and free hand to sandwich the Maître d's. He held it for a moment, locked eyes and smiled.

—The pleasure's all mine.

Bridget Wellington was seated at the long bar going over manuscript pages of a theater play. Her father walked over and planted a kiss on the top of her brunette head. After being seated and ordering their meal, Wellington asked her if she knew the student who had been videotaping him, Johnny Gobo.

55

—Is that why you invited me to lunch? Because you wanted me to talk to him, so he wouldn't film you anymore?

—I wanted to see you. That's the most important reason, but yes, I also did want you to talk to him, to ask him to lay off. I guess that's out of the question.

Bridget shook her head back and forth, ever so slightly, indicating her disapproval. Not that Wellington noticed, or would have cared if he had.

—He wants to interview me. He's probably going to try to make me look bad. He's going to accuse me of driving drunk and being with another woman.

—Don't you think of anyone beside yourself?

—I made a mistake. It happens.

—A mistake? Another *mistake?* How do you think Mommy's going to feel?

—Maybe you could talk to her.

—And what, tell her to forgive you for screwing around on her?

—No, just...tell her to not judge me so harshly. I'm under a lot of pressure.

—Do you ever wonder why she never wants to leave the house anymore? Do you? Or is politics all you care about?

☐☐☐ 3 ☐☐☐

Escorted by a campus security officer, Senator Wellington was led into a small production studio at New York University where a video camera was set up on a wheeled tripod. Johnny Gobo, who had just finished testing the lavaliere microphone, went over to greet the senator. A second student watched from behind the audio board.

—Hello, Senator. I'm Johnny Gobo.

Wellington extended his hand.

—It's a pleasure to meet you, Johnny.

☐☐☐ 4 ☐☐☐

The Wellington mansion was up in the leafy section of Westchester, in Bedford, slightly more than an hour's drive north of the city. Accessible only by a private road and surrounded by sixteen wooden acres, the formidable two-story stone structure was expansive enough to store a vast number of decorative objects but too large to foster a feeling of intimacy among the inhabitants.

The Wellingtons were sitting in the television room, the one room that was not seemingly set up or arranged for entertainment purposes. Though the television had been upgraded on a few occasions the rest of the furniture had not, giving the room a lived-in feeling that the rest of the house did not possess. The other rooms were as appealing, or lifeless, as those displayed in *Architectural Digest*, the magazine Candace put down as she went to the kitchen, a few paces away, to answer the ringing telephone.

—Hello.

—Hi Candace, it's Asher Mitchell. Is he there?

—Just a moment.

Candace walked back into the television room.

—It's Asher.

Wellington took the phone from his wife and walked through the kitchen into the hallway. He walked past the breakfast room, through the perfectly arranged dining room with its twelve high-back chairs and highly-polished mahogany dining table, through the entrance foyer with the pair of Greek marble statues of Diana and Apollo, and into the commodious living room where, after turning on a small Tiffany lamp, he sat on the edge of a 1940s divan his wife had purchased at auction.

—Asher?

—What happened at the interview, Senator? A friend from *The Daily Post* just called me. He said you punched Johnny Gobo.

Angrily, Wellington stood up and began pacing the room.

—That's bullshit! I didn't touch him.

—He said you went after him, knocked his camera over and broke it.

—That's a lie!

—What happened?

—There are certain things called fairness, decency and respect. Goddamn kid. I should have hit him! If I hit him, he'd know it. Wellington stopped his tirade and inquired cautiously,

—What is he claiming?

—That he asked you a question and you went ballistic.

—I got pissed off at him, I'll admit that. When I got up from the interview chair he thought I was coming after him, so he pushed the camera and tripod between us, and it got knocked over.

—Who knocked it over?

—He did. He pushed it in front of me and it got knocked over.

—Were you going for him?

Wellington paused momentarily.

—I hadn't made up my mind. Little goddamn fairy, hides behind a tripod.

—What did he say that got you so upset?

Feeling that Candace might be listening, Wellington turned his back toward the hallway and other rooms and spoke conspiratorially. — I'm not going into it. I got the tape, the videotape. So whatever he says it's worthless. I took the tape from the camera.

—He says that when he asked you if you were impotent you jumped out of your seat and went after him.

Wellington exploded.

—Who the hell does he think he is that he can ask me that kind of question?

—It's going to be in the paper tomorrow. The writer is claiming...

—I don't care what he says! Who the hell is going to believe some college kid, anyway?

□□□ 5 □□□

The New York Daily Post

Can Wellington Keep It Up?

New York University film student, Jonathan Gobo, claims that when Senator Wellington was questioned about an alleged affair, his impotency, and his use of Viagra, the three-time congressman punched Mr. Gobo, kicked over his camera and tripod, and stole the videotape from the camera, apparently believing that without the tape he could deny the interview happened.

Unfortunately for Wellington, an audio recording, rolling at the same time as the videotape, captured him saying "Come here, you little punk, I'm gonna kick your

Continued on page 3

□□□ 6 □□□

The following morning, Wellington was at his office going over a datasheet with a list of contributors' names and the dollar amount given. Along the border of the datasheet an aide had written either Y or N. This was to indicate whether the contribution was large enough to warrant a personal meeting with the senator. Wellington was reviewing the names to see if he would take the meetings or not. When his desk phone rang he glared at it before returning to his list of names. After a quick knock, his assistant entered. Wellington angrily tore his attention from the datasheet,

—Damn it, Keno, just say no comment!

—But sir…

—Keno! I told you, I'm not going to discuss my private life with the press!

—It's your wife.

—Oh. Thank you.

Wellington reached for the phone.

—Candace, hi.

—Should I believe anything on the news?

—Absolutely not. You know how the papers are.

—It was on TV, on POX.

—Well, they're lying. They picked it up from *The Daily Post,* and you know what kind of rag that is.

—What about the Viagra? I'm just a tad curious why you might have purchased it, since there hasn't been much need for it with us.

Wellington's nervousness made him take the phone, stand up, walk away from his desk and begin circling the work table in the center of the room.

—It wasn't for us.

—Obviously.

—That's not what I mean. I did buy it, but it was for a gag. I bought it for Dick Lofton, for his last birthday. Why don't we have a quiet dinner at home tonight?

—I was afraid you'd say that.

This annoyed him.

—Why?

—The only time you want to have dinner at home is when you're feeling guilty about something.

—Fine. If you don't want to have dinner, just stay so. I have work to do. I'll stay in the office.

Keno presented himself in the doorway.

—Senator?

—Hold on, Candace. What is it?

—Sorry, but Mr. Mitchell is on the other line returning your call.

—All right, thanks. Candace, I'll try to be home around nine.

Wellington pushed the button for the other line as he sat back down at his desk.

—Asher, why the hell didn't you tell me they had an audiotape?

—How was I supposed to know?

—That's your goddamn job, isn't it? To find things out, to keep me out of trouble? And how the hell did Gobo find out I had Viagra?

—I was going to ask you the same thing.

—It's got to be Pamela. She's the only one who could have said something. Let me call her. I'll call you right back.

After putting the desk phone back in its cradle Wellington went to his closet for his suit jacket. He extracted his cell phone from his breast pocket, flipped it open, went to Contacts, found her number and hit "SEND."

—Hello.

—Pamela. Hi, it's Richard.

—Oh, hi. I'm on my way to Capitol Hill. Are you in town?

Wellington sat back down at his desk. With his right index finger he doubled-clicked his computer mouse on the desktop folder "K Street." A half-dozen thumbnail photos appeared revealing a generously proportioned fortyish blonde in a hotel room in various stages of undress. Wellington doubled-clicked on one of the photos. It opened to full size and showed the woman in a red bra and a beige skirt blowing a kiss to the photographer. Pamela wasn't beautiful, but she had sexual appeal, and she seemed friendly and uncomplicated.

—No, I'm not. Um… this is kind of delicate…

—Are you talking about what's in the papers? I saw it this morning.

—Yes. Did you talk to any reporters about me?

—Why would I talk? I'm not particularly anxious for anyone to find out anything either. What do they know?

—I don't know. They may have a photo or some videotape of you, but not your name, as far as I know. As long as neither one of us says anything we should be fine.

—I hope so.

—I hate to be brief, but I have to go. I'll give you a call soon.

—Do. I miss you. Bye.

Wellington picked up the desk phone and dialed.

—Asher Mitchell.

—Hey, it's me. She didn't say anything.

—Did you order it online? That Gobo kid might have accessed your records that way.

—They can do that?

—Get your online records? It's illegal, but of course they can do it. If they can get into the Pentagon, they can get into your computer.

Pamela's folder was quickly closed and another folder, "Meds" was opened. The folder was highlighted and quickly deleted.

—That's what he did then, broke into my computer. That information's supposed to be safe. Now we have something we can sue him on!

60

—Is this the kind of lawsuit you want to pursue? "Senator Wellington sues college student over Viagra slander?"

—All right, maybe not. That's why he did it; he knows he's got me. He knows I'm a law abider and he's a criminal.

—Maybe he didn't access your computer. Maybe he was bluffing. At our age, plenty of men need a little help. He bluffed to see how you would react.

—Damn...

—Just put it behind you and move on.

—Easy for you to say. I've got to explain it to my wife.

□□□ 7 □□□

The Wellingtons were in the upstairs master suite getting ready for bed. Candace Wellington went into her dressing room, got out of her slacks and blouse, took off her bra, and put on a pair of silk pajamas and a bathrobe. Her dressing room—each had their own, at opposite ends of the spacious bedroom—contained a large walk-in closet, a full bathtub, toilet and double-sink, as well as additional cabinet and closet space. She washed her face and applied anti-aging face cream. Coming back into the bedroom, Candace found her husband sitting in the buttoned Chesterfield couch, nursing a Cutty Sark and soda as he watched television. On screen, a sexy redhead ran a finger suggestively along the spine of the silver Jaguar hood ornament. After finishing what was left of the translucent gold liquid in his glass, Wellington hit the mute button for the television and stood up to face his wife.

—Candace, I know the news was somewhat embarrassing for you.

—Humiliating would be more accurate.

—Okay, I'm sorry, but I think we have to keep our eyes on the ultimate goal.

—What exactly are you sorry about, Richard?

The senator sucked down the few lingering drops of scotch and crushed the remaining bits of ice with his molars.

—Her name is Pamela. She's a lobbyist. We had dinner and, well, we ended up going back to the apartment in Washington. That's it. It's over. It was a one-time thing.

—Why are you telling me this? To get rid of the guilt? Do you still have guilt?

—This isn't my fault. It's that kid's, that kid with the camera. If he didn't want to pry into my goddamn life, none of this would have happened.

—It happened before the kid with the camera, didn't it? What you mean is that I wouldn't have known and everything would be fine.

—No, that's not what I mean. I'm a public figure. Every time I turn around someone wants something from me, so I drink a little, blow off a little steam. Never said I was perfect. I think it's Connor Gazelle, or some of his people. That's who I think it is.

—Gazelle? Some kind of Democratic conspiracy to get you?

—That's right. It's an election year and Gazelle knows he doesn't really have a chance. He's a big-time Hollywood actor, right?

—So?

—Why do you think this kid is doing this? He's a film major at NYU.

—What does that have to do with anything?

—It has a lot. Every film major wants to go out to Hollywood and make it big. He probably thinks by getting something on me he'll get known and make a name for himself, which will help his film career. Hollywood is full of goddamn liberal Democrats.

—That's pushing it, don't you think?

—No, I don't. He pretends he's interested in my hunting. He's not. Doesn't give a damn about hunting, just wants to harass me, keep the pressure on until he makes me screw up. Well, you know what I'm going to do? I'll beat them at their game; I'll drop out of the race.

—What about your "ultimate goal?" Suddenly you no longer want to be president?

—Not if this is what I'll have to go through to get there. It's not worth it. What? You don't think I have other options? I've got plenty of other options.

—What I'd like is for us to have a conversation about something that doesn't involve politics. Do you think we could do that?

—Of course we can. I've always been able to separate myself from work...

Candace stared at him...

—What? Why do I always have to start the conversations? Let me put the news on, that's what I was waiting for.

Wellington picked up the remote and pushed "mute," reanimating the set.

—*Did you know that dieting could promote weight gain? Doctors say...*
Click.

—*...Senator Wellington has a reputation of being a womanizer...*

—That's a lie.

—*...much to the embarrassment of his wife, Candace, who rarely leaves their Westchester estate, and his children, Richard, Jr. and Bridget.*

Wellington clicked the flat screen to black and went into his dressing room where his jacket was hung on a hook of an old wooden

62

hat-rack that held no hats. Inside the breast pocket he found the cell phone and dialed his campaign manager.

—Dick Lofton.

—Dick, it's Richard.

—Hi, Senator.

Wellington undid his tie, walked into his bathroom and closed the door. Inside, he undid his belt, pulled down his pants and sat on the toilet.

—I want to have a news conference, tell the bloodsuckers my version, get it out there in the press.

—Mistake. Do you want to defend yourself against every accusation? If you do, you won't have time to do anything else. What you should do is act like you're not affected at all. Take Candace out somewhere fancy. Let the press see you enjoying life.

—Why? I had dinner with her tonight.

—That was sporting of you, but it doesn't do anything for us PR-wise. We need the press to see you out and about. And bring Bridget and Richie along.

—Richie's out west somewhere. I don't even know where he is these days.

—Then it'll just be the three of you. I'll find some event for you to attend, and I'll make sure you're seen holding Candace's hand and kissing her. That's the kind of photos we need.

□□□ 8 □□□

Keno greeted the tall, blonde woman with a handshake. He invited her to sit and excused himself as he stepped into Senator Wellington's office. Professor Samuelson gazed at the carefully selected news magazines stacked on the table in front of the waiting room couch. Not in a reading mood, Samuelson glanced up at the photos filling almost all of the available wall space. There were twenty or more photos of Wellington with what appeared to be other political leaders or businessmen, all dressed in dark suits accented with conservative ties, mostly red or blue striped.

Inside, Wellington had just finished reading: *One of the largest animals cloned is the guar, a large, wild ox species with horns and a hump-like ridge on its back. They live in the forests and bamboo jungles of Southeast Asia and India. Adult males have shoulder heights up to seven feet and weigh up to two thousand pounds. They're an endangered species because their habitat has dwindled. They were once hunted for sport.*

The senator looked up when his door opened.

—Senator, Professor Samuelson, the geneticist from Columbia University, is here.

—Oh, right. Tell him to come in. And if you could bring us some coffee, that would be great.

—Professor Samuelson is a woman.

—Really? I didn't realize that from the article. Well, tell her to come in.

When Keno went back for the professor, Wellington stepped from behind his desk to his closet for his suit jacket. He had just finished putting it on as Professor Samuelson entered. After shaking hands and some small talk, they sat adjacent to each other on the sofas, Wellington to the professor's left.

—Doctor Samuelson, let me tell you why I asked you here, and I thank you for coming. As you undoubtedly know, the senate has been looking into cloning for a number of years. I started doing some of my own research, which led to your article in *Scientific American* where you mention the Supreme Court decision Diamond v. Chakrabarty.

—I'm glad you're aware of it, because it will have far greater impact than Roe v. Wade. And not in a good way.

—I actually think there can be a lot of good from it. And that's what I wanted to talk about. I read about that sheep in Edinburgh and that got me thinking.

—Dolly.

—Right, Dolly. Besides the cloning of sheep, cows, pigs, monkeys, cats, and a horse, I've been reading about the cloning of a former hunting trophy, the guar. Since so many different animals have been cloned, I want to know what kinds of animals can't be cloned.

—Under the right conditions, just about every animal can be cloned.

—Okay, that's what I thought. What can you tell me about the Harvard mouse?

—If you know about the Harvard mouse, you know a great deal more than many. Why don't you really tell me what you're driving at?

—From what I understand, DuPont paid Harvard University to develop a mouse that was more resistant to carcinogens to use in their cancer research. By using genes from other species, including chickens and humans, they were able to produce a new or transgenic mouse. This mouse was later patented, which was what the Supreme Court decision was all about: owning the rights to any transgenically produced animal. In other words, by creating a gene-modified animal, DuPont now owns the rights to that animal as well as any of its offspring. What I'm wondering is if you have had any experience with the businesses end of cloning.

—Business? No. I'm a scientist. What kind of business are you thinking of?

□□□ 9 □□□

Later that evening, at the Ziegfeld Theater entrance on Fifty-Fourth Street, security men and a slew of handlers on cell phones or walkie-talkies communicated with limousine drivers as if they were airplanes circling Kennedy Airport. As soon as one limousine pulled out and the celebrity disembarked—with his or her date and or entourage—another celebrity was put on standby. The disembarked celebrity was given ten or twenty seconds in front of the photographers and the television sycophants before he or she had to move down the line and the process repeated itself.

Another long black limousine pulled up behind the other long black limousines. Inside, Senator Wellington finished the last sips of his scotch. His was dressed in a navy blue suit with a white oxford shirt and a red Jerry Garcia tie his son Richie had purchased for him two Christmases ago. Candace, at fifty-two, still maintained a trim enough figure to turn heads. She took her daughter's advice and wore a pantsuit in the dominant New York color: black. Candace allowed a bit of her own taste and femininity to show by wearing a blood-red top that showed a hint of cleavage. Bridget looked sexy and chic in a new pair of jeans and a distressed leather jacket, bought used at a Soho boutique at triple its original price.

The Wellingtons exited their limousine but were forced to stand still as cries for "Gwyneth" and "Russell" had cameramen and reporters pushing and elbowing each other to get closer to the stars. A few reporters, who couldn't get close enough to the movie stars, spotted the senator and rushed over. A thin, delicate hand of a fashionably unshaven man in his early thirties held a gray Uniball pen toward Candace and asked,

—Mrs. Wellington, do you know Pamela Hartley?

The senator glared at him and turned to his wife.

—Candace, you don't have to answer.

The media scribe continued,

—Any idea why she came out of your husband's apartment in Washington at seven in the morning?

Wellington stepped up to the reporter.

—I ought to break your damn face!

Another reporter jumped in.

—Senator, is Pamela good in bed?

As their limo still hadn't pulled away, Wellington stepped back, opened the door and beckoned to his wife. She looked at him, not quite understanding.

—Get back in.

—What are you doing?

—Just get in the damn car, Candace!

One of the reporters turned to Bridget.

—Ms. Wellington, how do you feel about your father's affairs?

Wellington, politely, but firmly pushed his daughter toward the still-opened door. She hesitated.

—Get in the car, Bridget.

When his wife and daughter were both in the car, Wellington closed the door so he could face the reporters alone. —Don't you have any respect?

—All I wanted to know is if Pamela Hartley is good in bed.

Bridget, watching through the window, recoiled slightly when she saw her father's fist fly through the air and connect solidly with the jutting, unshaven jaw of the reporter. He crumpled to the cement sidewalk in silence, his pen falling out of his hand and rolling uncapped against another reporter's black Doc Marten boot.

—Oh my God, he hit him.

Candace craned her neck so she could see past Bridget, but Wellington was quick and he stepped into the car, slamming the door behind him.

—Goddamn punk. That'll teach him.

Candace scowled at him and said,

—I don't believe you, I really don't.

—Why? They're going to say I hit him anyway, might as well get some satisfaction. Driver, why aren't we moving?

—Sorry sir, but there's a red light and cars are blocking me.

The limousine was Dick Lofton's idea. He didn't want his candidate to look inferior to the movie stars, so he ordered the black stretch.

—Richard, what you did was stupid. You should have just ignored him.

—They're accusing me of having an affair in front of my family and I'm supposed to do nothing?

Wellington reached into the liquor cabinet for the scotch.

—You *did* have an affair.

—So this is my fault?

—Whose fault do you think it is?

The liquor bottle was placed back in the cabinet.

—Okay, fine.

Wellington yelled up to the driver,

—Hold on! As soon as the car stopped, Wellington opened the door and stepped into the street. When the reporters saw him they rushed back, forming a semicircle of seven reporters around him. Wellington pointed at one who wore a blue blazer without a tie.

—You had a question for me?

—Did you have an affair with Pamela Hartley?

—Yes, I had an affair with her. Happy?

—So, you admit you had an affair with Ms. Hartley?

Pens scribbled on pads. Eyes checked levels on audio recorders.

—That's what I said.

—You *did* have an affair with her?

—What are you, deaf?

—No, I'd like to hear you say it again so there's no denying it.

—If it makes you feel better, I spent a night with Pamela. It's over with. She was a friend of mine before it happened, and she's a friend of mine still. Satisfied? This make you feel good?

Another reporter yelled out,

—Senator, who else have you had affairs with?

—All right, that's it. You bloodsuckers are never satisfied.

Wellington pushed two reporters out of the way to get back to the limousine. Once inside, Candace turned to him.

—What was that about?

—My fault, right? It's my fault, so why not tell them? Told you, might as well tell the rest of the world so they stop harassing me. You can read it in the papers tomorrow.

—That's just what I want to read in the school paper.

—You both know I had an affair.

Candace pounced on him.

—An? Singular? One affair?

—All right, Candace.

—Don't blame me when you're not reelected.

Candace turned away from her husband and looked out the window as the driver pushed into slowly moving traffic. When it picked up, the Wellington trio drove down to Bridget's apartment, the Devonshire House on East Tenth Street without uttering another word.

□□□ **10** □□□

The following day, Wellington sat in his office reading an online article about PPL Therapeutics, a company that Samuelson, the geneticist, had mentioned to him. Two quick taps on his office door and his assistant, Keno, stepped in closing the door behind him.

—Senator, Asher Mitchell is here, but you have a phone call I thought you might want to take first. It's Ms. Hartley.

—Oh, thank you.

Wellington picked up the phone and spoke in a pleasant tone.

—Hi, Pamela.

—What the hell did you do?

Wellington grew defensive.

—Nothing. I didn't do anything.

—Nothing? I'm all over the papers! What do you think my husband is going to say when he gets home tonight? And my kids, what are they supposed to think? Didn't you think?

—What was I supposed to do? Let things keep building and building? These damn people won't leave you alone. If it makes you feel any better, I did it defending your honor.

—*My* honor?

—Yes, of course. Who do you think I did it for?

—You did it for yourself.

—That's not true at all.

—You realize I can't see you anymore, don't you?

One of the three small silver framed photos on Wellington's desk caught his eye. It was taken on Bridget's college graduation day in front of the fountain in Washington Square Park. The smiling Bridget stood between her two parents, with her brother Richie next to Mrs. Wellington. Wellington lifted it and placed it face down on the desk.

—We'll just let this blow over and we'll be okay.

—You were really stupid to say anything, Richard.

—I'm sorry.

—Somehow I doubt that.

Click. The phone line went dead.

—Pamela? Shit.

Wellington went to the door and invited Asher Mitchell in. Instead of inviting him to sit, he went to his closet for his suit jacket before turning back to his legal counsel.

—Have you had lunch?

—Aren't you interested in what Police Commissioner Parker and Mayor Corpson said about you hitting Johnny Gobo, and about last night's incident?

—Not really. I assume you've taken care of it, correct?

—You're not too arrogant, are you?

—I'm busy is what I am. Ever heard of a guar?

—A what?

Later that evening, in his ride back to Westchester, Wellington dialed his campaign manager from his cell phone.

—Dick Lofton.

—Hey, it's Richard. I had a long talk with Asher Mitchell today. I've decided I'm not going to seek another term.

—I've heard that before. I'll believe you when you make it public. When are you going to do that?

—Soon, but not right away. I'm telling you because you should know. Just don't say anything to the press. I don't want them to think I'm stepping down because of them, and I don't want to be seen as a lame duck.

Outside the car window, a stream of cars in two lanes raced each other up the Saw Mill Parkway.

—Why? What's this really all about? Did you and Candace have another fight?

—No. I'm going to open a hunting ranch. I want to hunt lions, elephants, rhinos, wild game.

—How much have you been drinking?

—I'm not drunk. I want to clone them. They've cloned sheep, haven't they? Why not clone lions and tigers, and other wild and exotic species?

—You're moving kind of fast, aren't you? Dropping politics to clone lions? And where are you going to do this? Up in Westchester?

—No, in Africa. I've sent Asher Mitchell over there to find a suitable ranch because I don't want to clone just lions. I want to clone tigers and elephants, and other types of hunting animals.

—Senator, cloning a lion sounds…well, it sounds far-fetched, but let's say you can do it. Tigers are different. Tigers aren't native to Africa.

—Not yet, but they will be. Have you heard of the Diamond v. Chakrabarty Supreme Court decision?

—No.

—I won't go into all the details; I'll just tell you that the Supreme Court ruled, in essence, if a new organism or animal is created through genetic modification, that animal or organism would be patentable. What I want to do is to take animals that are difficult to hunt these days because they are increasingly rare or dwindling in populations, like lions and elephants, and clone them. I also want to take animals that aren't native to Africa, but which are great hunting trophies, like tigers and guars, and manipulate their genes in such a way that they'll be able to survive and flourish in Africa. Once we do that we'll patent the animal. We would own the rights to any kind of gene-altered or transgenic animal we produce. We would also own the rights to any of their offspring produced.

—What do you mean by own them? How?

—Own them like you own the rights to any other product, whether it's the secret formula to Coca-Cola or the software that runs Windows. Owning the rights to transgenic tigers or leopards or any other animal in Africa will be worth hundreds of millions, maybe billions. There'll be nothing like it in the world. We could also manipulate a gene or two of animals already native to Africa. Say we change a gene on a lion that we are able to clone; we could patent that animal, that lion. Any offspring of the lion we would own. If we become the first to produce cloned, huntable animals we will capture the market, and every hunting ranch will buy their animal products from us, from The Promised Land Ranch. That's what I'm going to call my ranch: The Promised Land.

—The whole thing sounds ridiculous to me, especially since you seem to be trying to turn yourself into some modern-day Noah.

—Ridiculous or not, it's going to happen. You should give it some real thought because I'm going to need investors. At this point, you're one of only a handful of people I'm telling about this.

□□□ 12 □□□

Ten days later, Wellington was in his office trying to formulate a succinct answer to the question: should the draft be reinstated? Some minority members of both the House and Senate had been trying to put together enough supporters to give it a formal hearing. Wellington wanted to make sure it was defeated before a vote was even considered. He realized it was almost always the poor and undereducated who were forced to fight for America, but a draft could turn the middle class and educated college students against politicians. As he had lived through the sixties and had future designs on the presidency, the last thing he wanted if he occupied the White House was a powerful and rebellious student class. A draft would have almost certainly prevented or shortened the wars in Iraq and Afghanistan, and wars were always good for business; therefore good for America. Anticipating questions from the press on this issue, he began to formulate answers when Keno knocked on the door, entered, and told him Asher Mitchell had arrived for his 9:30 appointment.

Mitchell never had a gray hair out of place or a loose thread dangling from his perfectly tailored suits, so it was a surprise for Wellington to see him wearing a safari jacket, polo shirt and blue jeans—all purchased at Paul Stuart before leaving for Africa. There was also a glow about Mitchell, and not all of it had to do with the sun. Though married, Mitchell had for a number of years been involved in a steady, thought casual, relationship with a younger man—in his thirties—who ran an art gallery on Fifth-Seventh Street. Mitchell had invited him to Africa, and this accounted for at least some of the effervescence he displayed. Wellington knew of the relationship, but never criticized or commented on it.

Asher took a seat at the worktable, opened his briefcase and handed Wellington a memory stick onto which he had transferred the photos from his digital camera.

—There's plenty of land, and cheap too. But there's no way you can casually walk in and quietly buy three hundred thousand acres. Africans hear some American wants a three hundred thousand acre spread they're suspicious. They think it's a ruse, that we're after oil or copper or diamonds.

—Didn't you tell them you wanted a hunting ranch?

—I did. But they didn't believe me. No one starts hunting ranches these days—doesn't make any sense. Why not tell them it's for you?

—It's too soon. The press will get a hold of it and it'll draw too much heat. And speaking of the press, how did they find out about Pamela?

—Why don't you tell me? She wasn't a one-time thing, was she?

Wellington didn't answer right away.

—Senator, with all due respect, you need to realize people are watching and keeping tabs on you. If you're seen with a woman other than your wife and it's not written about right away it's only because your opponents are waiting for a more opportune time.

—I know. That's why I want to get the hell out of politics and open up this ranch. Did you find anywhere that could be viable?

—I saw a big spread in Gwanda that looks pretty good.

—Gwanda? Isn't that by Kenya?

—Yes, to the northeast below Ethiopia, to the west of Somalia. Here, take a look.

Mitchell reached into his briefcase and pulled out two slightly worn maps. The first and larger was of Eastern Africa, showing Ethiopia, Somalia, Kenya, and Gwanda. The second map showed Gwanda with some handwritten notations and an X indicating the location of a ranch. Wellington looked at both without expression.

—What's wrong with Kenya?

—Nothing. It's just that your money will go much further in Gwanda, and it's one of the few English-speaking countries in Africa. If you're going to hire foreign workers, having English speakers will certainly

71

make things easier and less expensive. You won't have to train a bilingual staff or hire translators.

—What's the country like?

—Mostly open country with small villages scattered around, but plenty of land to hunt on. There are also some mountains and rivers which are quite beautiful. Total population is about three million. The capital city is Nakambu, which has about six hundred thousand people. The per capita income is less than eight hundred dollars, which means we wouldn't have to pay them much.

Wellington took the folded maps from Mitchell, walked to his desk, pulled open the bottom drawer on the right hand side, fingered through the hanging green file folders until he found an empty and unlabeled folder. He pulled it open and deposited the maps. He looked back to Mitchell who began speaking again.

—There are a few oil companies that operate on the coast. I think they pay their workers a dollar or two a day. DeBeers has one of their diamond mines there, and they pay about the same, as does Nike, who owns a factory in Nakambu.

Wellington came back to the table.

—Isn't that part of Africa rather volatile these days?

—Just about every country in Africa is volatile depending on what kind of resources they have.

—Okay, but just how volatile is Gwanda?

—There was one minor incident about four years ago. Apparently some villagers were upset because their water and farmland had been contaminated through years of oil spills and leaks. They began protesting and asking for reparations. Each week the protests were getting bigger and bigger until oil executives forced the military to crack down. A few Gwandans were killed and their leader, some power-hungry nut named Seisko Upendo, was sent to jail. But everything's okay now.

—Well, all right. And you saw something there that you liked?

—Yeah. There's one ranch, about two hundred sixty thousand acres. It's owned by an eccentric elderly couple, the Brumleys, whose families were part of the original British colonialists. He's nearly deaf and I think she's tired of taking care of him. She realizes they need a full-time nurse or staff, so they're planning to move back to England, where their son owns an estate. I had some video footage shot so you could take a look; unfortunately, I left it at home. I'll get it to you tomorrow.

—Good. I'd like to see the footage as soon as possible.

Connor Gazelle came out of his penthouse condo on Crosby Street in Soho. He walked up to Prince Street and waved to the owner of Savoy restaurant who was outside smoking. He continued walking to Lafayette Street where he raised a hand to hail a cab. A Pakistani cabbie picked him up and they drove north up Lafayette to Fourth Avenue. They passed Union Square, went up Park Avenue South and through the ramp that looped around Grand Central. When a red light stopped them on the opposite side of the loop, Connor pulled out his cell phone and dialed.

—Gazelle headquarters.

Gazelle's headquarters was a group of suites inside the Tribeca Grand Hotel. Zack Taylor, the campaign manager, tried to convince Connor it was much too plush for a political candidate. But Connor opted for the alluring atmosphere of the Tribeca, which was only a short walk from his apartment. Besides the usual business functions, there was access to the penthouse terrace, a one hundred person private screening room, a seductive cocktail lounge, an even more private lounge inside the lounge. The icing on the cake for Connor were the beautiful waitresses who, in order to extract larger tips, seemingly naively and innocently, bent low when placing cocktails on the tables so that the men could inspect, however briefly, their cleavage.

As an actor, Connor first made his name by portraying ordinary men who must act heroically or die when thrust into extraordinary circumstances: in other words, he played action heroes. Later, Connor became more politically conscious and veered away from action-hero roles. Nowadays, the image Connor wished to present to the public was that of an ordinary guy fighting against the machinery of political corruption. Zackary Taylor was happy to go along with this charade, but felt the props were all wrong. Ordinary men do not sip eighteen dollar cocktails during working hours. But what could he do, an ordinary man fighting against the machinery of celebrity culture?

The light showed green and the taxi began to move forward, up Park Avenue past the Waldorf Astoria.

—Zack, it's Connor. I've been talking to a friend of mine, Bob Hevens—a film producer—about helping us. Bob thinks releasing a movie that illustrates who I am just prior to the election will help my campaign. It might be enough to swing the election my way.

—We don't have time for any movie. Even if we did, I...

—We have seven months until the election. We'll shoot on digital video, which will be quick and cheap. Bob has been talking to some writers, and they're already working on a script. We should be able to have a shooting script in a few weeks. It'll take a few more weeks for preproduction and we shoot it. The shooting shouldn't last more than two to three weeks, a month at most. This isn't going to be a big Hollywood extravaganza. Add a month for post and a few weeks wiggle room, and we'll have plenty of time before the election to get it out.

As the taxi turned left on Fifty-Third Street, Connor smiled as a bus passed displaying an ad with a La Perla lingerie model adorning its side. She was posed feline-like on her hands and knees, in sheer black bra and panties. Her luscious lips were slightly opened and dark black hair cascaded over her bare shoulders. Connor had met her more than a year ago poolside at the Delano Hotel in Miami; she was in town for a fashion shoot. Being young, innocent, and not yet known, she accepted Connor's invitation to dinner. He surprised her by not attempting a seduction, a seduction she was quite willing to enjoy. Connor wasn't overly gentlemanly, he was merely patient: he knew that almost every time he was out in public with an attractive female, he was photographed and written up in the press. So he used this to his advantage. Many women believed the stories and expected him to fulfill his role as a legendary lothario. When he didn't, which was as often as not, they saw the man beyond the myth, gained some respect for him and told their friends. Later, when he ran into these women or their friends, many of them became much easier to seduce.

The Fifty-Third Street entrance to the Museum of Modern Art was crowded. This pleased Connor. He stepped out of the taxi and was immediately recognized. He played it nonchalant by continuing to talk as he made his way through the entrance.

—Connor, why don't you come down to the office so we can talk about this? I'd like to talk to you about it before I talk to Bob.

—I can't. I'm at MoMA. There's a film screening—part of the Maurice Pialat—retrospective they're doing, and afterwards there's a private reception. I told you about it already.

—Well good, enjoy yourself. I wouldn't want your political aspirations to get in the way of you having fun.

□□□ **14** □□□

Occasionally, Senator Wellington wanted some private time when traveling. When he did, he took the Acela Amtrak train to Washington instead of flying. This way, for a few hours each way, he knew he would be undisturbed. In the morning he could read the newspapers and in the evening he could relax with a scotch or three on the way back.

At Penn Station, with the other travelers, day-trippers and commuters, he waited until the track number was posted and announced. He walked down Track 7 stairwell onto the platform and into the train. The coach class cars were only partially filled. Moving beyond the first two and past the dining car, he entered the business class car directly behind the engine car. An elderly couple, both thin and dressed nicely, was looking at a German Fodor's travel guide of Washington, a mother and daughter sat a few seats ahead, three businessmen sat solo, and a single woman was seated next to a window, her dyed blonde hair was visible above the back of her seat. Wellington couldn't resist selecting the seat across the aisle from her. A quick glimpse at her legs told him she was attractive, so he made commotion putting his bag in the rack above the seats and taking out a *Foreign Affairs* and a *Wall Street Journal* from his briefcase. The woman turned in his direction. She looked to be in her early or mid-forties, and though no longer as stunning as she must have been in her younger days, she was still quite beautiful. Consequently, Wellington's glance fell to her fingers. there was no wedding ring. Her lips formed a bright red smile when she realized who she was looking at.

—Senator, what a surprise. I never expected to see you here.

Wellington smiled back at her briefly before saying,

—People must assume that the only place I exist is on television, because whenever they see me, it's always a surprise to them.

—It's not that. I was going to Washington to see you.

—Me? How did I get so lucky?

From the far end of the car, a voice called out,

—Tickets, please. Please have your tickets out.

After the train conductor punched their tickets and placed the stubs on the rail above their seats, the woman stood up and offered her hand.

—Senator, my name is Claudia Potter. Would it be too forward to ask to sit next to you so we don't have to talk across the aisle?

—I would be delighted.

Wellington stuffed his *Wall Street Journal* into the pouch of his front seat, freeing the adjacent seat. Ms. Potter extracted her *Variety* from her seat pouch, placed it on the overhead rack below her briefcase, and sat down next to Wellington.

—I called your office and your assistant said you would be in Washington for the next few days. I don't like to waste time, so I thought I'd make a bold move and come to see you in D.C. I never expected to run into you on the train.

—What did you want to see me about?

—The Promised Land. I want to put your hunting ranch on television.

Men, guns, and wild animals, it's exactly what we're looking for.

This surprised Senator Wellington but not in a good way. His face turned serious and sober.

—Absolutely not. This is going to be private. Who told you about The Promised Land, anyway?

Wellington started to regret allowing the blonde beauty to sit next to him, sensing it was going to be a long ride to the nation's capital.

—You're looking for investors, aren't you? And people talk, don't they.

—But I've only told a handful of people. Who told you about it? I'd like to know.

—Let's just say he's a billionaire businessman who usually gets what he wants, and he wants a piece of The Promised Land.

—Who?

—Seymour Blackstone.

—Sy knows about this?

—Yes. He hired me to turn VBS television into a major player, and that's what I intend to do. With Sy's help, we'll be able to provide you with the money to get this off the ground.

—This is not going to be televised. It's not going to be news. It's not going to be anything but a private ranch, completely away from the public eye.

—Tell me how you're going to pay for your startup costs? You need geneticists and researchers, and you have real estate and cloning costs, and lawyers' fees. Do you really think you'll be able to finance that out of membership fees? You've got all that to think about, and you're running for reelection at the same time?

—Who said I'm even running for reelection? I'm not.

Claudia Potter became didactic, as she was wont to do.

—Senator, I think you're a bright man, a very bright man. And I think you should take what I say seriously. This has the potential to be one of the most captivating shows on television. That's why we want it. We want shows that push the envelope.

—Hunting isn't for television. People don't want to see hunting and killing on TV. And, even if they did the FCC would never allow it.

—If the FCC allows people to sit home and watch other people fuck on TV, they'll allow hunting.

—I'm guessing you're not often accused of being too delicate, are you?

—Do you want me to pretend to be a wallflower, or do you want me to talk straight?

—You really think there's an audience for this?

—I guarantee it. Will there be obstacles? Yes. Will there be outcries?

Of course there will. Which is to your benefit—it's free publicity.

—And this would reach a national audience, correct?

—Yes.

—If you could guarantee that I was given a few minutes before each broadcast, I might be persuaded.

□□□ 15 □□□

A week later, Claudia Potter asked Senator Wellington to a breakfast meeting at the Regency Hotel in Manhattan. When he arrived, he was surprised to see a man, who appeared to be in his mid-twenties but was actually a decade older, sitting with her. Potter introduced them. They shook hands and took seats on opposite sides of the table.

—Senator, Adam's a geneticist.

Wellington was quick to pick up on the name, and on another day might have made a joke or Biblical reference. But he wasn't pleased with seeing a third party, and he wasn't going to make any pretense that he was.

—Didn't know you were bringing someone along, Claudia.

—I thought you two should meet.

A trim, silver-haired waiter approached and took the trio's breakfast orders. After handing off his menu, Adam spoke.

—Senator, my chief concern is getting enough product. It's not going to do us any good to have a hunting show, if, after the first episode, we run out of lions to shoot.

Wellington turned from the geneticist to the television producer.

—You're getting damn pushy, Claudia. I haven't even agreed to a show and you've got me talking with a geneticist?

—As I told you, I don't believe in wasting time. If we're going to do it we should do it and not just talk about it.

Adam waded in.

—Do you have your site secured, Senator?

—Not yet. I'm ironing out the details.

—You're going to have to work on that. That's a priority because it only makes sense to have the research and development facilities on site.

Wellington didn't even bother looking at him, his eyes burned into Claudia Potter.

—I'm sure you've had men jump through hoops for you. I'm not one of them. No one tells me what to do.

Abruptly, Wellington got up from his chair.

—You're leaving?

—Yes, I'm leaving. We do this thing in my timetable or not at all.

—But Senator...

—Goodbye.

He threw his linen napkin onto the table and marched off. A few steps away, a voice called to him.

—Senator?

Turning back, Wellington saw a man with helmet of black hair and two thick bushy eyebrows. It was state senator, Peter Morgan, who rose quickly from his chair and went over to Wellington. Morgan stuck out a hand for a shake but didn't get one.

—Do you have a moment?

—Why?

—It's about the election. Dick Lofton mentioned you weren't going to run, but that you were hesitant about announcing it. You are stepping down, correct?

—As I told him, I haven't had enough time to think it all the way through. It's just that I've been a senator for a good number of years and it's not an easy decision.

—I understand fully. It's just that the Democrats and Gazelle are starting to build momentum. So, the sooner you make your announcement the better for me.

—For *you*? Why'd you change from being a Democrat to a Republican?

—Because I now believe in the Republican Party. Their views are much closer to my own.

—I'll let you know about my decision when I make it. Until that time, I don't want to hear from you. Got it?

Morgan was taken aback by Wellington's tone. He stood there stone-footed and watched the senior senator exit.

Stepping out onto Park Avenue, Wellington pulled out his cell phone and dialed his campaign manager.

—Dick Lofton.

—What are you doing, squeezing me?

—What are you talking about?

—Morgan. I was having breakfast at the Regency, and he came up to me telling me to make my announcement. What gives?

—Senator, you can't tell me you're not going to run and not do anything about it, or expect me to just sit by idly. If you're not going to run we need to talk about it.

—I realize that.

—Do you? We have scores of people who have left positions to work for you. Don't you think we need to give them some notice? You're not helping anyone by sitting on the fence.

—Candace doesn't seem to want to live in Africa.
—I hope that doesn't come as a surprise. I need a decision soon. Are you stepping down, or not?

□□□ 16 □□□

VBS television offices occupied the Thirty-ninth floor of Worldwide Plaza at Forty-Eighth Street and Eighth Avenue. Claudia Potter's office faced west, giving her a vista of the plaza and fountain below and, beyond that, a glimpse of Ninth Avenue, the Hudson River, and parts of New Jersey. She was staring outward, contemplating Wellington's Promised Land Ranch, as Sarah timidly tapped on the door and entered. Sarah wasn't her given name. It was one she had selected when she first came to America from Hong Kong to study. She thought having an American sounding name would make it easier to fit in.
—Ms. Potter?
She turned to her.
—I told Mr. Gables you were too busy to talk, but he hung up and said he's coming over here.
—Well, I guess I'll see him, won't I?
No sooner were those words spoken than the enraged Teddy Gables was pushing through the partially opened door and stepping in. In an effort not to be noticed, the mousey Sarah ducked her head and scurried out the door. Potter didn't move to greet Gables; she stood defiantly with her back against the wide window.
—What the hell do you think you're doing, Claudia? When Sy Blackstone asked me about hiring you I told him I liked you because you had ambition, that you were a go-getter. That didn't mean I wanted you to kick me in the teeth.
Potter replied calmly.
—I didn't kick you in the teeth.
With that, she sat down giving Gables the opportunity to lean on the desk with both hands and holler menacingly at her.
—I'm not done! I woke up this morning and read in *The New York Times* that Claudia Potter is developing a hunting show. Who the hell told you you could develop any show without my approval?
—Are you through?
Despite his tone, Claudia was enjoying herself.
—No, I'm not. I called Sy this morning to tell him the *Times* piece was a mistake. He said what mistake, that you told him all about it. How the hell do you think that makes me look?
—I'm trying to get someone to either shit or get off the pot.

—Want to explain that in English to me?

—The hunting show I want is going to be developed in connection with Senator Richard Wellington. He's starting a hunting ranch in Africa. I thought that a hunting show would be perfect for us.

—Did you? Didn't think to discuss it with me?

Claudia Potter pushed her chair back, put her shapely right leg over her left, knowing Gable's eyes would dart downward to her teal skirt in a hope of seeing a glimpse of flesh. When he lifted his eyes she smiled quickly and spoke.

—No, I didn't because we're not anywhere with it yet. Right now, we're a channel that no one gives a damn about. I want to change that. The hunting show is going to be the first step. Problem is, Wellington doesn't know if he wants to do it or not. The only way to get him to make up his mind is to light a fire under him. I expect that in the next day or two he's going to be calling thinking I betrayed him. Once he does that I'll reel him in, and we'll start putting the elements of the show in place.

—Why didn't you tell me any of this before?

—Because I'm not going to come to you and ask for permission for everything I do. If I did you wouldn't want me to.

With his anger abated, Gables sank into one of the two cushioned chairs in front of Potter's desk.

—What's this show?

Potter stood up and addressed him like a not-particularly-bright student. Gables immediately regretted relinquishing his commanding position, but standing again would only obviate this, so he sat and listened.

—It's not just a show. I want programming that will make people aware of who we are. That's why I want Wellington and his hunting show. I want to use that show as our anchor. I want viewers to know that if they turn on VBS they'll see action, they'll see someone with a gun in his hand about to do something with it.

—Wonderful. We're almost at the bottom now and you want to push us into the toilet.

Potter's phone rang and she looked down at the blinking light. Outside her office, Sarah picked up.

—Claudia Potter's office. How can I help you?

A threatening voice boomed,

—PUT HER ON!

—Who's calling?

—Put her on the goddamn phone!

—She's in the middle of a meeting. Can I take a message?

—No, you can't take a message! Tell her it's Senator Wellington calling, and tell her to pick up the goddamn phone!

—Could you hold please?

Sarah placed the phone on hold and nervously entered her boss' office.

—Excuse me, Mr. Gable. Ms. Potter, it's Senator Wellington on the phone.

—Tell him...no, I'll take it. Excuse me, Teddy.

Potter pushed SPKR on her desk phone.

—Claudia Potter.

—Are you developing your own hunting show?

—Senator Wellington?

—You know damn well who this is!

Potter couldn't resist looking over to Gables before replying.

—You made it quite clear that you weren't interested. I don't have the time or patience to wait until you make up your mind.

—I never said I wasn't interested. I just needed time.

—Goodbye, Senator.

Potter pressed SPKR again and the line went dead.

—You hung up on him? Is that how you expect to get him?

—Why don't you leave it to me, Teddy?

Gables rose from his chair,

—Fine, do what you want. Apparently you already are.

Even before Gables was out the door Sarah was answering the blinking phone line again. It was Wellington, once again yelling for Claudia Potter. As soon as Sarah informed her, Potter closed her office door and picked up the receiver.

—Claudia Potter speaking.

—You've got some nerve, you know that?

—Does that mean you've made up your mind?

—Let's say that I have. Let's say that I want to do the show.

—I'm not sure it's not too late, Senator. We're thinking of building our own Africa set on the Paramount lot in L.A.

—Your own set? Well, you do that. If you're that stupid that you think you can build a set that will duplicate Africa, that will be suitable for real life animals and not drugged up zoo castaways, do it.

Click.

Potter smiled when the line went dead. She reached into her pocketbook for her purse, which contained the senator's business card given to her after hours of banter and flirtation on the train ride to Washington. Wellington's private cell phone number, handwritten on the back of the card, made her grin slightly. But she decided to keep this

professional—at least for the time being. Claudia Potter dialed the office line of her congressional leader.
—Senator Wellington's office.
—Tell him it's Claudia Potter.
—Hold please.

When his phone rang so quickly after he hung up, Senator Wellington suspected who was calling. Keno gave him the message, but he watched the minute hand of his watch make two full rotations before picking up the phone and speaking brusquely.
—What do you want?
—Can I buy you dinner tonight?

Wellington had looked at his calendar earlier in the day and knew he had the evening free, but didn't want to appear too eager.
—I can't do it tonight.
—Tomorrow?
—I think I'm free after nine on Thursday.
—Let's make it Thursday.
—Where?
—Jean Georges. Know it?
—Of course. At Trump Towers at Columbus Circle.
—Yes. I live above it. Shall we say 9:30?

□□□ 17 □□□

Across from the southwest corner of Central Park, high in the sky, an apartment door on the forty-sixth floor opened and two slightly intoxicated figures stepped in.
—...okay, it was a good meal, but hardly worth nine hundred dollars.
—You didn't pay for it, did you?

Wellington hadn't. Claudia Potter had picked up the tab and now she had Wellington where she wanted him. She let him take a quick look around the living room before dimming the lights. It was a neat and clean corporate-looking apartment with barely any personal mementos or artifacts anywhere. A moderately sized living room, with a couch and chairs and a television opened to a kitchen area with a small dining table. The selling point was the location and view: floor to ceiling windows that looked out on Central Park, which showed a scattering of lights, as did the buildings along Fifty-Ninth Street and up Fifth Avenue.
—Doesn't matter...I don't like to throw money away, even if it's not mine. Quite a view you've got here.

As Wellington stepped further into the living room to get a better look through the windows, Claudia Potter came up behind him and kissed the back of his neck.

—I like it best in the morning when the sun comes up over the buildings. If you're lucky, you'll get to see it sometime.

When he turned back to her, Potter brought her lips to his; softly first, and then with more passion. They kissed until she pulled back and took his hand, leading him out of the living room.

—Let me show you the rest.

With his free hand, Wellington scooped the roundness of her fleshy ass as he followed her down the hallway into the bedroom. Here, too, there were large windows looking out onto Central Park. Wellington gave a whistle of admiration.

—Now this is a room with a view.

—Why don't you take your jacket and tie off?

This made Wellington slightly uncomfortable and he tried to ease out of the bedroom without offending her.

—Not right now.

Potter didn't let him leave; she stood in front of him and started to undo his tie. Wellington grabbed her hands and pulled them away.

—All right, look, it's not like I don't want to.

Potter freed her hands, caressed his chest, and leaned in for a kiss.

—I don't care if you're married, if you don't.

Claudia kissed him.

—It's not that.

She reached for the zipper of his pants and he said,

—Don't you read the papers? My little man doesn't seem to work very well on his own.

Embarrassed by this admission, Wellington stepped away pretending to be more interested in the view. Potter wasn't easily dissuaded.

—Another time then?

Encouraged, Wellington turned back to his would-be seductress.

—I'd like that.

Claudia came up to him, pushed her lips to his and felt between his legs with her right hand. She found only softness.

—Would you like me to pick up some of those little blue pills for you?

—Would you? Because I am under a lot of scrutiny and it would be a lot easier if you do.

—I'd love to. It reminds me of the first time I bought condoms for my boyfriend in high school. You should have seen the pharmacist's face. He looked at me like I was some kind of dirty slut, so I winked at him and licked my upper lip with my tongue. He turned as red as a tomato.

☐☐☐ 18 ☐☐☐

Connor Gazelle was sitting on the soft gray sofa in his living room, across from three masterpieces of abstract art: a dark wine-colored Rothko center stage, a Brice Marden, from his Cold Mountain series, to the left, and a Sean Scully Wall Painting on the right. These paintings took his mind off a speech he now realized was destined for the proverbial cutting room floor. Early that week, Connor had been outraged to learn that the discrepancy between a CEO's pay and an average worker's had grown to more than five hundred percent. Feeling this was ammunition he could use, he told his staff to get him the names and financial figures of the highest paid CEOs. He was going to use the information for a speech on the rampant corruption of big business. The young intern who was tasked with providing the tiny factual details annoyed Gazelle by adding a few questions he though worth considering: did Gazelle realize the discrepancy between the pay for top Hollywood stars and bit actors, not to mention production assistants and even first time screenwriters, was often greater than CEOs and an average worker? Was he prepared to criticize the Hollywood establishment as harshly as he was the business world? If he wanted to ask CEOs whose companies had underperformed to give back portions of their salaries, was he prepared to ask Hollywood stars to do the same for films that lost money? Thankfully, a ringing phone pulled him out of his dilemma.
—Hello.
—*Mr. Smith Goes Back to Washington.*
—What?
—*Mr. Smith Goes Back to Washington.*
—Zack?
—Yeah, Connor, it's me. After talking with Bob, I watched *Mr. Smith Goes to Washington*. Why didn't you tell me that you wanted to do a remake of it?
—I wanted you to think it was Bob's idea. With all your anti-Hollywood attitude, I thought if I told you that it was my idea you would be against it.
—Maybe, but anyway I watched and loved it. We want to call yours *Mr. Smith Goes Back to Washington.*
Connor stood up and smiled to himself. Opposite the paintings and fireplace were three sculptures on specially made pedestals: a gilt bronze Bodhisattva, a gray schist seated Buddha, and a black stone

Ganesha, whose trunk Connor rubbed as he moved toward the dining area and terrace. The sculptures on pedestals helped delineate the living room area from the apartment's elevator entrance and the stairs to the floor above. On the opposite end of the room there was a floating wall with eight African masks and beyond that a media room. At the terrace window, Connor looked down at the Soho rooftops below as Zack continued.

—I like the whole idea of you reprising Jimmy Stewart's role. A sizable crowd out there wants the country to be what it once was. They're tired of career politicians; they're tired of lying, dishonesty, and corruption. If we can position you as throwback to Jimmy Stewart's era, we're going to do well, very well. That's why we need you to be on your best behavior, Connor. None of your philandering.

—Don't worry about my personal life.

—Trust me on this; people will be watching you much more than ever before. If you're going to have affairs, keep them…

    Connor's door buzzer rang.

—Zack, I've got to go. We'll talk about this tomorrow.

—Just remember what I….

    Connor disconnected the line and went to the door. He had met the woman ringing the doorbell two weeks earlier at the Museum of Modern Art. After the film screening, the galleries were opened to museum members and donors. While he was standing in front of a Barnett Newman zip painting talking with a public relations woman from the museum, Connor spotted a woman whose beauty made it impossible for his eyes not to follow her. The PR woman noticed this but pretended not to. It didn't matter to Connor. He ended the conversation as quickly as possible and went searching for the alluring siren.

    When he finally caught up to her, she was in one of the other galleries viewing an Agnes Martin grid painting. Her name was Kimberly Galway and she was even more captivating up close. Her eyes were blue-gray, direct and determined which contrasted with her delicate features. Her cheeks were thin, but not hollowed out; her upper lip was luscious and her lower lip even fuller, both painted with a soft red lipstick, which matched nicely with her reddish brown hair. From her delicate neck hung a simple thin, silver chain and from it a crucifix of Jesus. They talked for only a few moments, just enough for Connor to learn she was an actress.

    A few days later, Ms. Galway's agent told her Connor Gazelle wanted her to audition for the female lead in an upcoming film. When she auditioned, Connor was impressed but moved on to the next actress without commenting. A few days later Kim was pleasantly surprised when Connor called her and invited her to his Soho penthouse apartment.

When Kim stepped out of his private elevator, she did her best to mask her nervousness. Connor greeted her with a friendly kiss on the cheek before saying,

—I hope I was not too forward in inviting you here.

—No…I was surprised, I guess, yeah…but it's okay. Did I get the part?

—A final decision hasn't been made.

After a brief awkward pause, Kimberly took her eyes from Connor and looked at the three oil paintings on the wall.

—You have your own Rothko?

—I got lucky in life, what can I say? Do you want to take a closer look?

As Kim inspected the paintings, Connor inspected her. She deliberately didn't wear anything too provocative, as she wanted to convey a casual, yet strictly professional appearance. She was wearing blue jeans that were worn but not over-worn, and a white, button-down shirt, under a black blazer, and stylishly pointed black shoes.

After viewing the paintings, still feeling a bit nervous, Kim went over to the African masks. She wanted to feel the wooden face, but stopped before doing so and looked to Connor as if for permission.

—Yeah, you can touch it. Pick it up.

Kim took it off the small hook affixed to the wall, felt the ebony smoothness before placing it in front of her face and showing herself to her host. He smiled; she laughed and returned it to its place. Next, Kim walked inside the media room. When Connor wanted to watch movies, from either a 16- or 35-millimeter film projector, or digital video projector (all enclosed behind the back wall), a screen descended from the ceiling. This screen was the same width as the floating wall on the opposite side. When it was not down for viewing, the wall showed a large Shirin Neshat photo of Iranian women in burkas along a desolate sand dune. The left wall held shelves of DVDs and CDs. The right wall shelves held all the necessary devices to control audio and video. For viewing, there were two rows of four specially designed cinema chairs, and beyond them two black couches.

As Kim was eying the Neshat photo, Connor came up behind her and placed his hands over her shoulders. He felt her quiver slightly, but she didn't move away. Kim pivoted her head toward him and showed a perceptive smile.

—My agent told me to be careful around you.

—Did he?

—She.

—What did *she* say?

Kim turned away flirtatiously,

—Don't worry; I don't always listen to her.

Connor followed her out of the media room, and, as she proceeded to the sculptures, he went into the kitchen, calling out as he did,

—It's just that if we went out to a restaurant some people would want to meet me or want my autograph, or they'd call the press. They do that anytime I'm out with a beautiful woman. They'd get a photo of us, and the next thing you know we'd be written up as having an affair. That's the last thing I need with the election coming up.

Kim picked up a DVD on one of the pedestals and called into the kitchen where Connor was uncorking a bottle of wine.

—Is this any good, *Floating Weeds* by Ozu?

—You should watch it and find out.

Connor poured two glasses and returned to the living room where he handed Kim one.

—Are you into Eastern religion and Zen and Buddhism and all that? These are all Buddhas, right? What is this one, some sort of Hindu God?

She was looking at the center statue, a bronze, four-armed deity with a long trunk.

—Rub his nose, his trunk.

—Why?

—That's Ganesh—rubbing his nose is supposed to bring good luck.

Kim rubbed.

—It's smooth. How old is it? It looks old.

—It's from the twelfth century, the Hoysala Dynasty.

Connor came up beside her, put his wine goblet down on the side of the pedestal, lifted the statue and handed it to Kim.

—Wow, that's heavy…heavier than it looks.

She handed it back to Connor and he replaced it on the pedestal.

—What about this one, this Buddha, what year is it from?

—Actually, that one's a Ghandhara Bodhisattva from the third century. The other one is a Buddha.

—How do you know it's not a Buddha?

—By the way they're dressed. Buddha is always depicted in simple clothing, usually just a robe since he's found enlightenment. A Bodhisattva on the other hand, hasn't yet achieved enlightenment or reached Nirvana, that's why he's still wearing gold and jewelry. Buddha was from a wealthy family, so as a young man and a Bodhisattva, he is depicted with ornaments of wealth. Once he became Buddha, and reached Nirvana, he no longer possessed a desire for wealth or ostentation. Simplicity became his virtue. Do you want to sit down?

—I haven't finished looking at your paintings. Let me see those, first.

She was indicating two more paintings on the far side of the wide loft. On the south wall there was a small Gerhard Richter abstract next to a Richard Diebenkorn semi-abstract of Marin County. Connor smiled slyly,

—There's more upstairs in my bedroom.

Kimberly smiled back, but not slyly.

—You didn't expect me to view your bedroom tonight, did you?

—I didn't expect anything. But I didn't rule it out either.

□□□ 19 □□□

Over in Gwanda, after touring the Brumley ranch with the estate manager, Senator Wellington, Asher Mitchell, Keno Crawford, and Steve Lowell met with Mr. and Mrs. Brumley to discuss the purchase of their property. Lowell was an African American public relation guru from Washington. Before agreeing to sell, Harold Brumley, old and infirm, made certain the five families who lived on and worked the estate would be allowed to keep their houses. Asher Mitchell refused this request, but Steve Lowell thought it would be politically unwise to disrupt and upset the locals. Wellington sided with Lowell and the families were allowed to stay.

Afterwards, the quartet of Americans dined at Ibis, an upscale restaurant Ms. Brumley had recommended, in the capital city, Nakambu. During dinner, the men watched a number of nicely dressed dark-skinned beauties going upstairs to the lounge where music was playing. Once their check was paid the men went up to investigate.

While the older men sat at the bar drinking and talking of their plans for The Promised Land, Keno danced to Afro-pop music with a model from Nairobi. Wellington's treatment and feelings toward Keno ranged from professional, wanting him to act as a tight-lipped and dedicated employee, to cordial, even collegial at times. Keno felt slightly conflicted by this vacillation and subsequently almost never completely relaxed around the senator. But now that they were in another country, and on another continent, one Keno had wanted to travel to his entire life, he loosened up and was, at least while they were drinking, being treated as an equal. Perhaps this had something to do with the fact his three companions were all over fifty, married, white— well, two of them were white—and all of the women and men dancing were black and in their twenties or thirties. Keno was also the only one who recognized at least some of the music being played: Manu

Dibango, Fela Anikulapo-Kuti, Mzwakhe Mbuli, and Hassan Hakmoun.

After four dances Keno stepped outside on the veranda for some air. Their dinner waiter, Manlea, followed him outside. Ten minutes later, Keno returned inside and asked Wellington if they could talk. Wellington put down his Cutty Sark and soda and stepped outside where Manlea was still waiting.

—Senator, I'm sorry to bother you but Manlea infected his wife and child with the AIDS virus. Is there is anything that we can do to help him? If we could get them some antiviral drugs...

—Keno, let me talk to you privately for a moment.

Keno followed Wellington to the darker corner of the veranda.

—You've got a lot of gall introducing me and making him think I can get him AIDS drugs, when I can't.

—I just thought, if you're going to spend all that money on the ranch, maybe we could help one of the people over here.

—You want to be a diplomat someday, don't you?

—I'm not sure.

Wellington pointed his finger at the younger man's chest.

—Let me tell you something about being in a position of authority. The key is to not let your emotions get the better of you. Obviously you're having difficulty separating your feelings from your rational thoughts.

—It's not simply emotions, sir.

—I'm afraid it is. He sees anyone who can afford to eat in a restaurant like this as an easy mark. Gives you a sob story about his family and expects to cash in. You should realize that he sees us—maybe not you, because you're the same color as him—but Mr. Mitchell and I as wealthy Americans. We're not, but that's how he sees us. He figures he can extort money from us. This is good training for you. Like anyone else he should learn to solve his own problems, not get a handout. You can tell him whatever you want. If you're smart, you'll make your refusal sound compassionate.

—But Senator, if we just...

—Keno, that's enough. You're like a woman, you don't think, you go on emotions and feelings. That's a big mistake.

Wellington stared at him, making sure he comprehended what he said, before walking away. Manlea went over to Keno and extended his hand in gratitude.

—Thanks for trying. The two men shook.

—I appreciate it.

—Let me try again when we get back to New York, maybe he'll have a change of heart.

20

Yvette, a light-skinned African American, stepped from Connor Gazelle's private elevator into his condo, but there was no one to meet her.
—Helloooo?
Connor called from above the stairs.
—Be right down.
Yvette moved from the foyer into the living room. Like a movie star making his screen entrance, Connor descended the staircase slowly. Kim eyed his appearance from his feet upward: he wore soft suede loafers, tan socks, a pair of blue jeans, and a black button-down shirt. Italian cologne faintly scented the air.
—Yvette, hi. Thanks for coming by.
He gave her a quick kiss on her cheek.
—Thanks for inviting me.
—We didn't have much time to talk at the audition, and I wanted to talk to you because you're really talented.
Yvette got excited.
—Does that mean I have the role?
—It's between you and another actress. I thought it would be good to get to know each other a little, to see if we would feel comfortable working together. You look beautiful tonight.
—When I'm not acting or auditioning, I teach aerobics. I used to dance in a nightclub. That's how I stay in shape, dancing and aerobics. I'm just doing it until I get more roles.
Yvette's flawless chocolate skin had a faint rosy hue around her cheeks. She wore a dark blue skirt that wrapped tightly around her firm ass, and a black v-neck shirt that fit snuggly around the curves of her breasts.
—Can I get you a drink?
—Sure. It's almost like a museum or something with all these paintings. I took an art class at Pratt.
Yvette walked over to the paintings.
—But I never really got a lot of the stuff they were saying. I mean, what are these shapes, these rectangles, supposed to mean?
—Well, that's a Rothko, Mark Rothko, his paintings…
—I heard of him.
—He saw them as spiritual, all about the emotional state he was feeling or trying to express.
—Really?
Yvette dismissed this explanation and walked over to the Buddhist

90

statues.

—These are cool.

—Thanks. That's Ganesha, from the twelfth century, the Hoysala Dynasty.

—The wholesale Dynasty? Cool. I always try to get my things wholesale too.

Yvette laughed and caught Connor staring at her breasts. She smiled slyly and he spoke.

—Rub his trunk. It's supposed to bring you luck.

Yvette rubbed and spoke seductively,

—So, you think I'll get lucky tonight?

—Maybe.

She eyed the Bodhisattva.

—What happens if I rub this one?

—If you rub that one, I get lucky.

Yvette rubbed and smiled at him.

—Sounds like we're both getting lucky tonight.

She laughed again and sashayed past the African masks to look into the darkness behind the floating wall.

—Can I go here? Is that all right, me looking around?

—Yeah, of course, enjoy yourself. Let me get the light.

Connor hit a switch. When the room became illuminated, Yvette gave out a little chuckle.

—You got like your own private movie theater? I gotta get me one of those. Where's the popcorn machine?

—It's being repaired.

Yvette smiled.

—You almost had me. I almost believed you.

After a quick flirtatiously grin, Connor left the media room and went into the kitchen. Yvette followed him in and watched Connor reach up to the wine rack for a bottle of wine.

—Can I pick?

Surprised at the request, Connor turned back to her.

—Do you know wines?

—No, I just go by the label. I like pretty ones. Can I?

—Um…sure.

Yvette spun a couple of bottles around. Seeing one that grabbed her eyes, she pulled it down and turned the label so they both could see it,

—Chateau Petrus? Is this a good one?

A half-chuckle spilled from Connor's lips.

—What?

—Nothing. It's very good.

—You're not joking are you, because it says 1961? It's not too old, is it?

—That's the vintage…

—Oh, so does that mean it's good?

—Well, it's a…it's a very sophisticated wine…you might not like it.

—I can be sophisticated, let's try it. I want to try it!

Yvette bounded onto a counter stool. Connor smiled, and took two goblets down from the glass-enclosed cabinet above the counter. He shook his head slightly and before letting out a low sigh and saying to himself,

—A Petrus '61.

—Anything wrong?

—No. Petrus comes from the Pomeral wine region in Bordeaux.

—Bordeaux? Where's that?

—France.

—Oh.

—Petrus comes from a small vineyard, probably not even thirty acres. I took a trip there a few years back. It's made almost exclusively from merlot grapes.

—And like one family owns the vineyard, right?

Yvette's reply surprised Connor so he turned to look at his guest.

—Yes, how did you know?

—Lucky guess.

Connor looked at the wine bottle before looking back at Yvette. She wasn't quite smiling, but did show a playful expression on her face.

—You know a bit more about wine than I gave you credit for, don't you?

—Oh, I don't know anything.

—My apologies. You've drunk Petrus before I take it?

—Once or twice…for some reason men seem to want to impress me.

She giggled with a deep hint of sexuality.

—They take me out to fancy restaurants. After a few times a girl gets curious about the wine list.

—I bet she does. What else does a girl get curious about?

—You'll find out soon enough, won't you?

A corkscrew was mounted on the counter top. Connor gripped the bottle, aligned it with the corkscrew, and plunged the corkscrew into the cork. He yanked it out with a "pop." Uncorked, he grabbed the bottle, picked up the two glasses and turned to Yvette.

—Shall we go into the living room?

21

Keno had been sitting at his desk for the last half hour staring blankly ahead, trying to get up the courage to approach his boss. Finally, he abruptly got up, knocked once on Wellington's open door, and stepped in. The senator looked up.

—Could I talk to you for a moment?

—You can always talk to me.

Keno pulled up a chair opposite the senator's desk. Wellington capped the fountain pen he was using to edit a speech he would be delivering later in the week.

—Remember the waiter, Manlea, from the restaurant in Gwanda?

—That was weeks ago.

—I know. I've been keeping in touch with him and…

—You're been calling Africa from this office? Do you know how much that costs?

—I called him from home.

—Oh.

—He's, um, he's really desperate, and I told him a little about the idea for the TV show, how you're going to hunt animals and put it on TV… What if you were to hunt him instead of the animals?

Wellington leaned forward, not quite comprehending.

—Hunt him?

—Yes. He's willing to let you hunt and kill him, and put it on TV, if you'll provide AIDS medicine to his wife, his child, and his brother.

—He wants us to hunt him?

—I know it sounds crazy and I told him that but he wanted me to ask you. What happened to him was he went to see a prostitute while his wife was pregnant. He got AIDS from her and infected his wife, and their baby was born with AIDS. He feels horrible about what he's done. If he can save them, that's what he'd like to do. He knows that if they don't get any medicine they'll all be dead in a year or two. His brother also has AIDS. He's seen many of his friends die and knows how horrible a death it can be.

Wellington tapped the tip of the pen against the document on his desk before replying.

—You're talking about shooting a human being, Keno. We don't do that.

—I understand that. But he's desperate. Like a lot of Africans, he can't afford the cost of the antiviral drugs. He doesn't want his wife and child to die. He kept on asking me to ask you about it. I promised him I would. Could you think about it, and maybe ask Ms. Potter? It's her show, right?

—Let me think about it.

Wellington's desk phone rang. He looked down at the display name: A. Mitchell. He picked up the receiver immediately.

—Hi. What they say?

—Johnny Gobo agreed to drop the assault charge against you if you give him the right to use the footage he's shot. Here's the thing with him, he's planning to put together some kind of documentary. It amounts to little more than a school project, a senior thesis kind of thing. He doesn't have a lawyer, so I could probably tie it up in court for a while, certainly at least until after the election, and probably beyond that if...

—No.

—Listen to me. He's got the right to use the footage as long it's not for commercial purposes. It's for a school thesis, so it wouldn't be considered commercial. Essentially, I would be agreeing to give him the rights he already has, though he doesn't quite realize it.

—So we're just tricking him into dropping the charges?

—Right.

—That's fine with me.

—I also heard back from that reporter you punched, Dennis Paige. He said he'd drop charges if you give a contribution to his favorite charity.

—How much?

—Five thousand dollars. His daughter has cerebral palsy. He thinks giving to United Cerebral Palsy is better than writing about you.

—Can we use campaign contributions?

—We're not supposed to, obviously, but I'll find a way.

☐☐☐ 22 ☐☐☐

At Le Bernardin, Claudia Potter placed her decaffeinated coffee cup on the table. She reached into her pocketbook, found the bottle of blue pills and discreetly took one out. Just as discreetly, she reached across the table for Wellington's hand and deposited the pill in it.

Back at Claudia's apartment, when they were done Wellington rolled off of her and picked up his boxer shorts from the floor. He stepped into them and sat in the chair beside a telescope. Wellington put his eye to the eyepiece. Potter stood up, put on a red silk robe and turned on the bedside lamp. Wellington abruptly turned toward her.

—Hey, turn that off!

She ignored him.

—Do you really need to do that?

—What did you get a telescope for if you didn't want to look into other people's windows?

—I look into Central Park, that's why I got it. There's a hawk that I've been watching. He has a nest on one of the buildings on Fifth Avenue.

—Well, that's what I'm doing, looking for hawks.

—Are you? Or are you just trying to avoid the subject?

Potter sat on a vintage Art Deco chair upholstered in red satin and watched Wellington gaze at his unsuspecting constituents as he spoke.

—Don't you think hunting a person could impact us negatively? How's that going to look if the press says we're hunting someone with AIDS on my ranch?

She pulled open the drawer of a black lacquer art deco end table next to her chair and extracted a notepad and pen.

—You just have to see this as us bringing medicine to stricken Africans. The hunting is just a byproduct.

Claudia turned to a clean page as Wellington spoke.

—Byproduct or not, the drugs are expensive, up to twenty thousand dollars per year in some cases.

—That's retail not wholesale.

Wellington turned back to see her writing on the pad.

—You're talking about his wife, their baby, and his brother. That's three people. If they get the drugs we'd have to provide it to them for many years, for a lifetime. That's what he wants.

Potter wrote: SHOOTING AIDS PATIENTS CAN SAVE LIVES.

—But if we can get a show out of it.

—A show?

Potter put her pad on her lap and looked over to Wellington.

—He isn't the only African dying from AIDS. Hell, the entire continent is dying. If we could get a weekly show out of it. If we could hunt someone different every week, we might have something.

—Claudia, you're talking about hunting people, actual human beings.

Potter stood up, laid the pad and pen on the chair, and went over to Wellington. She ran her left hand through his thinning hair and sat down on the bed across from him.

—Who are going to die anyway. Don't look at it as killing Africans. You've got to see it as saving lives, because that's what we'll be doing. Take this guy, this waiter, we'd be saving his wife's life, his son's, and his brother's. That's no small thing, saving lives. The more people we hunt, the more lives we save.

—What about the legality of it? As far as I know you're not allowed to hunt people. Asher called you, didn't he? What did he say?

—He said we didn't have to worry about it. It's a foreign country which isn't under our jurisdictions or laws.

—Nonetheless, it would be on American TV.

—Let me worry about that.

—What about cloning lions? Is that off?

—No, not at all, but it's years away. With this we already have product we can shoot. It will give us a cash flow that will allow us to fund the cloning.

The senator stood up, found his trousers on the floor, picked them up and stepped into them.

—Where's my jacket? Is it in the other room?

They walked out of the bedroom together. In the living room his suit jacket was flung across the couch. He picked it up and put it on. Potter waited for him to adjust his tie before speaking.

—I hate to bring this up, but it wasn't cheap, the Viagra.

—Sorry you had to. How much do I owe you?

Wellington's left hand dove into his pocket for his cash.

—Four hundred fifty dollars.

Reacting sharply, he pulled his hand out empty.

—What? How much did you get, a truckload?

—Thirty pills.

—That's ridiculous, that's fifteen dollars a pill. I can get a girl to give me a lap dance for that price.

Potter looked cross.

—Does that work better for you?

She quickly cinched her silk robe, which had been open with her breasts visible.

—Not what I mean. Don't you think that's expensive? Fifteen dollars a pop?

—A pop? Is that what I am, "a pop"?

—No. This had nothing to do with you.

—I think it has something to do with me. Sorry I can't arouse you like a go-go dancer.

—It's the price I'm talking about. These pharmaceutical companies have gone too far. They know no one wants to complain publicly about the price but fifteen dollars a pill adds up. There's a good chance I'll be using Viagra for the rest of my life. The hell if I'm going to pay that kind of money.

—Do something then, you're a senator.

—Who the hell's going to sponsor a bill saying Viagra's too expensive? They'll laugh me out of the senate chambers.

—You don't have to mention Viagra, just target the pharmaceutical companies, the prices, under one umbrella.

—It's not that easy, they support me. They give me a lot of money for my campaigns.

—And you get a lot in return, don't you...don't you?

Wellington looked down at his watch: 10:43 PM. He went over and gave Potter a cold kiss on her right cheek.

—I'll call you.

□□□ **23** □□□

—Kim, hi. You look great. Come on in.

Connor greeted Kimberly Galway with a kiss as she stepped out of his private elevator. Having just come from teaching her class at a yoga studio on Spring Street, her cheeks blushed. She wore a light, black leather jacket, jeans, and a short-sleeve damask top.

—Do you want a drink? I've opened a bottle of chardonnay.

—I think we should talk first.

—Talk? You say that like there's something wrong. Is there?

—I don't know.

Connor looked over to the teak dining room table which had been set with placemats, silverware and candles.

—Why don't we sit down?

They went into the living room and sat on the couch.

—Sure you don't want anything to drink?

—No. Let me just say something...I had a good time with you when we got together last time and I...well I guess I'm a little confused.

—Confused about what?

—First off, about the movie *Mr. Smith Goes Back to Washington.* My agent told me you've already cast Reese Witherspoon.

Connor emphatically shook his head "No" and said,

—Not yet, we haven't made a decision.

—No?

Connor smiled with closed lips and reached for her hand. Kim didn't allow him to take it.

—Bob's talking to the studio. It's just about the finances. Is that what is bothering you?

—If you've already made a decision to go with Reese and you're pretending you haven't just so you can sleep with me again, that would bother me. It would bother me a lot.

—Well, we are leaning towards casting her.

—Leaning towards? Connor, are you just dangling this role in front of me so you can get laid?

He hesitated before replying.

—The studio wants an actress with a name and they don't think you have enough name recognition.

—Why couldn't you have just said that? If you had said that, I would have really admired your honesty, and I would have come here full of desire for you. But now I realize you're just like every other guy, you'll say whatever you need to for sex. That really turns me off.

Kim stood, walked to the elevator and pushed the button. This forced Connor to his feet quicker than he anticipated.

—Kim, just because we spent one night together doesn't mean I'm looking for a relationship.

—It doesn't mean I am, either. I just want you to figure out what you want. I don't want you to think you can spend a night with me, not contact me for two weeks, and expect to be together again.

—I just thought it would be nice to see you again.

—Okay, you've seen me.

The elevator door opened and Kim stepped in.

—Kim, hold on. Why don't we talk about this?

She allowed the doors to close between them without another word.

□□□ **24** □□□

From his office window, Senator Wellington viewed a Circle Line sightseeing ship cruise up the East River. This was the second ship he had seen that morning carrying tourists. A ringing phone brought his thoughts from Africa back to America. He went to his desk and lifted the receiver.

—Hello.

—Hi, it's me. I think the show's very doable. I'd like to hunt two or three people per show, probably three. For the season we'd have approximately twenty-five shows. That's a total of seventy-five people, which would cost us about seven hundred and fifty thousand dollars at most.

—How'd you come up with that?

—I'm estimating the cost of AIDS drugs per person for a year at ten thousand dollars. Seventy-five people times ten thousand equals seven hundred fifty thousand dollars. But that ten thousand dollars is retail. It probably costs drug companies at most five hundred dollars to produce the drugs, so we might be able to do it for substantially less.

—We're not going to get the drugs for five hundred dollars per person.

—No, we're not, but I think pharmaceutical companies might give you discounted rates if they know you aren't going to resell them in America.

—I doubt it.

—What about Asher, isn't he on the board of Merck?

Wellington picked up his fountain pen and wrote on a yellow legal pad, "Asher for drugs?"

—He isn't. His wife is.

—Could you see if he could help us out?

—Claudia, even if he can, you're assuming you can find seventy-five people who will allow us to hunt them.

—I don't think that's a problem. I've already set up a meeting with the people at Ogilvy. I want them to come up with radio ads that will convince Gwandans that if a man truly loved his family he'd be willing to die for them.

—What about the FCC?

—I checked. They have absolutely nothing to say as to what we're putting on TV. Here's what they've told me, I'll read it to you: "Because of the First Amendment of the U.S. Constitution, the FCC's authority to regulate the content of TV programming is extremely limited. Cable TV stations, such as CNN, HBO, and MTV are not licensed by the FCC. If a cable station is willing to carry a program, and advertisers are willing to support it, the FCC has no interest in the matter. If one of the participants should commit a crime on the show, even murder, it would not be an FCC issue. Rather, it would be pursued by the appropriate law enforcement agencies."

—Okay, but you said seventy-five people, that's seventy-five people who are going to die. Our end of the bargain is that we give them AIDS drugs for their families, right?

—Right.

—So how did you get seventy-five? Each family could have multiple AIDS victims, two, three, four, five or more people with AIDS. That's a hell of a lot more.

Claudia wrote "75? How many per show? How many per year?"

—Oh, right. I don't know how I screwed that up. But the principle's the same. I still think it's doable. We could cap it at no more than three people per family. In the audition process we could find out how many family members have AIDS and will need the drugs.

—But of course you're saying that you're going to supply the drugs for the rest of their lives. Suppose, and I don't want this but we need to be realistic, suppose that the show isn't the hit we expect it to be? Suppose it only runs for one season? We're stuck with paying for AIDS medicine for the rest of their lives.

—That's why we hire lawyers. In the fine print we say paying for AIDS medicine is valid only for as long as the show runs.

—But we're telling them we'll give their family members AIDS drugs for life.

—And we will, as long as the show keeps going. There's nothing wrong with saying that. It's perfectly legal. And besides, being hunted is better than withering away in a mass of sores and oozing pus, isn't it? Richard...?

☐☐☐ **25** ☐☐☐

A long black limousine slowed to a stop on the north side of Great Jones Street. Connor Gazelle stepped out of the back seat and walked to an apartment building. He wore a Prussian blue suit etched with thin white stripes and a baby blue shirt open at the collar. A bouquet of Sorbonne Lilies was in his left hand. With his right, he pressed the buzzer for 3C. The stairs up to the third floor were slightly slanted to the left or west as time, gravity and lack of building repairs had tweaked the original design. After buzzing him in, Kimberly awaited his climb at the top of the steps. She dressed as Connor had asked her to: in a slinky black dress and a pair of red heels. They kissed and stepped inside.

Kim's roommate, Sylvia, looked from an Ed Sorrel cartoon in the latest *New Yorker* over to Connor. She said hello and returned to the magazine. Connor had seen this ruse before: feigned indifference masking the burning desire to meet him. After Kim vased the flowers and placed them on the living room table, Connor surprised both women by taking out a small digital camera. The two women looked at each other before turning back to Connor as he spoke.

—I know, corny right? I just thought I'd get a quick photo of us before we went out for the night.

Excitedly, Sylvia jumped up and took the camera from Connor.

—I'll take it! Sit on the couch.

—I'd actually prefer to stand.

At only five foot seven, Connor was always slightly concerned with his height. Kim with her heels on was an inch taller than her suitor. So, for the photo, she took the shoes off, making Connor smile.

—I can't believe you'd want a picture with all the photos of you that have been taken over the years.

—Most of the photos of me are from the tabloids. They all seem so phony. This is the first time we're going out in public and...well, I just wanted to capture it.

After four photos—two with Kim, one with the two roommates, and one of the trio, by using the timer—Connor and Kim went downstairs and into the limousine. Connor popped opened the bottle of champagne that had been chilling.

—Are you trying to tell me something, Connor?

—If I'm not, I'm wasting a lot of money.

He poured them each a glass and placed the bottle in the champagne cooler. The glasses touched and the bubbling bubbly was sipped.

The movie star called up to the driver.

—We're all set.

The limousine moved gently away from the curb and rolled down the old, cobbled-stoned street. Kim said,

—So? Do I have to ask or are you going to tell me?

—Tell you what? I thought we'd drive over the Brooklyn Bridge and turn around and come back before we go to dinner. I love the view of the Manhattan skyline, especially when I'm with a woman as beautiful as you are.

—Come on, Connor. Do I have the role or not?

—Yes, you have the role, if you want it.

—What happened with Reese Witherspoon?

—It doesn't matter. I want you.

—What about the studio wanting someone with a name?

—By the time the movie comes out you'll have a name.

—Will I?

—Yes. What you said the other night, about what I wanted with a woman…well, it made me think. Not too many women stand up to me.

—So, you want me in the movie *and* you want to see me?

—Yes, if that's all right with you. I also have Bob Hevens working on getting you on a movie right away. We need to get you into as many movies as possible.

Kim's eyes lit up. In one quick gulp she emptied her champagne. She placed the champagne flue in the glass holder, placed her index finger on the bottom of Connor's glass and slowly moved it upward. After Connor swallowed his remaining champagne, Kim took his glass, placed it on another glass holder and then lifted her far leg over his legs to straddle him. She wrapped her arms around his neck, brought her lips to his and their tongues met in a dance of desire as the limousine drove through the magic of a Manhattan night.

 **26**

At VBS headquarters, six writers—four women and two men—filled in half of the twelve cushioned chairs surrounding an oval conference table. In the front of the room, Claudia Potter stood next to a

flipchart upon which she had reproduced her mantra:

WE ARE NOT HUNTING PEOPLE!
WE'RE HELPING AFRICANS!
THE MORE PEOPLE WE HUNT,
THE MORE PEOPLE WE HELP!

—Claudia, what about making some of the hunters women?
—That's an obvious consideration, one we're already looking into. But simply having women hunt isn't enough.
—We could have nurses...
—No. That's stupid. Nurses as hunters? It doesn't make sense.
—I think we need to give the women a reason to hunt.
—Such as?

A cell phone chimed.
—Hold on, let me get that.

Potter reached below the table into her pocketbook. Phone in hand, she moved from the table to gaze out the window. Traffic rolled up Eighth Avenue.
—Hello.
—Claudia, it's Richard. Steve Lowell just called from Gwanda. The radio ads were a disaster.
—Hold on.

Potter turned to the writers.
—Why don't you take five...I might be a few minutes.

She stood between the flipchart and the window, shielded from the eyes, if not the ears, of the writers.
—What happened?
—Apparently, they were slightly misleading. When Gwandans heard them they thought someone had found a cure for AIDS and the shit hit the fan. Two minutes after the first ad aired the phones started ringing and they didn't let up. Once callers realized they weren't going to get through to the station, they went down to our office on Churchill Street. A riot started and an old lady and two young kids were trampled to death.
—Were they able to sign-up any huntables?
—Unfortunately not. Steve doesn't want any more radio ads. He thinks it would be best to visit AIDS clinics and hand out flyers or leaflets. If we take a quieter approach I think we'll have better luck.
—We might not get the quality of individuals we're looking for.
—I wouldn't worry about that. Steve called a friend at CAA and they're going to send over some of their agents. In the long run this might end

up costing us less.

—Good. I'm with the writers now. I want to be certain we have suitable huntables when we're ready to shoot the pilot.

—Writers? Why do we need writers?

—We just can't shoot the huntables. We need to develop a storyline, something to pull the viewers in. Why, how did you see it?

—I guess I never really thought about it.

—That's why you're a senator and I'm a producer. Give me a call later, okay? She whispered,

—I have a little blue pill with your name on it.

Potter hung up and went over to the buffet table. All that remained of the catered breakfast boxes were a sesame seed bagel and some slices of pineapple. Claudia grabbed the last bagel, took a bite and went back to the front of the room.

—Where were we? Giving the women a reason to hunt, wasn't it?

A sexy blonde, with short, post-punk hair, raised a palm.

—Maybe they're getting back at past boyfriends who have...

Potter shook her head.

—Boyfriends? No, that's absolutely wrong. Then it's just mindless violence. I don't want that.

This struck one of the male writers as absurd.

—You don't want mindless violence? Isn't that what this show is?

—No, not at all. It's dramatic adventure.

Another writer spoke up,

—What if they were rapists or something?

—Hmmm. How do we know they're rapists?

—Maybe they've been brought there, you know, like what the English did in the eighteenth century, sending their prisoners to Australia?

—Okay, that's something to investigate.

—Or maybe they're escaped prisoners, murderers and the like.

—That gives it a vigilante spin: the average citizen seeking justice.

Claudia turned the flipchart page over. On the blank sheet she wrote, JUSTICE and underlined it.

A slouching, goateed man with shaved head raised his pen.

—I'm a little uncomfortable with people hunting other people.

—Okay, good. Work that into the script. Let one of the hunters have your concerns, have him be uncertain about shooting other Africans.

An overweight woman, who wanted the bagel Claudia had taken, interjected,

—I'm not sure I get any of this. You have these people, these huntables, as you call them, they're what? Just wandering around Africa? Africa doesn't have too many people walking around in loincloths carrying spears anymore.

Potter shot back, disdainfully,

—It's a TV show, it doesn't have to be factually accurate. And for your information, a lot of people still think of Africa as people in loincloths with spears.

—Even if they do, that doesn't explain anything. The hunters, I take it they're white, right? So, you have these rich white people shooting poor black people, is that it? Is that the show?

—What do you want? Rich black people shooting poor white people? How many people would watch that?

—Plenty.

—Can we not look at the color issue and just do a show about people hunting other people? Why is that so difficult? Aren't most shows about one person, or one group of people, hunting or using a gun, or guns, against another person or group of people? The only difference is that we're not calling them cops and criminals, or anything like that.

—What if the hunters are hunting poachers? There are people who illegally hunt and kill elephants for their ivory tusks and hunt black rhinos for their horns. We could have the huntables as poachers. The hunters going after them now have a reason to hunt them down.

—I like that very much. Now we have good guys and bad guys, good versus evil. That's something people can relate to.

Potter's cell phone chimed again.

—Hold on.

She went back to her pocketbook and pulled it out.

—Hello.

—Claudia Potter?

—Speaking.

—This is Tyrone Henderson from *The New York Times*. Are you planning to hunt people in Africa with AIDS?

Potter turned to the writers,

—Will you excuse me?

She stepped out of the conference room, went into an empty office across the hall and turned the light on before finding a chair.

—Mr. Henderson, I'm planning to help people.

—Help them how?

—I'm in the middle of a meeting. Can I call you back?

—Isn't it true that to qualify for the medicine or AIDS drugs, they have to agree to be hunted and killed?

—I think it would be better if we sit down and talk about this.

—You do realize that CNN just reported that Senator Wellington plans to hunt AIDS sufferers, don't you?

—Yes, of course.

—I'll call you in an hour. That should be enough time to get your story straight.

—Fine. Bye. Shit!

Potter fingered the speed dial button for Wellington. Keno answered and told her Wellington was out.

—He was there two minutes ago. Where did he go? It's extremely important.

—Ms. Potter, he told me not to disturb him. He's on the phone with David Diamond.

—David Diamond? Who is David Diamond?

—He's a political consultant.

—Does the senator know about the report on POX?

—Yes, that's why he's talking with Mr. Diamond.

—See if he'll take my call.

—Hold on.

□□□ 27 □□□

Inside his office, a frantic Senator Wellington leaned over the wooden work table as he listened to David Diamond on the Polycon speakerphone.

—A good idea? To whom, Senator? Hunting people with AIDS is a good idea?

—We're not just hunting them, we're helping them. We're going to help their families. Claudia Potter said that she would talk to the press before anyone found out and...

—Claudia Potter? Forget about Claudia Potter and anyone else! No one gives a damn about Claudia Potter.

The office door opened. Wellington turned quickly, a panicked look on his face. Keno offered up the palm of his hand as a silent apology. Quietly, he reclosed the door.

—All right, I messed up.

Wellington sat down at the table.

—Do they have proof? Is there any way they can prove that you've planned to shoot AIDS victims?

—What are you getting at, denying it?

—Of course we're going to deny it. We can't say you've planned to shoot AIDS victims. We need to get on the offense, blame someone else. What about Claudia Potter. Can we blame her? Say it was her idea, that you had nothing to do with it?

—She's got Seymour Blackstone behind her and all his money and media outlets. That won't wash.

—All right, but we need to attack someone. We don't want to be defensive. Obviously Gazelle is going to use this against you. We'll attack him before he attacks you. We need to put him on the defensive.

—How are we going to do that?

—Let me give our friend Will a call, he might be able to help us out.

□□□ **28** □□□

The New York Times

Wellington to Shoot AIDS Sufferers

Senator Richard Wellington has secretly purchased a large ranch in Gwanda, Africa where he plans to hunt AIDS sufferers. The hunting and killing of Africans with AIDS was to be shown on VBS television under the supervision of Claudia Potter, the executive producer. Neither Senator Wellington nor Claudia Potter's offices offered any comments. However, stock prices rose dramatically on the

Continued on page 8

□□□ **29** □□□

Zack Taylor sipped a Coke and Connor Gazelle sipped green tea, as they sat on opposite ends of a couch in the presidential suite inside Gazelle Headquarters at the Tribeca Grand Hotel. Yellow legal pads and pens were on the table in front of them. On the television monitor in front of them, Senator Wellington sat next to his good friend, Will O'Reilly, POX's star commentator.

—*Senator, let's get right into it. The New York Times claims you want to shoot AIDS victims. Any truth to that?*

—*Of course not. Will, it's sad, it really is, but this is what politics have become. I don't like to point fingers. I don't like name-calling. I don't like campaigns where one opponent personally attacks another. Unfortunately, that seems to be what is happening here.*

—*You're talking about Connor Gazelle, of course, the failed actor turned wannabe politician.*

—*Right. The Democrats, unable to field a legitimate candidate, have*

*selected a stand-in, an actor, someone who is used to playing roles,
which is what he's doing now. Gazelle is remaking the Jimmy Stewart
movie "Mr. Smith Goes to Washington." For those of you who don't
know the story, Mr. Smith is an honest, if slightly naïve, small town man
who is elected senator and goes to Washington to fight against the
corrupt politicians and big business. Gazelle believes that senators and
congressional leaders are manipulative and deceitful, and he's going to
change all that. Well, let me tell him something. Washington is a jungle
where only the strongest survive. In Washington your enemies smile at
you and wish you luck, but when you're not looking they stab you in the
back. They kill you in conference rooms; they destroy you with lies to
the press.*

Connor turned to his campaign manager,

—What the hell is Wellington doing, trying to help us?

—Let's just listen.

—*They leak sensitive information to third parties so that legislation you
are working on will be defeated. They tell untruths and half-truths about
you, and when you confront them they deny it. But Mr. Gazelle, a man
with no political experience, is going to come to Washington and
change all that. Gazelle has been living in La-la Land too long. In
Washington, in order to achieve anything, you have to know how to play
by the rules. Those rules make it necessary to sometimes lie or
manipulate the truth, to speak out of both sides of your mouth. If you
can't do that, you'll never accomplish anything.*

—Maybe this is some kind of new preemptive strike; he criticizes
himself so I can't criticize him?

—*Well said, Senator, well said. It might not be what our listeners
expected you to say but it is truthful.*

—*Will, I've never been afraid to speak the truth. Washington is a tough
town that requires a tough man who gets things done. That's what I've
done in the past and that's what I will continue to do.*

Connor turned to Zack Taylor.

—Get him on the phone for me.

Zack thought about this for a moment.

—What are you going to say?

—Just give me the goddamn phone!

—Hold on, I'll call.

During the broadcast, the call-in number to the O'Reilly show had
been periodically scrolling across the bottom of the screen. When it
came up again Zack dialed and got connected to a low-level staffer.
After being authenticated, Gazelle was put through to the show
producer, who told O'Reilly through his earpiece who was calling.

—Senator, my producer is telling me we have a special caller, Connor Gazelle, on the line. Mr. Gazelle, are you there?

—I certainly am.

—I take it you want to respond to Senator Wellington.

Zack stood up and nervously paced back and forth without taking his eyes off the television or his candidate.

—That's right.

—Go ahead.

—Wellington wants us to believe Washington is full of liars and manipulators, and that every politician is dishonest. He also believes that if you don't realize this you're an idiot. If that's how it is, I'd rather remain a decent and honorable man and lose the election than turn into someone like Wellington. But I'm not going to lose the election, because people aren't as bitter and cynical as Wellington wants us to believe. No one thinks politicians are like Jimmy Stewart. We're all aware of how things work, of the corruption in Washington and elsewhere. That doesn't mean we like it or want to stand for it. It doesn't mean we like those who are part of the corruption. Wellington does not care in the least about New Yorkers or their problems. If he did, he wouldn't be playing around in an African country. What's a senator doing in a foreign country, anyway? I'll tell you what he's doing. Wellington wants to hunt and kill AIDS patients on his Promised Land Ranch. He wants to put their murders on television for entertainment purposes. He thinks watching the less fortunate suffer and die will amuse the American public.

In the television studio, Wellington nervously crossed and uncrossed his legs before responding.

—Who told you I'm hunting people? Do you have any proof of this?

—Are you telling me The Promised Land Ranch isn't going to be used to hunt and kill AIDS sufferers?

—My ranch will help New Yorkers.

—How?

—There are lots of things I'll be doing to benefit New Yorkers.

—Such as?

—The good people of New York have my undivided attention. I've done good work for them in the past, and I will do even better in the future.

Wellington looked over to O'Reilly as if to say, "help me here" but O'Reilly did not react.

—Senator, what exactly are you going to be doing on this killing ranch of yours?

—It's not a killing ranch. It was never intended as a killing ranch. The Promised Land will help New Yorkers.

—You've said that. How is it going to help New Yorkers?
—*I think it's important for New Yorkers to know where we're heading. Unfortunately, now isn't the right time or place to get into details.*
—Because you're bluffing! Your ranch is for killing AIDS patients, and you have no way of helping New Yorkers. If you were concerned about New Yorkers you wouldn't be wasting your time in a foreign country.
—*If I didn't care about New Yorkers I'd probably be making a fictional film about a life that I want people to believe is my own. I'm not fictional! I'm real, and my ranch will help New Yorkers by cutting taxes.*
—How?

Finally O'Reilly jumped into the ring to save his fighter.
—*Connor, why don't we do this, why don't we have you come on my show?*
—I'd love to, Will. When?
—*Soon.*
—Good because I want to tell listeners...

O'Reilly gave an almost imperceptible nod to his producer and the phone line went dead in Connor's hand. Connor turned to Zackary Taylor with a winner's grin.
—I got him! See that, I got him!
—You were effective, but that doesn't mean we necessarily changed any minds, or won over any new voters. You know who listens to O'Reilly's show—his sheep. It's not like they're going to change their minds no matter what you say.
—Trust me, Zack. I know how to play the game. I'll show them.

□□□ 30 □□□

As soon as the show concluded, a red-faced Wellington stormed over the green room to confront David Diamond. The door banged open and Diamond jumped back from his seat on the couch.
—Why the hell did you tell me to go on Will O'Reilly?

Diamond responded timidly,
—You did well. It was a good show.

Wellington stood over him, menacingly.
—The hell it was! I was made to look like an idiot!

Diamond, diminutive, bespectacled, and physically slight cowered at the corner of the couch. Feeling like a bully, Wellington stepped away shaking his head. This gave Diamond an opportunity to stand up and play the pacifier.
—You didn't look like an idiot.

Senator Wellington sat dejectedly in a chair next to the television set, which was now off.

—The hell I didn't. Gazelle's asking me what I'm going to do with The Promised Land, and all I could come up with was some lame excuse about cutting taxes! Why didn't you tell me he was going to call?

—Will you trust me on this? We're winning this game.

Wellington regained his feet and went for the door.

—We're not winning. You fucked me, you really fucked me.

—Relax, Senator. You started off well. That whole bit about how difficult it is in Washington, how you need to be a real manipulator to get anything accomplished. I like that, it was refreshing.

—Of course, you like it! You told me to say it.

—Let me talk to Spellocanti, see what he's come up with.

The name surprised Wellington.

— Tony Spellocanti, the private investigator? You've hired him already?

Diamond smiled his diamond smile, which, for him, showed crooked, grayish teeth.

—It's an election year, Senator. Do you think I'm unprofessional enough to wait until some scandal erupts before I start working?

☐☐☐ 31 ☐☐☐

Instead of wearing one of his flashy custom-made suits for his appearance on *Will O'Reilly Live!* Gazelle went to Macy's and purchased what he considered a drab gray suit and a blue tie spotted with tiny white stars. As he sat next to O'Reilly in the television studio, he felt sartorially inferior. He wished he had worn one of his stylish suits and hadn't listened to Zack Taylor's suggestion to portray himself as a middle-of-the-road everyman.

—Good evening and welcome to *Will O'Reilly Live!* Our guest tonight is the New York Democratic nominee for the United States Senate, Connor Gazelle. Good evening, Connor, and thanks for coming.

—My pleasure.

O'Reilly's charming television smile was replaced with a devilish grin.

—Connor, if your last film, *The Life of Jacob Riis*, hadn't failed miserably, would you be running for United States Senate?

For the viewers at home, on the television screen a graphic with the word FAILURE appeared below Gazelle.

—It didn't fail miserably. It didn't make one hundred million dollars, but it...

The host ratcheted up his voice level.

—It was a FAILURE!

Connor remained calm.

—It wasn't. Jacob Riis was an important man, a great American, whose story needed to be told to those who were not aware of his legacy.

O'Reilly laughed haughtily,

—A great American? He took photographs of poor people living in hovels, in dark, dank alleys. They were living there because they refused to work, because they were lazy, good for nothing bums!

Instead of Jacob Riis famous images of New York from the 1880s, images from the South Bronx in the 1960s appeared on the television screen: two Puerto Ricans drinking wine on a doorstep, an African American stretched out on a filthy sidewalk with his hand wrapped around a bottle of beer in a paper bag, and three male Caucasians passed out sleeping in an abandoned building.

—They were working. They were working hard, but they had been exploited. That's what Riis' book was all about. Riis wanted to show, as the title of his famous book states, *How the Other Half Lives.* He did this by using photographs of the slums of New York, lower Manhattan. He forced the wealthy to take some social responsibility.

—You're wealthy, aren't you? I've been told that you are worth in excess of one hundred fifty million dollars.

—Not that much.

When Gazelle's net worth was mentioned, a graphic of $150,000,000 flashed on screen. This was superimposed on a smiling and tan Connor holding a bottle of champagne on a yacht in the Cannes harbor during the annual film festival. For a reaction shot, the camera cut to an elderly woman in the audience—she'd been planted— fingering her rosary beads as she mumbled a prayer to herself. The camera cut back to O'Reilly smiling smugly.

—You've earned as much as twenty million dollars for a single motion picture, haven't you?

—You have to remember that at least thirty-three percent goes to taxes, ten percent goes to my agent, and another big percent goes to my manager. There are plenty of others who get percentages as well.

—Nonetheless, you have made millions of dollars for acting in lousy films. How much of that did you give away to poor people?

An audio track loudly played the sound of the cash register "cha-ching" from Pink Floyd's *Money.*

—I never added it up.

—You know how much your agent gets, how much your manager gets, how much your makeup artist gets, how much your hairdresser gets, how much your manicurist gets, how much your gardener gets, how

111

much your pool boy gets, but you don't know how much you give away? Are you any different than the people you want to criticize? You made a film about how the wealthy mistreated the poor so that people would think of you as a good-deed-doer, isn't that right? That's your Hollywood image. In reality you're nothing like that are you? You're not helping out the poor. You're not giving your money away.

A bead of sweat slid down Connor's forehead.

—I've given money away. I've contributed to many causes.

—You gave a considerable donation to the "Buddhists For A Free Tibet," didn't you?

Gazelle was surprised at this knowledge.

—How do you know that?

On the television screen shaven-headed Hari Krishnas danced in bare feet and robes at Kennedy airport.

—Did you give anything to the Catholic Church?

On screen, clean-cut families walked into a small, white church. Inside, a father placed a five-dollar bill in a collection basket.

—That's none of your business.

From the church collection, the camera cut to a smiling Connor on the yacht at Cannes. The camera then cut to a hand, supposedly Connor's, slipping a fifty-dollar bill into the G-string of a topless dancer whose bare breasts were digitally blurred.

—Didn't you say that the resurrection of Jesus Christ was just a myth?

—No.

—*No?* Let me read something to you. "Every ancient culture had myths of death and resurrection. The Biblical story of Jesus rising from the dead was typical and probably came from the Babylonians' worship of Adonis. Most Christian or Biblical stories came out of, or were derived from, pre-existing pagan myths." Does that sound familiar?

—No.

—Well, it should. Those are your words from an article you wrote for a student newspaper when you at UCLA. How can you expect voters to trust a man who believes that the resurrection of Jesus Christ was a myth?

It quickly dawned on Connor that those were his words.

—Okay, yeah, now I remember. How did you get that?

On the television screen, an image of a much younger Connor, with long hair, a beard, and a tie-dye Grateful Dead t-shirt appeared.

—So now you admit it?

—I was studying philosophy of religion, and I was reading Sir James Frazier's *The Golden Bough*, and I...

O'Reilly responded with a sneer,

—I don't really care what you were reading. What I do care about is the deception that you're trying to pull on voters, on the American people.

—What deception? I'm not deceiving anyone. You're quoting a paper I wrote when I was a young man. I was eighteen or nineteen at the time.

—Isn't it true that instead of believing in the American God, in Jesus Christ, that you belong to an Asian cult? And isn't it true you worship Buddha in a private shrine in your own home?

—*The* American God? As far as I know Jesus isn't an American God, and has never been exclusively American.

—Don't change the subject. Do you worship Buddha in your home?

The television screen images showed a Chinese opium den filled with suggestively clad women, with one woman handing an opium pipe to a monk seated next to a statue of a seated Buddha. Three burning incense sticks stuck out of the Buddha's head.

—Worship? No. I have a statue of Buddha and other religious statues. I have a number of art objects. I've studied Buddhism and other religions because theology is important.

—Do you think a fat man sitting around all day is a good image for children?

—A fat man? What fat man? Buddha?

—Yes. O'Reilly shouted into Gazelle's face,

—Do you think this slothful figure is someone that children and young adults should emulate!?

Connor tried to remain calm and professional,

—I think you should watch what you're saying. Buddha is a holy and sacred figure for millions of people all around the world. He isn't sitting around, he's meditating; he's reached a state of Nirvana.

The host rolled his eyes and said,

—Whether you call it meditating, contemplating, daydreaming or just sitting around and farting, many Americans would call it wasting time. Do you think, with all the complexities in today's world, children should be taught to admire and look up to a man who tells his followers to sit around and do nothing?

—Who children admire or follow, study or contemplate, should be left up to their parents until they are mature enough to make decisions on their own. As far as imagery is concerned, a man sitting at peace is certainly as worthy of reverence as a man nailed to a cross.

—You're denigrating Jesus Christ! How can you say blubber boy Buddha is as great as Jesus Christ? That's sacrilegious. You're a god-hater, aren't you? Why do you hate America's God, Jesus Christ?

—I don't! I...

—Shut up! I don't want to hear anymore from a sinner. Let's go to the

113

phones and see what our viewers think. Go ahead, caller, you're on the air.

□□□ 32 □□□

The New York Tabloid

"Is Jesus Christ a Myth?"

United States Senate candidate Connor Gazelle claims that Jesus Christ is only a myth, one of many, according to the wannabe senator. The has-been actor says the life, death, and resurrection of Jesus Christ is "one of many fertility myths popular at the time." The failed thespian also admitted to having a shrine to Buddha in his home.

State Senator Peter Morgan, who was once rumored to be in line for Senator Wellington's congressional seat, stated that he was not surprised by Gazelle's lack of theology or morals, and added, "Unfortunately, this type of thinking is all too typical of Hollywood stars. Many celebrities take up and embrace secondary deities because there are no moral codes or commandments to follow. It allows them to act immorally, and at the same time claim to be spiritual." Morgan, who only recently changed from being a Democrat to a Republican, says that should Democrats decide to distance themselves from Gazelle, and in fact if they ask for his resignation, he would be available to run as a Democrat. Reaction from the Democratic

Continued on page 7

□□□ 33 □□□

Inside Gazelle Headquarters, Zack Taylor pointed to the *New York Tabloid.* The paper sat on Taylor's desk atop a pile of local newspapers, all of which condemned Gazelle. Connor stood in front of his campaign manager looking desperate.

—It was just some article I wrote for my college newspaper about how many Biblical stories were derived from pagan rituals. But it's all true. It's not like I made it up.

Doug Clifford, Zack's top aide, responded from his desk.

—We have to make a public statement about that. We have to issue an apology.

Gazelle turned to him.

—Wellington wants to kill people with AIDS! Why isn't anyone saying anything about that?

Taylor replied defeatedly.

—Can we prove it?

Knowing that they couldn't, Connor tried a different approach. — What about Peter Morgan? Who the hell is he to say Hollywood celebrities embrace secondary deities? What the hell is a secondary deity anyway?

Taylor spouted with as much contempt as anger,

—Forget about the secondary deities. Morgan is trying to oust you.

—Oust me? What do you mean oust me? He's a Republican.

—And before that he was a Democrat. Whichever way the wind blows that's where you'll find Morgan. You read his quote, "If the Democrats ask for your resignation." He's telling Democrats to get rid of you.

—Bastard.

Gazelle slumped into a chair. Zack came over and sat down on the couch adjacent to him.

—Connor, we need to get a picture of you coming out of church before next week's debate.

Connor got up and went into the kitchen to get himself a bottled water. Zack continued.

—You'll act like you didn't expect them. When they start asking you about God and religion, you'll just say something along the lines that religion is a personal matter and...

—It is.

—I know it is. Once the church photo is in the press, we attack Wellington at the debate.

Gazelle thought about this.

—I'm not going to come out of a church. That's bullshit.

—It's politics. And politics is bullshit. We all know that.

—That's why I'm different. I don't have to play the same games.

—Connor, if you want to be in the game, you've got to play by the rules! The rules say you've got to play up the God angle.

□□□ **34** □□□

Up in his home in Bedford, Wellington cloistered himself in his study reading and rereading the talking points David Diamond had e-mailed him. If anyone else had sent the notes, Wellington would have

115

dismissed them as ludicrous. But as Diamond had almost always been prescient he tried to see their merits. Nonetheless, his inner attorney was losing the case. He pulled his cell phone out of his pants pocket and dialed.

—Hello.

—David, it's Richard. I looked at your talking points. If I say what you want me to say during the debate they'll commit me, put me in an asylum.

—No they won't. I realize that they're radical, but...

—They're not radical. They're crazy.

—They're not. What I've written makes perfect sense. Articulating them will give you more press than you've ever had before. It will also show the country that you are the future.

—What makes you so sure?

—Because my talking points illustrate what the country wants. What the country needs. What the country is feeling. They just need someone to articulate them.

—I'm not so sure.

—Senator, if you don't articulate my plan sooner or later someone else will, and where will you be? You'll be kicking yourself because that person, whoever it is, will be seen as a brilliant man, a savior for this country, someone who saw the future and did what he could to bring it to fruition.

—It's damn risky.

—You asked for my opinion, my advice. If you don't want to listen, don't. Get someone else.

—All I'm saying is that we should talk about it, sit down and talk. Can you drive up here today?

Diamond replied with more than a hint of annoyance in his voice.

—What time?

—Hey, don't give me your goddamn attitude! These initiatives are extremely controversial. This is my life we're talking about. It's easy for you to write them up, but I've got to say them in public!

—I'm not complaining, just tell me what time.

—I'm here now, the sooner you get here the better.

□□□ **35** □□□

Bent Hall Auditorium at St. John's University was the venue for the Wellington/Gazelle debate. Wellington had insisted on this staunchly Catholic school because he knew the students would be on his side. The two candidates stood behind identical podiums in an

116

auditorium filled with students and press pundits. Their suits were dark and professional, nothing that would stand out as too expensive or chic. Gazelle's tie was blue with tiny white stars; Wellington's was red with slanting thin bands of white. The moderator, Charlie Rose, sat behind an oak desk facing the two candidates.

—Mr. Gazelle, the first question is for you. Let me start with a quote from something you wrote: "Prior to the writings in the Bible there were pagan miracles. Many of these so-called miracles found their way into the Christian Bible. There was, for instance, a Godman who changed water into wine. This was done before Jesus was born. There was also a pagan version of the great flood." There's more, but let's start with the first statement. Do you believe that before Jesus turned water into wine, there was a pagan who did that, and that Jesus was just a pale imitation?

—Many scholars, both secular and non-secular, who have studied the Bible and pre-Biblical history, have concluded that many of the myths, stories, and symbols in the Bible were taken from pagan rituals and myths. This isn't my opinion. It is a fact. But I'm not here to discuss religion. I do not feel religion should be a relevant issue in politics. A senator, or any politician, should not be looked upon as a spiritual leader. That's why there are priests and ministers and rabbis and lamas and imams. I think we should leave the spiritual domain for those who are qualified in that area. The Founders of this country believed in separation of Church and State. I believe the same thing.

Mr. Rose turned to the incumbent.

—Senator Wellington, do you feel that a politician's religious beliefs should play a role in politics? Or do you feel religion is a private matter that should be left up to the individual?

—I don't think you can separate a man from his religious beliefs, if he has religious beliefs. If you believe in God, in the Bible, you try to live your life in accordance with biblical laws.

The audience responded with enthusiastic clapping.

—Mr. Gazelle, would you agree with that?

—I do not feel that a person's religious beliefs, or non-beliefs, should be relevant to an individual's political beliefs. This university is filled with Catholic students, some of whom may not be aware of the controversy John Kennedy caused when he ran for president as a Catholic in 1960. At the time, many in the country were not prepared to accept Senator Kennedy because there had never been a Catholic President. Kennedy assured the voting populace that his religious beliefs would have no bearing on his politics. I believe the same thing. I am a non-believer, an atheist. I am not afraid to admit this in public, nor should I be. I think the voting populace today is mature enough to accept a candidate who does not believe in a God, or in organized religion.

There were boos and hisses from the audience. When the sounds of displeasure and mockery died down, the moderator turned to the other candidate.

—Senator Wellington, are voters ready to accept an atheist as a political leader?

Wellington worked hard to suppress a smile.

—I think if a politician wants to represent his state or his country, he or she needs to reflect his constituents' beliefs. I simply do not understand how anyone could neglect religion. I also do not trust anyone who does not believe in God. I don't think voters trust atheists either. What are we here for if not to serve God?

A loud applause erupted from the auditorium. Gazelle tried to speak up right away, but his words were drowned out. Mr. Rose waited for relative silence before he began his next round of questioning.

—Why don't we move away from the Bible? Senator Wellington, you have been accused of wanting to operate a ranch where people will be hunted and killed. Is this true? Do you want to hunt and kill people on your African ranch, on The Promised Land?

—I will answer your question, but before doing so, I would like to share a true story. On May 23, 1989, not too far from where we are this evening, LeRoy Jenkins, a family man with a wife and three small children, was walking home to his apartment in Fort Greene, Brooklyn. He had worked more than sixteen hours at two different jobs. He just wanted to sleep before he had to get up in the morning and repeat the process. Two blocks from his door, LeRoy Jenkins was held-up by two men, Buddy Pittman and Virgil Tate. Buddy and Virgil shot Mr. Jenkins dead, and used his hard-earned cash to buy crack cocaine. Buddy and Virgil were eventually caught and sent to prison. Seven years later they were both back out on the street. Two years later, Buddy was arrested for a second murder, and four years later Virgil was arrested for raping a neighbor's girl. They are both now in jail but they're going to get out. They are going to be on the street watching and waiting until they can rape or murder again. If it were up to me, criminals like Buddy and Virgil would never go free again. Unfortunately, there are liberals out there who are always coddling criminals. Liberals, like Mr. Gazelle, who believe that criminals should be allowed to watch TV, play cards, lift weights, and have conjugal visits while incarcerated. New York prisons are filled with thousands of prisoners like Virgil and Buddy who can't wait to get out and rape and murder again. Should these types of criminals be coddled by a soft criminal justice system? I don't think they should. The Promised Land Ranch I am creating will help me make this city, this state, and this country safer and more secure by reducing crime and eliminating criminals from the landscape. What I intend to do is transport violent criminals—murderers, rapists, terrorists, killers of police officers and firemen, the worst of the worst—to my ranch, The Promised Land, where they will be hunted down and killed for the murderous deeds they have done.

The auditorium became as silent as a monastery.

—Senator Wellington, did I hear you correctly? You want to hunt and kill criminals? Hunt them like animals?

—Yes. I'll repeat what I have said so that I am not misquoted. I want to send murderers, rapists, pedophiles, terrorists, and other violent criminals to The Promised Land, where they will be hunted down and killed. And I want this to be televised.

Connor Gazelle looked to Charlie Rose and to the audience, for faces that shared what he thought was not only a political blunder, but a statement of such inhuman audacity that surely no one could agree to it. But there was nothing to read; the faces hadn't had time to register emotion.

—Mr. Gazelle, your response.

—Why bother going to Africa to kill criminals? Why don't we let the criminals loose in Central Park and give New Yorkers rifles so they can hunt them on their lunch hour?

Without being asked to respond, Wellington jumped right in.

—Make fun of this if you like, Mr. Gazelle, but crime is not a joke to me. We've been fighting crime in this country as long as we've been a country. Has it helped? Have our streets and homes become any safer? No, they haven't. Are our children safe? Are our parents safe? Are we safe? Is anyone really safe? No. We are all, each and every one of us, frightened of vicious criminals. Why should this be? Why should we allow criminals to control our thoughts and actions? If my proposal does seem harsh, does seem cruel, ask yourself this: is it any crueler than having these vicious criminals hunting us? Make no mistake that is exactly what they are doing. They've got guns, knives, clubs, bombs, and lots of other weapons. In certain neighborhoods, residents are afraid to walk the streets after dark. They lock their doors and keep their children away from windows, in hope they'll make it through the night without some tragedy befalling them. How long are we going to continue cowering in fear of criminals? My job as senator is to help and protect the citizens of New York State. That's what I intend to do.

Gazelle shook his head to the loud round of applause that erupted from the audience.

—Mr. Gazelle, your response?

—After years of listening to politicians one gets somewhat inured to their...

From the audience, a dark, curly-haired student rose from his seat,
—Boring!

There was laughter and another voice called out,
—Atheist!

Gazelle continued.

— After years of listening to politicians one gets somewhat inured to their deceitful lies, their willingness to say anything to get elected. But this, this bloodthirsty desire to kill, shows me that some politicians will stoop to any level, say anything, to get elected. The death penalty has never been shown to reduce crime. But this isn't about reducing crime, this is about election through fear. Wellington believes he can frighten people into voting for him. The only proven method to reduce crime is through education and rehabilitation. But Wellington doesn't want to educate or rehabilitate. He wants to murder. Of course he hasn't mentioned how this is going to be paid for or even why criminals need to be sent to Africa.

Gazelle played into Wellington's hands just as David Diamond had told him. The moderator went right along, as well.
—Senator, if you were to send prisoners to The Promised Land, how would this be paid for?
—That is a good and important question. If we are going to be serious about crime and criminals, we need to think about the costs. Keeping a criminal in jail costs approximately thirty thousand dollars per year. Across the country we have more than two million people in jails and prisons. Think about that: two million people, more people than many nations. Two million multiplied by thirty thousand dollars adds up to an annual cost of approximately sixty billion dollars. What are we getting for our sixty billion? Are we getting justice? Is crime going down with any significance? No, it's not. We need to make this country safe again. Sending prisoners to The Promised Land is only the first step. As I just said, I want this to be televised. By televising the hunting and killing of criminals we will be able to generate income through advertisements. Advertising will give us the potential to bring in hundreds of millions of dollars. I want to use this revenue to fund social programs and cut taxes. The police, the fire department, teachers, and other public servants, will finally be paid what they deserve. These are the people who dedicate their lives to helping New Yorkers and other Americans. It's about time we do something for them. This will also help the elderly pay for costly medications. In short, everyone will benefit. Our homes and streets will be safer, and our tax burdens will be lessened. And perhaps equally as

120

important, we will all be able to see justice administered. Criminals will know that in New York, under what I would like to call "The Wellington Laws," there will be no second chances. Violent criminals once caught and convicted will never see freedom again.

Senator Wellington paused briefly.

—Before any of this happens, it is important for us to help the great nation of Gwanda. We will do that by helping their leader, President Mobley, deal with his country's horrible AIDS epidemic. In dealing with any problem it is necessary to be realistic. Just as it is impossible to prevent all crimes, it is impossible to cure all AIDS sufferers. But we are not deterred. We will allow AIDS sufferers from Gwanda to sacrifice themselves for their family members who also have the disease. Any Gwandan who allows himself or herself to be hunted will be eligible to have up to three family members get a lifetime supply of AIDS medicine. The revenue to pay for costly AIDS medicine will be earned from the most exciting reality-television show ever created. Yes, it is true that a small number of those who have AIDS will die, but these individuals are going to die anyway. We at The Promised Land Corporation, however, are going to allow them to end their lives with dignity and excitement.

A bewildered Charlie Rose looked to the other candidate.

—Mr. Gazelle, what do you have to say to that?

—I am overwhelmed, almost speechless. Wellington wants to hunt criminals and AIDS sufferers, and put it on television as entertainment? This goes beyond politics, beyond trying to make voters cower in fear. Senator Wellington seems to have lost his mind. As an individual, this saddens me. It makes me feel sorry for him and his family. From a political standpoint, I think this is a fortuitous moment. It shows voters just how sick and demented he has become and they'll be able to vote him out of office. Is this really what the world has come to?

▯▯▯ 36 ▯▯▯

When Connor got back in Gazelle headquarters, all eyes were on the television monitor awaiting the news anchor's verdict.

—*God is dead! Good evening and welcome to the eleven o'clock news with Jim Norris. Earlier this evening, Connor Gazelle, the actor and fading fast would-be politician stated that there is no God, and that religion should play no part in the government, or in personal affairs. Leading Democrats immediately distanced themselves from Gazelle. In a developing story, while watching tonight's senate debate, Cardinal John O'Farrell suffered what some are saying was a heart attack. Our*

*correspondent Penelope Coy is outside St. Patrick's Cathedral on Fifth
Avenue. Penelope?*

*—Thanks Jim. What we know so far is this: less than an hour ago, an
ambulance arrived at St. Patrick's Cathedral after someone from the
Cardinal's residence called Mt. Sinai Medical Center's hospital saying
Cardinal O'Farrell had been experiencing chest pains and may have
had a heart attack. Emergency technicians are still inside. As of yet,
there has been no announcement or comment from any medical
personnel or church official.*

*—Penelope, is the Cardinal's heart attack linked to the Gazelle
bombshell that God is dead?*

*—It's too early to tell, but the timing is too close to indicate any other
cause. One parishioner, who has been standing vigil outside Saint
Patrick's, said that if Cardinal O'Farrell dies Connor Gazelle will have
blood on his hands.*

*—Blood on his hands. Thanks, Penelope. In other related stories,
Senator Wellington announced a bold new anti-crime plan that could
save New Yorkers billions of dollars.*

Connor went over to the television set, turned it off and waited for
Doug Clifford to finish his phone call.

—Yeah, we saw it. Not yet. Gazelle just got here. As soon as they're
done Zack will call you, okay?

Clifford hung up and turned to his campaign manager.

—Zack, that was Senator Cavenaugh, again. I told him you'd call him
back as soon as you finished with Gazelle.

In his mind, Connor heard the death knell clang. Donald
Cavenaugh, the two-term Democratic senator from New York had never
fully endorsed Gazelle. He believed that actors should remain actors and
not pretend to be politicians. Cavenaugh had been criticized for this, but
now, in his mind, his instincts had been proven prophetic.

Gazelle asked Taylor nervously,

—What does he want?

Zack, shorter and wider than his titular superior, stormed over to
Connor and did his best to get in his face.

—What the hell do you think he wants? You go on TV and say you're
an atheist, and you wonder what Cavenaugh wants? Come on, Connor,
you're not that stupid.

—I was trying to be honest. Don't you think it's time that a politician's
religious views have no bearing on his political views?

—What I think, and what the public thinks, are two different things.
Anyway, it doesn't matter anymore.

—Good. It shouldn't matter. Now we can move on to the important things.

Zack shook his head, his eyes flush with disappointment.

—No, it no longer matters for you. You're out.

—Out? What do you mean *out*?

—You're off the ticket. As soon you said you were an atheist it was all over. They're already looking for a replacement for you.

—Who is?

—Not just Senator Cavenaugh. About a dozen Democratic leaders have called me and told me we have to dump you.

—I'm an atheist, so what?

—So what? You're not that naïve, so don't pretend to be! You represent New York State and the Democratic Party. If you think the Party's going to let you drag them down you're wrong. The Republicans would castigate you until they did major damage to the Democratic Party. We can't have that. There's no way we can support you.

—What makes you so sure voters won't support me? Wellington says he wants to kill people and put that on TV. Don't you think people are going to be more upset about that? Maybe we should just see how the media plays this out before you jump to any conclusions. Hold on, that's my cell.

Connor reached into his pants pocket for the ringing phone.

—Hello.

—Connor, it's Bob. I've got some bad news.

—Just what I need. What?

—They're putting *Mr. Smith Goes Back to Washington* in turnaround.

This drained Connor of all hope,

—You've got to be kidding me.

—I'm not. Everyone at the studio heard what you said. They think it's getting too risky. They're worried people will start protesting and that will hurt their other films.

—I don't believe they're canceling my film because I said I am atheist. If anything the publicity is an added bonus.

—Connor, be realistic, you know how these things go.

—I do now.

□□□ 37 □□□

—Don't you think you'd get a little bored, living with a drunk?
—Well... that's what I want.

In his media room, an unshaven Connor Gazelle pressed the pause button on the DVD remote. On the projection screen, Nicholas Cage and Elizabeth Shue froze. As he got up from the couch, Connor kicked over the empty bottle of Château Magdelaine. A few moments later, with a few wine stains now on his pajamas, Gazelle returned with a freshly opened bottle. He reseated himself on the couch, filled half of his goblet with the red elixir, sipped it, and pushed the pause button. Nicholas and Elizabeth came back to life. Cage said,

—*You haven't seen the worst of it. I knock things over... throw up all the time.*

Kim came into the room, grabbed the remote and pushed stop. The tragic couple from *Leaving Las Vegas* disappeared and the screen turned black. Connor looked up at Kim without saying a word. She walked over to Connor, took the wine glass from his hand, lifted the second bottle of Château Magdelaine from the floor, and returned to the kitchen. Connor called out,

—What do you think you're doing?

She came back into the room to face him.

—I'm pouring this down the sink.

Connor sat there glumly. With just about any other woman, Connor would have thrown her out of the apartment for such a defiant act, but the look on Kim's face told him she was steps away from leaving anyway, and he wasn't prepared to lose her. She waited for him to say something. When he didn't, Kim pushed her point home.

—I'll tell you what, Connor. For the past three weeks, you've been bent on self-destruction and sympathy. I'm not going to stay here and watch any longer. I'm going to go back to my apartment. When you're done with your pouting, you can give me a call. Maybe I'll call you back.

Connor stood up and walked over to her and softened his voice.

—What if we got out of town for a few days? It'll give me some time to think.

▢▢▢ 38 ▢▢▢

After deplaning at the Vineyard airport, Connor and Kim picked up their rental car, a sporty red Mustang convertible, and sped past the Hot Tin Roof nightclub, hung a left and then another left. With the sun shining down upon them and wind rustling their hair, they followed Barnes Road into Oak Bluffs for wine and other essentials before heading up-island where they were staying.

Three days later, from the vista of lawn chairs outside their Menemsha Inn cottage, Connor and Kim sat drinking wine, watching the slowly sinking sun transforming the blue sky into a tapestry of pinks and magentas and traces of purple over the Menemsha Bay. When the orange orb disappeared, Connor pulled out his cell phone and dialed his former campaign manager. Kim stood up, went behind him, bent down and kissed the right side of his neck before going into the cottage for a new bottle of vino.

—Hello.

—Zack, it's Connor. I've got some news. I'm going to run as an Independent.

—Connor, don't be stupid. Third party candidates don't have a chance.

—Maybe not, but I'm going to do it anyway. I would like to ask one favor though. Don't vilify me. I know whoever you choose is going to come out against me. I'd just like to be fair about it. Can you do that?

—The decision's not entirely mine and, as you know, you pissed off a lot of people. But I'll do what I can. Frankly, everyone would prefer not to mention your name at all.

—Is it Morgan? I've heard rumors that you're considering Morgan.

—Morgan's not a bad guy.

—Didn't you tell me that whichever way the wind is blowing, that's where you'll find Morgan?

—You didn't really call to argue politics, did you?

—No, you're right, I didn't. I called to tell you Bob Hevens is going to be running my campaign for me.

—Hevens doesn't know a damn thing about running a campaign. The only reason I agreed to work with him was because he was your friend.

—Maybe he's not a professional campaign manager, but in the three days we've been up here he was able to put together a fundraising concert for me at Madison Square Garden. We're calling it The Concert for Connor.

—I'll reserve comment. Who's playing?

—Eddy Vedder and Pearl Jam, Neil Young, The Dixie Chicks, Steve Earle, Bruce Springsteen, Patti Smith, Jackson Browne, Michael Stipe, the Beastie Boys, Henry Rollins, Billy Corrigan, Lou Reed, and plenty of others. It should be a great show.

—In other words every leftwing liberal you could think of.

—Thanks for the vote of confidence.

—Yeah. See you in November.

—Bye.

□□□ 39 □□□

Keno stepped in and closed Senator Wellington's office door behind him.

—Senator, Gabriel Patrick and Ray Langley, the guys who did the video interviews, are here to see you.

125

Senator Wellington took his eyes off of an endorsement letter from the National Rifle Association, praising him for his courage to hunt criminals.

—Okay. Send them in.

Dick Lofton had hired two young men to do videotape interviews. If this came back positive, he planned to do more interviews and use them in television commercials. The door opened and the two interviewers came in. Gabriel, the talker of the two, with walnut colored hair and eyes as blue as a robin's egg, took the encased DVD from his right hand and placed in his left, so he could shake the senator's hand. Ray, less sure of himself, tailed behind Gabriel and waited to be noticed. When Wellington's eyes fell upon him, he too extended a hand. They shook and said hello to each other. Gabriel waved the DVD in the air.

—Is there somewhere we can play it?

—Yes, there's a DVD player in that cabinet, behind you.

Wellington pointed to the cabinet in the corner of the room. Gabriel opened it and popped the DVD into the player and turned on the monitor. Ten seconds of color bars filled the screen before the edited footage of the on-camera Gabriel came up. He was standing in a city plaza, surrounded by tall buildings. With his jacket and tie, he looked like a cross between a professional news anchor and a student communications major at one of the local colleges. There seemed to be a slight grin or smile on his face as he went up to an older, balding man seated at one of the plaza benches reading a newspaper.

—*Hi, I'm Gabriel Patrick and I'm working for Senator Wellington. Could I ask you a question?*

—*Senator Wellington? Sure.*

Senator Wellington, Gabriel, and Ray took seats at the round table.

—*How do you feel about Senator Wellington's plan to send criminals to The Promised Land where they will be hunted and killed?*

—*Well, I think there comes a time in every politician's life when he realizes that he doesn't have just a job, what he has is an opportunity to make the country and the world a better place. I think Senator Wellington realizes this, and that is why he feels he needs to take the drastic step of sending prisoners to Africa to meet their fate. In a perfect world this would not be necessary; unfortunately, we do not live in a perfect world. So, to answer your question, yes, I do support Senator Wellington, and I wish him all the luck in the world. God bless him.*

Wellington turned to Gabriel with a wide, affirmative grin. Gabriel hit the pause button.

—That's terrific. He's good. Articulate and intelligent. That's the kind of people we need. This is exactly what I was hoping for.

—Yes, he was passionate.

—Okay, let's see the next one.

Gabriel pushed "Play." The second man interviewed was much younger than the first; he was perhaps thirty and wore a dark suit without a tie.

—*Senator Wellington? Well, I've always felt that he was compassionate, a man who wants the best for all of us. I talked to some friends about his plans. Some thought they sounded crazy at first, but the more we talked, the more we realized that he was going to do the right thing. I think criminals get away with too much. We have to start worrying about the good people, the people who don't commit crimes, the people who go to work every day, the people who care about their families and pay taxes. Who's looking out for them? Senator Wellington is. That's why I voted for him in the past, and that's why I'd vote for him again.*

Wellington was even more excited.

—Bingo. That's great. Where'd you find him?

—We went over to Daj Hammarskjold plaza by the United Nation, to get people on their lunch hour.

—I thought that looked familiar. He was excellent. Both of them were. See, no one believed me, but stuff like this shows that I am onto something. How many did you interview?

—Well, we were out there all day talking to people. We edited it down to the best three.

—These are good.

—Thank you.

—Roll the next one.

This interviewee was in her early fifties with reddish-blonde hair.

—*Could I keep the Wellington for Senate button?*

—*Sure.*

—*um...what was the question again?*

—*How do you feel about Senator Wellington's plan to send violent criminals to Africa?*

—*Oh...well, I guess I shouldn't say this but I've always thought Senator Wellington was sexy. I like a man like that, powerful, intelligent, forceful. A man who gets things done.*

—*And his plan?*

—*Oh right, sorry. It's a good plan. He's one of the first politicians, maybe the only one, who is really trying to do something. If we don't send them away, what are we going to do with them? Put them back out on the street? I don't want that to happen. I think if you murder someone, well, that's it, you don't get another chance. Murderers don't turn into choirboys overnight. If anything they get worse in prison. So, yes, I'm for Senator Wellington's plan.*

Wellington rose from the table and Gabriel and Ray followed suit.

—That was great. I can use this. You got them to sign releases, didn't you?

Gabriel answered reluctantly,

—I'm afraid we didn't.

Wellington looked at the interviewer with disappointment.

—Why the hell not? I want to use these for one of the campaign commercials I'm putting together. You should always get the contact information of anyone you interview, otherwise we can't use them.

Gabriel nodded, pretending to value this older man's words of advice.

—I know. I thought about that as soon as we finished.

—Do you think you could find them again?

Ray looked at Gabriel, who, much to his dismay, nodded in the affirmative.

—I think so, yes.

—Great. I want you to do that.

—We'll give it our best.

Wellington was warming up to younger man.

—Gabriel, I understand your father is friends with Dick Lofton. Lofton's a good man.

—Since when?

This surprised the senator.

—What?

—Nothing.

Wanting to remain amiable, Wellington ignored the perceived slight.

—I understand you went to Columbia University. What did you study?

—Corruption

—*Corruption?*

—Yes. It used to be that students would graduate without having a proper understanding of it and they'd be forced to figure it out on their own. Many got caught breaking the law and were sent to prison. Of course this reflected poorly on the University. Now they're teaching law students the best ways to break the law without getting caught. It gives you a real head start in the business world.

—Does that pass for humor in your circle?

—Occasionally.

—You know who likes a wise guy? No one. No one likes a wise guy.

Gabriel couldn't resist adding another quip.

—Some people do. Some people like wise guys.

Wellington's phone rang, but instead of picking it up, he turned from Gabriel to his quieter companion.

—What about you Ray, are you a student?

—I went to NYU for film.

—My daughter Bridget goes to NYU.

Gabriel, who had wandered over to look at the photos on Wellington's desk, pointed to the photo of Bridget with her parents.

—That's her, isn't it? She's very attractive.

—She gets it from her mother.

—Apparently.

—What the hell's that supposed to mean?

—That a man like you must have a beautiful wife.

—You know, I was a bit of wise-ass when I was your age, but I grew up.

—Does that mean I'll become a senator when I grow up?

Before Wellington could say anything, Keno had stepped back into the office.

—Excuse me, Senator. Ms. Potter's on the phone.

Wellington eyed Gabriel before turning to the other man.

—Nice meeting you, Ray. Do me a favor and get this guy the hell out of here.

☐☐☐ 40 ☐☐☐

A knock on her apartment door startled Bridget Wellington. She sat up from her prone position on the couch and called out.

—Who is it?

From outside the door a voice said,

—Open up and find out.

She got up and peeked through the door's eyehole. A tall, light brown haired young man touched his right thumb to his nose and wiggled his fingers at her. After a few wiggles he pulled his hand away and smiled. He wore black jeans, black boots, and a white shirt striped with blue.

—My name is Gabriel Patrick. I'm helping out on your father's campaign.

Bridget opened the door slightly.

—What do you want from me?

—We were talking, you know how men are, and we started talking about women, and I told him I wasn't getting laid very much, and he told me he had a daughter who I should look up.

129

Bridget started to slam the door, but Gabriel stuck his left boot inside the door before she closed it tight.

—Hey! What do you want to do, break my foot?

—Then get it out.

—I will in a minute, after we're properly acquainted. Let me start again. My name is Gabriel Patrick. You're supposed to say I'm Bridget Wellington. Go ahead, say it.

Bridget relaxed and allowed the door to open more fully.

—You already know who I am.

—Very nice to meet you, Bridget. Recently, I was talking to your father, Senator Wellington, and I told him how I wasn't getting laid very much, and he said he had a daughter...

She reached for the door handle.

—I'm kidding, I'm kidding. He didn't say anything.

—If you're working for my father I don't think we have anything to talk about.

—What if I told you I hate your father and everything he stands for?

—Do you?

—I'm not sure. I'm just wondering how you'd feel if I said it.

—What do you want?

—Love mostly. Money if you have it, but mostly love.

—Very funny. How'd you get up here? Didn't my doorman stop you?

—I knew he wouldn't let me up without knowing you, so I had to shoot him. If we're going to go out and have some fun I think we should go now before the police arrive.

—I'm studying.

Gabriel peeked into the apartment.

—Do you have a tutor? I could be your tutor.

—I suppose you think you're charming?

—Not at all, it's just that I've never seen such beautiful sadness in a woman's eyes.

—You think I'm sad?

—No. I think you're beautiful, but hidden in that beauty is a hint of sadness, and that drew me to you. I saw your photo on your father's desk and I told myself that you might be my one chance of happiness. If you turn me down you could damage me for life.

—Well, I guess you're going to be damaged.

Bridget closed the door. Gabriel stood there not quite shocked but surprised. He waited seven full minutes. The door did not reopen.

41

The following day, Bridget came home from class and checked her messages. She heard, "Hey Bridget, this is Gabriel. I guess it was rash and stupid of me to come by your apartment and expect you to drop whatever you were doing and go out with me. Well, I *am* a rash and stupid guy, but a woman as beautiful as you has a powerful attraction, so much so that I found out where you lived and impulsively went to see you. If I were like everyone else, the proper thing to do would be to continue working for your father and hope that I would get lucky and somehow meet you through him. Well, maybe that would happen and maybe it wouldn't. But maybe is not good enough for me. I'm not one of those people who wait for fate, or some other nonsensical force, to intervene. I think you need to go after what you want in life. That's what I did. *Fools rush in where angels fear to tread*...as the song goes. I guess I'm a fool, that's why I'm trying again. I'd still like to buy you a drink or dinner, if you'll let me. I found your number through AnyWho, mine's there too, if you want to call me back. If not, as Bogart said to Bergman in *Casablanca*, "We'll always have Paris." Of course, we haven't had Paris, have we? That's why you should call me, so we can create our own memories. Bye."

Bridget pushed the erase button on the answering machine.

42

In an apartment bedroom inside the Piano Factory in Hell's Kitchen, a telephone rang. After four rings the answering machine picked up and the caller began speaking.

—Gabriel, it's Senator Wellington. I know it's Saturday, but I need to speak to you about the interviews you did. It's been more than a week. Did you find the people or not? I'd like to use them for a commercial. Call me back at my office as soon as you get this.

Gabriel left the bedroom and walked to the kitchen. He dumped out yesterday's used coffee filter, put in a new filter, added freshly ground coffee, poured in an appropriate amount of water and pushed the ON button. In the living room he picked up the phone and dialed. After talking to an aide, he was connected to the senator and listened as Wellington's voice came through the line.

—Gabriel, what happened with those interviewees you were supposed to find?

—No luck.

—What do you mean, no luck? I need them. I told you I want to use them for a commercial.

—I ought to tell you before it blows up in your face, I made those interviews up.

—What? Why the hell would you do something like that?

—Because most of the people we asked were clueless. It's a rather an inarticulate populace, if you haven't noticed.

—What the hell is that supposed to mean?

—If you want to see the real tapes, I'll show them to you. More than a third of the people interviewed hadn't even heard of your proposals. Another ten or twenty percent said they didn't follow politics because it's always negative. Maybe five percent were in favor of what you want to do.

—Just because you're intelligent doesn't give you a right to be a smart ass.

—Who says I'm intelligent?

—I checked with Lofton, you got an academic scholarship to Columbia as both an undergrad and a law student. You graduated at the top of your class. That's not an easy thing to do.

—I cheated on my tests.

—The hell you did. Why'd you quit Kravat?

—What does it matter?

—You quit over a matter of principle, didn't you?

—Something like that.

—You made me sound pretty good. Ever done any speech writing?

—No.

—Ever worked on any commercials?

—No.

—Well, maybe you can help me, anyway. I'm expanding my campaign staff and I'm going to need some writers. You might be able to help us in that department.

—Writing speeches?

—Yes. I'd like to put you on my staff.

—I figured I was fired.

—No such luck. I'll see you at 9 AM on Monday.

□□□ **43** □□□

Up in Harlem, Claudia Potter was in the back of a Lincoln Town Car with a Nigel Wheeler, a top advertising creative director. After circling the neighborhood a number of times, their car pulled up cautiously in front of a group of men leaning against the chain link fence of the basketball court on One Hundred Thirty-Ninth Street and

Lenox Avenue. The ball players looked at each other with bemusement and curiosity as the dark tinted back window lowered, revealing Potter's blonde head framed center. She smiled and gave a quick wave in what she thought was a friendly way.

—Hi, how are you guys doing?

None of the men spoke. They gave only dead, blank stares.

—My name is Claudia Potter. I'm producing a commer...a video, and we're looking for a tough guy to be in it. Any of you guys interested in being in a video?

One man, who was sitting on the brownish colored basketball, stood up and drop-kicked the ball. It slammed against the door panel below Claudia's head. Claudia reactions were so slow she only ducked after the ball hit and was bouncing back to the kicker. They all laughed. Potter's head came back into view.

—There's money in it. Don't any of you want to make money?

Four of the men wore long white t-shirts. One wore a yellow polo shirt. Another one wore a denim jacket covering a Malcolm X t-shirt. He spoke up.

—What kind of video?

—Well, it's not exactly a rap video...it's TV. You want to be on TV?

Malcolm X t-shirt was about to respond but he was too slow. Another b-ball player, not the tallest, but the brawniest and meanest looking came right up to the car.

—Yo' man, what the fuck do you want?

Claudia nervously smiled at the man with the vocal toughness.

—I want a guy like you.

He put his hands on the car's roof above Potter's door and peered inside. Claudia retracted her head like a turtle.

—Yeah? Why the fuck is that?

Nigel uttered timidly,

—If you want us to leave, we'll leave.

—Okay, leave.

The driver looked to Claudia, who felt too intimidated to turn away from the man in her window.

—I don't see you leaving.

Claudia smiled.

—I just thought you might want a shot at being on television, in a commercial.

—Am I gonna be rapping? Because I got some rhymes I could drop on you.

Claudia shook her head as she said,

—No, that's okay. You'll just be looking mean.

133

—That's all?

He pulled himself out of the window, discouraged. Claudia pulled herself up to it.

—There's money.

He turned back to her.

—How much?

—With residuals it could be quite lucrative.

—How much?

—Every time the spot is on you get paid.

—How much?

—Some commercials run for years, which could mean a lot of money. Some commercials pay you as much as three thousand dollars to start.

—Yeah, and some pay millions, and some pay nothing. How much you paying?

—I'm Claudia Potter, and you are?

She stuck her hand out for him to shake. He thought about it, let her hand dangle for a few moments before extending his own.

—Robert Jackson.

—Nice to meet you, Robert. Would you like to go down to the studio and audition?

—You paying cash money? I don't do no checks. I need cash money.

—Okay, cash is fine. We can do that.

—A'ight.

Claudia quickly unlocked the door. Robert stepped in without looking back at his companions.

☐☐☐ **44** ☐☐☐

At the Sheraton Hotel's Metropolitan ballroom in midtown Manhattan, a spotlight shone on Mayor Corpson who was centered behind a lectern on a raised platform. Dignitaries, five to his right, six to his left, were seated behind their dinner plates. Approximately six-hundred police officers, dressed in their civilian clothes, had been listening to his speech and looking to him, or to the four large video images of his head and upper torso magnified on projection screens hung at each corner of the ballroom.

—...and now, without further ado, here he is, Senator Wellington!

An enthusiastic roar of clapping hands welcomed the senator. He rose from his seat, greeted the mayor with a handshake and a pat on the back, and stepped to the microphone.

—Thank you. Thank you very much. Please...take your seats...thank you...thank you...that's very kind of you...When I proposed...

Cheers, even some hooting and hollering continued for longer than could be reasonably expected. This was due to the police officers having utilized with great effectiveness the two open bars, one inside the ballroom and one outside in the hallway.

—...when I proposed the idea of...thank you. When I proposed the idea of having a dinner for police officers, my campaign manager was against it. He said I should only meet with campaign donors because those were the people who could help me raise the necessary money to continue my campaign. There is, unfortunately, a lot of truth to that. Nonetheless, I felt it was important to talk with New York's finest to show my appreciation for what you do each and every day.

More claps and cheers filled the ballroom.

—Thank you...thank you...please...let me continue...As you are well aware, crime affects each and every one of us on a daily basis. The New York Police force, each one of you, is the finest, not only in the country, but also in the world. Thank you...very kind of you...You've done everything you can to reduce crime, and you have been very successful. Unfortunately, crime hasn't been eliminated. It may never be eliminated. That doesn't mean we won't do everything we can to try to eradicate it. Some of you may be aware of my proposals which call for sending violent criminals, murderers, rapists, child molesters, terrorists, to The Promised Land where they will be hunted down and killed...thank you again...thank you...please take your seats...Sending criminals to The Promised Land has become controversial. Some people believe this is too harsh. They believe criminals can be reformed. Those who feel like that do not and have not worked with the violent, vicious thugs most of you have become all too familiar with. Let me give you an example. Three weeks ago, Samir Singh, a hard-working young man dropped his sister off at a friend's house in Long Island. He was returning to his family's home in Queens to let his brother borrow his car. They were a good, caring family, only citizens in this country for a few years. On the way home Samir saw two men in front of a broken down car on a side road. Because this country had helped Samir and his family he wanted to return the generosity and kindness. He stopped his car, got out and walked over to the men to see what he could do to help. The two men knocked Samir over the head, dragged him into the woods, took the keys to his car, took his wallet, his money, shot him through the chest, and stole his car. Samir just wanted to help, that's all, and he was killed for his efforts. The two men who did this were identified and apprehended by patrolman Kenneth Dillinger and patrolwoman Roberta Sanchez, who are seated here to my right.

The spotlight beam widened to include all three.

—Yes, go ahead, stand up, take a bow, you deserve it.

Dillinger and Sanchez did as commanded, eliciting great applause and cheers from their colleagues.

—Let me ask you this, what should happen to the men who killed Samir Singh? Should they be given a roof over their heads? Should they be fed three meals a day? Should they get television and conjugal visits? After their trial, they'll be sentenced to jail, but they'll eventually get out. That's right, make no mistake about it, those men will eventually get out of jail. Samir Singh will never see his family again. Never see his friends. Never see his girlfriend. Never have his own family. The two men who killed him will get out of prison. They'll get out and you'll have to catch them again. Because you know that once they are freed they're going to commit more crimes. I think that is wrong. I don't think they belong back on the street, ever. Animals that cold-blooded do not have the right to exist in a civilized society.

From the back of the room came a voice,

—That's why we're going to elect you!

One of his colleagues, Budweiser bottle in hand and a belly filled with shots of Jack Daniel's, began chanting,

—Wellington for President! Wellington for President! Wellington for President!

Wellington smiled.

—Thank you. I'm not running for president, but thanks...I appreciate your votes, but more than that I appreciate what each and every one of you has done to make this city, this state, this country a safer place. That's why I want to share with you one of my commercials. Some of you may have seen it because it's been airing for a few days. For those of you who have not, and even for those of you have, I want to show it to you tonight to let you know how I feel about New York's finest. Can we bring down the lights and roll it?

As the lights came down all eyes turned to one of the four projection screens. A tough looking convict—Robert Jackson—was uncuffed and allowed to walk through the gates of Sing Sing prison. A voiceover broke the ominous music.

—*His name is Trent Harding. After serving ten years for murdering a police officer, he's free. How long before he kills again?*

The commercial then showed Robert Jackson chasing a pretty young woman in a yellow dress down a deserted and dark city street. The woman realizes the street is a dead-end. She turns back to see Robert Jackson smiling menacingly as he pulls out a large bowie knife. The woman screams as Jackson grabs and rips her dress. Suddenly the action cuts back to the prison and Senator Wellington pushes Robert

Jackson into a prison cell, slamming the door behind him. The voiceover returns:

—*Senator Wellington wants to protect you and your family from thugs like this. Senator Wellington wants to make sure murderers never kill again. A vote for Senator Wellington is a vote for safer streets, safer communities, and a safer America. In Wellington's world, killers never walk free once they're convicted.*

When the lights came back up, Wellington stood authoritarian and proud behind the lectern. The entire room stood, cheered, clapped, hooted, and howled.

—Wellington! Wellington! Wellington!

—Thank you. Thank you very much.

—Wellington! Wellington! Wellington!

Senator Wellington raised his right palm to quiet them.

—Thank you. Thanks very much. I appreciate all of you coming tonight, and I appreciate all you've done to keep this great city and state safe for all of us. They're about to serve the meal, so let's eat up and enjoy ourselves.

—Wellington! Wellington! Wellington!

As soon as he regained his seat, waiters streamed in from the kitchen bearing trays with prime rib dinners. The shouting and clapping slowly faded out as the celebrants rushed from their tables to the reopened bars.

□□□ 45 □□□

After the meal Wellington handshaked his way through the crowd, receiving pats on the back, verbal congratulations, and good lucks. When he got into the hallway, Wellington tried to bypass the mass of beefy cops drinking down bottled beers at the second bar. A hand reached out to Wellington and didn't let go.

—Senator, hi. That was great, you know it was great. I mean it was great, that video, that commercial, and everything you said. I really liked it. It was great.

—Thank you.

A friend chimed in,

—He's right, Senator, I tell you a lot of us are behind you on this, we really respect what you're doing.

Senator Wellington nodded his head in gratitude.

—And I respect what you are doing. I realize just how difficult it is to be a police officer these days. I wish more people did.

—Thank you, Senator. If I could vote twice I would.

—Me, too, Senator. We're behind you one hundred percent.

—Hey, Senator, c'mere.

A short and stocky man, wearing an ill-fitting blue blazer and jeans, said in a hushed voice,

—Some of us are going over to Private Eyes, you want to come?

—Private Eyes? What's that?

—It's a topless bar. Like Scores, only cheaper. It's only a few blocks from here.

—Oh…thanks very much, I'd like to, I'd love to, but I can't. I have another engagement I must attend.

—I know the guys there, they'll treat you all right. It'll be my treat.

—Thanks again, but no.

Wellington turned his eyes to Gabriel Patrick who had trailed him out of the ballroom. He smiled, and motioned Gabriel over.

—Gabriel, this is…

—Tiny. Well, Alex, my name is Alex, but everyone calls me Tiny.

The cops corralled Wellington and his aide.

—Gabriel, why don't you join these gentlemen as my representative? They're going to Private Eyes.

—That sounds great…I wish I could go, but I can't. I have to meet someone.

—Nonsense. Gentlemen, this is Gabriel Patrick, one of my speechwriters. Gabriel, this is Tiny and…

—Tony.

Another hand was extended.

—I'm Pete, Senator.

—Tony, why don't Pete and Tiny and...

—I'm Tommy.

—And Tommy. Why don't you take Gabriel with you?

—You want to come, Gabriel?

—Any other night and I'd be happy to go but I can't tonight.

—You don't want to go to Private Eyes? What are you, a fag?

—I want to go, but there's a gymnast who wants me to help her work on her splits.

All the men laughed, save Wellington who looked at Gabriel crossly.

—Excuse me, fellas. Let me have a brief word with him privately.

—Sure, Senator. Sure.

Wellington placed his hand on Gabriel's lower back and gently pushed him back toward the elevator bank.

—Gabriel, it's damn important to have cops on our side. They want to go out and have some drinks and see some naked girls. I can't go with them, wouldn't look right. It's important I get their support. They deserve it for everything they do.

Wellington reached into his pocket, pulling out his billfold. Two fifties and six twenties were quickly peeled off.

—Here, take this; spend it on them.

Gabriel held up his hands in protest.

—But Senator, I really do have to meet someone.

—What is it, some chick got you by the balls? Call her and tell her you'll see her another time.

Wellington stuffed the money in Gabriel's suit pocket before continuing,

—Get them drunk, that's what they want.

—All right, look, it's not that I don't want to go, but these guys are drunk. They're only going to get drunker and probably start getting into fights. I'd rather not be there when they do.

—I don't remember asking you your opinion.

▢▢▢ 46 ▢▢▢

Gabriel Patrick and the brethren in blue came out of the Sheraton Hotel like a rugby scrum. They barreled across Seventh Avenue laughing and shouting for the cars to get out of their way. On Eighth Avenue, they pushed past swarming tourists that had exiting Broadway theaters and were now heading to their cars to take them back to New Jersey or Long Island or up to Westchester or Connecticut. At Forty-Fifth Street, a blue and red neon Private Eyes sign illuminated a doorman who held the door for the men. Inside, they paid the cover and headed into the Topless Lounge.

Centered in the dark room was a rectangular stage with two golden poles where two girls—they were never called women   plied their money-inducing theatrics. Gabriel took a seat at a small round table and looked around. Two Hasidic Jews were getting lap-dances next to each other at a square table. In the darkest corner, a large-gutted man, perhaps sixty, shared a bottle of champagne with a thin, small-chested, dark-haired girl who could have been his granddaughter. Along padded benches bordering the room, five more men were getting lap-dances. Minutes after receiving their first round of beers, Pete, Tiny, Tommy, and Tony found empty spots along the wall so they too could get lap-dances.

Gabriel felt a finger caress his cheek. He turned. No one was there. The opposite cheek was lightly touched. He turned again and saw no one. Spinning around fully he saw an incredibly seductive smile. She

leaned in and came within a millimeter of kissing him and licked her lips slowly. She ran her hand up Gabriel's strong chest before leaning forward and pulling her velvet dress downward, exposing the tops of her nipples. She spoke with a Russian accent,
—I'm Fantasy.
    Gabriel chuckled.
—*Fantasy*? Your parents must have been soothsayers to pick out a name like that.
—You want dance, handsome?
—Oh, I do, but lap-dances are like potato chips, you can never have just one.
    Tommy, only two feet away, getting a lap-dance, burst out laughing.
—Hey, did you hear that, Pete? Lap-dances are like potato chips, you can never have just one!
    Peter laughed, drunkenly.
—Yeah, I'm gonna get me a whole bag of lap-dances…extra spicy ones!
    Fantasy disappeared and a moment later a cute Asian with dyed blonde hair introduced herself as Tai and offered Gabriel her services. Gabriel took one look at her body and felt the crotch of his pants tighten. Decisively, he stood up and pulled out the wad of bills Wellington had given him. He placed it in the sexy Asian's hand.
—Tai, unfortunately, I have to leave. These men make this city safe for people like you and me. Will you give them your best service?
    Tai gave Gabriel a soft kiss on his cheek and slipped the bills inside her G-string.
—I like you…you come back?
—Just make sure you and your friends treat these guys right. Drinks and dances until the money runs out. And make sure Fantasy gives them a few dances, she's a stunner. Okay?
    Tai smiled,
—I save dance for you. You come back and me give you free dance.

□□□ 47 □□□

    The following morning, as Keno Crawford was quickly flipping through *The New York Daily Post* to see if the story had been reported yet, Gabriel came around the corner from the elevator on his way to Senator Wellington's office.
—Morning, Keno.
    He looked up solemnly.

—Did you hear?

—What?

—Robert Jackson, the guy from Senator Wellington's commercial, was killed last night.

—Killed? How?

—Beaten to death. Three big white guys were seen running from the body. They were drunk and laughing.

From inside the office a voice called,

—That you, Gabriel?

—Yes.

Gabriel looked toward the office and back to Keno. Wellington hollered again.

—Get in here.

Gabriel stepped in. Although his face was freshly shaved and his tie was not unloosened, Wellington's tired bloodshot eyes indicated he'd been up all night. He was at the round conference table with his own copies of the local papers. Gabriel took a seat.

—What happened?

—Some damn homeless bum is trying to blame the death of Robert Jackson on police officers. It's an out-and-out lie.

—How do they know it was police?

Wellington responded angrily.

—They don't! It wasn't. The homeless crack-head told some fire and brimstone preacher that he saw three big white guys go after Robert and beat him to death. Now this preacher is saying that cops did it. I don't think it's in the papers yet, but it will be.

—Do you think it's possible?

—Anything bad happens around this town and they blame the police. What the hell does a cop look like anyway? Do they all look the same? You went to a topless bar last night. What happened there?

—We had some drinks, watched the girls dance.

—Anyone asks, you weren't there. That understood? You didn't see any cops drunk either. Got that?

—Are you telling me to lie?

—I'm telling you I don't want a fiasco on my hands. I don't want some preacher blowing this up into something it isn't. I'm hoping that I can get your support on that.

—Where did it happen?

—On One Hundred Fifty-Fourth Street.

—Well, we didn't go anywhere near there.

—Did you leave the bar with the cops? Did you tuck them into bed? How the hell do you know where they went? Robert was a good kid who got caught in a bad situation.

—What did you want to see me about this morning?

—My son, Richie, is coming in later today, flying in to Newark. I want him to work on some of my commercials. He's a film director. I want you to meet him at the airport and take him to the Soho Grand Hotel.

—You want me to baby-sit him?

—No, not at all. I hope you don't mind but my daughter will be going with you.

—Bridget?

—Yes. How did you know her name?

—You've mentioned her to me a few times before, and I've seen her photo on your desk.

—Well, she'll be going with you. I'll get you a car and a driver. Shouldn't really need you there but if he disappears she won't tell me where he is, even if she knows. Something about sibling trust, not wanting parents to know. Anyway, I'm shooting another commercial and I want him to be involved. I'm trying to get him to straighten out his life, and I just need someone I can trust to keep an eye on him.

—Senator, I'm not going to spy on him or report what he says or does. I don't do that.

—I'm not asking you to. I just thought the three of you could go out to dinner together. It's on me. You might even like my daughter.

—I guess I can make the sacrifice.

—Senator?

Keno was standing by the doorway.

—What is it?

—There's a man from the *New York Daily Post* on the phone. He wants to ask you some questions about Robert, wants to know your reaction.

—Tell him I'm not available and get me David Diamond on the phone.

□□□ **48** □□□

Bridget and Gabriel ambled through Newark Airport Terminal A to await Richie Wellington's flight. They walked past a chain store for books, past a chain store for coffee, past a chain store for sunglasses, past a chair store for hamburgers. They had a half hour to kill so Gabriel suggested getting a drink. Inside a chain restaurant they went to the bar, pulled up stools, and ordered from the bartender. Once the drinks were placed in front of them, Gabriel clinked his glass of Jameson against Bridget's glass of white wine. They sipped and the glasses were placed back on the wooden bar.

—Bridget, let me apologize for coming to your apartment like I did.

142

Frankly, I'm surprised that you didn't tell your father you didn't want me anywhere near you.

—Normally, I wouldn't have, but I Googled you and didn't find any arrest warrants and well, apparently you're pretty smart…not that I go for that kind of stuff.

—You Googled me? What did you find out?

—You're a lawyer.

—I'm not. I was. I'm not any more.

—Why not?

—I got fired for beating up one of the clients.

—No, you didn't.

—All right, don't believe me.

—Why? What did he do?

—He was wearing too much aftershave. Don't you think men who wear aftershave should be beaten? I do.

—You're not going to tell me what happened?

—I was part of a team that was representing this corporate raider, a guy named Charlie Whorowitz. He bought Pacific Lumber in Oregon. The company had been in business over a hundred years and had a huge pension fund. Pacific cut trees down but they were also making sure they were growing as many trees as they cut down. When Whorowitz took over he wanted us to help his set up another company which he would use to buy Pacific Lumber.

—But didn't he already own it?

—Yes, but with the new company he could change management and change some of the company's structure. And that's exactly what he did, with our help. He forced the lumberjacks and woodworkers, and all the other union people, to either quit or work as non-union employees. Doing so cut their wages substantially and eliminated many of their benefits. This saved the new company millions. Whorowitz also gained control of the pension fund, which he used to set up another lumber company in the Brazilian Rain Forest. The long and short of it is that everyone made money—well, everyone except the workers. Naturally, they were pissed off. The workers at Pacific Lumber put together a committee who came to our office in New York to protest what had happened. One of the more senior guys was going on and on, about how he had worked for Pacific Lumber for twenty-five years and now he had nothing. His entire retirement pension was gone and he was screwed. We started yelling back and forth at each other and finally I had enough of his shouting, so I punched him in the face. He fell to the floor, and I started kicking him until someone pulled me off him and...

Bridget stared at him incredulously.

—Are you nuts, or stupid?

    Gabriel smiled before sipping his drink and replying.

—He deserved it. If he didn't like what his company was doing he should have just quit. Anyway, one of the senior partners thought I was a little too gung-ho, that I shouldn't have punched him or kicked him. I told him that I wasn't any different than anyone else, but he didn't like my attitude so I was fired.

—As they should have.

—Why? I can't stand people who complain about what happens to them. I mean, all right, maybe I shouldn't have hit him, but we were playing by the rules. Perhaps what we did wasn't moral or ethical, but it was legal and that's what counts. That's what corporate law is all about, what's legal. When I started out, a senior partner told me that there's no need to break the law because if you know the law well enough, there's always a way to bend it to accomplish whatever you want. If for some reason you can't find a law to support what your client wants, we tap a senator or congressman who we helped put into office and he changes the laws or enacts new legislation to suit our needs.

—No wonder why you're working for my father.

    Gabriel grinned, slightly.

—I'm kidding.

—Are you?

    He nodded.

—Just the opposite happened. I did do work for Whorowitz and he did buy Pacific Lumber and do everything I just told you, but no one came to see us about it, at least not me. After the deal went through I ended up in the hospital.

—Why, what happened?

—For a long time I had been feeling a lot of pain in my stomach and I started spitting up blood. After about a month, I finally had myself checked out. It turns out I was bleeding internally from a rather severe ulcer.

—You don't seem like the type.

—Beneath this confident façade there's a lot of turmoil.

—Why?

    Gabriel motioned to the barmaid for another drink.

—I was the firm's golden boy. They all loved me, thought I had a bright future, and I did. I worked my ass off in high school to get into a good college, and in college I worked my ass off to get into law school. I had this burning desire to be the best. I was this star kid—the kid everyone said was going to go far. My father was proud of me, my mother was proud of me. Everyone was proud of me. I was even proud of myself until I started working and learned what being a lawyer was really about. After my first year I realized I hated it, but I couldn't just quit. So I stuck it out for five more years, hating it every day.

—Why?

Gabriel watched the barmaid pour his drink before turning back to Bridget.

—I had done a few similar deals and they all boiled down to me helping these large corporations not break the law, but bend it enough so they could do whatever it was they wanted. It was all paperwork and numbers on the surface, but underneath, people's lives were being ruined. I knew that. Everyone knew that, but you were supposed to act like it didn't matter. It was all about helping the client, helping the client and advancing your career. In less than three years, I was making more than three hundred thousand a year. After five…well, I was making a lot. Whenever you're paid well it's easy to justify whatever it is you're doing. Somewhere deep inside I knew what I was doing was wrong, and that started eating at me. It had been eating at me since I started, really. Finally, it came to the surface, if you pardon the mixed metaphor. As I said, I ended up in the hospital, and after I came back to work I was supposed to start a new case. The time I spent lying on a hospital bed gave me time to think, and when I got back I told my boss that I didn't want to do it anymore. He asked me what I wanted to work on. I couldn't come up with an answer, so I asked for a leave of absence. They thought I was flaking out or something and told me to go see a psychiatrist.

—If you asked for a leave of absence, you didn't get fired.

—They didn't give me the leave of absence. They expected me to keep working, and I didn't. I stopped showing up, and after a while they gave me an ultimatum: either show up or get fired. So I was fired. It was a great relief. It really was. Two days after it was finalized I took a six-week trip to Ireland. Beautiful country, especially the west. It gave me time to get my head together. When I got back I didn't quite know what I wanted to do except not be a lawyer. My father's well connected. He ended up getting me a job with your father, which I didn't really want. I'm not even a Republican, but I did take some film classes and I thought it would be fun to do some interviews. I was actually rather rude to your father. It was my way of making sure he wouldn't want to use me again. But that backfired, and he hired me to do some writing for him. But enough about me. Tell me about you, or even your mysterious brother we're waiting for. I'm curious about a senator's son.

—Let me get another drink.

Bridget motioned to the barkeep.

—In some ways he lives in his own reality. Well, not his own reality, it's just, he went to NYU for film, but he didn't even graduate. He dropped out and moved to Colorado to study at the Naropa Institute. But he only stayed there for a semester before moving to Vail. He spends his summers working carpentry so he can ski in the winters. Or he was until recently, now he's living in L.A., Venice Beach. His girlfriend is trying to be an actress. Mostly, they just sit around and smoke a lot of dope. He wants to be a film director, but he doesn't want to go through all the steps you need to go through to get there. He kind of just expects someone to give him a job directing a feature film. It's never going to happen.

—I thought he was a director. Your father said...

—Richie says he's a film director because he's made one short film. My father tells other people he's a director because it's less embarrassing than saying his son doesn't work, and that he's still paying his bills.

—There are a lot of guys like him.

Above the bar were three television monitors. The center one showed CNN with closed captioning scrolling across the screen; the other two had baseball games on. The closed captioning on CNN caught Bridget's attention and she called to the steroid-inflated bartender.

—Excuse me, can you turn that up—the news?

The barkeep found the television remote and raised the volume.

—*...seemed to be just another random homicide has turned into something more mysterious. Early this morning the body of Robert Jackson, twenty-four, was found on One Hundred Fifty-Fourth Street in Washington Heights. Because he was shot at close range, and because nine hundred and twenty-four dollars were found on Mr. Jackson, police assumed he was just another young man cut down in the prime of his life because of drug related activities. However, detectives questioning Mr. Jackson's mother, Camille, with whom he lived at West One Hundred Forty-Eighth Street, found out that he was paid several thousand dollars for his work in a commercial for Senator Richard Wellington. Ms. Jackson claims Robert had never been arrested for any criminal activities, and had won a national talent search to be in the Wellington commercial. According to family members, Robert was planning to move to Los Angeles to pursue acting and music, his twin passions. Senator Wellington issued a statement saying he was deeply disturbed by the crime, and that Mr. Jackson was a fine young man whose talents, dedication, and love will be missed by all who knew him. The senator also vowed to find the killer, or killers, and bring them to justice, stating vehemently that once elected sending the murderer to The Promised Land would be among his first priorities.*

Gabriel had an intriguing glint in his eyes as he turned to Bridget.
—Someone's lying.
—What do you mean?
—I was told he was beaten to death by three big white dudes.
    A cell phone rang.
—Let me get that.
    Bridget reached into her small pocketbook for the device.
—Hello.
—Bridget, it's Dad. Richie just called me.
—He missed his flight, right?
—Worse than that. He's not coming.
—Why, what happened?
—How the hell do I know? He wouldn't say. All he said was he couldn't make it. Didn't even offer an explanation or an apology for screwing everyone's plans up. I just don't understand your brother, I really don't.
—That's just great. We came all the way out here and...
—Why don't you and Gabriel use the dinner reservations I made?
—Okay, but I'm mad. Bye.
    Bridget ended the call and turned to Gabriel.
—My brother's not coming, but we'll get a free dinner. I'm going to call him right now.
    Bridget flipped her iPhone back open, found Richie's icon and pressed. After a few ring tones a voice came through.
—Hello.
—Richie, it's Bridget.
—Hey, what's up?
—What's up? Daddy got you a flight, booked you a room at a hotel, and you just decide it's not worth your time?
—Hey, don't give me your attitude. I told him I couldn't make it because I didn't want to work with him. I'm not going to work on some lame TV commercial for something I don't believe in.
    Bridget got up from her stool and sat at one of the unoccupied booths with the checkered red and white tablecloths.
—Are you so good already that you get to pick and choose your projects?
—I'm not going to listen to this.
—No, of course not. Any criticism you get you just turn it off, as if you're the only one who knows anything. And maybe that's why you didn't come. You would have to prove your worth and maybe that's what you're afraid of, being judged, someone criticizing your work.
—Bridget, you've directed a couple of plays, and you're like an expert

now? Well, let me tell you something, directing a film is a lot more difficult than directing a play.

—But you're not directing a film are you? You're not directing anything. And who says directing a play is easier? How would you know anyway?

Gabriel watched the barkeep throw a white plastic bottle into the air and catch it behind his back. The bottle was in the shape and size of a regulation liquor quart bottle. The barkeep threw it up again and caught it between his legs. He was practicing for the bartender Olympics.

—Bridget, you know, I don't need another mother or another father telling me what to do. I've got my own project I'm working on. It's gonna be a documentary. It's like a behind the scenes look at skiers' off-season lives, you know like talking to them about working, doing whatever they do to get by, and cutting in scenes with them skiing the Back Bowls of Vail, or tree skiing, or flying off cliffs, or whatever. There are people from all over the world who come to Vail each year just to ski. They do whatever they have to do to get here. Just because they don't do the nine-to-five, doesn't mean they aren't as smart as anyone else. They just have different priorities. I'm going to start as soon as I find someone to give me the funding.

—I think it would be good for you to get the credit—to build up credentials instead of wasting your time. That's how you get people to support your projects.

—You get people to support your projects by doing good work, not by working on projects you don't believe in. What experiences have you had besides being in grad school? You're just hiding in grad school because you don't know what the hell else to do. What are you going to do once you graduate? Do you really think anyone cares about an MA in theater? It's a joke.

—Thanks for telling me my life's a joke.

—You called to tell me I'm a fuck-up, right? But at least I've had the courage to follow my convictions. What have you done? You started out in the film program, gonna be this great writer/director, but you changed from film to theater because you couldn't make it as a film student.

—That's not why I changed.

—No? Why did you change? You're the smart one in the family, right? But I don't see you doing anything.

—All I'm saying is Daddy gave you a great opportunity, and you blew it.

—If it's such a great opportunity, why don't you do it? You're a director, right? Isn't that what you studied in school? Maybe you're the one who's afraid—afraid of being judged. Did you ever think about that, Bridget?

Bridget hung up without replying and walked back over to Gabriel. He stood up and pulled out his wallet to pay.

—Can I finish my drink before we go?

—Sure.

Gabriel sat back on his stool.

—You can tell me about yourself. You're a student, right? What are you studying?

—I'm a grad student, and I'm teaching a class for freshmen and sophomores.

—What kind of class?

—A theater class, for directing.

—Are you working on anything now?

—Yes. A play called *Feeding the Machine*. It's set in the not too distant future where there are no longer any taxes, which sounds good, but there aren't any taxes because you have to spend a certain amount of your income on shopping. You have to spend a minimum of forty percent of your paycheck on something, doesn't matter what, you just have to buy something. The more you buy, the cheaper everything is. If you spend only forty percent of your income everything is regular retail price. If you spend fifty percent of your income, you get a twenty-percent discount. If you spend eighty percent, you get fifty percent off. If you spend one hundred percent, you get everything at five percent above cost. If you don't continue to buy, you can be arrested and sent to jail. Anyway, it's a comedy, and what happens is this young couple that loves to shop continues to buy until their entire apartment is filled. The only way in and out of the apartment is by crawling under the dining room chairs. Eventually, there is so much useless crap in the apartment that it all collapses on top of them and they're killed.

—They're killed?

—Yes.

Gabriel frowned.

—Very sophomoric, don't you think?

—No, I don't...I mean...well, the student who wrote it is a sophomore but...

—I get the metaphor, even though it's a bit obvious, but them dying, it's always easy for authors to tie up loose ends by killing off their characters. It's much more difficult to keep them alive.

—It's a comedy. It's not supposed to be an exact replication of life.

—I realize that. I just think it's more interesting when you put characters in situations where it looks bleak and hopeless and where it would be easy to kill them off, but where you make them go on. I can't go on, I'll go on. Right?

—But it would be an entirely different play.

—To me, dying is an easy way out. I mean, isn't that what we do? We've got to go on when we don't want to. We have to go on when we don't have the right answers, or any answers for reasons we don't know. We just keep living and we have to live with a lot of adversity, and most lives, most people, aren't conveniently summed up. We don't always know what they mean or what they're supposed to mean. Why are you smiling like that?

Bridget stared at Gabriel for a few more moments before speaking.

—Because you're not as much of a jerk as I first thought you were.

—With that kind of complement I'll go far in life.

Bridget let out a small chuckle.

—What are you doing the Thursday after next? Do you want to go to the Concert for Conner?

—Are you asking me out?

—Maybe.

—If I go, will I get a kiss?

—You might get more than a kiss.

—Is that a threat or a promise?

—You'll have to go to find out.

☐☐☐ 49 ☐☐☐

—Oh, god. I am so hung-over.

—Yeah, well, so am I. But you don't have to go to work.

—Maybe I shouldn't have ordered those last shots.

—No, probably not…

—I think I was high from how good the music was.

—It was a pretty amazing concert, wasn't it?

—Can you call in sick?

—Why don't you call in for me? He's your father.

—Did you tell him you were going out with me last night?

—Um…

Bridget arched up from the bed, leaned on her elbow and eyed Gabriel.

—I don't like him to know about my personal life.

Gabriel hesitated, looked guilty, and then said with a slight smile,

—I didn't say anything directly, but I did tell one of the other guys if I was late it would be because I would be screwing the hell out of

Wellington's sexy daughter.

Bridget laughed, rolled on top of Gabriel, gave him two quick hard kisses to the lips and said,

—If that's what you said, you'd better make sure it's true.

◻◻◻ **50** ◻◻◻

Peter Morgan's driver pulled his Lincoln Town Car up to Park Avenue and Fifty-Second Street. Morgan exited and stepped up the sand-colored steps of the Seagram's building. He did not bother observing the square fountain pools on either side, and did not tilt his head upward to look at the only structure in New York designed by Mies van der Rohe.

Inside the art-history-staple, he briskly stepped through the high-ceilinged atrium, past the security desk, and up and through the glass doors to the Four Seasons Restaurant. He did not pause to look at the large theatrical curtain filling the entrance wall: whether the circus scene was by Pablo Picasso or not was of no interest to him. He went directly into the Grill Room and presented himself to the Maître d' who had been told of his impending arrival by A.J. Steele. Steele was seated against the east wall on the restaurant in one of the booths. As Morgan approached, he stood to greet his lunch date. The handshake between the two men with industrialist sounding names was hawkishly eyed by a large rotund man seated across the room. A deferential and professional looking waiter waited two beats for Morgan and Steele to finish seating themselves before presenting himself. He handed Morgan a menu, solicited his drink order, half-nodded, and disappeared.

Morgan looked at the menu.

—Did you order?

—I was waiting for you.

Morgan perused the food selections as he spoke.

—I appreciate your generous campaign contribution, Mr. Steele.

—Not a problem. Once the Democrats got rid of Gazelle, PRP was happy to contribute. And, by the way, call me AJ. Everyone does.

A few moments later, the waiter placed Morgan's cranberry and seltzer in front of him and took their orders.

—Okay, AJ. What's on your mind?

—To come right to the point, Wellington is. What bothers me is his desire to execute prisoners.

This caught Morgan by surprise.

—Was I misinformed? I was told your company, Prison Resource Providers, is the largest prison company in the country. If so, why are

151

you against executing prisoners?

—I understand that certain criminals deserve to die; I just don't want to see this get out of hand. Right now, Wellington is talking about executing murderers. If this is successful it might lead to executing armed robbers, rapists, bank robbers, drug kingpins, and criminals of that sort.

—He's already said he wants to include more than just murderers.

—That's my point. Whether people realize it or not, prisoners are vital to our economy. Judges, lawyers, bail bondsmen, prison guards, food service corporations, and entire communities all make their living off of prisoners. This is true throughout the country, not just in New York. We can't afford to lose that business.

—There will always be criminals.

—But we don't want to lose those already in our system. The recidivism rate among convicts is about sixty-five percent. These criminals are our bread and butter. If the number of prisoners in our prison system goes down significantly it will significantly affect our bottom line. We simply cannot afford to give our product away just to appease a senator's desire to appear tough on crime.

—I understand what you're getting at. But I've been doing a good deal of polling and even though Wellington's proposals are controversial, it seems that those who are in favor of them are more likely to actually vote than those who are not. That worries me. If I can't be as tough on crime as Wellington, I'm not going to get elected. That's why I need to do something here in New York, like building a new prison where we could execute prisoners. Why do we need to go all the way to Africa? I'm going on the *Garry King* show in a few nights. I was hoping to announce my prison initiatives there for maximum coverage.

—If the only difference between you and Wellington is location, hunting prisoners in Africa versus hunting prisoners in New York, he's going to beat you. Wellington is an incumbent, and incumbents win ninety-five percent of races, so you need to find something different. You need your own initiative. You shouldn't have executions at all.

—If I don't, how will I get television revenues to reduce taxes and fund social programs? That's what people want.

—Peter, there's another way, a better way. Do you know Roger Zales, President of POX television?

—Not personally. I've heard about him, of course. He's a legend.

—Would you like to meet him? He can explain things much better than I can.

—If he can help, certainly.

   Steele looked across the moneyed room to the rotund man who had been watching them and gave a discreet wave. This was Roger Zales. Zales knew many of the powerful men and women in the room. After a few quick hellos he waddled over to Morgan and Steele's table, followed closely by their waiter. Handshakes and pleasantries were exchanged. Morgan scooted over in the booth and the waiter pulled the table back to accommodate Zales' girth. Once there was adequate room, Zales plopped his large frame down.

—Roger, I told Peter that he shouldn't bother with his own hunting programs, that there's a better way.

—That's right. Peter, we did some of our own research, and we found televised executions, while compelling at first glance, will never be more than a niche market. We don't think Wellington will be able to deliver the numbers he says he will, and therefore won't be able to fund his social programs. There is only one form of entertainment that has been able to sell anything and everything, and that's what we want you to use.

—What's that?

☐☐☐ 51 ☐☐☐

A blue sky, polo players on polo ponies on green grass, women in sundresses with hats, men with tan khakis and blue blazers with gold buttons, cocktails and hors d'oeuvres under a big tent. Those were the props for Senator Wellington's afternoon fundraiser on Hayground Road in Bridgehampton on the eastern tip of Long Island. It was evening now and the soliciting senator was at another fundraiser, this one for a more select crowd: the biggest donors from the afternoon's affair. They were at a private home on Lily Pond Road in East Hampton. As many were intoxicated from the events earlier in the day, few of them bothered to listen to Wellington's speech on the need to be tough on crime. They nodded politely when they thought they should, and when he concluded they clapped like an audience at Augusta, after a pretty putt. Afterwards, the guests dispersed to different parts of the house and estate. Some were out by the pool area, casually bantering and perhaps admiring the custom-built pool's intricately designed stonework and waterfalls, which blended in effortlessly with the flowers and shrubbery. A few guests wandered to the edge of the estate, down to the goldfish pond, which had a handmade wooden bridge. Others mingled closer to the house where a flamenco guitarist was playing.

Out by the pool and cabana, Georgina the hostess introduced the senator to her late-arriving billionaire husband, Calvin, the owner of a private equity firm.

—Senator, what are you drinking? I thought you were a man of the soil, a peat man. Don't you drink single malts?

—I usually drink Cutty Sark, but I do like single malts. Out here they're only serving white wine and I didn't want wine so I'm drinking Perrier.

Calvin shook his head and chuckled to himself.

—Come with me.

Wellington followed the billionaire through the crowd, nodding hellos and trading handshakes as he did. They stepped from the pool area and followed the gently winding flagstones through the neatly trimmed grass up to the veranda and into the main house.

In the living room a handful of people were talking and sipping cocktails, while soft jazz bracketed the background. More hellos and handshakes were exchanged. Calvin invited two other men to join them in the billiard room. On the far side there was a full bar complete with four stools. At the center of the room was a ten foot red-felt, pocketless billiard table.

The wooden bar had an array of the usual bottles: Absolut Vodka, Grey Goose, Tanqueray and Beefeaters gin, Cartavio Rum, Herradura Tequila, and other expensive brands. The upper shelves were reserved for the single malts. On the second shelf was a Johnnie Walker Blue Label, an 18-year-old Macallan, a 12-yeard-old Glenmorangie, a 15-year-old Laphroaig, a 10-year-old Aberlour, and a 15-year-old Balvenie. On the third shelf was a three-quarters-filled Bowmore 40-year-old. As Calvin reached for it, he informed his guests that it was a steal at nine thousand five hundred dollars a bottle. Next to it was an unopened 62-year-old Dalmore, which Calvin divulged was one of twelve in existence, and one of those twelve had sold at auction in London for more than twenty-five thousand pounds.

Wellington took one of the four snifters graced with the Bowmore and clinked glasses. As he tasted the precious single malt, he did some quick calculation in his head: the bottle was seven hundred fifty milliliters, about twenty-five ounces, and twenty-five went into nine thousand five hundred…His math was rusty so he rounded it up, twenty-five went into ten thousand four hundred times. Since he had approximately two ounces in his snifter, he figured he was sipping slightly less than eight hundred dollars worth of liquid. Wellington took another sip and picked a cue stick from the wall rack.

—Senator, what's this I hear about your bushy-eyebrowed opponent's plan to build his own prison in upstate New York?

Wellington had heard of this as well, but didn't want to discuss it.

—Morgan's just saying what he thinks he needs to say to get elected.

—And you're not? If you can build a prison in Africa, why can't he build one here in New York?

—Because mine will make money, his won't.

—No? I heard he was working with POX and they're planning their own television series to be shot inside the prison.

Wellington's cell phone interrupted them.

—Excuse me.

He pulled out the communication device from his breast pocket and placed it against his ear.

—Hello.

—Senator, hi. It's Steve Lowell in Gwanda.

This was a voice he wasn't expecting.

—Anything wrong?

—That's what I want to know. I just got a call from a reporter from *The Wall Street Journal* who wanted to know if was true that McDonald's was opening a branch just outside The Promised Land Ranch. Do you know anything about this? He said a whole town is being built. Is that true, and if so, why haven't I been informed?

Wellington, aware that the others were listening, stepped away from the billiard table.

—I was going to get back to you, but I've been busy. You might have forgotten, but I still am running for reelection. Anyway, Asher Mitchell is heading up development.

—I take it most of the real estate has been purchased, hasn't it? That's why you haven't told me—you knew I'd want to buy some land. I get the short end, don't I?

Senator Wellington turned to his host.

—Calvin, this is rather important. Is there somewhere private I could take this?

—In the den…you can take it in the family den.

He was led back through the living room, down a short hallway to a doorway that opened to the family room.

—Thank you.

The senator took a quick look around before seating himself on the white couch, which was accented with small, powder blue throw pillows. On a glass rectangular table directly in front of him was a stack of photo books: *In the Spirit of the Hamptons; The End, Montauk, N.Y.; Slim Aarons: A Place in the Sun; Bruce Weber's Blood Sweat and Tears;* and a stack of *Hamptons* magazines and *Dan's Papers*. The walls were white, as were the two wicker chairs topped with powder blue cushions. Across from the sofa, next to a flat-screen monitor, was a David Hockney print of a turquoise pool with a yellow diving board.

—Steve?

—Yes, I'm here.

—All right, as you know our Promised Land is about thirty miles of dirt roads away from Nakambu. Asher felt that if the show was going to take off, it wouldn't be long before tourists would want to see the hunting live and in-person. He talked with the country's leader, President Mobley and his top commander, General Msambee, among others, and well, the long and short of it is that we are going to develop a town around The Promised Land Ranch. It only makes sense.

—What does that mean, you're developing a town? What town? What exactly are you developing? Hotels, a post office, a bank, what?

—All those things, yes.

—What about the land? Has it all been bought up? That's why you haven't told me, right? You and Mitchell bought it all up.

—Get off your damn high horse, Steve. You're part of The Promised Land management team, aren't you? And that entitles you to a share of our profits, doesn't it?

—You mean you didn't buy this yourself? You and Mitchell?

—No, it's all under the aegis of The Promised Land Corporation, which includes you, unless you continue to make a big stink about it. Didn't tell you about it because the more people know, the more likely it was that the press would get a hold of it.

A bathroom door opened inside the den. Wellington turned to see Georgina and Calvin's thin, blonde, and pretty fifteen-year-old daughter, Bliss, a student at Choate. She sniffled once and rubbed her fingers under her nostrils. When she spotted the senator she froze, momentarily guilty. Bliss quickly recovered her calm, smiled, said a quiet hello and left the room.

—All right. Sorry for not trusting you. It just seemed...what exactly is going to happen? He mentioned paving the road leading to the ranch?

—Obviously we're going to have to pave some roads. You're not going to get investors to invest in some muddy puddle of a town, are you? We're putting roads in and everything you need to spur investments. As I said, Asher's handling most of the details. He thinks it makes sense to get some foreign investors as well. This will eventually be an international destination so having British and German and probably some Japanese and Chinese money, makes sense. It will make it that much easier to market later on.

The bathroom door opened again, and another girl stepped out. She was also young, slim, blonde and attractive. She didn't rub her nostrils but she did sniffle, and look like she'd been caught at something. Wellington spoke this time, trying to be friendly, perhaps even flirtatious.

—Anyone else in there?

This made her even more nervous.

—Um…no. I was just going to the bathroom.

Senator Wellington was well aware that the toilet hadn't flushed, but said nothing more as she slipped past him.

—How did this change from a hunting ranch to a town? Do you have a name for the town yet?

—Paradise. Probably the Town of Paradise. Claudia's running the name by Sy Blackstone. He seems to believe that setting up some kind of stadium, or coliseum, to watch the hunting will increase viewers.

Wellington decided to investigate the bathroom. It was as clean as the maid had left it, with three small, unused bars of lilac scented soap in the soap dish, a fresh roll of toilet paper, and two white washcloths atop two white bath towels on a rack.

—A coliseum? What, like the Roman Colosseum with the lions and the Christians?

—Yes, something like that. It makes sense to have some sort of arena to herd the huntables into so their termination can be viewed by the maximum amount of people. It also will help with bringing in tourists, and keeping them happy by having their accommodations close by.

Wellington came out of the bathroom and peaked through one of the den's windows. Unfortunately, with the growing darkness and distance to the pool area, there was nothing to engage his imagination. He sat back on the couch to finish his conversation.

—But I thought there were going to be accommodations, lodges and such on The Promised Land Ranch?

—There will be, but the way I see it now, they'll be just for the actual hunters and family members. Anyway, that wouldn't handle enough people. Starwood is putting up a hotel, and I think Claudia's talking to Disney about some type of entertainment complex. It's all come about rather quickly as you can tell.

—What does President Mobley have to do with any of this?

—You don't think he's going to let us just waltz into Gwanda without taking on a local partner, do you? That's rather standard whenever you deal with a foreign company, I mean country. Asher has set up a company for President Mobley and General Msambee called the M&M Corporation, Mobley and Msambee. It will allow us to funnel funds to them so that we won't have any government interference.

—What about the families we said we were going to keep on the land? There are about five families living on The Promised Land Ranch—the ones we decided it would be good to keep to build public relations.

—They're going to have to go.

—Where am I supposed to put them?

—Jesus, Steve! Get rid of them, it's that simple! We can't have them on the ranch—that's just going to be for the hunters.

—This is exactly the wrong thing to do. I know you want investors and all that, but you need to think about the native Gwandans as well.

—What do you want, some shantytown? How the hell are we going to get investors if we show them our main attraction is filled with poor Gwandans in broken down shacks? We're doing these damn people a favor by modernizing their country. The least they can do is get off the land.

—Hey, I'm all for investors, you know that, it's just that if we show some good faith, it'll help us in the long run. It's important to make them think we care about them. I thought the whole point of me coming over here was to avoid that, to avoid upsetting the natives.

—We are avoiding them, that's why we're moving them. Do you think they'd be comfortable with restaurants and tourists spending money when they have none? Of course not, that's why we need to get rid of them. You should be able to see that.

—All right, whatever.

The doorknob to the hallway door turned and a drunken duo pushed in, mouth glued to mouth. Her hands ran inside the front of his white linen shirt and his dove beneath her white pants to grab her thin, almost fleshless ass. They pushed in further completely unaware the room was occupied. Wellington looked at them, amazed. He recognized his thick black hair and his swarthy complexion. He was one of the Argentinean polo jockeys. Wellington didn't recognize her. She was older, perhaps fifty, perhaps a bit younger, it was difficult to tell as he only got a quick glimpse of her skin pulled tight across her face. He let out a brief cough…uhmm. Neither heard, or responded if they had, so he did it twice more. Uhmm…uhmm. The woman turned first. Wellington couldn't put a name to the face but he had seen her before. She was one of those pencil-thin women he always saw at social functions, always with a drink and a breezy laugh. She seemed more annoyed than embarrassed. Without a word they took their hands off each other; she tucked in her shirt and he smoothed back his lust-inspiring hair. The door was swung on its hinges back and forth and Wellington was alone again.

—Steve, I'm not trying to be harsh, it's just that, for some reason, I don't know, maybe you've gone native on me or something.

—Maybe I have gone native, or maybe it's just that I'm over here for months now and I have to see these people every day, and I see the poverty and hardships that they have to endure.

—Are you going to start crying to me? Because if you are, if you're not happy, you can leave and we'll find someone else.

—I'm trying to give you an accurate portrait of the people over here. A lot of them are worried. They're talking about their land being taken over, and how they should start doing something about it.

—We're not taking over anything, we're providing jobs.

—Yeah, but word of mouth is powerful here. You've got agitators saying that what happened in South Africa and Zambia is going to happen here. The whites come in and take over, and the blacks are little more than slaves.

—What the hell does skin color have to do with it? You're black, aren't you?

—Yeah, but...

—You want me to send some more African Americans over there? Do they think I couldn't find some blacks who will do exactly what we're doing? Are they so damn naïve to think that people with white skin are evil, and that people with black are good, and decent, and will treat their people fairly?

—Well, it...

—Look at Rwanda, the Congo, Zimbabwe, Somalia, and the Sudan. It's blacks killing blacks, and blacks getting rich off of other blacks. And it's not just in Africa, it's the same thing in New York and Chicago and all over the world, so don't give me that same old color of skin cliché. It's not about black and white, it's about green. You would do well to remember that.

—All right, fine. Getting back to my original question. What do I tell this reporter?

—Tell him that we're trying to help improve the country, and leave it at that. It isn't your role to do his work.

□□□ **52** □□□

Two nights later, Senator Wellington sat at home watching Peter Morgan on *Garry King Live*. Candace came into the television room, handed her husband a bowl of chocolate, chocolate chip ice cream and took a seat on the couch with her own bowl of ice cream.

—*Mr. Morgan, what about sending prisoners to The Promised Land? How do you feel about that?*

—*My opponent is correct in understanding that crime and prisons are just too expensive, too much of a drain on taxpayers. But do we really want to have any Americans, even prisoners, under the control of a foreign government? Why can't Americans, and New Yorkers in particular, take care of their own criminals? The truth is Senator Wellington doesn't know what to do about prisoners and the high cost of crime—that's why he wants to kill them. That to me is both immoral and just plain wrong. The way it is now, prisoners are locked away for years, sometime decades. Because of budget cuts there are no educational opportunities available for prisoners. So what do they do? They lift weights, look at pornographic magazines, and they are forced to join gangs. Prisoners build up hatred and anger and rage. Too often this spills out into violence—prison stabbings, knifings, rapes, even murders. When prisoners leave prison they are still filled with anger and rage and violent tendencies. Only now the chances of them getting a job or interacting successfully in society is even more unlikely.*

—What should be done to change this?

—Prisoners need a strong incentive. One that will make them want to better themselves, one that will encourage them to educate themselves, one that will prepare them for their eventual release from prison.

—How do you propose we do that?

—We will start off by building an entirely new prison upstate, where…

—A new prison? That's going to cost taxpayers hundreds of millions of dollars…

—It won't. POX television and Prison Resource Providers, a private and well-respected company, have agreed to pay half the cost for the prison. This prison will be equipped with cameras and microphones in every prison cell, in every hallway, and in every room. Even the prison yard will have video and audio recording devices. This way we will be able to watch every move a prisoner makes. Prisoners will be monitored and videotaped 24/7.

—For what? Why do you need to videotape them?

—For a television show. The footage will be edited down to a nightly television show tentatively entitled "American Criminal." On "American Criminal," the prisoners in the prison will be the worst of the worst: murderers, armed bank robbers, drug kingpins, hit-men, mafia bosses, rapists, and others sociopaths. Viewers will have the opportunity to watch real life hardened criminals in a competition. Inmates will compete against each other to see who gets the most points. Points will be earned for educational activities, religious activities, and activities that build social skills. For example, an inmate would win points for enrolling in a program that would help him earn a GED. If a prisoner started reading the Bible on a daily or weekly basis he would gain points. If one inmate taught another inmate to read, both would gain points. If prisoners created their own prison choir, this would also gain them points. Fifty percent of the points will come from the deeds

the criminals do. The other fifty percent will come from viewers at home voting on their favorite criminal. Viewers will be able to see which criminal have been making the best effort toward rehabilitation, and have the best chance of success once they are paroled. It will also work the other way: if a prisoner joins a prison gang, or commits violence, he will have points deducted. These votes will continue on a running tally until the end of the season.

—And what happens then? What is going to motivate these violent thugs?

—The possibility of having sex with a pornstar.

—Sex with a pornstar? You're joking, right?

—No. The inmate who racks up the most points at the end of the season is the winner. We will have a winner for each of the three television seasons, fall, spring, and summer. The winner will spend a three-day weekend in a specially designed apartment inside the prison having sex with a pornstar. The prisoner and the pornstar's sexual escapades will be filmed 24/7 and we will sell various live viewing packages: a two-hour package for ninety-nine dollars; a full-day package for five hundred dollars; and the entire weekend for twelve hundred dollars. Once the weekend is over, the tapes will be edited and sold as individual DVDs for the home, or available on video-on-demand channels. This will easily net hundreds of millions of dollars, which will be used to cut taxes and help fund social programs. And best of all it will motivate prisoners. Every prisoner will be on his best behavior, because he might get the chance to sleep with a pornstar. I don't think there can be any greater motivation for criminals. As for the viewers, many women find convicts scarred with jailhouse tattoos very sexy and male viewers will get a deeper knowledge and insight into real life pornstars. We think this will be a big hit.

—This is...you're serious about this? Prisoners, murderers perhaps, having sex with pornstars? Don't you think voters will find this immoral or just plain wrong? Why should prisoners get any kinds of rewards?

—Gambling is immoral or wrong to many, isn't it? If I held a high-stakes poker game in my home for thousands of dollars a hand, I would be arrested, because gambling is illegal, right? It's illegal, unless, of course, the government sanctions it through its own gambling parlors: New York State Lottery, Lotto, Powerball, and other games of chance, or places it in specially regulated areas: Las Vegas or Atlantic City or on an Indian Reservation in New York or Connecticut. So, what is right or wrong, moral or immoral, is defined by whether the government gets a cut or not.

161

—But pornography is different. Many, if not most, adults will say that pornography is immoral.
—They say that publicly, but last year some seven hundred million pornographic movies were rented.
—Seven hundred million?
—Yes. Hard to believe, isn't it? But those are the actual numbers. Pornography is an enjoyable diversion for consenting adults. GE and AT&T, two of America's biggest and best-known companies, have made hundreds of millions of dollars supplying pornographic movies to their customers through their cable television companies. All the major hotels, Hilton, Hyatt, Sheraton, Marriott, Holiday Inn, and all the rest, make pornographic movies available to their clients. The Internet was built on pornography. Google and Yahoo, and many other Internet companies, wouldn't have become multibillion-dollar businesses without the advertising revenue generated through pornography.
—Would it be safe to say the difference between you and Senator Wellington, between the Democrats and the Republicans, is now one between sex and death?
—Damn it!

Wellington grabbed the remote and brought the screen to black. Looking around, he realized that Candace was no longer in the room. Hearing her in the kitchen he hopped up from his chair and went to find her. She placed her ice cream bowl in the sink and turned to her husband.
—That bastard Morgan, he's a degenerate! Wants to give prisoners the right to have sex with pornstars.

Wellington went to the cabinet for the Cutty Sark. Candace took a glass down from the cabinet, went to the refrigerator for some ice cubes, and handed it to him. Wellington took it from her without thanks.
—But he won't be able to do that, will he? And aren't you ahead of him in the polls?
—That doesn't mean anything—things change! No election is over until it's over. Just what I need another phone call.

He reached into his pocket for his ringing cell phone.
—Hello.
—Senator, hi, it's Asher. I just met with General Msambee. He wants to know if we would be willing to hunt Gwandan criminals in addition to hunting the AIDS victims, and whether we'd be able to get a TV show out of it.
—We can't do everything. Let's get one show up and running first and take it from there.

Three-quarters of the glass was filled with scotch before

Wellington brought it to the sink and added a topping of tap water. He swirled the cubes around with his index finger and walked out of the kitchen into the breakfast room. Though it was dark in there, he didn't bother turning on the light. It was better this way to see through the large windows into the yard and surrounding woods.

—All right. But I also got a call from the Chinese Minister of Culture, he wants to know if we would be able to execute some of their dissidents. I think we should at least plan ahead, think about other tie-in shows.

—Asher, I can't be a savior to the world. Didn't you tell Msambee about the plans for the town?

—No, because we're still going over some of the finer points.

—Well, maybe if you and Claudia Potter talk to Msambee together he'll understand.

—Potter? I'd rather not deal with her.

—Why not?

—When she was over here last week she had a couple of huntables shot. I didn't think we were moving so quickly on that.

—She did what? Goddamn it! I'll talk to her.

—Please do, because now that huntables have been killed it's making our relationship with the natives that much more contentious, especially since Potter refused to give the dead men's wives their AIDS anti-viral drugs.

—Jesus Christ! You straighten out Msambee. I'll straighten out Potter.

□□□ 53 □□□

—How about a drink after my speech?

Seated in the first row of the Tishman Auditorium at the New School for Social Research on West Twelfth Street, the attractive Japanese student body president whispered back to her questioner with a mix of disdain and disillusionment. —Mr. Gazelle, I never have drinks with anyone older than my father.

Gazelle quietly chuckled. —Do you have a sister, preferably a young one, who isn't quite so conservative?

—Don't you have a girlfriend?

—She's out in L.A. working on a film.

—I'm sure after your speech there'll be plenty of students who will be happy to join you.

—Of course there will, but will they be as cute as you are?

The student leader turned her eyes from the priapic Gazelle and focused her attention on the Director of Liberal Studies who stood at the

163

center of the stage behind a lectern. The director was praising Gazelle's "iconoclastic political vision" and his "relevant third party candidacy" to an attentive audience of students.

Once the introduction was concluded, a beaming Gazelle strutted to the stage.

—Thank you. Thank you very much. I have been to many colleges and universities in New York State to talk with students, because students are America's future. Many young people have expressed to me their dismay with the present political system. They are tired of seeing their friends and family members going off to wars to fight for oil companies and other corporate interests. They are tired of reading about global warming, acid rain, melting icecaps, and the depleted ozone. They are tired of seeing megastores coming into small towns and wiping out all of the local businesses. They feel, and rightly so, that politicians are not responsive to voters. They feel politicians have become little more than corporate pawns. But I am not here to argue whether politicians are for sale or not. That is as obvious as the cement on the sidewalks of New York City. The question we need to ask is: *can anything be done*? Or are we beyond the pale?

Gazelle halted, letting his audience think for a few moments.

—In the 1960s and early 1970s, hundreds of thousands of students, and millions of Americans, took to the streets and campuses to protest the Vietnam War. They went and marched on Washington to protest the corrupt and dishonest leadership of this country. Those protestors forced the President and Congress to listen and to make changes. But this is not the 1960s, and students today do not think and do not act the same way we did back when I was young. We need, you need, to find your own voice, your own way of making changes. And you have done that with great skill. Your generation is the Internet and Social Media Generation. Perhaps many of you are not overtly political, but you have, nonetheless, changed the world with your use of the internet and social media networking. These tools are more powerful than television or the press in changing perceptions and influencing politicians and corporate strategists.

Gazelle paused to take a drink of water from a glass on the inside shelf of the podium.

—If corporations are responsible for pulling the strings that run Congress, we need to forget about politicians and go directly to the source: corporations. There is one voice that corporations listen to above all others, that of the almighty dollar. Corporations listen only when money is at stake. Knowing that, what do we do? Every corporation today relies on computers and e-mails. For big corporations, losing electronic communication could cost them thousands perhaps hundreds of thousands or millions of dollars a day. If we can interrupt corporations' businesses—not illegally or through vandalism or violence—but legitimately, they will be forced to listen, and they will be forced to consider their actions more fully. How do we do this? It's rather simple, actually. We do it through what I would like to call E-Floods: tens of thousands, maybe hundreds of thousands of e-mails and text messages sent directly to corporate leaders. Imagine the CEO of Halliburton and other top officers, for example, arriving at their offices and finding fifty thousand, or one-hundred thousand, e-mails in their Inboxes and thousands of text messages on their personal and work phones. Not only would these corporate officers be angry as hell—and I think it's about time we made these people angry—their computers would have probably crashed. Once the computers had crashed it would be necessary for someone from the IT department to go through all the e-mails to find out which ones were related to business and which ones were in protest. That could take days. During this time, the corporate headquarters might not be able to communicate electronically. The CEO would lash out and want to know what right an average American had to disturb his plush existence. This is what we need to do! We need to disrupt their lives. CEOs feel their only responsibility is to their shareholders. This is wrong. When America engages in military action many corporations earn hundreds of millions, even billions, of dollars off death and destruction. People die, families are devastated, countries are ruined, and someone is getting wealthy from this. Around the world hatred for America grows, and yet these corporations claim no responsibility. Multibillion dollar corporations claim their only responsibility is to make money for their shareholders. This is wrong! Corporations must be held accountable for their actions, not just to their shareholders, but to the lives of those they affect! If they can have young men and women sent off to fight and die for their corporate profits they need to be held accountable!

Loud cheers filled the auditorium. Shouts of "Connor!," "Connor!," "Connor!" rang out. Gazelle paused and eyed two pretty young women seated in the first row. After a few moments the cheers subsided and he continued.

—Okay, how do we get fifty thousand or one hundred thousand, or even one million e-mails and text messages sent at the same time? We need to have each and every one of you get together with your friends and families to form E-Groups. We would have primary E-Groups and secondary E-Groups. The primary group would contain at least eleven e-mailers, ten people plus oneself. These are people who you would contact anytime someone from outside the primary group contacted you. Those outside your primary group would be considered secondary e-mailers. Here's how it works: once a target has been picked, on my website, www.GazelleForSenate.org, I post the name of the corporation, a list of the e-mail addresses of the top corporate officers, and their phone numbers. On the date of the E-Flood, I send e-mails and texts to the ten members of my primary group. These ten members send the same type of messages to ten others, that's one hundred. Those hundred send ten messages, that's a thousand. Those thousand send ten messages, that's ten thousand. Those ten thousand send ten, and that's one hundred thousand. Those one hundred thousand send ten and that's a million e-mails and texts. Everyone who visits www.GazelleForSenate.org will be able to do the same: hundreds, thousands of people sending out E-messages to their E-groups, and those people sending out E-messages to members of their E-Groups. This could give us hundreds of thousands, perhaps millions, of E-Warriors. But who do we target? That's the question I want you to consider. I don't want my campaign to be a top-down organization where you have to take directions from me. I want everyone to feel that they have the power to enact change. If you have something you're passionate about, if you have a corporation you want to target, an idea you want to express, send me an e-mail. I also want you to send e-mails to reporters, bloggers and anyone else who can reach a wide audience. But this shouldn't be used simply to be disruptive or negative. Not all corporations are bad or evil. Some corporations are making efforts to be good global citizens. Some corporations, for example, have stopped hiring child laborers around the world. These things should be applauded. I do not want to make a mockery of, or try to hurt or embarrass this great country in any way. I want to help make America as great a country as it can be. These e-mail groups, and E-Floods, are simply a way to give people back the power that has been stolen from them. I have my own ideas about who we should target but I want to hear from you. Any suggestions? Who do you think should be our first target?

Dozens of hands rose into the air. Connor pointed to a student with an "Anarchy" tattoo on her left arm.

—Yes?

—What about Bechtel? They turn blood into dollars. They're vultures, who make their money off the war dead.

—Okay, good. Who else?

—Wal-Mart! They eliminate Mom & Pop stores in small towns, they refuse to pay living wages to their employees, and they refuse to pay medical benefits to a vast majority of their employees. They also drive down wages of competing companies.

—An obvious choice, but a good one. Who else?

A very conservative looking student stood up and Connor pointed to him.

—Yes?

—The Carlyle Group. They are one of the biggest war-profiteers through their defense contracts that sell arms all over the world. They're filled with former politicians and ex-military men, some of the most blood-thirsty people in America.

—You're absolutely right. Who else?

—Kissinger Associates.

—Excellent choice. I wish the rest of Americans were as well informed as its students. I will consider what each of you has said, and what others have said. Within a week, I will post the decision on who to target for our first E-Flood on my website, www.GazelleForSenate.org. So, please visit my website, sign up, and start to form E-Groups so we can move forward on this.

□□□ 54 □□□

Three chocolate-colored miniature men stood on Claudia Potter's desk. The dolls were made to resemble African tribesmen wearing loincloths. After eying them, the designer, Jerry Zycoff, spoke to the woman who had ordered them.

—As you can see, we made them in three sizes, the twelve-inch, the twenty four-inch, and the thirty six-inch. We felt that if they were any larger they would scare kids. Let me show you how they work.

Zycoff reached into a large brown bag and took out an X-acto knife. He grabbed the middle-size doll by the head and stabbed it in the stomach causing red liquid to slowly spill out. Claudia Potter momentarily shuddered at this violent act, but composed herself before speaking.

—Obviously, that's not real blood, is it?

—No.

Zycoff replaced the cap on the X-acto and placed it on the table.

—It looks authentic enough, but it's a non-toxic, non-staining liquid made from sugar-based ingredients that are edible and tasty, so the kids will have fun licking it off the dolls.

The red liquid was slowing dripping down the doll's torso onto the table. From a second brown bag, Zycoff pulled out a sponge and some paper towels. These were used to clean up the prototype. After the doll was wiped clean, the paper towels were tossed into the brown bag and two small bottles, one red and one flesh-colored, were extracted.

—But once you stab them, won't they be useless?

—No, not at all. You simply pull the head back like this and pour in more "Bloodd."

An unseen hinge in the back of the neck allowed the dolls head to be pulled back, revealing a hollow internal tube. Before the red liquid was poured in, Jerry took a small paintbrush, dipped it into the flesh-colored bottle, and used it to paint and seal the puncture wound. He waited a few moments for it to dry before pouring in the fake blood.

—But won't it just spill right back out?

—No. The first bottle is a sealant. I sealed the puncture hole with it. It's also non-toxic. This way you can stab the dolls over and over again. Since you want to use these for your promotional deal with McDonald's we thought having refills would generate more revenue. The refills, which we call Bloodd with two ds, should be available for about a dollar. You could either use them with the dolls, or kids could just freeze the Bloodd and suck 'em like Popsicles.

Claudia brought a scowl to her face,

—So, they're only for stabbing?

—Yes. Why? You sound disappointed.

—What about shooting them? The dolls are supposed to be for kids to shoot with their guns.

—You didn't tell me that. You said you wanted dolls that children would be able to hunt.

—Yes, but not with knives. These dolls are being used to get the kids interested in our television programming and our Promised Land video game. Kids will see targets on screen and they'll have the ability to shoot them interactively. Shooting can be done interactively, stabbing can't. Don't you see that?

There was a quiet knock on the door before Sarah's head leaned in.

—Sorry, Ms. Potter, but it's Senator Wellington on the phone. He called twice. He's really upset. I told him you were busy, but he said to get you anyway. Do you want to talk to him, or should I tell him you're in a meeting?

—Would you excuse me for a moment, Jerry?

—Okay.

—Sarah, could you get Jerry some coffee?

She nodded and Jerry followed her out of the office. Potter sat down at her desk and picked up the phone. When connected she had a friendly lilt in her voice.

—Hi, Richard.

Wellington shouted into the phone,
—DID YOU SHOOT THE HUNTABLES?!
—I didn't shoot anyone.
—Did you have them shot!
—Yes. Why?

Back in his office, Wellington was standing and fuming, yelling into his desk phone.
—*Why?* Why the hell do I have to hear what you're doing from Steve Lowell?
—I don't particularly care for Steve.
—Your feelings for each other seem to be mutual, but you know what? I don't really give a damn about how you feel for each other.
—What did he say?

Wellington settled down slightly and took a seat at his desk.
—He said when you were over there you had the huntables shot.
—Volunteers. We're not calling them huntables anymore, we're calling them volunteers. Marketing feels it sounds better, I told you that.
—Huntables! Volunteers. I don't give a goddamn what you call them. Who told you to shoot anyone?
—It was a test run for our advertisers. Why do you sound so shocked?
—Because it's my ranch and I don't know what the hell's going on there.
—You told me you wanted me to take care of the programming of Promised Land Television, didn't you? Well, what do you think that means? How am I supposed to get advertisers and product placement people interested if they have no idea what our show looks like?
—How did you get to move on this so fast? Last I remember you told me they were too skinny to be on TV, and that you were trying to get marijuana for them to smoke, so they would get the munchies and eat more and get fatter.
—I was, but I thought it would be a public relations nightmare if the press found out we were getting them stoned before shooting them. I had some meetings with the people from McDonald's regarding tie-ins and it hit me, why not feed them McDonald's? Everyone knows how fattening that food is, so why not give it to the volunteers? I talked to them and they agreed to supply the volunteers with free Big Macs, French fries, and milkshakes, if we gave them a higher percentage on the dolls.
—What dolls?
—They're promotional tie-ins. I'm developing dolls that look like volunteers for kids to shoot. They'll be available at McDonald's with a purchase of a Happy Meal. I using them to get kids interested in The

Promised Land video game Asher is developing.

—Christ, maybe it's better I don't know about any of this stuff. So, why won't you give the women antiviral AIDS drugs?

—I have to think about budgets, don't I? You know how difficult it is to get AIDS drugs in the first place? I don't want to just hand it out like it's candy.

—Candy, my ass. And don't give me that about budgets.

—Okay, maybe it wasn't totally monetary. I didn't like their attitudes. I was prepared to give the woman the drugs, but they had this, like this chip on their shoulders, like I was doing something evil or something. All they had to do is show me a little respect and everything would have been fine.

—A little respect? You're turning this into a personal matter? What the hell's wrong with you? If we're going to have a future in Gwanda, we're going to have to treat them with a certain amount of respect. You seem to think that just because we've got Mobley and Msambee working with us we're not vulnerable. You keep your attitude up and we'll never have a show over there.

—So you're taking Steve's side?

—I'm not taking anyone's side. Do you want me to tell Sy we're bogged down in petty grievances? Damn it, Claudia, we're developing an entire town around The Promised Land and you're trying to scuttle it because of a personal matter, because some dumb widows didn't give you respect?

—I put a lot of hard work into this and no one gives me any credit. Creating a new show isn't easy. Everyone expects you to fail. There are a million things that could go wrong and…

—Hold on, I've got another call. It's my wife.

Wellington picked up the other line.

—Hi Candace.

—Hi. I just got off the phone with Bridget. She dropped out of school.

—Why?

—To work for Greenpeace.

—You've got to be fuckin' kidding me. Greenpeace? Jesus, that's all I need.

☐☐☐ **55** ☐☐☐

Peter Morgan and Roger Zales sat across from each other in Zales' midtown office. Zales filled out a plush and soft cushioned red chair. Morgan sat on a matching red sofa. To Morgan's left, the wall displayed more than two dozen award plaques. In the corner of the room, a trophy

170

case was filled with Emmys and other trinkets of acclaim. Zales' administrative assistant placed a coffee service on the table in front of the men and exited.

—Peter, I understand your meeting with leading Democratic leaders at the Hyatt went well.

—I guess it did, much to my surprise.

—Why are you surprised?

—In our initial meeting you convinced me that I needed to do something bold and different. But I'm still not sure pornography is the way to go. I do know that the Democrats need a change, and that's what I told everyone at the meeting. Before I started speaking, I thought they would laugh me off stage, but they didn't. I'm not sure if they really believe in pornography or if they're supporting me because at this point they have no other choice.

—Peter, if we're going to have a relationship, if POX is going to continue to back you not just now but in the future, we need to know we can trust you, and that you believe in our vision.

—Trust me? You don't trust me? Didn't I go on *Garry King* and say what you wanted?

—Yes, you did great. That's why Hubert respects you so much. He thinks you have great potential, and if you play your cards right one day you could occupy the oval office.

—I hope so. But can I ask you a question? Why is Hubert so interested in pornography?

—Peter, pornography is a ten to fifteen billion dollar industry that is little understood. There are so many players, so many different corporations and people involved, that no one really know just how much money it brings in, but the low end is ten billion. That's more revenue than Hollywood movies, more revenue than all of the professional sports teams combined.

Zales took a sip of his coffee, placed on the table in front of him and stood up. He walked in front of his wall of awards.

—I won't pretend to be a modest or humble man, I'm not. These awards on my wall and these trophies weren't given to me for my good looks. They were given to me because I have the ability to anticipate the desire of viewers. I have to know what they want even before they are able to articulate it. I also have to know what advertisers will support, because without advertising there can be no television. I haven't always been right, but in over forty years in television, I've been right more often than just about anyone. I'd like to give you a bit of history, if you don't mind.

—Go ahead. I'm happy to listen.

Zales plopped back down onto the couch.

—In the 1890s, when the Lumière brothers, Auguste and Louis, invented film they did it out of love. They were in love with the flickering images, and the newness and originality of what they were creating. In the earliest movie-making days a director was given a few weeks to shoot a film before he was put on the next one. Louis B. Mayer, Samuel Goldwyn, Darryl Zanuck, D.W. Griffin, and the Warner Brothers, Harry, Albert, Sam, and Jack, turned film into a big business. They made stars out of particular actors and actresses, and out of the directors, but they kept it a business run by men who knew and loved film. The studios those great men created were all eventually bought up by corporations. Eventually the corporations themselves were purchased by even bigger and more powerful corporations. Now almost every movie produced and distributed theatrically is owned by six multinational corporations.

As Zales was talking, Morgan had been eying the awards, trying to read the inscriptions.

—Do you want to take a closer look?

—No, I'm listening, I'm just looking around as I do. Continue, please.

—Okay. When the music industry began, almost a hundred years ago, it was much like the film business: run by people who loved music. There were hundreds of music labels. Eventually those small labels were bought up by bigger companies, which were in turn purchased by bigger and bigger companies. Publishing followed a similar trajectory. Even fifty years ago publishing was still a gentlemen's game, something wealthy men of taste pursued. There were dozens of publishing houses, most with a distinct vision. If they made a profit they were happy, but mostly it was for love of books. Eventually those publishing houses were bought up by bigger and more powerful companies. I'm not sure if you know it or not, but the same six multinational corporations that own the film business own the music business and own the publishing houses. Do you think the owners of these corporations care about the aesthetic value or artistic merit of film or music or books the same way the originators did?

—Very doubtful.

—That's right. They could give a rat's ass about a particular film or novel or music track. What they care about is making money. When they talk, they don't talk about films or music or books, they talk about product, about content. Everything you see or hear or read is product or content. Twenty-five years ago you had about fifty corporations controlling the destiny of the media world. Fifteen years ago there were about fifteen. Ten years ago there were about eight. Today, were down

172

to about six: Time Warner, Disney, General Electric, Viacom, Comcast, and our parent company, News Corporation. These six multibillion-dollar media conglomerates control just about every aspect of film, music, and books, and they also control television, radio, magazines, and newspapers. By controlling the media, they control the intellectual thoughts of the country. These corporations are so wealthy and powerful they exert a greater influence on the world than heads of state and leaders of nations.

Zales poured more coffee into Morgan's empty cup.

—Thank you.

—My pleasure. Where film was a hundred years ago is where pornography is today. A pornographic film can be shot in a day or two. The men and women are almost interchangeable, and there are hundreds of companies and hundreds, thousands, of distribution points. Pornography is still a business run by people who care about pornography *as* pornography. Unlike every other industry, right now there are no dominate players. That will change. The six big media giants, global corporations, worth hundreds of billions of dollars, with tentacles that reach around the globe, are locked in fierce competition with each other. Do you think in this competitive world that these global giants can afford to ignore ten to fifteen billion dollars worth of product, of content? Do you think any of them believes the merging and acquiring of media corporations is finished?

—I'm sure they think about their competitors all the time; and they are all afraid of being bought up and eliminated.

—That's right. Each media giant is afraid that their competitors will eliminate them. But the public doesn't think about that. The public sees pornography as sexually explicit movies. To the media giants sex had nothing to do with it. Pornography is content. The men and women who run the media corporations may not like pornography, and they may not watch pornography, but you can be damn sure they watch every move their competitors make. Whether pornography is moral or immoral is irrelevant. They have jobs to do, and their jobs are to protect their shareholders and increase the value of their stock. Each of them is afraid that if they don't get involved in pornography, their competitors will and they will be left behind, and eventually they will be bought out.

—So the prisoners and pornstars are what...a first step?

—Yes. We want to dominate the pornography industry before any of our competitors do. But the selling of these movies is itself only a first step.

—What's the second step?

—Advertising.

—Advertising? How are you going to advertise? Advertise what?

—Let me give you a little scenario. A super sexy woman walks into a Victoria's Secret store. She picks out some hot lingerie and goes into the dressing room to try it on.

—I don't think you're allowed to try on lingerie.

—This isn't reality, this is the movie. She looks at herself in the mirror, at her pointy pink nipples. As she's admiring her own breasts, her Verizon cell phone rings. Calling her is her boyfriend, a rugged bare-chested carpenter wearing a worn pair of Levi's who has just gotten off work. She flirts with him and takes a photo of her breasts with her camera phone and sends it to his phone getting him all excited. After hanging up, she purchases the lacy material, exits the store and goes to a shoe store where she buys some Steve Madden shoes. She goes to another store to buy Coco Chanel perfume. Later, she gets into her brand new Audi and drives home. Our bare-chested carpenter rushes home in his Ford pickup truck sipping Gatorade. Back at his apartment he showers using Dove soap and Vidal Sassoon shampoo. After showering, he steps into his Calvin Klein underwear, a clean pair of Levi's, and a pair of Kenneth Cole shoes. As he's brushing his hair he listens to a Rolling Stones CD. Once he leaves his apartment, he buys flowers and wine. He proceeds to a suburban house where we see the girl's Audi. Inside, they open a bottle of Robert Mondavi wine and listen to a Lady Gaga CD on her Bose CD player. The woman pops a pornographic DVD into her Sony DVD player. In bed they watch the pornographic video on her Panasonic flat screen television while they make love. Do you see how many products I've mentioned in what will take maybe two minutes of film?

—Who says those companies want to be associated with pornography?

—They won't, not in the beginning. I'm looking down the road a bit. And this won't be on network television. It will be on pay-per-view, on the internet, and on personal communication devices, and, of course, on traditional home videos and DVDs. In the beginning we'll start with smaller companies, those that might not have broken into the mainstream yet; those that are trying to grab a bigger piece of the market. Instead of a Rolling Stones CD we have some indie band from some new label or some rap group. Instead of Levi's we have the guy wear something from American Apparel, or an even less well-known brand. Eventually American Apparel clothing becomes cool with indie rockers. High school and college kids, wanting to imitate rock stars, start buying and wearing American Apparel because the young always want to do what is considered cool, whatever will piss their parents off, and whatever seems to be anti-establishment. When Levi's realizes no one wants to wear their jeans because they aren't cool anymore, their market share will tumble and their stock price will start to go down. When that happens, stockholders will start complaining, and when they do, Levi's is going to have to find a way to get people to buy jeans. If that means having pornstars wear their jeans that's what they are going to do. The same scenario follows with other products. Maybe instead of the carpenter drinking Gatorade, when he's having sex with his girlfriend, he reaches for a can of Red Bull.

—Because Red Bull is big with twenty somethings…?

—Exactly. They get into their sex thing and they're going at it like real athletes, as he's doing her, he reaches for the Red Bull to refresh himself. He takes a drink and his energy levels soar. Red Bull becomes like Popeye's spinach: you're okay without it, but if you want to be a sex god you'd better have your Red Bull. So he drinks the Red Bull, and he's full of wild sexual energy and his girlfriend goes crazy. Maybe for kicks he spills some of the Red Bull on her breasts and licks it off. Low and behold Red Bull becomes even more popular with the college crowd. I can even see it turning into a college euphemism, instead of saying "I hooked up last night," or "I got laid last night," college kids will say, "I got Red Bulled last night!"

—So we're really just seeing the tip of the iceberg here, aren't we?

—Yes. When other caffeinated beverages see how well Red Bull is doing, they will have their own products put into pornographic movies. In one movie you'll see the stars reaching for a Red Bull drink, in another you'll see the pornstar reaching for a different kind of caffeinated beverage. Eventually, you'll see pornstars reaching for a Coke or a Pepsi or a Gatorade or a Vitamin Water and when that happens, pornography will have become mainstream. It will be owned and controlled by the large media giants. Pornography will just be one more piece of product. Pornography will have been reduced to content.

—You've put some thought into this, haven't you?

—Hubert's a multibillionaire because he works with people who see the future. My job isn't just to focus on what is going to be on television today, I need to understand where television will be in five or ten years. Hubert saw something in me, and I see something in you. And that's why I mean it when I say that if you play your cards right you could end up in the oval office. But before that happens, we need to know you'll be our spokesman, you'll carry our message with conviction.

—I've showed you I can do that.

—I know. But now we need to ramp up what we're doing. If we're going to build a prison where prisoners are televised 24/7, and allow one of them to have sex with a pornstar, we need to make viewers comfortable seeing pornstars as regular people. That's why we need for you to bring a pornstar on your campaign tours.

—You can't be serious.

—Do you really think Hubert or I have time for jokes?

—Well, no but...who's the pornstar you want me to work with? How do I know she's not some bimbo who can't even speak in complete sentences?

—Her name is Cassidy Canyons. She's a beautiful, articulate Latina woman, which will help with the minority vote. She's also a college graduate who ran her own real estate company in Westchester before realizing she could make more money through pornography. We're not just going to throw you up there with a pair of tits. We have a hell of a lot more invested in this than you do.

—You couldn't find anyone with a more appropriate name?

—We thought about that but it doesn't make sense to disdain the names and the culture pornstars represent if we want to use them and promote them. We need people to get used to pornstars' names. We want this to be positive not negative.

—Do you have a photo of her?

—No, but I can show you her website.

—All right.

Roger went over to his desk and Peter followed. He brought up his browser and typed in CassidyCanyons.com. A moment later, the two men were staring at Ms. Canyons' naked body and massive breasts.

—Wow...she's ah...she's quite provocative.

—Yes, she's stunning.

—Well, I'd like to meet her...privately...before I agree to anything....just to see if I'll be able to work with her.

—We have a corporate suite at the Waldorf. You can use that to meet her.

—I'd prefer somewhere less visible. I don't want to run into people I know, which might happen if we use the Waldorf.

—The Waldorf suite is fine. I've used it myself. It will be worse if you're seen slinking into some out of the way hotel or motel. Business people have these type meetings at the Waldorf all the time.

□□□ **56** □□□

After hearing from his wife that their daughter was dropping out of school and joining Greenpeace, Wellington immediately called Bridget. She, however, used her caller ID to identify her father's call and decided she wasn't ready to talk with him. Without success, he tried her a half dozen more times before he left the office. At the end of the day, as he was being driven back to Westchester, Wellington dialed Bridget once again.

At Gabriel's Piano Factory apartment, a ringing phone became a coitus interruptus. Bridget, who was on top, looked over to the phone on the bedside table. Her father's name was displayed. Impulsively, she reached over and picked up the phone.

—What?

—Are you going to throw your life away on something stupid?

—It's not stupid! The environment is very important! Do you know what global warming is doing to the world?

—Bridget, even fourth graders know what global warming is doing. Why the hell do you want to give up your education for that?

—Because someone needs to do something.

—How much are they paying you?

—That's not important.

—No? You think you can support yourself working for Greenpeace? Your apartment alone costs more than two thousand dollars a month. Can you afford that while you're saving the world?

—You can't buy me. I'm not going to stay in school just to please you.

—You want to drop out, then drop out. But before you throw away your life, I'm going to have someone call you about a job...

—What job?

—Hold on, I've got another call.

Wellington's fingers worked the little buttons on his phone as his driver raced him up the West Side Highway.

—Hello.

—Senator, it's Asher. I'm back in Gwanda and we've got problems with the volunteers.

—Hold on.

Wellington again pressed a phone key. Outside his window lights from the George Washington Bridge were visible.

—Bridget, I've got to take this.

—Well, take it. I never told you to call me.

—You'd better watch your attitude. I don't like it.

—Well, don't call me.

Wellington stabbed the Call Wait button with his right index finger and brought the phone back to his ear.

—What's the problem, Asher?

—We're starting to invest a great deal of money over here, and if we're not going to have volunteers to shoot all our efforts are going to be in vain.

—Why the hell wouldn't we have volunteers to shoot? I thought that's what they wanted?

Wellington's driver, Charles, shot a quick glance at Wellington through the rearview mirror. The senator gave him a hard cold stare back.

—It is. But when the women whose husbands were shot didn't get their AIDS drugs right away they got angry and started protesting. There's this guy, Seisko Upendo, who has become their leader. He's charismatic, doesn't have AIDS, and he's telling Gwandans not to allow us to hunt them and not to work for The Promised Land corporation. He's already gathered a substantial following.

—Upendo?

—Yeah. Anyway, he's smart. He gives speeches and people listen and cheer. He wants to prevent us from finishing building the coliseum because he knows that's what will be used for the hunting and to bring in tourists.

—What is he really doing, holding out for a cut? Find out how much he wants.

—It's not going to be that simple. If we could just pay him off I would, but he's one of these goddamn righteous sons of bitches who really believes in helping his country. I'm not the only one worried; General Msambee's worried, too.

—Why the hell don't they arrest him for disturbing the peace or something? There've got to be some charges they can throw at him.

Charles turned the radio on. Mozart's Concerto for Piano No. 17 in G Major was playing softly. The volume was brought up just enough to give the appearance that he wasn't listening in on the conversation.

—We talked about that. Putting him in jail is just going to cause greater disturbances and possibly riots, maybe even bring in the international press. We don't want that.

—Have Steve make sure those who have lost their husbands get the AIDS medicine right away.

—I have been working that angle, but there's been the usual bureaucratic bullshit in getting the AIDS drugs into the country. Just make sure Claudia doesn't get in the way, she's starting to annoy a lot of people.

—I'll talk to her.

—Thanks.

Wellington snapped his cell closed and looked up at his driver.

—Charles, how's your wife? Is she better?

She hadn't been sick. It was his thirty-six-year-old daughter who had been.

—Fine, sir, thanks for asking.

The rest of the trip was silent, save for the interweaving of the flute, piano, and strings, and when the piece was finished, the voice of Candice Agree announcing the soloist.

☐☐☐ **57** ☐☐☐

Bridget exited the VBS building at Worldwide Plaza and took the E train down to Soho. At Spring Street she emerged from the underground tunnel and made her way to Agent Provocateur, a lingerie store on Mercer Street. She looked at various undergarments before selecting the "Abracadabra," a pink and fuchsia bra and brief. She took the E train back to Hell's Kitchen. At the Amish Market on Ninth Avenue she purchased fresh salmon, asparagus, and rice. Her next stop was the Ninth Avenue Vintner for a bottle of chardonnay.

Inside Gabriel's apartment she took off her old underwear and put on her new lingerie under her interview outfit: a white blouse tightened at the waist with a red belt, and a knee-length skirt sashed with rows of small scarlet waves.

In the kitchen she opened the bottle of wine.

At 8 PM Gabriel arrived. They greeted each other with a kiss. Gabriel took off his suit jacket, placed it on the back of a dining room chair and pulled his tie off. In the kitchen he found a wine goblet and brought it into the living room, where he sat down next to Bridget and poured himself a drink. Bridget stared at him for a few moments.

—You've got a funny look in your eyes. Is everything all right?

Bridget thought about what she wanted to say for a few moments before responding.

—I went to see a woman my father knows at VBS television. I wasn't even going to meet her, but I figured I'd go just to get my father off my back. She wasn't as horrible as I thought she would be and, well, she offered me a job and I accepted. I'm going to be the Special Assistant to the Head of Programming.

Gabriel tried to read Bridget's face.

—What about Greenpeace. I thought you were all gung-ho about working with them?

—I was…sort of, but they pay like ten bucks an hour. VBS offered me one hundred thousand dollars a year.

—One hundred thousand? You're joking?

—No.

—You realize what your father's doing here, don't you? He's buying you.

—He's just helping me out. If I stay in school, what happens when I graduate? And if I work for Greenpeace, what would I really be doing? You know I can't live on ten dollars an hour.

—Why would you want to do that? I thought you hated what your father was doing?

—I do, but this way I'll get to see The Promised Land in person. We're going to go over there.

—Are you doing it because you want to work in TV or because you want to go over to Gwanda?

—I don't know…that's what I've been trying to figure out. I don't have the answer right now. Right now I'd like to get drunk and screw. Do you want to?

—I want to know what's on your mind first.

—Make love to me first.

—That's just avoiding it. What's going on?

Bridget got up from the couch.

—I bought some lingerie today after I took the job.

She unbuttoned the top few buttons of her blouse to show him her new bra.

—Do you like it?

Gabriel looked at her without response.

—I was going to make this big meal and was going to do a sexy little dance for you…

—Why? Did you feel you had to seduce me about the job?

Bridget considered this before sitting back down.

—Who knows, maybe I did. Maybe I'm taking the job because I want my father to like me. How come you never told me about your parents?

—What does my family have to do with this?

—You know all about my family and I know nothing about yours. Why can't I know about yours? Maybe your father bought you too. He bought you this apartment, didn't he?

—Why do you want to know about my father now?

—If you don't want to tell me you don't have to.

Gabriel took a long drink of the white wine.

—My father always told me to get rich, because if you're rich money won't solve all your problems but it'll solve most. And I believed him. Or maybe I didn't believe him, but what else did I know? My mother was no help either. They were divorced. She lived in this big apartment on Park Avenue and Eighty-Third, and he lived up in Rye, in Westchester. She used to go to parties and drink. That was enough for her and her friends, charity parties, fancy clothes and champagne. With my father it was always about safety—have money and you're safe. But safe from what? He was just a timid little man who was afraid to do

what he really wanted. That's why I quit being a lawyer. Didn't want to be my father. I didn't know what the hell I was going to be. Didn't care. And I got that job with your father, told you I didn't know why I took it. I did. I knew from the start. I want to write a book about him, a book about the people I came from, the rich and the powerful. I thought here's my perfect opportunity. But I've always felt like a phony.
—Why?
—Because your father thinks I'm helping him, and I am, don't get me wrong—I'm not sabotaging him, I can do the work, and do it well, but I hate pretending to like him. And if I was being false to him, I was also being false to you. How is it going to make you feel when I write about your father? I won't do it until he wins the election, but it probably won't be pretty. I don't like the man, don't like what he stands for. Don't like politicians as a breed.

Bridget looked at him almost with contempt.
—What am I, just another chapter in your book? Are you using me like you're using him?
—No, not at all. I love you.
—You never told me that.
—Well, maybe I should have. You mean much more to me than any book. So if you don't want me to write anything, I won't.
—There's a lot about my father you don't see. To you he's just a symbol, a symbol of something you hate, a politician. But at least at one time he tried to do something, wanted to do something. That's more than you, isn't it?
—You're going to trash me?
—Why, are you sacred? He's not perfect, okay. Who is? You hate politicians but someone's got to take the job, and it isn't always easy to get done what you want to get done. I don't even want to talk about this now.

Bridget started to rise, but before she could get fully to her feet, Gabriel reached for her hand.
—No, it's good. I want to hear what you have to say. Please, tell me.

Bridget sat back down. She looked at her glass of wine and poured what was left of hers into Gabriel's glass.
—I grew up my whole life listening to him and his friends arguing about what they were going to do, or what they wanted to do, or what they wished they could do. This made me wonder why my father spent so much time away from home, trying to do things that he never seems to get done. He always said he was trying to provide for his family, and to make the world a better place, but how could he be doing that if he just left my mother alone all the time, and left me alone, or just with my

brother.

—You paint a different picture than the man I've been observing.

—People could say the same thing about you, couldn't they? They could say you're just a guy who gave up, because that's what you did, isn't it? You quit your job because you didn't agree with what they're doing. If you really cared, maybe you'd do something from the inside, something as a lawyer. But you're not, are you? You're just going to write a book about how horrible a man my father is. Why don't you do something better than that? Anyone can criticize someone else. It's a lot harder to do something yourself, to try to do something that makes the world a better place.

Gabriel nodded in agreement.

—All right, maybe I won't.

—I think you should write it because maybe he would read it. I think he's completely blind to what he does to others. I don't think he really notices. He says he wants to help the world, and one time I believed that.

—And now?

—I think he's like all the rest of them. It's about power, getting power and more power or just trying to hold on to what they have. And despite all those things he does or says I still love him, and it just screws me up inside because how could I love him if I know he lies all the time, even to me?

Suddenly there were tears in her eyes.

—Are you okay?

—I'm not crying.

With his thumb, Gabriel wiped her tears away and gave her a quick kiss.

—It's okay.

—It's not me, I'm not thinking about me, it's my mom. You don't know what it's like for me when I go home and I see them there. It's like he hates to be there and she's completely unhappy, and I'm caught in the middle. My brother doesn't even come home anymore. I feel so bad for her because she thinks that there's nothing she can do. She wants to leave my father but she never will. She doesn't have the courage. She feels that her life is over and she's not old. She's still very pretty. What am I supposed to do? What? I've got to think of my mom just sitting home afraid to leave, and I got to think of my father saying how he wants to kill prisoners and hunt Africans, and my brother's all screwed up in his own way. And now you, I say I want to make money and you say don't. I can't please my father; I can't please you. How am I supposed to feel? Am I supposed to ignore everything?

—What can I do?

—Maybe I shouldn't take this job, maybe you're right, but it's not always easy to do what's right. Sometimes, I just want to stop fighting everything and take the easy way out, even if I know I'll regret it in the end.

—Tell me what you want from me, and I'll do my best to give it to you.

—Can we just stop talking for a little while? I don't want to talk anymore. Can we go to bed? Can we just go into the bedroom and can you just hold me and tell me you love me?

—I do. I love you very much.

—I wish you would tell me that more.

Gabriel kissed and led her to the bedroom.

□□□ 58 □□□

The following morning Gabriel, dressed nattily in his best suit, arrived at the office at 8:15. After greeting Keno, who had also been there close to an hour, he knocked once on the senator's open door and entered. Wellington was at the worktable with a map of New York divided into its political counties.

—Senator, I was wondering if I could talk to you for a few minutes.

—Are you just going to stand in the doorway, or are you going to come in?

Gabriel came in and stood in front of the table.

—I've been dating Bridget for the last few months.

—Yes, I know. My wife Candace told me. I was wondering when you or Bridget were going to tell me so I wouldn't have to keep pretending that I didn't know. You're not asking for her hand in marriage, are you?

—Nothing like that. I, well, I want to be honest with you, sir. When I started working with you it wasn't for the purest of reasons. I didn't particularly care for your politics, but I needed a job. I thought it would be a good experience to see how things worked firsthand. It has been a good experience, learning-wise, but I think it would be wrong for me to continue on here. I don't want to deceive you, and I also don't want to just resign without telling you why. I'm going to continue to see Bridget and I don't want my relationship, or lack of it with you, to affect my relationship with her.

—What is it that you don't like about me?

—It's nothing you haven't heard before. You're proposing to shoot people with AIDS. You're proposing to send criminals to Gwanda and shoot them for a television show.

Wellington stood up angrily and took a step toward Gabriel.

—Think you know what's best, do you? You're like a million other people. You'd make the world a better place if you only had the chance, right?

Gabriel stepped backward toward the couch.

—I never said that.

Wellington went to the door and closed it.

—But it's what you believe, isn't it? Guys like you are a dime a dozen, always blaming politicians.

—What guys like me? You have no idea what my thoughts and feelings are, my philosophy, so don't generalize.

—No? If you're dating my daughter I have a pretty good idea of what your thoughts are.

—Do you? What are they?

Wellington sat back down at his worktable.

—Bridget believes that if we just help the poor and disenfranchised everything will get better and problems, crimes, will magically disappear.

—She's not that simplistic.

—What I want you to do is to write up a proposal of what you'd like me to do. If you were in a position to change things, if you were a senator, tell me what you would do. Tell me how you think we can solve these problems.

This surprised Gabriel,

—You want me to...you want me to continue to work for you?

—You think you know what's right, don't you? Let's see you come up with some of your own proposals. Or do you prefer to sit around with your friends and complain about how horrible the world is, how lousy politicians are?

The door opened slowly and Keno stepped in and stood there. — What is it?

—Asher Mitchell's on the phone.

—Tell him I'll be right with him. Gabriel, I'm asking you to stand up for your beliefs. Can you do that? Or will you spend your life complaining from the sidelines?

—I'm not complaining from the sidelines, I'm...

—Don't answer me now, think about it. Give it some real thought.

Wellington reached for the Polycon and pushed the active line.

—Asher, what's up?

Gabriel stood there slightly dismayed that the talk hadn't gone as expected.

—Senator, I just got off the phone with Steve Lowell who says General Msambee has been secretly meeting with Upendo. Seems Upendo's

184

better organized than we thought. He's got thousands of followers. Steve thinks Msambee is using Upendo to stir up trouble.

—Why would he do that?

Wellington looked up at Gabriel when he realized he was still standing there. Gabriel quickly turned and exited.

—Steve thinks General Msambee might be trying to wrest control from President Mobley. If Upendo acts up Msambee will have more reason to flex the military's muscle and assert his power. That's usually the first step if you want to stage a military coup d'état.

On his white writing pad he wrote MOBLEY and underlined it twice.

—Christ. I'd better give President Mobley a call, see what he knows about this. This might require a face-to-face meeting. I'm too busy to get over there right now, so you or Claudia, or both of you, might have to go talk to him.

Keno was back in the doorway looking brightly anxious. He needed to interrupt but didn't want to appear too intrusive; he spoke quietly.

—Senator?

—Not now, Keno.

—But sir, Police Commissioner Parker's press secretary is calling. They've made an arrest in the killing of Robert Jackson.

—Oh.

Wellington nodded and Keno stepped out of the office.

—I'll take it. Asher, I've got to go. Find out what you can.

He pushed the blinking phone line.

—Hello.

—Senator, it's Harrison Silver. Police Commissioner Parker wanted me to let you know we've made an arrest in the killing of Robert Jackson.

Wellington stood up with excitement.

—Really? Fantastic. That's good, very good, what I've been waiting to hear. Thank God. I can really use the publicity.

—We've been working very hard on the case and...

—Yes, I appreciate that. I appreciate that very much. I'm going to announce a press conference.

—That's a bit premature because...

—Don't worry, Silver, I'll make sure Parker's mentioned. I'll need the names of the arresting officers. I'll have my assistant contact you. Thanks again.

—But, Senator...

Wellington disconnected and called out,

—Keno?

He was back in a flash.

—Yes?

—I want you to set up a press conference down at City Hall. I want all the major newspapers and networks there.

—At what time?

—Set it up for noon, one o'clock. I want it on the six o'clock news. But, hey, you know what, let's not do it at City Hall. Let's do it uptown, at the precinct headquarters of the arresting officers. It'll be good to show the minority community that we support them. We'll have it up there.

—I'll make the arrangements.

□□□ 59 □□□

By the time Wellington arrived at the 30th Precinct on One Hundred Fifty-First Street there was a sizeable crowd of reporters and news cameramen assembled and facing the entrance to the station house, where a podium, with a nest of microphones, had been placed. Harrison Silver greeted Wellington as he stepped out of his Lincoln Town Car, Keno in tow.

—Hi, Senator. Harrison Silver.

Wellington shook his hand.

—Where are the arresting officers, Detective Mallory and Detective Torinsky? Are they here?

—Yes, up on the platform waiting for you.

—Great.

Wellington saw the uniformed officers and went up to shake their hands.

—Detectives, thank for your hard work and dedication. We need more men like you.

The taller of the two officers, Torinsky, said, somewhat sheepishly,

—I can't say I feel too good about it.

—Why not? Of course catching a killer, well, I'm sure it gives you a distorted view of humanity; nonetheless, without men like you the city wouldn't be as safe as it is.

Keno tapped his watch and said,

—Senator, if we want to make the six o'clock news we'd...

—All right, all right.

Senator Wellington straightened his tie, turned around and took three steps forward to the bushel of microphones as the flashbulbs began flashing.

—Good afternoon. The police department, with the help of detectives to my right, Detective Thomas Mallory and Detective Joseph Torinsky, has made an arrest in the sad and brutal murder of Robert Jackson. I wanted to say a few words about that before I allow the detectives to speak. A few months back, I pledged to do what I could to make this city and state as strong and as crime free as possible. Today we take a decisive step in that direction. When I began my campaign for reelection I put together a series of commercials. In one of these commercials I had the great honor to work with a gifted young actor and musician, Robert Jackson. A few days after the commercial aired, Mr. Jackson was gunned down in cold blood. It was a ruthless and brutal murder that stopped a young man in the prime of his life. It robbed Robert Jackson's family and friends of the joy he had brought them. Now, because of the dedication and hard work of Detective Mallory and Detective Torinsky, we have been able to apprehend the killer responsible for this horrendous murder. Some of you may know of my plans to send murderers to The Promised Land where they will receive the justice they deserve. Upon conviction, I would like to send the murderer of Robert Jackson to The Promised Land where he will be executed on Promised Land television.

Senator Wellington turned to face the arresting officers,
—Detectives, why don't you tell us how you apprehended the suspect?

Detectives Torinsky and Mallory walked forward, unaccustomed to the glare of flashbulbs in their eyes. Torinsky spoke for both of them.
—Thank you, Senator. Um...well, the a...the suspect was um...he was turned in by his seventh grade teacher. After questioning him we had no choice but to arrest him.

Wellington tilted his head with puzzlement, as if he hadn't heard correctly.
—Did you say seventh grade teacher? Just how old is the suspect?
—Billy is twelve.
—Twelve? A kid? He's just a kid?
—Yes. That's why we were wondering why you wanted to have a press conference.

Wellington's eyes darted to the press secretary, Harrison Silver, and back to the news crews. He did his best to keep his composure as he spoke.
—Excuse me, folks. There seems to have been a slight misunderstanding. Thank you all for coming. As soon as we straighten this out, we'll, um...thank you.

Completely flustered, Wellington walked off as a reporter shouted after him,
—Senator, are you going to execute a boy?

There was no reply. But this didn't stop a second reporter from shouting,

—Senator Wellington, isn't killing a twelve-year-old a little too young, even for you?

Wellington slammed through the police precinct door. Press Secretary Silver, quick on his heels, followed him in. Once the door closed, Wellington grabbed Silver by the neck and threw him against a wall lined with wanted posters.

—JESUS FUCKING CHRIST! Why the hell wasn't I told that he was a kid! A goddamn kid! A twelve-year-old! I just told the entire world that I want to kill a kid. Fuck!

Wellington took a step away from the diminutive press secretary, tried to calm himself by running his hands through his hair, but this didn't work. Seconds later his fury rose again and he used the knuckles of his right hand to push Silver up against the wall.

—What the fuck did you just do to me?! Why didn't you tell me he was a kid!?

—I thought you knew!

—Bullshit! You knew damn well what you were doing!

Wellington turned and walked away. Silver hurried after him.

—That's not true at all. You haven't let anyone get in a word edgewise, I...

The senator came back at him,

—Fuck you! You're a liar! Jesus, a kid! A goddamn kid! All right, hold on, let me think about this. Obviously we can't execute a boy.

He saw Keno standing by a uniformed officer with his cell phone in hand, dialing. Wellington went over to him.

—Keno, you should have looked into this.

—You had me booking the press...

—I don't give a damn what I had you doing! You look out for me, that's your damn job! Who the hell are you calling? Hang up and get me David Diamond!

—That's who I was calling.

—Oh. Thank you.

When the voice at the other end of the line said hello, Keno handed off the phone.

The Village Voice
Kill Killer Kid!

Senator Wellington, the crime-crusading congressman, has vowed to kill a twelve-year-old boy, Billy Tyler. The tot, not yet in high school, has been accused of killing Robert Jackson, an out-of-work actor with one commercial to his credit. Wellington wants the boy to be sent to his Promised Land Ranch where he'll be hunted down, shot, and killed. "Slaughter-'em-for-safety" Wellington was quoted as saying: "Upon conviction I would like to make the murderer of Robert Jackson the first to be sent to The Promised Land

Continued on Page 4

David Diamond's head was bald and shiny, save for a horseshoe of hair, cut extremely short, which wrapped around his head just above his ears. He came into a holding pen inside the 30th Precinct carrying a briefcase and a big bag from Kentucky Fried Chicken. He placed the food on the table in front of an African American boy and his father, who was reading *The Village Voice*.

—Don't believe what you read in the papers, Mr. Tyler.

—It was on the chair. I picked it up while we were waiting for you.

Billy Tyler, who had been held in a special juvenile cell overnight, eyed the KFC bag voraciously.

—Go ahead, it's for you.

Billy extracted a bucket of fried chicken, a pint of mashed potatoes with gravy, and two large cups of Coca-Cola.

—I appreciate your bailing Billy out, Mr. Diamond.

—Thank Senator Wellington. He's the one who made all the arrangements. I just came down here to make sure it all went smoothly.

—We thank you both.

Billy, with a drumstick in his mouth, wasn't thinking about thanking anyone.

189

—Senator Wellington was very much offended that your son was mistakenly arrested, and wishes he could be here personally. Unfortunately, his present duties and commitments prevent him from doing so.

Mr. Tyler watched Diamond take out a yellow legal pad and pen from his brown leather briefcase and place them on the table in front of him. The room was bare, save for the table and chairs; Diamond sat on one side, Billy and his father on the opposite.

—I'm a little curious why the senator would first say Billy should be hunted down and killed, and end up bailing him out.

—That was just a misunderstanding. Senator Wellington had been given false information. The important thing now is to make sure Billy stays out of jail.

—That's what we want.

They both turned to Billy who looked guilty. He stopped eating for a brief moment before continuing after the men were again eyeing each other.

—To do that we have to move quickly. We can't just say that he was playing around with a gun and it went off.

—But that's what happened, and that's what he told his teacher, Ms. Waddles, that he was playing around with a friend and the gun just went off.

Diamond looked down at the preliminary notes written on the pad. After reading the first and second pages, he flipped the pad open to a clean sheet. As Diamond questioned Billy he jotted down notes.

—Let me worry about that. Now Billy, let me see, did you know Robert?

In a few short minutes, Billy had already eaten the drumstick and half a breast of chicken, and now was working the potatoes and gravy with a spoon.

—I saw him around. He used to hang out.

—Okay, he hung out. Hung out doing what?

—Nothing, just hanging out.

Mr. Tyler took a plate and set himself up with a meal: two breasts of chicken, potatoes, a roll and the other soda. He used the plastic fork and knife to cut into the tender breast, sprinkled some salt from its little package, and put a large piece of white meat in his mouth and chewed.

—He had to be doing something. Did you see him drinking? Did he sit and drink beer?

—I don't know.

—But he didn't not drink beer, right?

Not quite understanding the logic of the sentence, Billy looked to

190

his father who responded for him.

—What?

—He didn't not drink beer. You can't say that every day he didn't have a beer, right?

Mr. Tyler looked at his son who answered.

—I don't know.

—It is possible that he drank beer, and maybe some whiskey, when he was hanging out, right?

—I guess.

Diamond wrote, DRINKING and next to it DRUGS? He turned back to Billy.

—So, we have him drinking. What about drugs? Did you ever see him do drugs? Get high?

—Not really.

—Billy, I don't want you to lie, but if we say you shot Robert Jackson for no reason you're going to go to jail, and jail isn't nice, especially for a handsome, young boy like yourself.

Mr. Tyler wiped his mouth with the paper napkin and responded.

—Mr. Diamond, he would go to jail? I thought the worst case would be juvenile hall?

—Even at juvenile detention there are big boys, seventeen, eighteen years old that have been locked away for years. Some are murderers full of rage and sexual desire. It's a scary place. No place for a boy. Billy, you don't want to go there, do you?

—No.

—Okay then, let's find out what really happened. Since Robert was hanging out he obviously didn't have a full-time job, and if he didn't have a full-time job he had to get his money from somewhere. It's quite possible that he made money selling drugs. You'd agree that it was possible he was selling drugs, wouldn't you?

—I don't know.

—There are drugs in your neighborhood, aren't there, Mr. Tyler?

Tyler didn't like the implicating tone in Diamond's voice, and by eating the fried chicken he felt he had fallen right into the stereotype Diamond assigned to him. Nonetheless, there was little he could do besides responding with a somewhat defiant tone.

—There are drugs in every neighborhood.

—Exactly, and your neighborhood even more so. Drug dealers usually hang out on street corners waiting for people to come by to buy drugs. So what it looks like is that Robert was dealing drugs, and what Billy did—Billy, you're against drugs, aren't you?

—Yeah.

—Okay, I think what we're realizing is that Billy didn't want drugs in the neighborhood, and since no one else was doing anything, Billy realized it was up to him to protect the neighborhood. So, he decided to take matters into his own hands. Is that right?

—Go ahead, Billy.

The boy had turned away from Diamond and was working on a fresh chicken breast.

—What?

—Tell Mr. Diamond that you didn't want drugs in your neighborhood.

—I didn't want drugs in my neighborhood.

Diamond wrote this down.

—Good. Because you knew a dangerous drug dealer was starting to corrupt your neighborhood, and knowing that the police wouldn't do anything...no, wait, strike that, we can't criticize the police, that won't play well. You wanted to help the police, isn't that right? You felt it was your patriotic duty to help this country, didn't you?

Billy looked to his father for guidance, but didn't receive any. —I guess.

—Good. It was your patriotic duty to get rid of the drug dealers. You would agree to that, wouldn't you?

—I don't know.

—Mr. Tyler, I'm just trying to help your son.

—Billy, tell the man that you were trying to protect your neighborhood, your family, and friends.

—I was trying to help my friends.

—Okay. Billy, after you shot him, you saw that the problem hadn't been stopped or averted, so you told your seventh grade teacher, Ms. Waddles, because you realized that you needed additional help. That's right, isn't it, Billy?

—Um...

—Billy, just say yes to whatever Mr. Diamond says.

—Yes.

—Okay, good. So you told Ms. Waddles that you shot down drug-dealing scum.

—How come the senator said he was a good guy?

—He was mistaken. Robert Jackson was a dangerous man who, if left to his own devices, would almost certainly have brought violence into the neighborhood. There's also a strong possibility that Robert would have killed to support his drug addiction, and to protect his drug-dealing turf. So, in many ways, what you did was noteworthy.

—Um...Mr. Diamond, Billy didn't actually tell his teacher. His friend Byron did.

192

Byron's name was jotted down.

—All right, I'll talk to Byron when we're through. Billy, what I'm going to do is write up a statement for you to sign. Did the police, did you sign anything for the police?

Billy looked to his father who answered for him.

—They asked him to, but I told him it was better not to. I wanted to talk to a lawyer.

—All right, good. You know what, hold on. Let's think about this, we can't say that Billy took matters into his own hands, that's not believable at his age. Let's see, One Hundred Fifty-Fourth Street is a dangerous street, isn't it?

Billy nodded in the affirmative.

—Sometimes.

—Okay, and you had to walk past it every day on your way to school, didn't you Billy?

—Yeah.

—On your way to school and back you often saw people hanging out, among them was Robert Jackson, correct?

—Yeah.

—And it's well-known, that drug dealers often recruit young kids to sell drugs for them, and they do this by becoming friendly with them, and that's what Robert Jackson was doing, wasn't he? He was trying to gain your confidence, so that he could recruit you to sell drugs. That's what he did, right?

—Um...

—You used to talk to Robert, didn't you, Billy? Didn't you occasionally talk to him?

—Sometimes, yeah.

—Okay. Robert was trying to be friendly so he could get you to sell drugs for him. But you refused, didn't you? You never agreed to sell drugs for Robert, did you?

—No.

—And when you refused to sell drugs, Robert started menacing you, right? Billy, were you ever afraid of the bigger kids?

—Sometimes.

—Of course you were. And Robert was big and scary and tough, right?

—Um...I guess.

Diamond had been quickly writing this all down, as if he were an inspired short story writer. Finally he rested his pen and looked directly at the boy.

—Robert wanted you to sell drugs, and when you refused Robert threatened you. You were so scared you started carrying your father's

193

gun. Right?

—Um...

—And when Robert tried to take the gun—forcefully take the gun from you—it went off and Robert was killed. That's what happened, isn't it? You would agree with that, wouldn't you? Mr. Tyler, I'm trying to help you and Billy.

Tyler could barely conceal his scorn for Diamond, his straightforward and unabashed manipulation of the truth, especially since this was being done in front of his son, who seemed to be almost as oblivious as Diamond to the subtle nuances of expression he used to convey his disdain.

—Go ahead, Billy, tell Mr. Diamond that's what happened.

—That's what happened. Robert tried to take the gun and it went off.

—Okay, good. It's important that you remember that, remember the way things actually happened. I'm going to write this up, have it notarized, and then I'll have a copy sent to you for your signature. It's just a legal formality; nothing to worry about. But it is important to remember it just as it is written, because I think we all realize that we can forget details over time, and that's why we write details down. You did a brave thing, and Billy, I know that this has been a long and difficult ordeal for you. I'm sure you're eager to get back home and relax, but you need to remember and memorize exactly what's written. I'll be in touch soon to go over the details with you again, and to get Byron's contact information.

Diamond stood up, quite pleased with himself.

—Mr. Tyler, I think we're going to be able to beat this. When we do, it may be difficult, but I'm going to try to get Senator Wellington to give Billy some sort of medal commemorating his fight against drugs. I greatly appreciate both your efforts here. Billy is a real hero.

Billy now joined his father who had also risen.

—I'm a hero?

—Yes, you are. Mr. Tyler, let me give you some cab money home.

—That's okay.

Shiny-headed Diamond reached into the briefcase and took out a large manila envelope stuffed with cash. Tyler put up his hands in refusal.

—No thanks.

—Take it, you deserve it.

Diamond pushed it into Mr. Tyler's hands giving him no choice but to accept the hush money.

—I realize that it's not a lot, but since you had to take a day off from work...

—But...

—Please, you've been quite helpful to our cause. Thanks again. And thank you, too, Billy. He patted Billy on the head.

—Good-bye, and stay safe.

—Thank you.

—We'll talk soon. Bye.

As the father and son were exiting, Billy looked back to see Diamond biting into a chicken leg he wished he had taken with him.

◻◻◻ 61 ◻◻◻

At POX studios in midtown, Roger Zales was leaving his office for his morning staff meeting when his cell phone began vibrating. Extracting it from his pants pocket he gazed at the illuminated name. It was Peter Morgan. Zales stepped back inside, closed the door, and walked back to his desk, where he plopped down in his padded chair.

—Hello, Peter.

The voice came on excitedly,

—Did you see the news?

Zales calmly replied,

—Wellington and the kid?

—Yeah. It's great, isn't it? Almost assures us of victory, does it? Tomorrow I want to hit the press full speed. I thought I'd give POX my first interview.

—Slamming Wellington for his comment isn't a good idea.

—Why not? He says he wants to kill a kid.

—Got to think of our future. Don't want to criticize now what we may have to do later.

—Why would we ever want to kill a kid?

—It's not a viable market now but it might be in the future. If so, we don't want to be seen as flip-flopping. And, anyway, we need you to stay on message. After your appearance with Cassidy Canyons on the *Today Show* and *Good Morning, America* your poll numbers have gone up significantly.

—Well, yeah, because everyone likes Cassidy. She's terrific. If I'm not careful, I'm going to fall in love with her myself.

—I don't want you two getting involved. It wouldn't be good for her image. I ought to let you know now that we've run into a few bumps in the road, but nothing we can't handle.

—What bumps?

—Our lawyers have heard from the lawyers of women prisoners. They're claiming that by only allowing male prisoners to compete to sleep with pornstars we're being discriminatory. Women prisoners want the opportunity to sleep with a male pornstar. Gays and lesbians are also upset. Each group is threatening a lawsuit if they don't get a chance to sleep with a pornstar.

—What about…have you thought about giving them all their own shows?

—Yes, we're looking into that. But there has been opposition here from some executives who do not want to see homosexuals having sex on a POX affiliate.

The fat man stood up and went to the shelf by the window, lifted the lid of a box of fresh Cuban cigars, took one out, and ran the long brown Montecristo under his nose as he watched the traffic struggle north up Sixth Avenue. His doctor had forbidden him to smoke cigars, but he did like to sniff, just to remind himself of their sweet taste.

—But what about Wellington? I say nothing?

—If asked, say it was a terrible tragedy and leave it at that, leave it to the press. They'll come down hard on him by themselves. I'm sure Gazelle will also try to come out against him. At some point, we made need to get into execution-TV. That's why we need to remain objective now. It's called playing fair. Being fair and balanced is what this station is all about.

—All right.

Zales placed his precious possession back in its box and sat back down, as standing too long often tired him.

—If the press questions you, say you're praying for the family.

—Which family, the kid killed or the shooter's family?

—Doesn't matter. Just say you're praying, that's the important thing—say you're praying.

▢▢▢ **62** ▢▢▢

Claudia Potter and Senator Wellington shared a table at Druids on Tenth Avenue and Fifty-Second Street. With less than ten tables, a long wooden bar and brass foot-rail, the restaurant invoked old New York without being trendy. Behind the bar was a blowsy blonde that reminded Wellington of Pamela, his former flame. Every time he sipped his scotch he shot a quick glance over to her, only half paying attention to what Potter was saying.

—Richard, I'm not saying politics is my arena. All I'm saying is that I think we could use the unfortunate incident with Billy to our advantage.

Wellington cut into his steak, chewed, and swallowed before speaking.

196

—The sooner Billy is forgotten the better. They have me saying I want to kill a kid. If you think I want further association with that you're wrong.

—I think this could be a real gift. Billy already has exposure from the newspapers and TV. I think we could expand that to markets outside the Metro area. If you say Billy accidentally killed someone it shows guns are dangerous, guns are wrong. But if you're able to show that Billy was acting in self-defense people will sympathize with him. Who hasn't felt afraid at times and wished they had a gun? We all have. We need to play that up.

Wellington finished the last of his steak, laid his knife and fork together on his plate, wiped his mouth with the white napkin, and deliberated for a few more moments before replying.

—What would you want him to do?

—Demonstrate how to use Promised Land rifles and handguns. We'll have him show other kids how to hunt and shoot the volunteer dolls. He's killed a drug dealer, hasn't he? The fact that he's black is an added bonus. I want to hire him to go across the country demonstrating how Promise Land rifles work. Eventually, I want to take him to Gwanda to shoot a commercial that demonstrates Promised Land rifles at the actual ranch, so that we can tie this in with our interactive dolls and video games.

The senator from New York pondered this. Before he could entertain negative thoughts, Potter pushed her point home.

—This will work for all of us. He's the perfect spokesperson, and he'll give you the added publicity you need to win the election.

Wellington nodded slightly, making Potter feel she had made progress. She took a self-congratulatory drink of her sauvignon blanc.

—I have to meet with the Mayor Corpson and Police Commissioner Parker tomorrow to see what they're going to do about Billy. If he's not charged, you can have Billy and take him to Gwanda.

□□□ 63 □□□

Two weeks after the charges against Billy Tyler were dropped, Billy and his young friend Byron were with Bridget Wellington and Claudia Potter at the coliseum grounds at The Promised Land Ranch. When completed, it would be one of the biggest sporting arenas in Africa, with enough seats for ninety-thousand people. The coliseum was shaped like giant parentheses ( ) and had a "playing field" of more than three times the size of a football field. In order to protect the viewers, bulletproof glass was being built to encapsulate it. One end of the coliseum was open. The opposite end had a painted backdrop that depicted trees and other local flora. In front of the backdrop there would be real trees and wild savannah grass, and a small pond with live crocodiles. When the volunteers were let into the stadium, they would be told if they made it to the other end they would be freed. But once they got close they would find there was no chance of escape: they would either be shot or eaten by the hungry crocodiles. To make the viewing experience even more enjoyable, each group of box seats had at least two interactive hunting rifles. The volunteers would have electronic bullseyes affixed to their chests, backs and skulls and viewers would have the ability to hunt the volunteers and score points electronically.

With the quartet was Sergeant Springs, a former U.S. Army officer and six volunteers. Billy and Byron, holding rifles almost as tall as they were, looked up at Ms. Potter as she explained their duties.

—Okay boys, we need you to do some more practicing, but today instead of using the video games we used in New York, we want you to practice shooting volunteers. You should aim for the targets you see on them.

Claudia pointed to the red and white bullseyes painted on the volunteers.

—That's how you score points. When they run, you shoot them.

Billy looked at the men who, to him, looked not only sad but also too sick to run anywhere.

—They're volunteers?

—Yes. That's what we're calling the Africans we're going to be shooting. Sort of like, well, like the way you shot Robert Jackson. You knew he was evil, so he had to be eliminated. The same thing applies to the volunteers.

Billy wasn't convinced.

—Ms. Potter, my father said they didn't do anything, that's why he didn't want me to go.

—But your mother wanted you to go, didn't she?

—Only because we needed the money.

—And you want to earn that money, don't you? If you keep asking silly questions you won't, and your mother will be mad, won't she?

Byron tried to help his friend out by saying.

—But Ms. P., they didn't do anything.

—They did. What the volunteers did was kill rare and valuable black rhinoceroses, and they plan to kill more unless they're stopped. They've also stolen jewelry from wealthy women. Basically, they're just...they're bad people who must be stopped. I don't really want to get into a debate with you about this.

Potter looked over to Bridget and said,

—Feel free to help me out here. You can answer some of Billy's questions as well as I can.

Bridget came up behind Billy and Byron and placed her hands on their shoulders.

—Actually, I have many of the same questions myself.

Claudia Potter returned to her arrogant self.

—We're not here to ask questions. If you have questions they can wait until we get back to New York. Right now, we're under time constraints, so we need to get going on this. Boys, why don't you go with Sergeant Springs? Sergeant Springs was a member of the Army's elite 101st and served in Iraq. He'll help you learn to shoot Promised Land rifles like real army men.

Sergeant Springs' gut had expanded since his military days had ended. After two tours of duty in Iraq he went home to Oklahoma where he was born and raised, but he was unable to feel comfortable with civilian life. Suffering from war-induced nightmares, he did a variety of drugs, got into fights, and was unable to hold a regular job. Consequently, with an Army buddy, he signed up with a private military company in Iraq where he earned four times his military pay. Seven months later, after an RPG ripped through his friend's chest, Sergeant Springs opted out. Eventually, he heard about The Promised Land and he went to Gwanda where he was offered employment with The Promised Land Corporation. As Sergeant Springs was still unable to sleep peacefully, he spent most nights drinking in a Nakambu pool hall until he was so drunk he was able to stumble home and pass out.

After another night of countless Tollie's lagers, he was red-faced and bleary-eyed, dressed completely in camouflage gear. He pulled down his cap, sheltering his eyes, as he addressed the young boys.

—Fall in, soldiers!

Bridget watched Billy and Byron march toward the video crew who were setting up for the commercial. Instead of following them, as Potter expected her to do, Bridget turned to Potter with an angry look. Claudia was standing in front of a table that had been set up with a landscape blueprint of the coliseum. It showed the box seats, the trees, rocks and other physical elements. She was looking at where the cameras would eventually be placed.

—Ms. Potter, Sergeant Springs told me Billy and Byron's guns are real. That's not true, is it?

—The guns *are* real, but the bullets are rubber.

—How can you do that? How can you give young boys real guns?

—I told you from the start we were shooting a commercial for Promised Land TV. The whole point is to make it look real as possible. Fake guns will look phony and our viewers won't believe what they're seeing is real.

—Why do you actually need me here? Am I doing anything besides babysitting Billy and Byron?

—Bridget, you're not babysitting. Both of the boys like you, and you have an important role in making them feel comfortable and happy.

Potter came around the table to Bridget's side and placed her arm over her shoulder. She tried to walk Bridget toward the video set. Bridget resisted and shrugged her shoulder free.

—I told their parents a senator's daughter would be watching over them. They were happy to hear that. And anyway, once we start filming that's when your expertise comes in. You have experience directing younger people, right?

—But I'm not directing this, am I? Scott is, isn't he? And he told me to stay the hell out of his way.

They both looked over to where the boys were lying on the ground with their guns propped up before them as they listened to Sergeant Springs' instructions. Twenty yards from them, Scott, the cranky and gruff director, was talking with Piero, the director of photography, about the placement of the camera.

—Don't worry about Scott; he just talks tough. What I want you to do is make it feel real. Scott has never worked with kids. You have. Your job with Billy and Byron is to psych them up. You make sure they're really getting in to what they're doing, make it so they really want to kill. Later in the week, when we have the actual volunteers shot, I want you to work with the boys in case they feel uneasy about anything.

This shocked Bridget.

—What do you mean actually shot? You're going to shoot some of these men?

—Yes, that's the whole point in coming here. Billy and Byron will only pretend to hunt the volunteer. We will have actual retired soldiers off-camera who will do the actual shooting. That's why we need them to look and feel comfortable with The Promised Land rifles. You have to realize we're doing these men a favor—they are volunteers after all. It's just, I'm wondering emotionally, if Billy or Byron will have any problems. Personally, I think Billy will be fine, after all this wouldn't be the first time. Byron might not be as well-adjusted. What do you think?

—I think they'll both be perfectly happy. What twelve-year-old boy wouldn't want to go to another country and kill someone?

The boys were standing up now looking scared, not quite sure what

200

they were doing. They wanted to please the adults but their inner voices told them shooting other men was wrong. They looked at each other, uncertain what to do.

—Bridget, we're trying to help these men's families. If you're not for helping people you shouldn't have come over here.

—Helping them?! Bridget was almost screaming now. —You're killing them so you can get ratings for your TV shows, which you are only using to sell advertising that sells products that most people don't need!

—I was rebellious when I was young, too. We all were. You'll see when you get older it's much better to join the system than to fight it.

Bridget walked away, toward the entrance of the coliseum.

—Where are you going? Bridget, get back here!

Bridget turned to face Potter. She raised her right hand and stuck her middle finger in the air and said, —Fuck you!

□□□ 64 □□□

For transportation in Gwanda, Bridget had been given the official vehicle of The Promised Land Corporation, a GM Hummer. Although GM was no longer manufacturing them, Potter was able to locate six Hummers through a company that had bought up the last surplus vehicles. At first, Bridget refused to even get into the Hummer because she hated what the cars represented, but without any other means of getting to and fro, she had no choice but to test out and drive the four-wheel behemoth. To her surprise and chagrin, she found that she actually enjoyed driving it. She liked being up high and she liked how protected she felt inside it. But she wasn't thinking of any of these things as she raced back to Nakambu and her hotel.

Once inside her room at the Safari Park Hotel, Bridget jumped on her bed, grabbed the phone and dialed. A voice grumbled,

—Hello?

—They're planning to shoot some of the Gwandans.

—Bridget?

—Who did you think it was?

Back in New York, Gabriel turned on his bedside light.

—I was sleeping. It's the middle of the night here.

—I forgot. Tell me what you think of...

—Hold on a minute...let me just get up...

Gabriel sat up and looked to the clock, 3:13 AM.

—I'm thinking of going to talk to Upendo, he's this rebel leader who...

—I've heard about him.

—What if I went to see him and told him Potter plans to have Gwandans shot?

—He knows that.

—But only vaguely. He doesn't know the details. He's going to be at The Promised Land Coliseum tomorrow to give a speech, and the next day they're going to shoot real people.

—Says who?

Bridget pulled off her hiking boots and socks and unsnapped her pants. Feeling as dirty morally as she was physically, she wanted a shower.

—Potter, that's who. If I tell Upendo exactly where it's going to happen he could be there to stop it, or at least protest it. The other time they shot a person he only found out afterward. This way I could probably save the guys being hunted.

—I understand your concerns, but I wouldn't put too much faith in this guy Upendo.

Bridget's pants were down at her ankles, almost ready to be kicked off, when she sat back on the bed. —When did you get so cynical?

Gabriel was awake now, sitting at the edge of the bed in his underwear.

—Why don't you come home?

—And do what?

—Bridget, you don't really think you can actually stop what's going to happen, do you?

—Maybe. I don't know...

—Don't be naïve about this.

—I'm not.

—You're sounding like it. Potter and your father are in cahoots with President Mobley and General Msambee and a number of global corporations who have invested millions, hundreds of millions of dollars, to develop The Promised Land Ranch and the Town of Paradise. If you think they're going to let Upendo, or some other rebel stop them, you're wrong.

—So, we're supposed to just let them? Upendo has a lot of people over here that support him.

—If you're successful in getting Upendo to stop the hunting of Gwandans, where is that going to leave you in relation to your father? First off, his reelection bid is very much linked to him eventually shipping prisoners over to The Promised Land. If you prevent that he's going to probably lose the election. Don't think he won't blame you. Maybe he won't say as much, but he will. Do you feel strong enough to oppose your father?

—I'm not opposing him.

—Of course you are. It's exactly what you're doing. And maybe you're only doing it for your own Freudian reasons, wanting him to acknowledge you or something.

—You think it's that simple?

—Not at all. I think it's complicated, and I think he's a powerful man who has spent his life playing political games. You haven't. Don't take this the wrong way, but you're a complete greenhorn in this. And even if your father won't fight you like he would someone else in the same position, the people he's connected with will. This is their life. This isn't some college course in political science. You're not in the classroom anymore.

—You don't have to lecture me.

—I just think you need to think this through. Think about what it means to reach your objectives. And do you know what your objectives are?

—Yes, to get them not to shoot Gwandans.

—But that's my point. It's not that simple. You can't say, "Don't shoot the Gwandans with AIDS," or have some little protest and they see the light and stop their plans and that's the end of it. If they don't shoot the Gwandans, what happens? What happens to the hundreds of millions of dollars people invested in The Promised Land? What happens to your father's reelection bid? What happens to all the people working for him? What happens with Claudia Potter and the TV people? What happens to the Gwandans with AIDS? What happens if...

—All right, all right, you made your point.

—Bridget, I just want you to have your eyes open going into this, because if you don't you're going to get hurt. You're probably going to get hurt anyway. You should know that going in.

—You're five years older than me and you act like you're a hundred.

—Maybe.

—So, what should I do?

—I think you should come home and move in with me.

—No, really.

—I'm serious. Do you want to live with me?

—You bring that up now?

—You asked me what I wanted.

—No, I didn't.

—All right, you didn't. And okay maybe I'm cynical and bitter, or maybe I'm not. Maybe I'm just selfish as hell and miss you, and want you with me.

—Do you really want me to move in?

—Yes. I've got enough room here for both of us, and even if there weren't enough room I'd still want you here.

—I can't really think about this now. There's the big protest planned for tomorrow outside The Promised Land Ranch and Upendo's going to speak.
—You'd rather think about Upendo than us?
—I was hoping you would support what I'm doing.
—Bridget, don't be like that.
—I'm sorry, but I just can't stand by like everyone else. I've got to do something.
—What are you going to do?
—I don't know. I'll call you tomorrow.
—Bridget…
—Bye.

□□□ 65 □□□

With her thoughts divided between wanting to stop Claudia Potter from having AIDS sufferers killed and thoughts of returning home to Gabriel, Bridget wasn't able to fall asleep until after four in the morning. When she finally did, she slept until after ten, which would have made her late for work, had she decided to go to work. She hadn't. Bridget had decided that she wouldn't work for Claudia Potter or The Promised Land Corporation. Instead, she would try to help those who were going to be hunted. To that end, she had planned to get to The Promised Land Ranch to hear Seisko Upendo's speech. By the time she got there, Upendo had already begun. Careful not to have his listeners physically block the entrance to the coliseum, Upendo stood to the right of the entrance, on a small, crudely constructed platform.
—When the slave ships came over and stole our people we blamed the white man. But it was also the tribal chiefs who worked together with the white man; the tribal chiefs betrayed their own people. Today we are again being betrayed but it is not just the leaders. President Mobley and General Msambee are betraying their people by allowing The Promised Land Corporation to hunt and kill the most vulnerable amongst us: those suffering from the horrible disease of AIDS. But every worker who walks through these gates to help build The Promised Land Coliseum is also betraying his people. I know you need money to feed your families, but that money has blood on it. Foreign companies have been coming to Africa and stealing our natural resources for hundreds of years: they have taken our raw material—our diamonds, our copper, our coffee, our oil. They make billions and billions of dollars and leave us with ruined and unusable land and contaminated water. Now they want our most precious raw material—our people. They tell us they will save our

families from AIDS if we allow them to kill our brothers and sons and fathers. Don't believe them! Don't let yourself or your family members be killed! We all need to come together to stop The Promised Land Corporation from killing our families and destroying our country!

There were perhaps five hundred people listening to Upendo, and three cameramen and four news reporters recording the event. Bridget was one of the few whites. Being young and pretty, she stood out. One of Upendo's men made his way to her and asked who she was. After talking, the aide slipped up to the stage whispered in Upendo's ear. A few moments later he announced to the crowd,

—We even have here among us a spy from America. We have the daughter of Senator Wellington, the man responsible for wanting to kill our people.

Bridget almost fainted. She couldn't believe they didn't know she was there to protest her father's corporations. Feeling shamed and embarrassed, she made her way to the side of the platform, where she spoke to one of Upendo's top men. She told him that she supported Upendo and would like to say so publicly, if allowed. They didn't trust her at first, but she pleaded and the conviction in her voice made them change their mind. Upendo allowed her to walk to the stage and stand next to him. They talked for a few minutes and Bridget was able to convince the African leader of her belief in his cause. Consequently, he handed her the microphone and Bridget began speaking.

□□□ **66** □□□

Within an hour of Bridget's speech, news agencies around the world had picked up the story. By the time she got back to the hotel later that day, ten messages had been left from her father. Not realizing why he was calling so urgently, she feared something horrible had happened at home. Bridget rushed up to her room to place the call.

—Hello.

—Dad, it's Bridget. What happened? Is everything all right?

He shouted into the phone.

—What happened?! You were on television with the goddamn rebel leader! How do you think it makes me look, my own daughter protesting my ranch and my company?

—You're worried about how you look? What about the people who are going to be killed?

—Don't get wise with me, Bridget. Do you want me to have someone send you home?

—Send me home?

—That's right. You're a foreigner. General Msambee found out about you and was furious. He couldn't believe you were my daughter. He said if you're seen speaking with Upendo again, they're going to revoke your visa and send you home.

—Let them. I'll have a good story to tell the press when I get back to New York.

—You stay away from him! Do you understand me?

Click. Bridget hung up the phone.

—Damn her.

Realizing the futility of calling her back, Senator Wellington quickly dialed his last hope, catching him at home.

—Hello.

—Gabriel, it's Senator Wellington. Are you aware of what Bridget is doing?

—With Claudia Potter?

—No, with Upendo and the protestors. Do you know about her protests?

—Vaguely.

—I want you to go over there and bring her home. She won't listen to me, and I don't want her to get into any trouble.

—I think you need to trust her and let her do what she needs to do.

—Damn it, Gabriel! This isn't fun and games! This whole thing could turn deadly serious. She could find herself in jail or worse. They're playing for keeps over there. Suppose some kind of violence erupts? Are you so damn naïve to think something like that couldn't happen? That the police couldn't, or wouldn't, crack down on the protestors? That someone might get shot and killed? And that someone might be Bridget?

—I'll talk to her.

—I don't want you to talk to her! I want you to go over there and bring her home!

—Is that an order?

—I'd do it, but she won't listen to me. It'll only make things worse. If you love her and are concerned about her safety, and you'd better be, you'll go over there and bring her home.

—I'll go, Senator, but I'm not promising anything. If I feel it's too dangerous for her, I'll try to persuade her to come home. But the decision is hers.

—You're not much of a man, are you?

—What's that supposed to mean?

—It means that when I was growing up, a man was a man. He did what he was supposed to do, and a woman listened.

—And if she didn't, what would you do? Slap her around? Or would

206

you keep her up in a house in Bedford and make it so she wouldn't leave?

—Don't you wise off to me! I've got a goddamn daughter who I don't want to see hurt. Now, get your ass over there and bring her back.

After Connor Gazelle's constant talks of E-Floods at college campuses, many students and many bloggers began to talk seriously about becoming E-warriors. They went to Gazelle's website, www.GazelleForSenate.org and voted on which corporation they felt should be the first targeted. When the votes were tallied, HexxonMoble was the dubious winner. Connor wrote on his website: "During the Iraq War, in a three year period, HexxonMoble has made over one hundred billion dollars profit. One hundred billion dollars profit from the blood of patriotic soldiers and innocent civilians. This is one of the reasons government officials, big business leaders, defense contractors, and construction firms did not want the war to end—it was just too damn profitable. It was difficult enough to get a war going in the first place, so once it was up and running, the last thing the masters of war wanted was to see it end."

August 29th was selected as the date of the E-Flood. This day was chosen in memory of the victims of Hurricane Katrina and the flooding of New Orleans. The e-mail's subject line was: Blood Money. Inside the email was the message: "From your greed flows a river of blood. For every dollar you put in the bank there is an eye, an ear, a hand, an arm, a leg, a body buried in the sand." When the levee of e-mails broke, more than a million emails flooded HexxonMoble's world headquarters outside of Dallas, Texas, and almost as many text messages flooded personal and work phones. Within three hours, electronic communications at the headquarters had to be shut down. For two days, HexxonMoble was unable to contact the outside world electronically. To respond to this emergency, new and secret e-mail accounts were setup for the top executives. But unbeknownst to the executives, one of the IT people responsible for setting up the accounts was sympathetic to the E-Flooders. He leaked the new e-mail addresses to Gazelle who posted the e-mail addresses on his website. This set off another E-Flood.

These actions caught the attention of the press and made Gazelle a hero to many on the political left. HexxonMoble, the world's most profitable corporation, wasn't about to allow some actor and would-be politician threaten their bottom line. Three days after the E-Flood, Connor Gazelle was arrested and taken down to the Tombs in lower

Manhattan. While he was waiting to be bailed out, his apartment was raided and ransacked. His computers disappeared and anything of value—books, photos, even dishes and glassware—were thrown to the floor in an effort to break or destroy them. His desk and dresser drawers were opened and the contents were spilled to the floor where they were kicked and stepped upon. His media room was virtually destroyed. DVDs and CDs were opened up and thrown on to the floor, the cases broken, stepped on, and crushed. Even his 16mm and 35mm prints had been taken from their film canisters. The films were opened up and the contents pulled out and thrown all over the floor as casually as confetti.

HexxonMoble lawyers also contacted the Department of Homeland Security (DHS) and had Gazelle labeled a "potential terrorist." This allowed for his cell phone, home phone, and offices phones to be tapped and monitored. Additionally, DHS had Gazelle followed day and night. This wasn't done discreetly. They wanted Gazelle to know he was being watched and followed. After all, HexxonMoble was not the only corporation concerned with E-Floods. Many other large corporations immediately contacted various members of Congress and members of the Executive branch, to make sure something was done to stop future E-Floods.

The official charge against Gazelle was "Incitement to Vandalism," the vandalism being the willful and deliberate attack on HexxonMoble's "virtual" property—their website and e-mail accounts. There was also political pressure put on Connor's jailers to make sure he wasn't bailed out quickly. They wanted him to spend the night in jail, a night in a crowded holding pen filled with drunks, derelicts, career criminals, and the mentally retarded. Connor was too scared to even try to sleep. After yelling for his lawyer one too many times, he was told by one of the bigger and meaner regulars, "You scream one more time, motherfucker, and you're going to have my black dick up your white ass. Got that?" This quieted Connor for the rest of his stay.

After being informed of Connor's arrest by Bob Hevens, Kim booked the next flight back from Los Angeles where she'd been working on a film. She was waiting for him when he was finally bailed out the following afternoon. When they returned to the apartment, it looked like teenage crackheads had been living there for a month. The last and perhaps most painful desecration of his property was to his Rothko painting. It was easily worth tens of millions of dollars. The smell of urine led him to a puddle of piss underneath the painting. Connor looked at the canvas and was certain someone had pissed all over it. Connor turned to Kim.

—I guess I was pretty naïve, wasn't I?

—But you showed E-Floods can be effective.

—But at what price? Look at this place. This is just the beginning. I have no desire to be a martyr. I'm too old for that. And you'd better be careful too, you can be sure they are watching you.

The phone rang. Kim turned to Connor.

—Should I get that?

—No, I'll get it. It's probably the press. Hello.

—Connor Gazelle?

—Yes.

—My name is Father Peter, I'm calling from St. Patrick's Cathedral.

—Father Peter? How can I help you?

—Cardinal O'Farrell would like to meet with you.

—With me? Why? This isn't some setup, is it? I've got enough problems right now as it is.

—This isn't a setup. Many members of his parish have told the Cardinal they do not like what Senator Wellington is saying about executing criminals, and they also do not like Peter Morgan's push to make pornography a staple of primetime television. Many Catholics would like to endorse you, but they are leery because of your atheism. If you could at least show that you think about God they would be more willing to vote for you.

—I appreciate the call, but I think it would be a mistake to start talking about religion again. I don't want to run as a religious or non-religious candidate. If I met with Cardinal O'Farrell that will bring up the whole religious controversy again. I want to prevent that.

—Don't you think if you two met it would send a strong message to voters?

—As I said, I don't want to make my candidacy about religion. Please explain to Cardinal O'Farrell my position. I'm sure he will understand.

—Is there any way I can persuade you to meet with the Cardinal?

—I'm afraid there isn't.

—Well, okay. Good-bye.

—Bye.

As Connor was speaking to Father Peter, Kim had picked up Connor's statue of Ganesha, which had been knocked to the floor and broken into three pieces. She places the pieces back on its pedestal and turned to him.

—Maybe it's not a bad idea to meet with Cardinal O'Farrell. You'd probably pick up a lot of votes that way.

—Frankly, the timing is a little suspect, if you ask me. I get arrested and suddenly I get a call from the Catholic Church? They probably think it's a perfect time for me to renounce my atheism. Well, that's not going to happen.

68

Two days after speaking with Senator Wellington, Gabriel Patrick landed at Mobley International Airport at 7:30 AM. As he stepped past customs, a half dozen young kids offered to find him a taxi. Gabriel felt wealthy handing the shortest boy a Gwandan five-dollar bill. Though it was only equivalent to about fifty US cents, it was enough for the boy, perhaps nine, to eagerly and with great enthusiasm wheel Gabriel's bag from baggage claim to the taxi pickup. A pat on the boy's head and Gabriel was in the back seat of the car and moving into traffic.
—Morning, sir. Where to?
—The Safari Park Hotel.
—Very good. Are you with the press?
Gabriel's unshaven and rumpled appearance made this as good a guess as any.
—No, why?
—I thought you might be here covering what happened out at The Promised Land Ranch.
—No. What happened? Were there more protests?
—Yesterday, the police got into a fight with some of the protestors. Killed one of them.
—Someone was killed?
—One of the Gwandans For Independence rebels. Police shot him.
—*Him?* So it was a man, not a woman, right?
—Yeah, a man. But they kidnapped a woman. It was on the radio. The senator from the United States, his daughter. They said they're going to kill her.
—Bridget?
—Don't know her name. Seisko Upendo's men, the Gwandans For Independence, kidnapped her.
—Fuck! Get me to the hotel as quickly as possible.

69

When Gabriel arrived at the Safari Park Hotel, the desk clerk told him it was urgent he call Senator Wellington at home. In his room, Gabriel dropped his bag on the floor and went to the phone. He immediately recognized the voice that picked up.
—Wellington residence.
—Keno, it's Gabriel. What happened?

—Upendo and the Gwandans For Independence are holding Bridget ransom for fifty million dollars worth of AIDS drugs.

From inside the television room came a deep voice.

—Keno, who's that?

—It's Gabriel.

Wellington came in the kitchen with a Cutty Sark and soda—his third—and snatched the phone from Keno's hand. He had been with Candace in the television room, trying not to panic while they listened to CNN for any scrap of news.

—If you didn't waste your goddamn time getting over there, Gabriel, this wouldn't have happened!

— I just got here, Senator. How was I supposed to stop her kidnapping? Did you call President Mobley to see what he can do?

—Of course I called him! He doesn't know where the hell she is! That's why I need you, and I don't want you to screw this up!

—You're not coming over here?

—I've got to try to raise the ransom money, won't be able to do that from Africa. If I can get over there, I will. In the meantime, you try to find out where the hell she is. Don't trust anyone. You call me as soon as you find out anything, anything at all.

—Should I talk to Mobley or Msambee, tell them you sent me?

—No, forget about them. I don't trust them either. Steve Lowell is dealing with them in an official capacity. See what you can find out behind the scenes. Keno?

He was standing outside the television room, peering in on Candace who was doing her best to prevent a nervous breakdown.

—What's the kid's name, the waiter's name that you know? Do you have a phone number or an address that Gabriel can use to contact him?

—At home. I have his number at home. I don't have it with me.

—Well, get going. Get Charles to drive you home and get Gabriel that number.

—Yes, sir.

As soon as Keno exited, Wellington spoke back into the phone, — Gabriel, Keno will get you the name of someone who lives in the city there. Contact him—see if he knows anything. Talk to people—see what you can find out. You're at the Safari Park, right? I'll have Keno call you as soon as he gets home. Let me go, I've got another call.

—Bye.

Wellington pushed the call waiting button,

—Hello.

—Senator, it's Bill Schmegman.

—Bill, thanks for getting back to me. I realize that fifty million dollars

211

worth of AIDS drugs is a vast sum to anyone.

—Senator, I'd love to help you on this, and I'm going to recommend to the board...

Wellington walked into the dining room, trying to shield Candace from hearing any information that he thought would cause her further stress.

—Hey, Bill, don't start shitting on me with this! I don't want you to recommend anything! I want you to tell your board members that you have to do this. That you have no choice not to do this! That you...

—It's not that simple...

—Give me a list of your board members. I'll call them right now.

—I can't give you their...

—Goddamn it, Bill! We're talking about my daughter's life! If I don't get the names from you, I'll get them from Asher.

—If you'd let me finish, I was going to say that I'm not supposed to give out the private phone numbers of board members, but I'm doing it for you. I just sent you an e-mail with their numbers. Undoubtedly, some of them won't want to face this issue, so I prefer if you didn't let them know I gave you their phone number.

—I won't.

—One other thing, are you aware that Claudia Potter called me from Gwanda and told me not to release the AIDS drugs to you or to the rebels?

—That goddamn cunt!

Wellington hung up and called his mistress who was treating herself to an early morning massage at spa at the Safari Park Hotel. When her cell phone rang, the masseuse picked it up and handed it off.

—Hello.

—Claudia, did you tell Bill Schmegman not to give AIDS drugs to Upendo?

—Richard, Bill's not going to give you the drugs anyway. I hope you realize that. Because if they do, they know that every HIV positive homosexual and drug addict will start kidnapping people, and where will they be?

—I don't give a damn about other people right now!

—I know, that's why I'm doing this. It's important to not lose focus. I have no problem with giving the drugs to Upendo and his people, but let's be smart about it. We don't want this to happen again. And Richard, you have to realize that this is tremendous publicity, publicity we couldn't buy, and not just for The Promised Land, for your reelection as well.

—You disgust me!

The phone line went dead in Potter's hand.

70

Over at 740 Park Avenue, Asher Mitchell sat on one of two identical Chippendale chairs, relaxing in his midnight blue silk smoking jacket and slippers. He sipped a Remy Martin as he leafed through Sotheby's Important American Paintings, Drawings, and Sculpture catalogue. His wife had left a yellow sticky note with a question mark on a page with a Maurice Prendergast watercolor. Estimated at between one hundred and one hundred fifty thousand dollars, she felt it was undervalued and would look perfect in their library. Mitchell began to read the description when a house phone interrupted him. He picked it up from the side table.

—Hello.

—Asher, it's Bill Schmegman. I just got off the phone with Wellington.

The catalogue was closed and placed on the other Chippendale chair on the opposite side of the table. With a credit card sized remote, Asher lowered the volume on the Chopin playing on the Bose music system.

—And?

—Obviously we can't give away fifty million dollars worth of product.

Mitchell stood and walked across the hardwood floor of the living room and took a closer look at the George Innes Hudson Valley landscape hanging above the inlaid cherry bombe chest-of-drawers. The maid must have touched it while dusting because it was slightly off-center. He adjusted it and went to the window to look down on Park Avenue as he listened.

—Did you tell him that?

—Of course not, I'm not that stupid. I'm stalling for time.

—That's not going to work.

—I know; that's why I'm calling you. You're his lawyer, and the husband of a board member.

That reminded him. Asher's boyfriend, the gallery owner, had for years been trying to get Asher to take a greater appreciation in contemporary art. When his wife, who visited Christie's and Sotheby's almost weekly, mentioned the American paintings exhibit currently on view, he had asked her to pick up the latest contemporary art catalogue. Asher looked around the room for it, and there it was atop the coffee table.

—Bill, if you don't do something, there's a good chance they'll kill Wellington's daughter.

—I'm aware of that. If that happens and we're blamed we'll have a public relations nightmare on our hands, and our stock will be in the toilet. Is there any chance you can talk to him, Asher? Reason with him?

—What about the other pharmaceutical companies? Can't you work together? You know the CEOs of the other companies, don't you? Give them a call; see if they can help you.

—I have. None of them have returned my phone calls. They're ducking Wellington, and they're going to duck anyone who tries to force their hand.

—What do you want me to do, Bill?

—I'm not opposed to doing something, but fifty million dollars worth is out of the question. I just don't want to have this come back and bite us in the ass. If anything happens to his daughter, Wellington will try to fuck us. There's been talk in the past about Congress forcing pharmaceutical companies to produce generic AIDS drugs. If that happens, we'll be out hundreds of millions, maybe even billions. We need to find a way to at least make it look like we're doing everything we can.

Asher Mitchell sat down on the sofa and began to flip through the Sotheby's catalogue.

—Bill, I don't really want to have to do your thinking for you on this one.

—I'm not asking you to. But I am asking for your help, and I would, of course, compensate you.

—How much?

—How much would you want, Asher?

—I don't think ten percent is out of the question.

—Ten percent of what? Of the fifty million? That's five million dollars. You're crazy.

—Then go talk to him, Bill. See what he does. See if...

—If you can get us out of shipping the antiviral drugs, and making sure Wellington won't enact legislation that will force us to create generic AIDS drugs, I might be able to persuade the board to go as high as, say, half a million.

Asher Mitchell closed the catalogue and went back to the end table for his Remy Martin.

—Bill, don't nickel and dime me on this. I could be saving you hundreds of millions of dollars.

—I could go possibly as high as one million, but that would be contingent on you preventing Wellington from enacting legislation in the future. That's key. Otherwise it's not worth it.

—I can't predict the future.

—I'm not asking you to predict, I'm asking you to prevent.

Mitchell rolled the mahogany-colored liquid in the snifter before breathing it in through his nostrils. Upon reflection, he spoke.

—I don't want this to be traceable. You can set it up so that it goes to my wife. End of the year bonus or something.

—All right, Asher, just keep Wellington out of my hair because he's...

—I'll try. But let me go, I've got another call. Goodbye. Hello.

—Hi Asher, it's Claudia.

He put his drink down.

—Claudia? What the hell is wrong with you? You told Bill Schmegman not to release the drugs?

—Come on, Asher, you know Merck isn't going to release fifty million dollars worth of AIDS drugs.

—Maybe not, but do you think Wellington wants to hear that you're trying to prevent it?

Wellington's phone call forced Potter to conclude her massage early than desired. She was now strolling through the hotel lobby toward the elevator.

—Bridget's going to be all right, Asher. Upendo's smart enough not to kill a senator's daughter.

An elderly couple, who had just returned from breakfast and were waiting for the ride upward, turned disdainfully toward Potter. Realizing she might lose reception on the elevator, Potter stared back before returning to a soft cushion chair in the lobby to complete her call.

—That's great. We'll all go out for margaritas until he's ready to release her.

—Don't be cynical, Asher. The thing is, and I don't want to seem callous here, but this is actually a good thing. Or it can be. Once the kidnappers are caught they could be our first volunteers. It'll show how The Promised Land takes care of business. And it will give us a hell of a rating.

—Is that all you're thinking about?

—If Bridget could get shot, slightly wounded, nothing life-threatening, but something that draws blood. Maybe if her arm got cut or something like that. If we could find a way to get that on camera, that would be perfect.

—You should be thinking about how to get Bridget out of there safe and sound.

—I am, but that doesn't mean I have to lose sight of our main focus.

—Good-bye, Claudia.

—Don't be like that, Asher, It's not every day that a senator's daughter gets kidnapped. I want to beat the networks at this. If we do, it will be a real coup for VBS. These are the kinds of stories that can really make a network's reputation and a person's career.

—Goodbye, Claudia.

□□□ 71 □□□

Wellington's driver Charles raced Keno from the Wellington mansion back to his apartment on West One Hundred Third Street in forty minutes. Once Gabriel received Manlea's number, he dialed it a half dozen times in ten minutes without getting any answer. Gabriel quickly left the hotel and jumped into a cab to take him to the Ibis Grill. When Gabriel walked into the restaurant, he saw a man taking dining room chairs down from dining room tables and putting them on what looked like a freshly mopped floor. Gabriel guessed that this might be Manlea. He was right. With his AIDS showing its first signs, the general manager, who liked Manlea but didn't want him interacting with customers as a waiter, instead of firing him allowed him to stay on as the morning porter. Gabriel walked up to the man.

—Hi. Are you Manlea?

—Who are you?

—My name is Gabriel Patrick. I'm from New York. Keno Ahmaden said he might be able to help.

—Hi.

They shook hands.

—Keno's a good person. I can't say the same about Senator Wellington.

—Well, I'm here because of his daughter, Bridget.

—The kidnapping.

—Yes. Is there anything you could tell me about the Gwandans For Independence? Anything that might help get Bridget free? Do you have idea where they're hiding her? I was hoping you could tell me some things about President Mobley and General Msambee.

—Like what? I don't even know if Mobley is talking with Msambee.

—What do you mean?

—Some people are saying that even before the kidnapping, Upendo had been meeting secretly with General Msambee, and they might be planning something.

—What would they be planning?

—I don't know. Not too many people over here like The Promised Land Corporation. Maybe Msambee realizes that if he wants to stay in power he might have better chances with Upendo than with President Mobley.

—What do you think the chances are of Upendo letting Bridget go free?

216

—Would you? She's a big prize, isn't she?

—Do you think he's planning to kill her?

—I don't mean to sound unsympathetic, but why else would he have kidnapped her? The chances of Upendo getting fifty million dollars worth of AIDS drugs are almost nonexistent. If he kills Bridget there's going to be trouble, isn't there? Maybe that's exactly what he wants. Destabilizing the government, and hoping for some kind of coup d'état or revolution, is probably the only way he's going to stop people from being hunted, isn't it?

□□□ 72 □□□

When he returned to his hotel, Gabriel's key card wouldn't let him back into his room. Angered, he went to the front desk where the clerk stood and looked down on the lower counter where he had surreptitiously hid a copy of a local newspaper, the *East African Standard*, which he wasn't supposed to be reading while at work.

—Excuse me...

The clerk, lost in the lead story about Bridget Wellington, looked up at Gabriel.

—What the hell's going on here? I went out for an hour. I come back, go up to my room, 309, put my keycard in the door and it won't open.

—Let me check that for you...

The clerk went over to the computer and pressed the appropriate keys.

—Hmmm...I'm showing that room as unoccupied.

—It's my room. Why would it be unoccupied? I haven't left.

A tall, balding man in his late fifties, stepped out from the inner office. The clerk quickly closed the newspaper.

—Excuse me, you're Mr. Patrick, correct?

—Yes, why?

—I'm the manager. We upgraded you to a two-bedroom suite, room 702.

The manager took over at the computer. He punched in the appropriate numbers to encode a new key-card for Gabriel's room and handed the card across the counter.

—I hope it's not a problem. Ms. Potter said it would be okay.

—Ms. Potter?

Gabriel looked completely confused.

—Claudia Potter from VBS television. She said they needed a bigger room for the lights and cameras.

Now Gabriel was gravely concerned.

—Lights and cameras? Did something happen to Bridget?

Before getting an answer he rushed for the elevator.

□□□ 73 □□□

Up on the seventh floor, Gabriel sprinted down the hallway past video equipment road cases and pushed through the partially opened suite door. In the living room, two chairs had been set up for an interview. A cameraman was placing a video camera on its tripod.

—Where's Claudia Potter!

—Who are you?

—Is Claudia Potter here or not?

—Dude, I don't mean to be rude, but would you mind waiting outside until I get her?

—Where the fuck is she?!

Claudia Potter stepped out of the bedroom with a big smile and extended her hand as she approached Gabriel.

—Hi, Gabriel. I'm Claudia Potter.

Gabriel panicked and yelled,

—IS BRIDGET ALL RIGHT?!

—Yes, at least as far as I know.

This calmed him, but also added to his confusion.

—Then what are you doing here?

—We'd like to interview you.

—Me? Why?

Two other women, whose hair was dyed blonde like Potter's, stepped out of the bedroom. One was dressed more professionally, that was Perky Perkins, the other one, Suzy Kasmir, slightly more casual, held a pen and a pad. Potter continued.

—Because it's a good story, compelling. A senator's daughter doesn't get kidnapped every day, and for her boyfriend to come to Africa and rescue her, that's quite exciting.

Potter turned to the other women who were now smiling and nodding in sync.

—I'm sure you know Perky Perkins from *Tonight's Entertainment!*

—No, I don't.

A bejeweled hand was extended. Gabriel didn't reach to greet it.

—And this is Suzy Kasmir.

Not wanting to be rebuffed with her own handshake, Suzy gave a short little wave.

—Hi, Gabriel.

—Suzy's from *People* magazine.

—You didn't tell me he was so cute. I'd love him for the cover without his shirt.

A desirous Potter gushed,

—Gabriel, would you be willing to take your shirt off if we could get you the cover of *People*?

Gabriel looked at them like they were nuts. By now the cameraman had taken the camera off the tripod, placed it on his shoulder and was filming Gabriel, who couldn't quite comprehend why he would be doing so. Potter picked up on this.

—It's okay, he's not with *People,* he's just part of the documentary team.

—What documentary team?

—We want to document Bridget's rescue for a separate broadcast. It'll be tremendously exciting. The camera crew will follow you around until you save her. You'll be a real hero.

Gabriel pivoted toward the door and exited.

Flustered, Potter turned to her writer,

—Well, don't just stand there, go after him!

Suzy skipped out of the room and ran down the hallway, calling out,

—Gabriel, are you and Bridget engaged? Is she the best lover you ever had? ...Gabriel?

Potter's assistant, Sarah, stood timidly by the bedroom door holding the telephone.

—Ms. Potter, Richie Wellington's still on the phone. Should I tell him you'll call him back or...

—No, I'll take it.

Potter walked over, took the phone, went into the bedroom and sat down on the bed.

—Hi, Richie, sorry about that. Gabriel Patrick was here. Have you met him?

—No.

—Well, that's okay. We don't really need a scene when you two meet.

—Ms. Potter, I haven't agreed to write anything yet.

—I realize that. But you do know that we can do the movie without you, don't you?

—Yeah, but like she's my sister. I know her better than anyone.

—That's exactly why I want you to do the deal with VBS. But we will need exclusive rights.

—When would I get the money?

—Why don't we do this, I'll have one of my associates fly out to Los Angeles and meet with you. Would that be okay?

—I guess.

—Good. I'll have him bring one of my top writers.

—Writers? I thought I was writing the screenplay. Didn't you say I was the writer?

—Yes, that's why we're hiring you, but film is a collaborative art form, the more writers you have the better it is.

—But what am I doing if you have other writers?

—You'll be able to give us information on Bridget, that's very important, and we'll be able to attach your name to the movie. You'd like that, wouldn't you?

□□□ 74 □□□

Peter Morgan lived in Deer Park, Long Island and represented New York 4th Congressional District. He set up his campaign headquarters in Babylon, a short drive away from his home. Since his involvement with Roger Zales and POX television, however, he wasn't spending much time on Long Island. More often than not, he was in Manhattan. To cut down on his commuting time back to Long Island or up to his senate office in Albany, Morgan allowed Zales to lease him a suite at the Waldorf Astoria Hotel. Technically, it was against campaign laws to accept such a gift, but Morgan skirted the law by not having the suite under his name. The suite was leased to a POX employee and Morgan was given the room key.

Zackary Taylor had grown increasingly distressed by Morgan's cozy relationship with Zales. When he found out about the apartment, he felt it was time to straighten Morgan out and get him to distance himself from POX and his stance on pornography. In addition to being infuriated by Morgan's moral laxity, Taylor have been given an advance copy of *The New York Times* Sunday Magazine cover story on Peter Morgan. Since it was nearly impossible to get Morgan to come out to his own campaign headquarters, Taylor went to see Morgan at the Waldorf. After knocking and being let in, Taylor angrily waved the magazine in Morgan's face and threw it down on the living room coffee table.

—Do you know about this?

Morgan looked at the magazine where he was photographed with a provocatively posed Cassidy Canyons. The title of the article was: *"Is This the Future of Politics?"*

—I was going to offer you a drink, Zack, but I guess you're not here to be sociable.

—No, I'm not.

Morgan looked back down at the article and over to Taylor.

—I'm guessing the article isn't flattering.

—No, it's not. It's about how POX is using you to make pornography more mainstream with a new cable channel they're calling POX PORN. Do you know about this new channel?

—Yes. A little.

— A little? Let me make sure you know what kind of shows they want.

Taylor opened up the magazine, found the article on Morgan and read.

—*"Use Your Head to Give Good Head and Get College Credit, Too!"* *"Cunnilingus Techniques and Tongue Exercises for Men."* *"Discovering and Uncovering the Clitoris."* These are the type of television shows you want to be associated with?

—Zack, I'm looking to the future. Roger has a much better understanding of where we're going to be in five or ten years than you do. I want to be part of the future, not part of the past.

—Did you think about the abuse and violence toward women because of pornography? Did you talk about child abuse and pedophiles?

The suite was large enough for a living area with a couch and chairs, and there was also a dining area where a laptop was opened. Morgan went over to it and closed the cover. He did not want Zackary Taylor to see the online article on WebMD.com he'd been reading.

—Don't preach morals to me. You job is to get me coverage, right? That's what a campaign manager is supposed to do. Right now, Roger is doing a better job than you are.

—Did he get you the *New York Times* article? Because they're saying Gazelle is the most trustworthy candidate because he's talking about the issues, healthcare and education and taxes and…

—I don't give a damn about *The New York Times*.

A ringing cell phone caught Morgan's attention.

—Excuse me. He quickly rushed to the dining room table and picked it up.

—Hello.

—Peter, it's Roger Zales. What's so urgent you left me eleven messages?

—Hold on.

Morgan turned to his campaign manager.

—Excuse me for a moment.

Peter Morgan went into the bedroom and closed the door behind him.

—Roger, I got a present from Cassidy Canyons. Can you guess what it is?

—No. What?

—Herpes! She gave me herpes.

There was silence on the other end of the phone.

—Did you hear what I said, Roger?

—Yes. I'm sorry to hear that.

—I bet you are. You fuck! She said you gave it to her!

—Well…um…I might have.

—Goddamn it, Roger! Couldn't you have told me you were screwing Cassidy and to stay away from her?

—I didn't know you were interested in her.

—Don't give me that crap. You've seen her. Anyone with a cock is interested in her.

—But you're married.

—So are you. I mean, what the fuck were you thinking?

—Watch your language, Peter.

—How do you expect me to react?

—You deal with it and we move on. I'm not too happy about having herpes either, but some little filly gave it to me at the last Republican National Convention, and I've had to deal with it.

—Roger, if I didn't think I had a future with you and Hubert I would have come over there and kicked your ass.

—I didn't tell you to sleep with Cassidy. And if you don't think we can find someone to replace you in five minutes, you're wrong.

—Yeah? Then replace me.

—Peter, do you really want to do this? Do you really want to challenge me? Because I'm sure you realize you're not the only politician on my payroll, and that New York isn't the only senate race we're involved in.

Morgan considered his options for a few brief moments.

—All right, fuck it. Let's just drop it and move on. But I want you to get rid of Cassidy Canyons.

—I can't.

—Why the hell not?

—Well, when she told me I had infected her, I felt horrible. I told her I'd make it up to her. And I have, or I will. She's going to be the public face of POX PORN.

Zackary Taylor, who had been listening outside the door, had heard enough. He tapped once on the door and entered. Morgan turned toward him as Taylor spoke.

—Let me talk to Roger.

—Why?

—Because if he and I don't come to an understanding I'll make sure the Democratic Party stops supporting you.

Morgan spoke back into the phone.

—Roger, I'm with Zack Taylor. He'd like to talk to you.

—Put him on.

Morgan handed off the phone.

—Roger, I think it's about time we sat down and talked, don't you?

—About what?

—You may be able to use Morgan to push your programs of pornography, but I'll be damned if I'll let you use the Democratic Party to do so.

—Is that right?

—Yeah, that's right.

—Put Peter back on the phone, please.

—I want to know when we can meet.

—I heard what you said. Now put Peter back on the phone.

Zackary Taylor thought about this for a moment before handing the phone to Morgan.

—Roger?

—Peter. I want you to fire Taylor. And I want you to do it now.

—Fire him? Really?

—I'm not going to be told what to do by some lowly campaign manager. Through POX and with my own personal contributions, I've given millions of dollars to the both the Democrats and the Republicans. Who does Zackary Taylor thinks he is? I don't want to hear from you again until Taylor's fired. Got that?

—Um....yeah, I'll take care of it.

Morgan hung up and looked to Taylor.

—I heard. I'll save you the trouble, Peter. I quit. It's about time I got away from filth like you and Roger.

—Zack, I'm sorry, but you brought this on yourself. Did you really think you could tell Roger Zales what to do?

People

BRIDGET WELLINGTON'S HUNKY HERO!
By Suzy Kasmir

Senator Richard Wellington's daughter, Bridget, is being held by armed and dangerous revolutionary rebels who have vowed to slaughter anyone who stands in their way. But at least one man knows not the meaning of fear. Gabriel Patrick, one of America's sexiest bachelors, has traveled to the darkest heart of Africa to bring Bridget Wellington back or die trying. Mr. Patrick, a broad-shouldered six-footer with chestnut hair and a winning smile beneath penetrating sky-blue eyes plays piano and paints when not busy pursuing his law career. This heartthrob and former gridiron star fell for the exquisite Ms. Wellington after seeing the statuesque beauty's production of Tennessee Williams' "Long Day's Journey Into Night." Though no wedding date has been set, sources speculate that the couple is planning a lavish...

—Candace, do you really need to read that?

In the Wellington's living room, Candace, seated on the divan, threw the magazine down and stood up. —What am I supposed to be doing? You don't want me to read anything. You don't want me to watch anything on TV. You don't want to go over there. You don't...
—What are you going to do over there?
—More than I'm doing here.

Candace walked to the double doors at the far end of the living room and stepped out to the patio and pool area. Wellington went after her, saying as he stepped on the cement of the patio,

224

—You go over there and there's a good chance they'll try to kidnap you.

—No one's going to kidnap me.

—You don't know that! I'm having enough trouble raising their demands here. It'll be a hell of a lot more difficult over there.

Beyond the pool, which was now covered with a blue tarp, a stone wall corralled the neatly trimmed lawn. Beyond it, there were acres of untamed woods that had started to change color due to the fall weather and the cool October air. There was not another home in sight; nonetheless, Candace felt trapped by the wall and turned from it to angrily face her husband.

—If the drug company won't give you the AIDS medicine, why don't you just raise money and buy the drugs?

—Raise fifty million dollars?

—If they give you millions for your reelection, why won't they give it to you for this?

—It's illegal. You can't use the money for...

—They're threatening to kill Bridget and suddenly you're all law-abiding?

—I'm always law-abiding.

—Spare me. What if the drug companies don't give you the drugs?

Wellington walked back to the house.

—They will.

—But if they don't, what are we going to do?

The senator stopped at the entrance to the living room.

—Candace, the last thing I need right now is your pessimism. You'd think you could give me some support.

—What about you giving me some support? I turn the TV on and you tell me to turn it off. I pick up a magazine, and you tell me to put it down. Honestly, Richard, what am I supposed to do?

Wellington's ringing cell phone interrupted them. He quickly pulled it from his pants pocket.

—Hello.

—Senator, it's Gabriel.

—Did you find anything out?

Wellington mouthed the word "Gabriel" to Candace as they had been desperately awaiting his call.

—I need you to set up a meeting for me with President Mobley. And I'll also need Claudia Potter's number.

—Why? What's your plan?

—It's best that you don't know.

—Why?

—Senator, I'm not going to take a chance of someone finding out.

Maybe my hotel phone is bugged, I don't know. I'm not going to chance Bridget's life.

—Can you tell me anything about it?

—The Gwandans For Independence plan to assassinate President Mobley.

—Who told you that?

—I found some things out. I've been breaking my ass over here, and I'm not going to get into details over the phone. Can you get me a meeting with President Mobley or not?

—I'll set it up.

—Senator, make sure you don't tell him anything. Don't mention what I just told you.

—Why not?

—Just don't. You just got to trust me on this.

—All right, but you'd better not screw up. It's my daughter's life we're talking about.

—Yeah, and the woman I love.

□□□ 76 □□□

The following afternoon Gabriel stood waiting in the Marble Room of the Presidential Palace awaiting President Mobley. Most of what he could see of the palace was marble. Why this room had been given this particular title eluded him. Twenty minutes later, President Mobley stepped in, closing the door quietly behind him. Gabriel stood to greet him. A quick handshake and both men were seated on chairs in front of an opulent but unused and seemingly unneeded fireplace.

—I appreciate you taking the time to see me, President Mobley.

—Senator Wellington said it was extremely urgent.

—It is, so I'll make this as brief as possible. First off, we at The Promised Land Corporation want to thank you for all you've done for us. If you think The Promised Land Corporation can do anything to help stop the assassination do not hesitate to ask for our help.

A puzzled expression mapped the president's face.

—What assassination?

—Yours. That's why I want to personally thank you for granting me this brief interview. It's not often a speechwriter gets to meet the person for whom he has to write an obituary. Is there anything particular you would like Senator Wellington to say at your funeral?

—My funeral? Who told you that there are plans to assassinate me?

—Obviously, you're aware of the Gwandans For Independence plan to assassinate you.

—No. Why would they want to kill me? What have I done? I've tried to help my country.

—By allowing AIDS sufferers to be hunted and killed?

—General Msambee was in charge of most of that.

As Gabriel hadn't brought a briefcase to Africa with him, he had to buy a new one prior to his appointment. From it he had taken a clean white notepad and pen. He placed the pad on his knee and looked solemnly at the president.

—Unfortunately, the Gwandan people believe the ultimate responsibility resides with you.

—They're mistaken.

—Hmmmn.

—What?

Mobley watched Gabriel write NOT RESPONSIBLE on the pad.

—I'm just thinking how to work that into the speech, how it was not your responsibility to help the people of your country. Perhaps it would be better not to mention AIDS at all and just focus in on the good things you've done in the...how long has it been since you became dictator?

—I'm not a dictator.

Gabriel wrote NOT A DICTATOR in large letters so that President Mobley couldn't miss them.

—My mistake. I was told there had never been an election in this country since you took office.

—That doesn't make me a dictator.

—I'll note that. Getting back to your achievements, I have a few questions. How do you think the people of Gwanda will remember you? Do you think they'll see you as just another corrupt African leader?

Although Mobley's skin was almost as dark as a moonless midnight, Gabriel thought, for just a moment, that he could see a reddish anger rise to the surface.

—You'd better watch what you're saying, young man.

—I mean no offense, it's just what people have been saying, and I want to be accurate. Don't worry, I've worked with other politicians. I know how to gloss over your misdeeds to make you look saintly.

President Mobley didn't quite know what was going on, and was starting to become fearful.

—Who told you about this plan to assassinate me?

—A number of people, but you had to know you weren't well liked, right? Senator Wellington has no illusions about his popularity. He knows he is unloved, but he also knows that since so few people vote in America, he only has to win over a small percentage of the overall populace to remain in office. And here, where there is no voting, it couldn't have mattered to you whether the Gwandan people liked you or not.

—You think you're smart, don't you?

Gabriel tossed the pad on the table, capped his pen and stared with determined eyes at President Mobley.

—I'll tell you what I really think. You've got a serious situation on your hands and if you screw it up—if you treat it like it isn't—you could end up dead or you could find yourself in the middle of a civil war.

—So, now you're being serious?

—I was serious the moment I walked in here. I just wanted you to think about a few things. Now that you have, we can proceed accordingly.

—Proceed? What are you talking about?

—It was a big mistake for Upendo to kidnap Bridget Wellington. It's going to be a bigger mistake if you think you can just arrest him and that will be the end of it.

—Is that what this is all about?

—Even if you put Upendo in jail, you're still going to have to deal with the people and the forces he represents. Putting him in jail will probably only fuel their fires. Almost twenty five percent of your adult populace has some form of AIDS. What are you doing about it? You're planning to have them hunted and killed. That's why people are rising up against you, because they either have the disease, know someone who does, or know it's only a matter of time before they get the disease themselves. When they do overthrow you, you'll go down in the history books as just another African leader killed because he didn't know when to stop thinking about himself.

President Mobley stood up and reassumed his royal prerogative.

—Who the hell do you think you are?

Gabriel remained seated and calm.

—You might think of yourself as wealthy and powerful, and you are wealthy and powerful, but to The Promised Land Corporation you're just a puppet. They say dance and you dance. You're their house nigger.

—I ought to have your throat cut!

—Don't take it personally. We're all someone's nigger. That's just how it goes. We want to pretend we're not, but in the end we're all tied into the bloody mess of a world together. When you think you're not, when you think you're too high and mighty to bend down and tie someone else's shoes, that's when you start to get into real trouble.

—Is that what you're doing?

—What I'm doing isn't important, what you're doing is. Very few people are given the chance to make a difference in the world. You were given that chance. And what did you do? You decided to enrich

228

yourself at the expense of your countrymen. You got wealthy while others suffered and died. You claim to be a religious man, a man of God. How do you think He will judge someone like you?

—That's between me and Him.

—Yes it is, and some day you'll have to answer for your deeds.

Gabriel reached for his pad, put it back into his briefcase and stood up to leave. President Mobley couldn't believe that this young upstart was dismissing him.

—What would you have me do?

The briefcase was placed on the black and white marbled floor.

—Set up a meeting between Seisko Upendo and myself.

—What will that do?

□□□ 77 □□□

Making the arrangements for Gabriel to meet Upendo was tricky. Numerous phone calls were made before the Gwandans For Independence relayed a message to Gabriel to wait in the lobby of the Safari Park Hotel. At precisely 6:14 PM he was to walk outside where a black Land Rover would be waiting to pick him up. When the car arrived, Gabriel climbed in the backseat. There were two men up front and one in the back, all with black ski masks that left only their eyes visible. Gabriel was quickly hooded with a hood without eye holes and the car sped off. Twenty-five minutes later, the Land Rover was abandoned and he was hustled into the back seat of a second car. This car was driven in stop-and-go city traffic until it too was abandoned and a third car was utilized. Finally, after about two hours of driving, Gabriel was led out of the car and into an unremarkable suburban home where, after being denuded of the hood, he found himself sitting across a kitchen table from Seisko Upendo. Upendo wasn't as big or powerful looking as expected, but there was concentration and purpose in his eyes.

—Gabriel, President Mobley said you would be able to help us get the AIDS drugs for the Gwandan people. How are you going to do that?

—I'm not.

—You're not?

—Mr. Upendo, no one is going to give you AIDS drugs, not fifty million dollars worth, not fifty thousand worth. I know you don't want to hear that, but that's how it is.

The two top lieutenants of Upendo, standing beside the table with pistols in holsters, couldn't believe what they were hearing. After all that they had been through, they expected that Gabriel was going to be the answer to their prayers.

—Then what are you doing here?

—The world has gone to hell and I don't really think it's going to get any better. In fact, I think it's going to get a lot worse. Nonetheless, every now and again you find someone who defies logic, who is aware of how screwed up everything is and still believes in trying to make the world a better place. If you would have said that a scrawny, little man could force England out of India without firing a shot, no one would have believed you. If you would have said that a South African black man, thrown into dark prison cell and sentenced to life in prison, would one day emerge to dethrone his white oppressors and rule his nation that, too, would seem impossible. But Mahatma Gandhi and Nelson Mandela accomplished those deeds. So someone like you, who is doing everything he can to help his fellow man, his nation, well, you are a rare and unique individual. Maybe you won't end up being as triumphant as Gandhi or Mandela; it's possible you might end up martyred, like Steven Biko or Patrice Lamumba. The important thing is that you're trying.

—And that's why you're here?

—What's happening between you and President Mobley is a no-win situation. I know you're trying to help your country, but you won't be able to hold Bridget forever, and you're never going to get enough AIDS drugs to save your country. For Mobley, putting you in jail might solve his problem temporarily, but it will probably make things worse in the long run. If there are revolts and fighting, The Promised Land Corporation, and all the other corporations who have invested in your country, will pull out, causing greater instability. I agree that what The Promised Land Corporation wants to do is evil; nonetheless, in these days, to paraphrase John Donne, no country is an island. Gwanda, like every other country, needs outside investors. That's just how the world works. What you need to do is find a way to allow the investments to serve your country, and not just the wealthy or political elite.

—I thought you were here to save Bridget?

—I am, but I'm not going to be able to do that if I don't help you, am I?

—How are you going to do that?

☐☐☐ **78** ☐☐☐

Later that evening, at the darkened Wellington mansion, a ringing phone broke the night's silence. Candace, always an extremely light sleeper, especially now, awoke immediately, and grabbed the receiver.

—Hello.

230

—Mrs. Wellington?

Senator Wellington turned on his bedside lamp.

—Yes?

—It's Steve Lowell, in Gwanda. She's free! Bridget's free!

—Oh my God!

She turned to her husband,

—Bridget's free! It's Steve Lowell! They freed her!

Before she could instruct him, Wellington was already fumbling for the remote and bringing CNN to life.

—*...moments ago, Bridget Wellington, the senator's daughter, was freed from the rebel group, Gwandans For Independence. In a dramatic rescue, swarming government troops surrounded the Gwandans For Independence safe-house and captured the leader, Seisko Upendo, and dozens of his forces. Unbelievably, no shots were fired and there were no casualties or injuries. The senator's daughter had been held for more than three weeks. Claudia Potter, a spokesperson for The Promised Land Corporation, for whom Ms. Wellington was working, is with us. Ms. Potter could you tell us how this remarkable rescue came about?*

—*VBS television and The Promised Land Corporation have been working quietly, but determinedly, behind the scenes with President Mobley.*

—Give me the phone.

Wellington took the phone from his wife.

—Steve...what happened? How did you get her free? Can we talk to her?

Candace turned her eyes and ears to the television.

—*Ms. Potter, why was Bridget Wellington shouting that Seisko Upendo was innocent when she was freed?*

—*Obviously the stress of being held captive for so long got to her. She may have been brainwashed—that's not uncommon with kidnappers— especially with someone who has been known to side with the oppressed. I think these last few weeks in captivity sent Bridget over the edge and she's probably suffering from Stockholm Syndrome like Patty Hearst.*

—*So you don't believe Ms. Wellington when she said Upendo is innocent?*

—*No, of course not. He's obviously guilty and a very dangerous man. We got lucky today.*

—*My sources indicate Gabriel Patrick was the one who was able to locate Upendo and the rebels. What can you tell us about him?*

—*Gabriel, as everyone should know, is Bridget's boyfriend. He came over here seeking my advice. I did what I could to help the lovers*

*reunite. He is a brave and beautiful man. His story, his and Bridget's
story, is being turned into a made-for-TV movie for VBS television
called "Bridget and Gabriel."*

□□□ **79** □□□

As soon as Upendo was handcuffed and placed inside a police
vehicle, members of the Gwandan police took Bridget from the house.
With screaming sirens, she was raced to the Safari Park Hotel. Inside
her room, she immediately called her parents.
—Hello.
—Dad, it's me. They're putting me on a plane back to New York. I only
have a few minutes before I have to leave. Can you pick me up?
—Of course we can pick you up. Tell me what happened.
—I don't want to talk about it. I'm flying into Kennedy.
—How did Gabriel get you free?
—He didn't! He's a liar! I hate him! He lied to Upendo. Upendo's a
good guy! I don't care what you say, and he didn't kidnap me. It was all
my idea.
—Your idea?
—Yes. I told Upendo to kidnap me so no one else would be killed. It
was just a way to get the press involved. But Gabriel tricked Upendo.
He set a trap. As soon as Upendo revealed where I was, President
Mobley's men surrounded the house and captured him.
—Good for Gabriel.
—Dad! He's a jerk! I hate him!
—He saved your life.
—He didn't save my life! Upendo was never going to hurt me. I just
wanted the world to know what was happening so no one would get
killed. He was just trying to help his people, and now he's probably
going to go to jail. You'd better find a way for him to go free.
—We'll talk about that when you get home. I'm just glad you're safe. I
love you.

□□□ **80** □□□

Bridget cleared customs at Kennedy Airport only to find herself
staring at a swarm of news-thirsty press people. There were television
reporters, newspaper reporters, magazine reporters, bloggers,
cameramen and camerawomen, gossip hounds, and the merely curious.
They eyed her like a pack of hyenas watching a baby lion that had
strayed from the herd. When Bridget didn't make a move forward they

came at her shouting questions. At the last moment, Senator Wellington appeared with three burly, uniformed police officers who acted like football linemen on a sweep play. They swung in front of Bridget and pushed through the throng of reporters knocking and elbowing anyone who dared to step in their path. Wellington led them to a private room where his wife was waiting. As soon as she saw Bridget, Candace broke into tears. Wellington joined the two of them, and even he had tears in his eyes as the family hugged for a few tense minutes before Candace spoke.

—What happened to your eye? It's black and blue. Did Upendo hurt you?

Bridget shook her head back and forth, indicating "no."

—Upendo didn't touch me! Upendo hasn't done anything wrong! It was the press at the airport in Gwanda, some stupid cameraman, trying to get in front of all the other reporters and cameramen, hit me with the lens of his camera.

—Let me get some ice.

Candace, happy to play the role of the caring mother again, went to a buffet table which held sandwiches and sodas. She took a napkin and placed ice cubes taken from the soda tray into it. Wrapped up she attempted to place it over Bridget's eyes. Bridget shrugged it off.

—I'm all right!

Candace still looked concerned.

—I was so frightened for you. Gabriel was brave, wasn't he?

—No, he wasn't! Can we not talk about him, Mom? I don't want to talk about Gabriel. I hate him!

Wellington was overjoyed that his daughter was safe, but he was also cognizant of the press outside the door.

—Bridget, I understand that you're exhausted, but maybe a few words…it will help me with my election.

—Richard, is that's all you can think about?

—The reporters aren't going to leave until they get some photos and a few words. That's why I think…

—Well, you go talk to them! Why does she…

—Candace, if you didn't cut me off, I was going to say that when I go out to talk to the reporters, you two should have the security men take you the back way to the car.

—Oh…

—Is that okay, Bridget?

She nodded agreement without looking at her father.

Wellington didn't actually expect his daughter to face the reporters. He was glad she didn't want to, as this would give him an opportunity to speak with them, get his picture in the papers and on the news, and most of all to gain the sympathy of millions of potential voters. He took his prepared statement out of his suit pocket, read it over once more, and stuffed it back into his pocket before giving Bridget a kiss and exiting the room to face the reporters.

□□□ **81** □□□

The New York Tabloid

Bridget Wellington Freed!

After his daughter Bridget was flown back to safety, Senator Wellington promised to do everything in his power to have the rebel leader, Seisko Upendo, put to death. Senator Wellington said, once elected, Mr. Upendo will be the first person executed at The Promised Land Ranch. The execution will be broadcasted live on VBS

Continued on page 11

□□□ **82** □□□

When he returned to New York, the first thing Gabriel did was call Bridget. She refused to speak with him. Nonetheless, every day he continued to call her, both on her cell phone and at her parents' house, but she still refused to talk. Gabriel contemplated renting a car and driving up to Bedford, but wasn't sure if that would make matters worse, so once again he dialed the Wellington household. Candace answered the phone.

—Hello.

—Hi, Mrs. Wellington, it's Gabriel. Could you try her one more time?

—Hold on.

Candace took the back staircase up the eighteen stairs, walked down the hall, knocked twice on Bridget's bedroom door and peeked her head in. Bridget was sitting like an angry ball in a cushioned chair, with her knees up to her chest and her arms wrapped around them.

—It's Gabriel again. Why don't you talk to him?

Bridget thought about this for a moment, relaxing her posture, letting her feet touch the floor.

234

—Can I take it in your room?

—Of course.

She rushed down the hallway to her parents' bedroom, leaped on the bed, reached for the bedside phone, and yelled into it.

—How could you?

—How could I what? Save you?

—Betray me! You didn't save me! You never saved me! It was my idea. The whole thing was my idea! Upendo didn't want to kidnap me. After the police killed one of his men, I convinced him to pretend to kidnap me, that way the world press would know what was going on there, and we could stop the killing of Gwandans. But you had to screw it up, didn't you?

—Tell me what you thought was going to happen? That they'd give Upendo the fifty million dollars worth of AIDS drugs, and that would be the end of the problems? How far did you think it through?

—When people are drowning you don't think about the future, you dive in and try to save them.

—That's just naïve thinking, you have to...

—Screw you.

—Bridget, don't do this. I love you. I did this for you.

—You didn't do it for me, so don't say you did! You're a big hero now, but nothing has changed in Gwanda. You think you've saved me but a lot of Gwandans are going to die because of what you did. Great job, Gabriel, you should be proud of yourself.

—Bridget, please...tell me what you would have done.

—I would have fallen in love with someone else, someone who cared more about others than about himself.

—I did try to do something good. You've got to believe me. You have to wait and see what will happen.

—And you've got to believe me when I say I don't want to see you anymore.

She slammed the phone down, buried her head in the down pillow and began to cry.

□□□ **83** □□□

Two days later, Wellington returned from work and found Candace sitting in a semi-darkened living room with a near-empty bottle of white wine. Since she rarely drank, and never alone, it was obvious something was wrong. He looking at his wife and asked,

—What happened?

Candace didn't respond.

—Where's Bridget?

She looked up at her husband and answered bitterly,

—She left. She went to California, to stay with Richie.

—And you just let her go?

—Let her go? She made up her own mind. When I saw a taxi pull up in the driveway I thought he must have been lost, and Bridget came down the stairs with a suitcase. She was despondent. She's been crying her eyes out all week.

—Because of Upendo or Gabriel?

—Because of everything. She was in love with Gabriel and hoping to help Upendo, and none of it worked out. She blames you, because if it weren't for you they'd still be together.

Wellington was now fuming with anger,

—This isn't my fault. I'm not going to let you blame me. The world isn't a perfect place! I can't help it if an entire continent is infected with AIDS. That's not my fault. I can't help it if people kill one another. I play a small role in the world. I'm just doing what I can.

—No, you're not. You're doing whatever pleases you.

—Sure, everything's my fault. Believe that, if it makes you feel better.

Wellington went into the kitchen for his own solace. For the first one he didn't even bother chilling the Cutty Sark with ice. He poured a third of a glass, drank it back, and refilled half a glass more before retrieving the ice from the refrigerator. Ice added, he swirled it around with his index finger and sipped. For the next hour or more, he remained in the television room, drinking alone.

Candace slept in one of the spare bedrooms, and when she finally awoke, with her first hangover in many years, Wellington was already in the city.

□□□ **84** □□□

After Kimberly Galway finished her early morning yoga class, she stopped at Dean & Duluca on Broadway where she bumped into a friend who inquired if she had seen the morning paper. She hadn't. After procuring two bagels and two cappuccinos, she picked up a copy of the *Daily Post* and returned home. She dropped the paper on the kitchen table in front of Connor, who was on the telephone.

The New York Daily Post

Gazelle Disses O'Farrell!

By Anthony Markel

For the last few weeks, Cardinal O'Farrell has been trying to reach out to the embattled Independent candidate for Senate, Connor Gazelle, but Gazelle refused to meet the holy leader. The Cardinal, in an effort to save the soul of the lost heathen, invited Mr. Gazelle to a private meeting at St. Patrick's Cathedral. The failed actor informed a spokesman for the church he had no time to waste with obsolete religious groups. Gazelle claimed God has no place in politics, and he wanted nothing to do with any church groups or anyone stupid enough to believe in organized religion.

Continued on page 12

Connor looked at the headline and nodded to Kim, indicating he was aware of the front-page news. When he got off the phone, he walked past the living room and over to the dining area where Kim had the bagels on plates and two glasses of orange juice to go with the morning pick-me-ups.

—That was Bob Hevens. He saw it, too. I never expected Father Peter would get the press involved.

Connor sat down and bit into his bagel just as the phone rang. The cream cheese spilled out and hung off his lower lip. He wiped it clean with a napkin, took another bite and washed it down with a taste of the orange juice.

—Do you want me to get it?

—No, let the machine pick up.

After a few moments, a voice responded to the answering machine message.

—Mr. Gazelle, it's Father Peter from St. Patrick's Cathedral. I don't know if you've seen the *Daily Post* today but there is a very negative front-page article about you and Cardinal O'Farrell. I want you to know I had nothing to do with the article and I feel terrible because...

Somewhat reluctantly, Connor went over and picked up the phone on the living room end table.

—Hello.

—Mr. Gazelle?

—Yeah, I'm here. I saw the paper.

—I feel terrible about it and Cardinal O'Farrell is deeply upset.

—What happened?

Connor sat down on the living room couch.

—The writer of the article, Anthony Markel, I'm afraid I trusted him, and he deceived me. When I told you it was my idea to get you and Cardinal O'Farrell together that wasn't quite true. It was his idea. He made me believe it would be a good idea for the two of you to meet and talk.

—It's rather interesting that a reporter comes to see a priest and...

—He didn't come to me as a reporter. He's a new parishioner. He acted very concerned and often called asking after the Cardinal's health. Eventually he started asking about you. He told me I should get Cardinal O'Farrell to talk with you. He seemed very genuine. Cardinal O'Farrell seems to believe Mr. Markel knew what he was doing from the beginning.

—Yes, I'm sure he did.

—Perhaps, but I still don't see how he could know that you would not want to meet with Cardinal O'Farrell.

—He didn't. He didn't have to. The reporter just wanted a story he could use to discredit me. If I talked with Cardinal O'Farrell he could say I was just doing it to get votes. If I didn't meet, well, you've seen what he's written. Do you know who owns *The New York Daily Post*?

—No. Why?

—Hubert Merdedok. It's politics, Father. He was using you for political reasons.

—I see.

—Your only mistake was trusting someone. In my book that's no mistake at all.

—I appreciate you saying that, Mr. Gazelle.

—And I appreciate your calling. Goodbye.

—Bye.

The phone was dropped onto the couch and Connor joined Kimberly back at the breakfast table.

—So, Father Peter was set up?

—Looks that way. He's a priest and a nice enough guy, who was only trying to do something good. Unfortunately, he doesn't know what's going on. He doesn't see the bigger picture.

—Neither do I. What is going on?

Connor looked at the bagel, wanted a bite, but decided to wait to eat until he finished his phone call.

—Hubert Merdedok owns the *Daily Post* and POX and hundreds of other newspapers, magazines, and television stations around the world. Who's his candidate? Peter Morgan.

—How does this help him?

—Those who vote for Independent candidates more often than not vote Democratic, if there is no third party candidate. So every vote I get is potentially a vote Morgan won't get. Merdedok knows that, that's why he has his people go after me. The reporter didn't know what I would do or think, but he did realize that my atheism has alienated voters. That was his angle. If I had met with Cardinal O'Farrell he would have just said something to the effect that I was trying to scam voters by pretending to have found God.

—But why is Merdedok backing Morgan? Isn't Merdedok a Republican?

—Political parties have nothing to do with it. If Wellington wins the election that's going to be a big boost for Seymour Blackstone and VBS. VBS competes with POX. If VBS wins, Merdedok and POX lose. It all comes down to dollars and cents. That's why Merdedok's people will do anything they can to win, even if it means lying to and deceiving a priest.

—So, what are you going to do?

The proverbial light bulb illuminated in Connor's head.

—Wait a minute, do you know what I just realized? There's a damn good reason Father Peter was calling me.

—What?

—The reporter, where's the paper?

Connor jumped up, and in doing so knocked the table, spilling his cappuccino.

—Shit.

He raced to the kitchen for paper towels. After the coffee had been sopped up Kim followed him back to the kitchen where Connor picked up the newspaper.

—Anthony Markel, that's his name, he's the one who wrote the article. He's got something on Father Peter. That's why he's calling me. Markel's blackmailing Father Peter.

—What are you talking about?

Connor went to the couch to pick up the phone. With his caller ID, he found the number for St. Patrick's Cathedral rectory and quickly dialed.

—Hello.

—Father Peter? It's Connor Gazelle.

—Oh, hi again.

—Anthony Markel, the reporter, does he have anything on you? Was he

trying to blackmail you? Did you know him when he was a boy?
—No.
—You never knew him? He didn't go to your church as a young boy, did he? He wasn't an altar boy, was he?

Kim's scornful look forced Connor to turn and walk away from her.
—I'm not sure what you're implying, but I don't like it.
—Forget I mentioned it. Do you have his number? I'd like to talk with Mr. Markel.
—I won't give you his number, but I will call him because I want to get this straightened out.
—Tell him I want to talk to him right away.
—Goodbye.

Connor ended the call, satisfied, even a bit smug.
—What was that all about?
—Just what it sounds like. Markel's a reporter, right? What do reporters do? They dig up information. He's probably got something on Father Peter.
—What?
—Father Peter's a priest, right? Since when does a priest start hanging out with reporters?
—Who said they were hanging out?
—Markel knows Father Peter is a pedophile.
—He's a pedophile?
—That's right.

Kim shook her head, dismayed by the stupidity of his statement.
—Jesus, Connor, how can you say that? You don't know anything about him.
—I suppose you think there are no more pedophiles in the church, that...let me get that.

The ringing phone was already in his hand.
—Hello.
—Connor Gazelle?
—Speaking.
—This is Anthony Markel. Father Peter just called and told me you urgently needed to speak to me.
—That's right. What do you have on Father Peter?

Gazelle pushed the phone's speakerphone button and placed the phone upright on the table so Kim could listen in. Though not yelling, he was leaning into the phone, almost like a bully belittling a smaller boy.
—Father Peter is a pedophile, isn't he? That's why you got him to call

me, right? You're blackmailing him. Hubert Merdedok put you up to this, didn't he?

Markel replied calmly,

—And what did I hope to gain by having Father Peter talk to you?

—You thought I would get together with Cardinal O'Farrell, and you would use that to slander me. Well, it's not going to work you friggin' pervert! You don't have the decency to turn in a pedophile, do you? No, not you, you'd rather use him to get a story. People like you disgust me! You can forget your story because I'm going to call the police and report Father Peter as a pedophile. He's not going to get away with this and neither are you!

Connor reached over and jabbed the phone's OFF button with his index finger knocking the phone across the table and onto the polished wood floor where it slid against the windowed wall. Kim glared at him.

—What's gotten into you?

—Decency, that's what got into me.

He went over and picked up the phone and walked into the kitchen.

—These people disgust me.

Kim followed him, annoyed.

—Connor, you just can't call someone a pedophile without any proof.

—Proof? The goddamn Catholic Church is riddled with sexual perverts.

Connor took the phone book out of one of the drawers and opened it to the blue pages. After eying the local precinct numbers, he found the appropriate one and dialed.

—Connor, what do you think you're doing?

Kim tried to take the phone out of his hand. He turned his shoulder forcing Kim away.

—Leave me alone.

A voice came on the line,

—Fifth Precinct.

—This is Connor Gazelle. I want to report a pedophile.

—Connor Gazelle the actor?

—That's right.

—Let me get a detective.

A few moments later Connor heard,

—Mr. Gazelle, this is Detective Simon. How can I help you?

—Father Peter from St. Patrick's Cathedral is a pedophile.

—He molested you?

—*Me?* No, not me.

—Well then, how do you know he's a pedophile?

—Because Anthony Markel is trying to blackmail him. Markel works for the *Daily Post*. He told Father Peter if he didn't get me together with

Cardinal O'Farrell that he would expose him.

Kim rolled her eyes, not quite believing what she was hearing.
—I'm not quite following. What does Cardinal O'Farrell have to do with any of this?
—It's politics. He wants to get a story out of it.
—I still don't follow, Mr. Gazelle. Because a reporter wants a story, Father Peter is a pedophile?
—Why else would he try to get us together?
—Do you have any proof that he's a pedophile? Do you know anyone who he abused?
—He might have abused Anthony Markel.
—Might have? Mr. Gazelle, accusing someone of being a pedophile is a very serious charge. You can't just say someone is a pedophile without proof.
—He's a priest, isn't he? Out of the blue a priest calls a politician? Doesn't that make you suspicious?
—Any priest who calls a politician is a pedophile?

Gazelle yelled into the phone.
—What are you, dumb? Don't you get it? Don't you see what he's doing?
—No, I don't.
—This will be a big scoop! Markel forced Father Peter to call me. If he didn't, Markel was going to report that he was a pedophile!

That was enough for Kim. She came up behind Connor, snatched the phone from his hand and hung up. He spun around, angry. —What the hell are you doing?!
—What am *I* doing? What are you doing? Are you stupid? Think for a minute! Think about what you're saying.
—Give me the phone.
—No. Take five minutes and think about what you're doing.

Connor took a step toward her. Kim put the phone behind her back and pushed him away with the other hand.
—Are you thinking, Connor? Are you?

He hesitated and began to think. When doubt finally entered his mind it was like an earthquake shattering the foundations of his cement brain. Out of the remaining crumbled blocks of thought, he tried to rebuild.
—What the hell did I just do?

Gazelle sat down on the couch and buried his head in his hands, scarcely believing his actions. Kim stood and looked down at him, like a mother would an errant child.
—You'd better call the reporter back and tell him you made a mistake.

242

Otherwise he might put it in the paper.

—I don't have his number.

—Use your caller ID again.

Connor scrolled through the phone numbers until he found the one that he needed. Very humbled, he dialed.

—Hello.

—Anthony? It's Connor Gazelle. I jumped to conclusions. I shouldn't have called Father Peter a pedophile.

—It's a little late for that now, don't you think?

—Why? You're going to put what I said in the paper?

—Don't you think the public has a right to know what kind of person runs for office?

—I made a mistake. I'll admit that. But if you put that I called Father Peter a pedophile in the paper, that's going to cause him a great deal of pain and embarrassment. It's also going to hurt the Catholic Church.

—Mr. Gazelle, you called Father Peter a pedophile, and you called me a pervert, and now you want my help?

—It's like *Chinatown*. Do you know the movie *Chinatown*?

—You're blaming the Chinese? What do the Chinese have to do with this?

—No, it's just...in that movie when Joe Mantell's character says to Jack Nicholson, "It's Chinatown, Jake, it's Chinatown"...meaning that...

—Mr. Gazelle, you've made a very serious accusation and now you're invoking movie quotes?

—All I meant is that it's politics. Politics makes you say and do things you wouldn't normally say or do. It made me say something I shouldn't. I'm hoping you can understand that.

—And I'm hoping you can understand New Yorkers don't want you.

85

The New York Daily Post

Gazelle Calls St. Pat's Priest Pedophile!

By Anthony Markel

Failed actor, turned would-be politician, Connor Gazelle has struck out against the Catholic Church once again. Gazelle, not satisfied with potentially giving Cardinal O'Farrell a heart attack, has called one of St. Patrick's most highly respected priests a pedophile. Father Peter has spent his entire life trying to help others, and not once in his devotion to God and to the Church, has he been accused of any untoward activities. It seems that Mr. Gazelle believes every priest is a sexual pervert who has

Continued on page 13

86

During Bridget's time at Richie's apartment in Venice Beach, in an effort to numb her mind, she sat or stretched out on the couch watching television. It didn't matter what was on, as long as it wasn't political. Daytime soaps, evening soaps, reality television, all were used, but to little effect. She also tried sleeping her days away. In the evening, when Richie and his girlfriend were home, Bridget walked to the beach and sat there alone listening to the waves crash on the shore.

Richie had begun to worry about his younger sister, and was trying to allow her time and space to relax, but he was also getting slightly impatient. On the eleventh day of her visit, he waited for her to awake. When she did, he brought her a fresh cup of coffee. As he hadn't done this on any of the other days, it was a surprise. Bridget thanked him, sat up on the couch and sipped.

—Bridge, are you all right? Is everything okay?

His tone implied that it wasn't.

—Yeah, why?

—I know I'm not supposed to ask or put any pressure on you, but like you've been here for almost two weeks, and I'm just wondering what you're up to, what you're planning to do.

—Nothing. I'm going to be like you, just hang out.

—I'm not just hanging out. I'm working on my script.

—What script?

—You probably don't want to hear this, but Claudia Potter is paying me to write about you. That's why I need to know if you are going back to Gwanda when they shoot Upendo.

This alarmed and frightened Bridget.

—Shoot him? Who said they were going to shoot him?

—That's what's going to happen to him. They did like this quick trial so they could do it. He was found guilty and now they are going to use his execution to officially open The Promised Land Coliseum. I already talked to Ms. Potter, and it's all set up. Daddy's going to be there, too.

—He didn't kidnap me.

—He said he was going to kill you unless they got fifty million dollars worth of AIDS drugs. You may not think that's kidnapping, but everyone else does.

—Only because I told him to.

—Either way, he's going to die. Plus, it will also make a good ending to the movie I'm making with Ms. Potter. This way we can say justice was served.

Bridget got up off the couch so she could yell at Richie.

—Doesn't it bother you that The Promised Land is all about hunting and killing people for entertainment?

—Okay, yeah, it's horrible. Is that what you want?

—No, it isn't what I want! I want people to do something.

—Well, go back to New York. You saw Gazelle with all those protestors on TV the other day. You can go back and join them.

—Maybe I will. I only came out here because I didn't want to be in New York with Daddy and his election coming up. I had all these press people wanting to interview me, and I just didn't want to deal. I thought it would be better out here, but it's not. I can't get away from it, can I?

—I guess not. But are you going back to Gwanda or not?

☐☐☐ **87** ☐☐☐

The skybox suites at The Promised Land Coliseum had been sold-out one month after going on the market. On this bright and sun-filled day every seat was filled. There were tourists, travelers, and corporate revelers from around the globe. Champagne was flowing and banquets of food were being gobbled up. On stage, an African singing group finished performing. Claudia Potter, who was sitting on stage next to Senator Wellington, who was seated next to President Mobley, walked to the podium.

—Good afternoon, and welcome. My name is Claudia Potter, and it is my pleasure to welcome the ninety-thousand people here at The Promised Land Coliseum.

A great roar rose from the crowd.

—It is also my pleasure to welcome the millions of you watching us live on VBS television. Today, we celebrate the culmination of a dream. Today, in the Town of Paradise, we officially open The Promised Land Coliseum, a coliseum that would not exist without the vision of Senator Richard Wellington, and the support and encouragement of President Mobley. When I first met Senator Wellington, he spoke of wanting to find a way to help people less fortunate than himself. He wanted to lessen the tax burden of his constituents and make their lives safer and more secure. We see before us the fruition of that hard work and dedication. Senator Wellington has done what all political leaders have wanted to do from the beginning of time: he has found a way to not only reduce crime and eliminate criminals, he has found a way to use criminals to help fund social programs. In short, he has been able to make crime pay. This would not have been possible without the help of the honorable and dedicated Gwandan people, their fearless leader, President Onan Mobley, and his trusted right hand man, General Msambee. Their efforts and goodwill have been invaluable. I would like President Mobley to have the opportunity to say a few words before we commence with the first Promised Land execution.

As President Mobley stood up, sounds of applause filled the coliseum. The Gwandan president gave Potter a quick kiss on the cheek before taking the podium.

—Thank you, Ms. Potter. It is indeed a great day in Gwanda, especially here at The Promised Land Coliseum, in the town of Paradise, a town that did not exist a year ago. The Promised Land is not only a beacon of hope and a living example of what perseverance and determination can accomplish, it is in many ways a symbol, perhaps even a microcosm, of America itself. We Gwandans are forever indebted to Senator Wellington, Claudia Potter, Asher Mitchell, Steve Lowell, and many of their colleagues who worked tirelessly to make The Promised Land a destination, not only for Gwandans and other Africans, but also for Americans and tourists from around the world. There are representatives from more than two hundred international corporations here today, more than two hundred of the finest corporations in the world. When I was a boy, Gwanda was just a small country of farmers and small businesses. Those days are gone. Many Gwandans now have the privilege of working for The Promised Land Corporation, one of the finest corporations in the world. Our first executionee, the man you see blindfolded and chained to the pole in the far end of the coliseum,

Seisko Upendo, had the impudence to try to kick The Promised Land Corporation out of Gwanda. Seisko Upendo had the audacity to try to force pharmaceutical companies to make AIDS drugs available to indigent Africans. Seisko Upendo did not realize that if Gwanda wants to compete in the global economy, if it wants to position itself as a modern nation, we must learn to emulate and imitate America's wise and benevolent business leaders. Upendo Seisko failed to realize that by allowing The Promised Land Corporation to televise the hunting and killing of our citizens we would be able to increase the Gross National Product of our nation. Claudia Potter told me I could personally earn tens of millions of dollars in television fees over the next few years. All I needed to do was offer a steady supply of Gwandans who were willing to be hunted and killed.

President Mobley paused to take a quick look over at Wellington, Potter, Mitchell, and David Diamond, before continuing.

—A great American once said, "Ask not what your country can do for you. Ask what you can do for your country." Gwandans are doing that by sacrificing themselves for their country and for The Promised Land Corporation. Since our first sacrifice, Seisko Upendo, is well known to all of you, it is only fitting that his executioner should be as well known. That is why I ask Senator Wellington to honor us by being the executioner of Seisko Upendo.

Wellington turned almost as white as snow, saying to himself.
—Me?

President Mobley clapped his hands together. The crowd followed Mobley's lead and began clapping.

—Senator Wellington, on this bright and beautiful day, the nation of Gwanda would be forever grateful if you could demonstrate just how rewarding killing can be, by using one of your patented Promised Land rifles to slaughter Mr. Upendo.

The senator looked to Claudia Potter and Asher Mitchell for explanation of this unexpected turn. Both shrugged, unaware of what was going on. Wellington knowing the cameras were on him and the broadcast was live, walked over to President Mobley, shook his hand and patted him on the back as he spoke into the microphone.

—That's kind of you, very kind of you Mr. President, but I think it would be more fitting if I allowed a Gwandan to have the honor.

Senator Wellington attempted to return to his seat. Mobley's forceful tone stopped him.

—Senator, we want you.

Wellington turned, looked at President Mobley and spoke with as much authority as he could muster.

—No, really, have someone else.

—Senator Wellington, every Gwandan wants you to be the first to kill at The Promised Land Coliseum.

—Thank you, Mr. President, but as I said, I believe it would be more honorable to allow a native of the great country of Gwanda to be first.

—Senator, since this is your vision, it only makes sense that you are the first executioner.

—Mr. President, might I have a private word with you?

Senator Wellington stepped forward and gently but firmly pushed President Mobley to the side of the stage, where they were no longer facing the cameras.

—What the hell are you doing, Mobley? Don't you realize there are television cameras and millions of people watching?

—Of course I do. That's why we're here, isn't it?

—Then get someone to kill Upendo.

—Senator, all you have to do is aim the rifle at Mr. Upendo's head and pull the trigger. It's so simple even a child could do it, right?

—Mr. President, you either get someone up here to shoot that bastard or you're through!

The crowd was growing impatient, wondering what was happening. President Mobley left Wellington on the wings, walked to the podium and spoke into the microphone.

—Senator Wellington, I am giving you one last chance. Either kill Seisko Upendo or I am going to let him go.

Wellington was torn. Walk to the podium? Walk to his seat? Just leave? Sensing his indecision, President Mobley verbally poked him a final time.

—Senator, you've asked others to kill. We now ask you if you are willing to practice what you preach. Will you kill Seisko Upendo or not?

Wellington, as angry humiliated and full of rage as he'd ever been, stormed off the backstage. Seconds later, Claudia Potter ran after him.

At the podium, President Mobley had a slight smile on his face.

—Ladies and gentlemen, Senator Wellington has left us because he is unwilling to do what he wants others to do. Senator Wellington wants to televise the killing of AIDS victims and criminals, but he refuses to do the killing himself. Why is that? Asking another to kill is simple enough; it's slightly more difficult to do the actual killing yourself. Since Senator Wellington will not kill Seisko Upendo, I am going to unchain Mr. Upendo and set him free. I am also going to ban The Promised Land Corporation from Gwanda. I will set Mr. Upendo free today because he is not a traitor to this nation, but a great patriot, one who has shown me the error of my ways. I am grateful for what he has done, for allowing me the chance to correct my past mistakes and misdeeds. From this point forward, this coliseum will not be used for hunting and killing. It will be used for sporting events, soccer tournaments, World Cup games. Any foreign company that does business in Gwanda will have to pay an AIDS tax, which will help pay for the horrible epidemic that has engulfed this country and this continent.

Backstage, a stagehand had the misfortune of eyeing the enraged senator. Without warning, Wellington punched him squarely in the jaw. When he was on the ground, Senator Wellington began kicking him until security forces grabbed and pulled him away. Potter came down the stage stairs and tried to take control, yelling to security,
—Leave him alone! Don't touch him!

The two security men, familiar with Potter quickly unhanded Senator Wellington. The stagehand got to his feet moaning. Although he wanted to attack Wellington, the guards' presence held him at bay.
—Richard, what were you thinking? Why didn't you shoot him?
—Think it's that easy, Claudia? Millions of people watching me? Think it's easy to kill someone with the whole world watching?
—You pull the trigger, and The Promised Land is in business and you're reelected. You don't pull the trigger and we're fucked. Now we're fucked!
—You think I want Candace's accusing eyes on me for the rest of my life? Think I want Bridget's? How the hell do you think it would look if a senator's caught killing another man in another country?
—It would look good. It would show the world what you're made of. What are you going to do now? Do you realize how much money is invested over here? Do you think these corporations are just going to write it off?

Wellington was reeling, as if in a nightmare. He wanted to strike out, to hit someone, something.
—Fucking Mobley!

By now David Diamond and Asher Mitchell had come backstage. Diamond was the first to speak.
—Senator, don't panic. We can use this, if you play it right.
—Play it right? What the hell are you talking about?
—You need to tell the press that God spoke to you. That he told you not to shoot Upendo.

Potter shot a glance at Mitchell, who looked as skeptical as she felt.
—God spoke to me?
—Yes.

—That's ridiculous. I can't say that, no one will believe me.

Diamond persisted,

—Believe me they'll believe you. All you have to do is tell them God told you to save Upendo's life. That it was an act of mercy.

—The press will eat me alive. They'll say I'm just spinning.

—Senator, you either tell them God spoke to you or you concede the election to Morgan.

□□□ **88** □□□

The New York Daily Post

WELLINGTON BALKS!

Senator Richard Wellington can talk the talk, but he can't walk the walk. Yesterday in Gwanda, Africa, Senator Wellington showed himself to be a coward and a hypocrite. The soon-to-be-ex-Senator demonstrated his inability to practice what he preaches. Having based his reelection campaign on the necessity of sending criminals to The Promised Land to be killed, Senator Wellington couldn't do the deed when given the chance. If he

Continued on page 5

□□□ **89** □□□

Roger Zales was ecstatic with Wellington's political stumble. It seemed to him that his candidate, Peter Morgan, had all but sewn up victory. But Peter Morgan had grown much more politically savvy. He realized that one mistake, even a big mistake, didn't assure him of victory. Therefore, instead of discussing Cassidy Canyon and the new shows, as they had planned to do, Morgan asked Zales if they could talk confidentially and privately. Zales invited Morgan to his home in Conyers Farm, in Greenwich, Connecticut. When they entered the living room, Zales poured them each a cognac. Morgan wasn't in the mood to drink; his mind was racing, but he took the snifter in his hand anyway. Zales, ignoring his doctor's advice, lit a big Cuban cigar, blew out a cloud, and smiled before speaking.

—Can you believe it, Peter? Two days ago it looked like Wellington had the election wrapped up, and now, my friend it's all yours.

Morgan was deadly serious and wouldn't allow himself to act so lightheartedly.

—It's not mine yet, Roger. People are disappointed with Wellington because he didn't have the balls to execute someone who deserved it. That doesn't mean they'll vote for me. Not unless I can find a way to show voters I'm not a coward like Wellington.

—What do you want to do, shoot someone?

With steel-eyed determinism Morgan looked at his mentor.

—Roger, do you have what it takes to be president? Not a senator, anyone can be a senator, but a president?

—But you're not running for president, at least not yet.

—Right, not yet. But to get there you've got to think ahead. You've got to prove yourself, and you prove yourself by showing you're willing to shed blood. Every president has to show the world he's willing to kill, otherwise he won't be respected. Anyone who doesn't know that knows nothing of history.

—What are you saying?

Morgan swirled the liquid in his glass before meeting Zales eyes.

—I think shooting someone is the only way I can assure myself of victory. If I can find a justifiable reason to use my gun—I'm licensed to carry—it will be enough for me to beat Wellington.

Zales put his own drink on a bookshelf, in front of a first edition of Dale Carnegie's *How to Win Friends and Influence People*. —What did you have in mind?

—I'm not sure yet, that's why I asked you to invite me here. I needed somewhere private. Am I going crazy here, or am I...I mean what do you think?

They sat down next to each other on the black suede couch. The house was completely silent as Zales had told his wife not to interrupt them for any reason.

You're not crazy. It's an important election.

—It is. And just because I said I want to shoot someone doesn't mean I have to kill him, I don't want to do that. I just want people to know that, put in a situation, I will act responsibly.

—If you are going to shoot someone, I think it would be better if he weren't black.

—I'm not shooting a white guy; voters won't go for that.

Zales sucked in on the cigar, held the smoke for a few moments, and let it out away from his visitor, toward the entrance doorway.

—I was thinking of an Arab or a Muslim. Someone with dark skin and a beard, someone who looks like a terrorist.

—How do we do that?

—What we need to do is find someone who is already under suspicion, or maybe some Middle Eastern student who is poor or having trouble with his visa and doesn't want to be sent back to his country.

—We have five days before the election.

Zales gave a slight nod, indicating that he understood and wasn't worried.

—I have people who can help, but we'll have to find a way to make it look like he's trying to mug you or something. You'll be a victim acting in self-defense.

—All right, but how?

Zales nodded, took another puff, stood up and paced the floor back and forth twice before stopping and facing his candidate.

—Here's what we do: we find someone from the Middle East, we have him car-jack you outside your home. He tells you to get out of the car, but what he doesn't know is you're packing. You get out of your SUV and shoot him once. Don't have to kill him, just shoot him in the leg or something.

This was considered, but Morgan shook his head.

—No one's going to willingly let me shoot them for a carjacking, that's probably a ten-year sentence.

—What about…you catch him trying to siphon gas from your SUV, no big deal, he's got a tire-iron, but you've got your gun. You don't shoot him, you clobber him over the head with the butt of the gun. This is even better than killing him—you had the opportunity to do so, but you showed good judgment, compassion. This has big headlines. After the election, we have charges quietly reduced to a misdemeanor, he gets parole and we slip him some cash.

This excited Morgan.

—Can you set that up?

□□□ 90 □□□

Wellington hadn't been sleeping. Even the bags under his eyes were developing their own droopiness. The election was a big enough concern, but having The Promised Land Corporation kicked out of Gwanda was even more troubling. If the companies and investors who financed his dream had been solicitous during the creation process, it was only because that's how things are done. But now with hundreds of millions, perhaps billions, at stake the kid gloves were off. Wellington was just another errand boy who would be treated as such until he could remedy the situation. Asher Mitchell was sent out on damage control to a meeting with the biggest investors. When he came back, as was customary, he presented himself first to Keno who greeted him before stepping into the inner office and notifying the senator. A moment later, Keno stepped back out and Asher came in, closing the door behind him.

—Morning, Senator.

—How'd it go?

Wellington really didn't have to pose that question as the answer was evident on Mitchell's downtrodden face. They both pulled up chairs and sat at the round worktable.

—Sy Blackstone was the most vocal of the group. He's furious about what has happened. He wants us to find a way to remove President Mobley.

—Did you talk about how?

—It may be necessary to get the military or the CIA involved, but that's complicated. We'd have to come up with a viable reason.

—One that I could explain to the American public, presumably.

—Yes. There are still Americans in the country. We talked about having one of them kidnapped, or killed, and having that require a military response, but we're trying to avoid that. I've been trying to set up a meeting with General Msambee. We may be able to work with him. But it's not easy because, obviously, we can't let President Mobley know. Mobley's not naïve enough to think moves aren't being made against him.

—This puts me in an awkward position because I'm still fighting to win the election, and I've been playing up the religious angle, saying God told me to spare Upendo's life. I can't very well come out and say that I still fully expect to have The Promised Land operational in the future. And maybe I don't even want that, the whole thing is tearing my family apart.

—It's too damn late to get sentimental, Senator.

□□□ 91 □□□

After a long day of speeches, ending a very long week of speeches, Connor Gazelle's last speech of the day was at the Wadsworth Auditorium at Geneseo State University. As usual, some of the students came up to meet and talk with Gazelle, and inevitably, someone suggested going for a drink. As Connor was making the best of his final campaign days and nights, he eagerly agreed and a small group of politically active students took him to their favorite bar, The Idle Hour. Over pitchers of beer, Connor hit it off with the two graduate students, Linda, and her roommate Andrea. After a couple of not-so-sly sexual innuendos about a *ménage a trois*, Connor discreetly invited the young coeds back to his hotel for a nightcap. They were more than game. Not wanting to be seen leaving with them, Connor gave the barroom a warm good-bye, asked everyone to vote for him, and exited the bar.

As agreed, fifteen minutes later Andrea and Linda left the bar and began walking back to campus. A block away, they were picked up by Connor's SUV, which was being piloted by Bob Hevens. The Country Inn in Mount Morris, where Connor was staying, had been selected earlier in the week because of its proximity to the campus, and because it had a large jacuzzi inside the bedroom suite. Before picking up the women from the bar, Connor phoned ahead to a campaign staffer and told him to turn on the jacuzzi and make the usual arrangements.

When they arrived, two bottles of champagne were chilling in ice buckets. Connor popped the first open and poured three glasses. As they were already intoxicated and laughing, it didn't take the much prompting to get the young women out of their clothes and into the hot tub. Connor was a little slower getting undressed, as he was busy eying the women. Submerged up to their breasts, their nipples appeared to be floating on the bubbling water. When he stepped into the hot tub, Gazelle put his champagne down by the side of the jacuzzi. It felt like he was back in his Mulholland Drive glory days. Underwater, a hand reached between his legs for his cock and gave it a quick tug. He looked over and Linda was laughing. Connor smiled and turned to Andrea.
—You've got a naughty friend.

Andrea looked at Linda and asked her,
—What did you do?

Linda took Andrea's hand and showed her. They all laughed and Connor reached for the bar of soap, which he lathered up in his hands and began soaping the women's breasts, first Andrea's and then Linda's. As he was massaging Linda, he moved in and kissed Andrea. After massaging Andrea's breasts he kissed Linda.

Andrea called out,
—Group kiss!

In the middle of the tub, three pairs of lips met. Andrea opened her mouth to allow Connor's tongue to explore, and a moment later he moved over to Linda's open mouth.

The phone rang and Connor froze. He looked at the women and put a finger to his lips.
—Sssh. That's probably my girlfriend. Don't say anything or splash around. If she hears you I'm dead.

The phone continued to ring. Connor stepped out of the tub, grabbed a towel and wrapped it around his waist.
—I'll tell her I can't talk because I'm in the middle of a meeting with my campaign manager. Don't say a word. Okay?

The phone rang again. Connor picked it up from the bedside table.

—Hello.

—Connor, it's Bob.

Gazelle exhaled and relaxed.

—I hope you're not enjoying yourself too much because Morgan's been shot.

—Shot? What happened?

—He's dead. Roger Zales just called me. Turn on your TV. I'm watching it now on the news.

The television was in the corner of the room. Connor found the remote and turned on the set. Andrea and Linda remained in the jacuzzi sipping their champagne.

—...for a special bulletin. Police reports have confirmed that Senate candidate Peter Morgan has been killed! About thirty minutes ago, at 10:43 P.M., police responded to shots being fired outside Rayo's, a small, exclusive restaurant on the Upper East Side of Manhattan that is popular with politicians, celebrities, and members of organized crime. According to Roger Zales, he and Mr. Morgan were returning from dinner when they spotted a man, later identified as Mohammed Alibaba, siphoning gas out of Mr. Morgan's SUV. When Mr. Morgan confronted Mr. Alibaba he was hit over the head with a tire iron. Mr. Morgan fell to the ground bleeding profusely, but was able to pull out his licensed .38-caliber pistol and shoot Mr. Alibaba. Unfortunately, he only nicked him in the leg. Mr. Alibaba was able to strike two more powerful blows to Mr. Morgan's skull before Morgan, covered in blood, fired one last shot striking Alibaba in the right eye, killing him instantly. An ambulance rushed Morgan to Beth Israel Hospital North, but doctors were unable to save him.

That at least was the official police report. A neighborhood couple that witnessed the attack tell a different story. According to Jose Garcia, Mr. Alibaba had been standing by the SUV for a half hour with a gas can and a rubber hose, as if waiting for someone. When he saw Mr. Morgan and Mr. Zales approaching he began to pry open the gas panel with a tire iron, in an attempt to siphon gas. When Mr. Morgan was only three feet away, Mr. Alibaba turned and smiled, and as he did so, Morgan pulled out his gun and fired, hitting Mr. Alibaba in the leg. Mr. Morgan was about to fire again when Mr. Alibaba defended himself with the tire iron. He was able to strike Mr. Morgan in the head; this caused Morgan to fall to the ground. When he realized Morgan was going to shoot him again, Mr. Alibaba again struck Mr. Morgan with the tire iron. After which, Mr. Morgan fired a final shot that killed Mr. Alibaba.

Gazelle silenced the set and spoke into the phone.

—Bob, did you say Zales called you?

—I did. He says he can get Morgan's supporters to support you as long as you don't mention anything about God and religion in any of your speeches.

—Morgan's been shot and killed and the first thing Zales does is call you? What a sympathetic guy.

—He doesn't have much time. He's worried about Wellington and VBS winning, which would hurt POX. If Morgan's supporters back you there's a chance you could beat him. Zales also told me that PBS has some video footage on Wellington that could be helpful for us.

—What video?

—Apparently some student at NYU shot some footage of Wellington a while back. PBS has been waiting for the right time to air it. It's going to be on tomorrow night. I think, if you play your cards right, we have a viable chance at winning. That's why we need to talk about how we're going to handle the next few days.

—All right.

—I'll call the front desk and have them put on a pot of coffee so we can talk about his. I'll be over to your room shortly.

—Actually, I'd prefer to come over to your room. Give me a few minutes…better yet, make it a half hour and I'll be over.

—Connor, get rid of the women. This is impor…

Connor placed the phone back in its resting place and turned to the women.

—Now, where were we?

□□□ **92** □□□

—*Tonight, in our Young Filmmakers series we bring you three short films by New York City students: one from New York University, one from Columbia University, and the third from John Jay College. Jonathan Gobo, our first filmmaker, has put together a short video on Senator Wellington. Jonathan, why don't you say a few words on why you chose Senator Wellington as your subject?*

—*Well, I don't know if I necessarily chose him—at least it wasn't a premeditated decision—it sort of presented itself.*

—*How so?*

—*I was visiting my girlfriend Sadie's grandparents, the Quigleys, upstate near the Adirondacks, and we were walking in the woods with her grandmother, who's like this birdie, she likes to look at all types of birds. Anyway, I had my video camera with me because I wanted to*

256

make the Quigleys a video. While we were walking, we came upon a large buck on the ground that had been shot and was bleeding from the neck. He wasn't dead, but he was dying. We wanted to save him, but there wasn't really anything we could do. Later on, back out on the road, we saw some hunters, and I wanted to ask them some questions, wanted to see if they were the ones who shot and abandoned the deer, but they were really rude and wouldn't answer any of my questions, so I just followed them.

—Did you realize Senator Wellington was among the hunters?

—Not at first, because he was dressed in hunting fatigues, and they were passing around a bottle of Jack Daniel's. They had a deer strapped to the car, and they were taking photos of it and laughing. Since they wouldn't answer my questions I started filming. When they left I just followed them in my car and kept filming. Later on, when I talked to one of my professors, he suggested I continue to film Senator Wellington to see if I could develop a narrative out of the footage. So that's what I did.

—Shall we take a look?

Up at the Wellington mansion, the senator looked over to his wife.

—Goddamn sneak. He followed us. I mean what the hell is that?

—You didn't know you were being filmed?

—I wasn't paying attention.

—Because you were too intent on getting drunk.

On screen, Wellington and two other men passed around a bottle of Jack Daniel's along a wooded roadside. The video cut to a desolate roadside restaurant. Wellington and his two hunting pals got out of their SUV and drunkenly stumbled toward the entrance of the eatery.

—Okay, so he got us going into a restaurant, big deal...

—And now he's got you coming back out.

—Damn him.

—What arc you doing?

One of Wellington's companions unstrapped the deer from the roof of the SUV and attempted to pull it off. The deer, bloody and heavy, didn't move easily. Wellington and the third man helped the first man pull the deer off. The first man, now with a better grip on the dead animal, pretended to be dancing with it and waved one hand to a large man standing in the doorway of the restaurant.

Candace shook her head.

—Is that supposed to be funny? That's disgusting.

—The bartender didn't believe Harrison shot a deer, that's why we were showing him.

—He had eyes, didn't he? Didn't he see the deer on the roof?

—We were just having some harmless fun and that sick kid followed us.

257

That ought to be against the law, filming someone without their knowledge. You follow anyone around with a camera long enough and you'll see them do something embarrassing.

Wellington pulled out his cell phone and dialed.

—Hello.

—Asher, it's Richard. Are you watching it?

—Yeah. It's not good. The kid found a loophole. It's on PBS. That's public broadcasting.

—I know damn well what it is! You told me he wasn't allowed to show the goddamn footage!

—He agreed not to show the tape on commercial television. A public television station isn't commercial. He's probably not getting paid to show the film; therefore, he has a right to show it.

—You told me he couldn't show the goddamn thing! It makes me look like a goddamn fool!

—There's a chance we could sue him.

—Sue him? This isn't about money. I don't give a goddamn about the money. Once it's on you can't take it off, can you? Once people see it you can't...oh, Jesus...

The footage abruptly cut from the wooded wilderness to a city, Washington D.C. Wellington was again walking unsteadily, this time coming out of a restaurant with his right arm draped across the shoulder of a blonde woman, equally as drunk.

—So that's her? That Pamela woman? Or is that someone else? At least she's better looking that the deer, despite her bleached blonde hair.

—Senator?

—I'll call you back, Asher. Turn it off. Give me that!

Senator Wellington grabbed the remote. A push of the button silenced the screen. Candace got up and left the room. Wellington followed her into the kitchen.

—It wasn't supposed to be on. It wasn't supposed to be aired. That's Asher's fault.

—It's Asher's fault you were drunk and your friend was dancing with a deer? It's Asher's fault you're stumbling out of that restaurant with some bimbo?

—This is not me. This is just politics. PBS loves liberals and they resort to nasty tricks like that. Why do you think they waited till just before the election?

Candace eyed him disdainfully, perhaps even with hatred. Wellington stood there, embarrassed and disgraced, unable or unwilling to offer further excuses for his behavior. Candace walked away, back through the house and up into the bedroom she did not share with her husband.

□□□ 93 □□□

At the University of Buffalo, the city's mayor shouted to the capacity crowd,
—Buffalo, we're talking proud, because we've got Connor Gazelle here with us tonight! Give him a big hand!

□□□ 94 □□□

—Rochester Republicans, let's show Senator Wellington how we feel by giving him a big round of applause!

□□□ 95 □□□

—Binghamton, put your hands together for Connor Gazelle!

□□□ 96 □□□

—Hello, Watertown, please give a warm welcome to Senator Wellington!

□□□ 97 □□□

—Lake Placid Democrats, here he is—Connor Gazelle!

□□□ 98 □□□

—Poughkeepsie, here's the man you've been waiting for—Senator Richard Wellington!

□□□ 99 □□□

—Utica, let's have a warm round of applause for our next senator, Connor Gazelle!

□□□ 100 □□□

—Here he is, Huntington, our present and future senator from New York, Richard Wellington!
—Thank you, thank you very much. This has been the longest,

strangest, and most difficult campaign I have ever been involved with. I want to thank each and every one of you for your support. After Mr. Morgan was killed, I got down on my knees and prayed. I asked God what I should do, what course I should take. God wants America safe, safe for the hardworking men and women who pray to him. God wants criminals to be put away so that they never go free again. On Tuesday—Election Day, two days from now—I ask you to pray to the Lord and ask him who you should vote for: a God-fearing Christian or an atheist. The choice is yours.

□□□ 101 □□□

—Good evening, Albany! Let's have a warm round of applause for our next senator, Connor Gazelle.

—Thank you, thank you very much. When I began my run for the United States Senate, I felt that I was a long shot at best. Nonetheless, I campaigned because I felt it was important to stand up for what I believe in. I try, like most Americans, to live in harmony without trying to exploit or take advantage of others. I try to live by the Golden Rule, doing unto others, as I would have them do unto me. Unfortunately, sometimes it seems that power and greed and corruptible seed seem to be all that there is. Peter Morgan wanted to make a mockery of prisoners, by putting them on television. He died tragically and violently. I do not believe violence solves anything. Violence only causes more problems. Senator Wellington has also preached violence, and now he is pretending to have found a new faith in God. I think we can all see through this hypocrisy. The only way we can stop additional violence is if we...

BANG!

Connor fell backwards and hit the stage with a thud. The shot was so sudden that pandemonium only broke out once blood started flowing from his Connor's skull. When it did, it spread in expanding ripples like a heavy stone breaking the surface of a placid pond. The crowd screamed, scattered and surged toward the exits. The only person not running away was the shooter. He dropped the gun and raised his hands in the air. Two police rushed and tackled him at the same moment, one grabbing his arms, the other grabbing his waist. The first officer pushed the shooter's face to the floor. The second officer roughly twisted the gunman's arms behind his back and tightly clasped handcuffs around his wrists.

—Repeating the top story. Last night, as he was giving a speech at the State University of Albany, Independent senate candidate, Connor Gazelle was shot by a crazed gunman. He is alive, but he is in a coma. Local correspondent Hillary Clydesdale is outside William Kennedy Memorial Hospital in Albany with the latest on Mr. Gazelle. Hillary, what can you tell us?

—Pete, apparently the bullet that grazed Mr. Gazelle's skull did not go deep enough to hit vital brain functions. In fact, doctors are not yet sure if it was the bullet that caused the coma or if Mr. Gazelle's falling backward and hitting his head on the wooden floor with such force that caused it. Although he remains in a coma, doctors are cautiously optimistic that he will pull through this. In fact, just this morning his left eye blinked.

—He blinked?

—Yes, doctors are not sure if it was an involuntary blink, or if he was winking at his beautiful girlfriend, Kimberly Galway, or at one of the pretty young nurses who was standing by his bedside. Whatever the cause, doctors see it as a positive sign.

—What can you tell us about the shooter?

—Paul Hille is a fundamentalist Christian who was paroled from jail two years ago after serving nine years for the attempted murder of an abortion doctor. At the time of his first arrest, Hille said he believed his action would be rewarded in Heaven. Though Hille is well known in fundamental Christian circles, the Christian community largely dismisses Hille as a fringe character that maligns their organization.

—Turn it off.

Click.

Senator Wellington, David Diamond and Asher Mitchell were huddled together at the senator's New York office. Mitchell looked at Wellington who looked at Diamond whose confident, even arrogant, air was gone. Nonetheless, they looked to him and hoped he has some special insight on what to do.

—Senator, I don't know how we handle this. Gazelle getting shot is about the worst possible thing that could happen to you. If he lives, this is going to get him all kinds of sympathy votes.

—Is a brain-dead candidate a legal candidate?

—Unfortunately, yes. I've checked. There are no precedents, so, constitutionally, even if he is in a coma or brain dead, technically he's alive so he's a legitimate candidate.

—So, what do you suggest I do?

—I think you need to go on television and ask people to pray for Gazelle. You do that and voters will see that you're a politician, but you're also human. That might be enough for you to pull this out.
—I don't know. There are too many sympathetic people out there. That's the problem with America, too much sympathy.

□□□ **103** □□□

In Gazelle's hospital room, Kim looked from the unmoving Connor to the television.
—*Good morning and welcome to the Special Edition Election coverage on POX News. The results are in. Connor Gazelle has become the first person in history to be elected to the United States Senate while in a coma. The election also claims another dubious distinction: the lowest voter turnout in New York State history. Only eighteen percent of eligible voters bothered to cast ballots. Pundits are saying the combination of Wellington's hypocrisy and Gazelle's atheism, on top of the killing of Peter Morgan, was just too much for most voters, many of whom are tired of all politicians. One voter said that even if Gazelle is brain dead, he may still be the wisest man in Congress.*

□□□ **104** □□□

At the Wellington mansion, Candace stood idly by a living room window, watching a bushy-tailed squirrel gather nuts for the coming winter. Senator Wellington sat at his desk in the library writing a form letter that he would send to each of his staff members thanking them for their support.
A phone rang.
Wellington waited for Candace to answer it. She did not move from the window. The phone rang four times before the answering machine picked up. Even though the machine was in the kitchen, the house was so silent Wellington heard part of the caller's message through the partially opened library door. After hearing, "...call the White House," he immediately rose to his feet, walked out of the library, and looked into the living room. He was expecting Candace to turn towards him. When she didn't, he yelled to her,
—Didn't you hear the phone?
Candace did not respond or even look in his direction.
Wellington walked through the dining room, past the breakfast room, and into the kitchen, where he pressed the message button on the answering machine.

—Senator Wellington, this is Arthur Mack, Communications Director for President Swinemore. The President would like you to call the White House at your earliest convenience. The number here, in case you do not already have it, is...

Wellington quickly dialed the given phone number.

—This is the White House, how can I direct your call?

—This is Senator Wellington, for President Swinemore.

—Hello, senator. Just a moment, please.

Two minutes later, a southern voice came on the line.

—Wellington?

—Hello, Mr. President.

—All of us down here were real sorry to hear of your loss.

—I'll survive.

—I'm sure you will. As you probably know my Secretary of Education, Burt Lawrence, is stepping down at the end of the year to become President of Yale.

—I did hear that.

Candace tiptoed into the dining area to hear what was being said.

—I think it would be a shame to lose two good men in the same year. That's why I'd like you to consider being my Secretary of Education.

—Secretary of Education? That would be a great honor, sir. Certainly I will consider it. Without question.

—Fine. I was hoping you would. They'll want to go through the normal vetting processes. As soon as that is concluded, I'll make the announcement.

—Thank you, President Swinemore.

—Thank you Senator, and good-bye.

—Good-bye, Mr. President.

Elation filled Wellington. He raced from the kitchen, past the breakfast room, through the dining room and into the living room. His wife was nowhere to be seen. He called out.

—Candace!

When he didn't get a response, he shouted up the grand staircase, toward their bedroom.

—Candace, where are you? They want me to be Secretary of Education. Candace?

Hearing a noise he stopped and listened. Outside in the driveway a car engine started up. Wellington ran to the front door, opened it and saw Candace behind the wheel of the black Mercedes. She saw him and started to pull away. He ran out after her.

—Candace, hold on!

Candace stopped and rolled the window down. Wellington came

around to her door.

—Where are you going?

—I'm leaving.

—Leaving? Leaving what? Leaving me?

—Yes.

Senator Wellington almost refused to believe his ears.

—How can you leave me? They want me to be Secretary of Education.

—I heard. That's why I'm leaving you. You'll never change, and if I stay here neither will I.

—But this is what we want, this gives me another chance, this puts me back in the game.

Inside the house the phone rang again. Wellington looked toward the opened front door and back to his wife.

—I should get that. It might be the White House.

—I'm sure it is.

They both looked at each other, knowing...

—Candace, I...

—Goodbye, Richard.

He watched her pull away.

When the driveway was vacant, Wellington felt like he had been punched in the gut by a heavyweight prize fighter. He stood in the cold autumn air among the bare trees, gray sky, gray stone house, and gray stone wall, filled with a sudden and unexpected sadness.

By the time he came back inside he had forgotten about the ringing phone. Slowly he found a chair in the living room next to where Candace had been standing. Wellington gazed outward. The sky was turning from slate gray to charcoal. The phone rang again but he did not go for it and no message was left on the machine. A half hour later, or perhaps longer, Wellington was sitting in a darkened room. The phone rang once more. He turned on the tableside lamp so he could see. Not with enthusiasm or desire to talk but out of habit he went to the kitchen and picked up.

—Hello.

—Richard, it's Claudia, I have wonderful news! General Msambee staged a military coup and took over.

Wellington didn't respond.

—Richard?

—I'm here.

Claudia Potter was so full of enthusiasm she barely noticed how deflated his voice sounded.

—I mean I guess it's sad that both President Mobley and Upendo have been killed, but that's an internal issue—it has nothing to do with us.

264

See the thing is General Msambee, I guess it's President now, President Msambee talked with Sy Blackstone and some of the other big investors, and he's interested in reestablishing The Promised Land. He thinks it can really work this time. Msambee also promised to have the military lock up anyone who tries to stop us from hunting volunteers. He wants a bigger percentage, which is understandable, a bigger percentage of the television revenue that would be generated from hunting volunteers and criminals. The important thing is to get it going again. Sy's going to be more hands-on this time, and he's going to make sure we have as much money as we need. What do you think? Now that you're no longer a senator it should be perfect.

—President Swinemore just asked me to be Secretary of Education.

Potter paused and then quickly plowed on. —Who says you can't do both? With Sy wanting to take on a greater role and with Msambee in there you wouldn't have to do as much, and if you're going to be Secretary of Education, obviously you're going to be in Swinemore's inner circle. That will help us persuade him to send undesirables from all fifty states to The Promised Land.

Wellington looked into the blackness beyond the kitchen window. He saw a faint reflection of himself in the glass. —I don't know.

—This is a golden opportunity, it really is.

—Let me think about it, Claudia. Give me a day or two to think about it.

—All right, but remember, with those two do-gooders gone, there'll be nothing to stop us.

—Probably not.

—Richard, it's really like a dream come true. And isn't that what The Promised Land is all about, making your dreams come true?

The phone was lowered onto its cradle and the line went dead. Wellington's legs felt leaden as they took him past the breakfast room, past the long mahogany dining room table, through the foyer and into the living room where he regained his chair. The tableside light was turned off. Senator Wellington sat silently in the darkness thinking about Candace, thinking about the blank unhappiness in her face as she drove off, thinking about Bridget, how she hated and no longer wished to speak with him, thinking about Richie, who wasn't much more than a memory, an occasional voice at the end of a phone line. He tried to conjure up an image of them all together, smiling, happy, like something he had seen in a movie: a family at the beach throwing a football or a frisbee, or his family at dinner laughing at a joke he had told. He went as far back as he could, but there were no images to be found. He thought about what Claudia had said, about making one's dreams come true. Was life, was America, was The Promised Land really all about

265

making one's dreams come true? And what did this mean anyway? What did it mean to have a dream come true?

□□□ 105 □□□

Candace found herself driving south on Saw Mill Parkway feeling elated that she had finally made a move, but also incredibly mournful that her marriage was over. Tears dribbled from her eyes as she followed the Saw Mill to the Henry Hudson Parkway. Before she knew it she was in Manhattan. She drove over to Sutton Place where the Wellingtons had an apartment. The doorman hadn't seen her in a long time, perhaps two years, and had almost forgotten who she was. Inside the tastefully decorated living room, she picked up the phone and called her daughter.

Bridget had just gotten off the phone with a news reporter who wanted to know her thoughts about Upendo's death. She didn't respond to the reporter, and after talking briefly with her mother, she hung up, feeling that her world was collapsing.

In the living room, her roommate, Halley, was watching television. Bridget didn't say anything to her as she left the apartment. She came out of the Devonshire and walked west on Tenth Street. When she passed Fifth Avenue she didn't bother looking south to Washington Square Park where the Arch was lit up with white lights. She continued on Tenth, past the Gothic Church of the Ascension. When Tenth dipped south on a diagonal at Sixth Avenue she passed the red bricks of Jefferson Market Library. Her only thoughts were to get away from the pedestrians filling the streets. She continued past Greenwich Avenue, past Waverly Place, past the Three Lives & Company Bookstore, past Seventh Avenue and a few steps later West Fourth Street. She walked beyond Bleecker Street and a swarm of laughing students. As she walked, she thought of the water, the vast Hudson River. She walked past Hudson Street, past Greenwich Street, past a man with two small poodles on leashes. At the end of Washington Street she could see a glimpse of the dark river. She walked past the final street, tiny Weekhawken Street, only one block long. The West Side Highway was the only barrier between her and the water. She walked up a block to Charles Street for a crossing point. When the traffic in both directions stopped at the light, Bridget walked across the highway. She saw the small blue lights illuminating Hudson River Greenway, the Bike Path and, jutting out into the water, Pier 45.

Far across the water, New Jersey was lit up with white lights like a Christmas display. The pier was dark and empty, which made it feel peaceful to Bridget. She walked past the blue lights, out onto the dark and vacant pier. A cold wind ripped into her face. She walked past the dark lawn on the pier, a lawn that had been green and alive with people in the spring and summer. She walked until a cold metal barrier at the end of the cement pier stopped her progress. She looked down into the black water and saw a field of dark wooden pier-posts sticking up black in the ebony water like gravestones in an abandoned cemetery. The water, black, silent, and peaceful, lapped up against the cement pier poles, again and again, like a quiet voice calling to her. Bridget climbed over the barrier and stood on the edge.

Before throwing herself into the cold water, Bridget looked into the blackness and thought of all that had happened: her own kidnapping; her father losing the election; the killing of Upendo; her parents breaking up their marriage; her mother sitting alone and crying to her on the phone; her brother lost in his own confusion; of Gabriel...

Thoughts of Gabriel turned her eyes from the darkened water back toward the city. Beyond the low rise apartment buildings of the West Village, the white lights at the top of the Empire State Building, caught in mist and low clouds, illuminated the sky like a holy halo. Bridget climbed back over the railing and onto the pier.

She walked back down the pier, back across the dead winter lawn, and back to the bike path. She began walking north. The dark cold air felt good to her. She continued walking. Further north, she passed another watery graveyard of wooden pier-posts sticking upward, almost like accusatory eyes looking up from a time that was. She walked past Chelsea Piers, past the Heliport, past the Javits Center on her right. Before she knew it she was approaching the Intrepid and Forty-Second Street where she recrossed the highway.

□□□ **106** □□□

At his apartment in the Piano Factory, Gabriel was awoken from his sleep on the couch by the front door intercom. He struggled out of his dreamlike state and pushed the intercom button to answer.
—Yes?
—A Ms. Wellington is here to see you, sir. Shall I send her up?

Gabriel was so surprised to hear her name he was momentarily flustered.
—Um...Yeah, sure.

Still half asleep, Gabriel looked around the apartment. It was in disarray: empty beer bottles, a half empty bottle of Jameson, a dozen books that had been opened and discarded because he had been unable

267

to concentrate.

When the light tap on the front door came he opened it and saw Bridget standing there sadly beautiful. Because neither of them knew what to say at first there was an awkward pause. Bridget broke the ice.

—Are you going to invite me in?

—Sorry.

Gabriel stepped back, let her in and closed the door behind her.

—Your face is all red. Are you all right?

—Yes. I was walking. Walking and thinking. Can I have a glass of water?

—Okay. Sit down and I'll get it.

Bridget sat on the sofa and Gabriel went into the kitchen. When he returned, he handed Bridget her glass of water. He took a seat next to her and watched her take a small sip before she said,

—You brought President Mobley and Upendo together, didn't you, when you were over there, to get me free.

—You're blaming me for what happened?

—No…of course not, not at all. I just want to know what happened. What Mobley did, telling my father to shoot Upendo. That was your doing, wasn't it?

—Does it matter?

—Are you angry with me?

—Why would I be angry? It's not like I tried to save you only to be told to fuck off.

—Gabriel, I'm sorry, okay? Why didn't you tell me what you were doing? I wouldn't have acted the way I did.

—*Me?* Why didn't I tell you? I was worried to death that you were going to be killed, and I…

—I tried to tell you. I left a message on your answering machine.

—That was really nice of you, leaving a message! Problem was I was in Gwanda, wasn't I?

—How was I supposed to know that?

—There's been a good deal of time since then.

—I was in California.

—Oh, okay. That explains everything. You were in California and people in California don't have telephones and…

—Would you shut up? I realize I made a mistake. I'm here because I love you, and want to say I'm sorry for not trusting you. I tried to help the Gwandans who were going to die, who were going to be killed, and I tried to call you. I felt horrible not being able to talk to you. I cried thinking about you, thinking about what you must be going through, thinking about how I couldn't wait to see you to explain what had

268

happened. And when I finally see you, you're helping President Mobley and having Upendo captured and arrested. How do you think that made me feel? You could have come over and said something, couldn't you? But, no, you wouldn't even talk to me. You just told Mobley's men to take me to the airport. How do you think that made me feel!

Small hot tears dribbled down her cheek.

—And the press was all around, and I had to sit on a plane for twelve hours and there was more press in New York and my father and I...what do you think it was like having all those police around and all those reporters? I just had to get away, I couldn't think straight. What did you expect? Do you even care about me?

—Of course I care about you. I went over there because I loved you; because I thought you were the woman I would spend the rest of my life with.

—Really?

—Yes.

There was a pause, as both uncertain of their next move.

—How did you come up with your plan?

—I didn't have any plan when I got there. All I knew was that I had to do something to get you free. I convinced Mobley that it he let The Promised Land Corporation kill his people he would be overthrown and killed. I convinced Upendo that there was no way he was going to get the AIDS drugs. I told them the only option they had was to work together. That's all I did, persuade them to work together.

—Why couldn't you have told me when I was freed?

—I wanted to...but it was Upendo. He didn't trust you.

Bridget was shocked.

—Upendo didn't trust me? He said that?

—Not like that, he trusted you but he thought you were too honest. He thought that if we told you what we had planned it would have been all over your face, and you wouldn't be able to lie as easily as the rest of us. You had too much innocence and your father would have known. He wouldn't have come back and our plan wouldn't have worked.

Bridget stared into Gabriel's eyes for a moment before speaking again.

—Was that your plan, the raid, and what Mobley said at the stadium about the African AIDS tax?

—Yeah, most of it. I wanted to believe it could happen. I guess we all did. That's what it was all about, that big kickoff with your father, the whole plan was to have it backfire on him so President Mobley could kick The Promised Land Corporation out. Everything seemed to be going the way we hoped, but somehow I guess we all forgot about

General Msambee. I never thought Upendo and Mobley would end up being killed.

—Are you blaming yourself?

—I don't know…

—It's not your fault. Upendo did what he could to try to save his country. He risked his life for me. But so did you, Gabriel, you risked your life for me.

—Bridget, I'd give my life for you. Before I met you, I was a bit of smartass, and very cynical. I didn't really care about anything. I was just hoping to make money by writing a book about the faults of others. But being around you changed me. You lived your life to do some good. I over-think everything. You just go out and do it. You saw what was happening over in Gwanda and you didn't wait to ask others what to do, you just did something. I could never have done that, and I certainly wouldn't have tried to help Upendo or Mobley if it weren't for your influence on me. You tried to make the world a better place and maybe you didn't succeed as well as intended, but you tried…that's all you can ever do.

—Kiss me.

When their lips touched, the floodgates of their passions, long blockaded, burst open. They reached and grabbed each other as if they had never touched before. Soon they were naked—she wet with desire, he almost bursting out of his own skin with his erection. Gabriel was almost too excited to stop, but he did. He pushed himself away from her and got up off the couch.

—Let me get a condom.

Bridget grabbed his hand, stopped him from leaving.

—No.

—What are you saying?

—I don't want you to wear a condom.

This excited him so much it felt like his cock, already at maximum length, extended another inch. He got back on the couch, lay on top of her, and after more kissing and fondling, and a slow, gentle push, he was inside of her, as deeply as he could be. He held himself there and looked down at her naked body, not lit pretty with candles or by a fireplace like some Hollywood fantasy, just pure naked passion with ordinary lights, but still beautiful. He began to push himself into her and pull himself out, in and out and in and out. Bridget smiled at him above her, his chest taut, his arms strong and muscular spread beyond her shoulders, holding his upper torso aloft. Gabriel moved his hips and loins into her and as he did she whispered….

—I want your baby.

Gabriel thrust into her as deeply as he could.

—Say it again!

—I want your baby.

—Say it again!

—I want your baby!

He pushed into her, harder and faster.

—Scream it!

—I want your baby! I want your baby! I want your baby!

Gabriel pumped into her again and again and again. Bridget matched his strength and power with her warmth, softness, and inner silkiness. With Gabriel pumping into her, Bridget wrapped her arms around his back and dug her nails deep into his flesh. They made love— in and out and in and out, and in and out and in and out. As he was just about to release Gabriel restrained himself, arching his back and thrusting his hips into her. Bridget screamed with delight as she began to orgasm. She pulled herself to him, and when she came she grabbed him so tightly they spilled off the couch and landed on his back on the hardwood floor. Bridget sat on top of him and began going up and down and up and down, and up and down. As he looked up to her, Gabriel saw Bridget's breasts were rising and falling in opposite rhythm from her hips going up and down and up and down. Bridget let out a deep moan for her second orgasm. Gabriel wrapped his arms around her waist and spun her around so he was on top. From this position, he thrust himself into her, in and out and in and out, and in and out and in and out. Bridget stared into Gabriel's eyes as she began to orgasm again, and as she was coming Gabriel exploded inside of her like a Macy's Fourth of July fireworks celebration.

As they lay together dripping with sweat in blissful happiness, inside Bridget's private and beautiful promised land, a multitude were engaged in the only race that truly matters, the race to conception: they wiggled their little tails and raced up and into her fallopian tubes, hoping and desperately trying to be the one sperm cell that would be embraced and united with an egg.

Nine months later, to Bridget and Gabriel a beautiful baby boy was born—a child they named Upendo, the Swahili word for love.

Fade out.

POSTSCRIPT

Well, there you have it. I hoped you liked it enough to want to watch it again. For those few who haven't seen the film yet, I suggest renting it as soon as you're done reading this. I'm not saying it was perfect. Far from it. But there were some good scenes and some good acting. Of course, there are plenty of things I wish I had done better. But we can't change the past. We can recut films, but as this was the version that went out to the public, I'm going to leave as is.

The editing took nine months, just enough time to allow us to put the finishing touches on the film and have it ready for a theatrical release before the end of the year, which is necessary to be eligible for the Academy Awards. Even though they had agreed to a five-hour film, my producers pressured me to cut as much as possible. The final length was four hours and thirty-eight minutes—still very long for a Hollywood film.

We opened on the second to last weekend of December. Critical reaction was strong from the start, and this started a buzz for the Academy Awards. Among the initial awards we won were a Best Picture award from the New York Film Critics and a Best Director from the Golden Globes. This was a dream come true in many ways, but it was also a nightmare as it threw me into a whirlwind press cycle that I had no desire to be part of. Every day or nearly every day, I was doing interviews: newspapers, magazines, radio, television, I did them all. I wouldn't have minded doing it so much if the questions were relevant to the film, but almost always I was asked about the various stars I was working with. No matter how many times I said I would not answer personal questions I got them anyway. Not all film reviewers were so superficial, of course, but most were.

I think, even if the film didn't have any merits on its own it would have been nominated for Academy Awards simply because of the numerous stars involved. I was grateful that Brian Dennehy won the Oscar for Best Actor. Dennehy allows us to sympathize and perhaps understand a man who has blindly chased the American dream only to lose everything of value in the end. Catherine Zeta-Jones had a different goal with her role. In movies, the leading characters traditionally follow an emotional arc where, by the end of the film, each character is supposed to have learned a valuable lesson. This may be true in movies but sadly, it is often not true in life. Ms. Zeta-Jones understood this and didn't try to portray Claudia Potter with a sympathetic side. She played her as being as ruthless in her desire to capture her own American dream in the end as she was in the beginning. That is why the Academy awarded her the Oscar for Best Actress. Christopher Doyle won for Cinematography because his overwhelming brilliant artistry is evident in every frame he shot.

No one was surprised when the duet with Bob Dylan and Bono won the Best Original Song award for *Mixed Up, Confused, Promised Land Blues*. Their performance of the song at the Academy Awards made many in the audience deliriously happy, and the evening was shaping up to be quite a memorable one. For that reason, I was apprehensive about the Best Original Screenplay Award, the first award I was personally up for. I knew I had a chance to win, and this meant saying a few words to the academy and to the world. The academy doesn't like political speeches. They like and expect you to play the game—to thank the Academy, your spouse and family, your agent, the producers, the actors, and everyone else involved with the film. I did think about doing that, as all those involved with the film—my dedicated and hardworking crew, the actors, producers, Kyle, and Gwendolyn for her patience with me—all deserve thanks. But there were larger issues here. I thought if I did win I would probably never again get the chance to address more than a billion people. Therefore, I questioned whether I should play it safe or not. After all, an Academy Award is an instant payday worth millions. If I won, I knew my financial problems would be solved. I would be able to write and direct virtually any film I wanted—within limit, of course. But if I did do that, if I did play it safe and thank Hollywood, I would be praising an organization I grew up loving but one I had grown to despise.

When my name was called as the winner for Best Original Screenplay, I gave Gwendolyn a big kiss and walked up to the podium to do what I felt I had to do. The co-presenters of the award were Jennifer Jason Leigh and Steve Buscemi. After giving Jennifer a kiss on the cheek, and shaking Steve's hand, I took the Oscar from him and placed it on the edge of the stage. My speech, as most of you know, caused a great deal of controversy, but not everyone remembers exactly what I said, so I have reprinted it here.

Although I greatly appreciate the admiration expressed for my film and for my writing, I cannot accept this award. After thinking long and hard about this, I have decided I cannot be part of a corporate mentality that seeks to trivialize every artistic endeavor, a corporate mentality that seeks to reduce all filmic values to purely financial statements. Although there have been many outstanding films and performances celebrated tonight, these are aberrations and have nothing to do with Hollywood's true aim.

The Academy Awards are a lie.

The Academy Awards give the illusion that those responsible for producing movies care about movies as something other than a merchandizing product, when in reality what is produced here is as disposable and is used for the same purpose as toilet paper. Hollywood movies have one aim today: box-office dominance.

The highest grossing in Hollywood history, Avatar, Titanic, Star Wars, E.T., Transformers, Spiderman, and Forrest Gump are complete and worthless crap with absolutely no redeeming value. These films are the equivalent of McDonald's junk food. They are not junk food for the body, they are junk food for the mind and soul; they are "junk-films." The film Super Size Me showed how sick one becomes from eating a steady supply of McDonald's food. The same is true for the mind: a steady supply of junk-films rots and sickens the mind. These junk-films are what Hollywood sells to the world. Their dominance, both domestic and international, makes it nearly impossible to see valuable films because there is a finite amount of screens available for viewing. When ninety percent of cinemas are devoted to junk-films it is nearly impossible for filmmakers of vision to have their films shown or to find films where genuine and complex human emotions are expressed.

Not only is Hollywood poisoning the minds of Americans with their junk films, Hollywood is poisoning the minds of people around the world. Hollywood dominates every foreign box-office, robbing these countries of their own culture. It also makes Americans believe that the thoughts and emotions expressed in Hollywood films should be embraced by every culture around the world. In my youth, my understanding of the world was enriched by seeing films from France, Italy, Germany, Poland, England, Sweden, Japan, Russia, and many other countries. Filmmakers such as Jean Luc Godard, Francois Truffaut, Federico Fellini, Michelangelo Antonioni, Roman Polanski, Rainer Werner Fassbinder, Werner Herzog, Akira Kurosawa, and Ingmar Bergman were known to just about everyone who saw films on a regular basis. Today, the general public would be hard pressed to name a single foreign film director. This isn't an accident. And it isn't because other countries have stopped making significant films. It is nearly impossible for foreign filmmakers to establish a broad audience by having their films seen in the States because they simply cannot compete against the money and marketing power of corporate Hollywood films.

I realize in saying this, I am kissing goodbye my career as a Hollywood filmmaker. That's okay. Hollywood is practically devoid of

274

*individuals who will stand up for what he or she believes in. Almost
everyone involved with this industry is afraid to risk their million-dollar
paychecks. I have lived long enough in obscurity, relative obscurity, to
have no need or desire for wealth and fame if it comes from renouncing
my beliefs and accepting those of a corporate Hollywood. I don't care
about making millions of dollars. I don't care about being interviewed
for television or magazines or newspapers. I do not care about meeting
celebrities. What I care about is film as an art form. Such thoughts are
no longer valid here.*

*There are people in this room worth ten, twenty, fifty, even
hundreds of millions of dollars. There are even some here worth
billion—hello Steven and George. These people, instead of using their
wealth and the power that comes with it to do something important or
noteworthy, they continue to churn out the same stale and mindless
product. Their desire is not to create meaningful and emotionally
complex films that reflect the growing complexity in our world and our
personal relationships, but to reduce thoughts and expression to the
intellectual level of a sixteen year-old boy, and not a particularly bright
boy at that.*

*Filmmakers have allowed their industry to be taken over by
accountants and bookkeepers. By accepting this award, I would have to
agree to that arrangement. In good faith, I cannot do so. I have too
much respect for the great filmmakers who came before me to surrender
to those who are making every effort to destroy the greatest art form
ever invented: film. Therefore, not only will I not accept this award, I
am resigning my membership from the Academy. Thank you, and good
night.*

As I was speaking, I noticed Jack Nicholson in the front row
wearing his trademark sunglasses and grinning from ear to ear. Since he
found my speech so amusing, I decided to send him my Oscar. I took
one last look at the little golden man standing on the edge of the stage
before taking two quick steps and booting it in the Joker's direction.
Jack reached up for it but it was too high. It hit the tips of his fingers and
went behind him, bouncing off the head of Woody Allen who was
sitting in his usual seat in the middle of the second row. Sorry Woody. I
felt bad that he was cut and bled all over his very funny muse seated
next to him, Scarlett Johansson, and that he had to be rushed to the
hospital, but I am happy he never sued me.

My cell phone vibrated as soon as I stepped off the stage. Kyle
wanted to know if I had lost my mind. I didn't want to deal with him so
I hung up. Instead of doing the backroom interviews that every award

winner is expected to do, I left the Shrine Auditorium. A moment later, Gwendolyn called. She was surprised by what I said, but pleasantly so. She asked me where to meet. Like everyone else, I had a limousine for the night. I told Gwen to come outside. Once she did, she gave me a big kiss. We jumped into the limo and I asked our driver take us to a local bar where they would be showing the ceremony. The driver had been watching the ceremony on the limousine's television and said he knew the perfect place for us.

Once we arrived, the driver came inside with us and introduced us to the bartender and his friends who greeted me like Mickey Rourke at the end of *Barfly*. I wanted to get drunk, but Gwendolyn didn't want to drink at all, which was disappointing because I wanted to celebrate. For more than a month she had been on some new health kick where she wouldn't drink at all. I bought myself a shot and a beer and we turned to the television set up in the corner of the bar. When *The Promised Land* won for Best Director there were many boos heard on screen, but in the bar the patrons roared with approval. Undoubtedly, many academy members wouldn't have voted for the film if they knew what I was going to say. When we won Best Picture there were more boos from the television, but I didn't care. I was with the woman I loved, and I had said what I wanted to say.

When the ceremony ended, Gwendolyn and I moved away from the bar and settled in at a corner table. We just wanted to relax and enjoy ourselves. Unfortunately, someone told the press where I was, and before long photographers and reporters descended upon the bar. I didn't want to answer any questions so I had our driver take us back to our bungalow at the Beverly Hills Hotel. There were numerous messages. Half a dozen were from Kyle demanding I call him back, others were from various press people. There were also a number of messages from friends and some of the actors from *The Promised Land*. The actors were mostly supportive of what I said, and there were many who implored me to attend the various parties. Although there were plenty of people I would have liked to see, I didn't want to spend the night explaining my action, or more accurately, my words. The truth is, I was always happy when I was with Gwendolyn and I didn't want to share my time with her with anyone else. I also didn't have any desire to be part of the pyrotechnics that surround any awards ceremony. We also hadn't been able to spend much time together lately, due to my press commitments for the film, so we locked ourselves away from the world and got into bed.

The next morning, Kyle knocked on our door at 7 AM. Although he was pissed off about what I had done, he said every network, and all the various talk shows, wanted to book me. After all, how many Academy Award-winning filmmakers had denounced the academy from the stage? I almost gave him a heart attack when I told him I wasn't going to do any press. He said I was committing career suicide (as if I hadn't done so already). My declining to do any press started the paparazzi feeding frenzy.

A few hours later, when we came out of the Bel-Air to head back to New York, the paparazzi were waiting. I had rented a brand new red Mustang. Gwendolyn and I hopped in and sped off. Five press cars and a motorcycle followed us trying to get photos. In an effort to lose them, we got on and off the highway. We were going well over 100 mph at times, but still we couldn't shake them. Finally, I gave up, drove to LAX and allowed them to photograph us, but I didn't answer any questions.

As soon as we landed at Kennedy Airport, we were besieged by more paparazzi. Again I refused to speak to anyone; nonetheless, they followed us all the way into the city. From that day forward they continued to hound me. They would wait outside our apartment building and try to get a photo or two if I stepped outside. At first Gwendolyn and I tried to pretend they were not there when we went out, but it's very difficult to feel comfortable with paparazzi photographing you every time you stepped out of your house, even if it was just to go to the bodega to get the morning paper. Doing something more public, like going to dinner, or to music clubs, became virtually impossible.

There was also another reason for concern. When we arrived back home from California, Gwendolyn told me the real reason she hadn't been drinking: she was pregnant. This seemed almost too good to be true, but it was. She hadn't told me sooner because she didn't want me to worry about a pregnant wife, or the possibility of a baby, with all the pressure of the Academy Awards. In the beginning of January, Gwendolyn missed her period. At first she thought she was late and didn't give it much thought beyond that. After eight weeks without having a period she began to suspect something was up. Without telling me, she went out and bought one of those home pregnancy tests. She was in a state of disbelief when it came back positive. She tested herself every couple of days over the next two weeks and then went to her doctor who told her she was indeed pregnant. She kept her secret for two months. I had never asked her what happened during her abortion in France because I didn't think she wanted to relive the ordeal any more than she already had. She had told me that her French doctor said could no longer have kids and I accepted this fact. Apparently, her body had found a way to heal itself.

A few weeks later, we had an ultrasound done and we found out the baby was going to be a boy. Since we met on Martha's Vineyard and spent so much time there, we wanted to have the baby's name reflect the island. Gwendolyn toyed with a number of different names, among them were Tisbury, Aquinnah, and Quiddick, short for Chappaquiddick, but even in these pretentious baby-naming times, those names sounded ridiculous to me. I decided to go to the source. It is generally believed an English explorer, Bartholomew Gosnold, discovered the island in 1602 and named it after his daughter, Martha. Consequently, we decided to call our son Bartholomew, Bartholomew Gosnold McManus, which has a nice ring to it, doesn't it?

After the Academy Awards, I continued to receive numerous requests for interviews from the press, but I ignored them all. I did, however, respond to many of the universities and colleges that asked me to talk with their students. As I'm a lifelong New Yorker, I went to New York University first, and after to Columbia University and City University, and finally to the New School. There were members of the press who tried to sneak into my first talk, so I made it a contract stipulation that only students would be allowed in the lecture halls. I also told the professors and students that I would only talk about my films or other films, and I would not talk about my Academy Awards speech or indulge in any celebrity gossip. I told the students, I believe actors desire and deserve private lives. Actors share and give of themselves through their work. I do not think we have to right to ask for more. If they want to share more—and plenty do—then that's their prerogative, but those who do not want to share their personal lives should be left alone. I also believe the more we know of an actor's personal life, the less effective the actor is on screen.

By the time I arrived at the Cannes Film Festival in May, many European filmmakers were eager to meet me because they were happy an American filmmaker had finally publicly acknowledged how Hollywood and America tried to bullyingly dominate world culture. Unfortunately, paparazzi in Europe are as relentless as those in the States. It was, after all, Federico Fellini who created the first of the breed, Paparazzo, in his film *La Dolce Vita*. Many Europeans expected me to make another big speech, to say something about corporate America or American imperialism. I had no desire to do so. European history is much longer and bloodier than America's, and almost every European power has a history of dominating or trying to dominate other countries.

When I won the Golden Palm I said two words. "Thank you." I

didn't say more because I was tired of the press' scrutiny and felt the less I said, the fewer questions would be asked. I was immensely grateful that we had won, but I hated everything that went along with winning. I hadn't realized the Faustian bargain of giving up one's soul for fortune and fame had changed. Now, in addition to losing my soul, I was supposed to surrender every aspect of my personal life to the public.

When we returned from Europe, we went to the Vineyard for the summer. Although I started work on a new screenplay, I wanted to be with Gwendolyn and wanted to enjoy the summer sunshine. Many of the up-island beaches are clothing optional but they are not as free and open as they once were. To avoid the eyes of the ever-present press, Gwendolyn and I had found a secluded spot up in Gay Head not too far from where Jacqueline Onassis used to live. It was very private, and it was quite delightful for it to be just the two of us. Gwendolyn's stomach had expanded by this time and her face emanated radiance and joy. It was quite pleasing for me to see her swimming nude in all her pregnant glory. Unfortunately, we soon found out we weren't alone. Some paparazzo with an extremely long telephoto lens had somehow followed us and snapped photos of us swimming and sunning ourselves in the buff. The photos were sold to various tabloid magazines. Gwendolyn was quickly dubbed "Gorgeous Gwen", and when the two of us were together we were referred to as "Blaskdolyn." Adding insult to injury, Gwendolyn began getting solicitations from various T&A magazines like *Maxim, Stuff,* and *Playboy*, asking if she would pose for them after she had the baby. I was even asked to do some shilling myself. The Gap wanted me to be in one of their ads, as did American Express. Did I look that desperate? Did they think I had no integrity at all?

When the school started up in September, I started touring campuses again and talking with students. A few weeks later, on October 21, Bartholomew Gosnold McManus was born. Two days later, we brought the little lump of love home with us from the hospital. Certainly, this was the happiest day of my life. His arrival made my years of struggle, the years of uncertainty, the years of failure and rejection worth it. I had missed out on fatherhood the first time around, but I wasn't going to let that happen a second time. Not only was I a new father, I had a beautiful, intelligent, and successful wife, and I had become what I always wanted: a successful and respected film director.

For Christmas, Gwendolyn wanted to visit her parents and siblings to show off our new baby. With a young child, we didn't want to fly, so we rented a Lexus. I picked up the rental and drove back to our building to get Gwen and young Bartholomew, and to load in our bags and presents for Gwen's nieces and nephews. It seemed impossible to believe, but as soon as we began packing up, a BMW with a paparazzo and driver, pulled up next to us. The paparazzo immediately started snapping photos of us. I figured once we drove away he would leave us alone, but I was wrong. We were followed. Here it was Christmas Eve, it was snowing, and we still couldn't catch a break. Gwendolyn thought they wanted to capture us wherever we were having Christmas as the seasonal photo with Bartholomew would be worth more than a regular photo. We went through the toll booth at the tip of Manhattan only to get stuck in traffic in the Bronx. I had to bide my time until the Henry Hudson Parkway turned into the Saw Mill Parkway. When it did, I wove in and out of traffic like a suburban dad pretending to be a stunt driver, which meant that when the speedometer pushed past seventy miles per hour, Gwendolyn started screaming at me to slow down. We did, after all, have Bartholomew strapped into the back seat. When we veered onto the Cross County Parkway, I eased up on the gas. This is just what the paparazzo was waiting for. The BMW raced up to our car and, in an effort to get closer to snap a photo, they banged my back bumper and we were knocked onto a long patch of black ice on the edge of the traffic lane. We slid toward the guardrail and...

My daughter Lily was sitting by the bedside when I opened my eyes. My head was bandaged and my ribs were throbbing with pain. Everything felt very foggy. I asked Lily what happened. Tears formed in the corner of her eyes and she said I had been in an accident. I don't why, but I tried to get up. I couldn't. My body was too weak. Lily called for the nurse who came in, took one look, and called the doctor. The female doctor told me I had been in a coma for three days. She asked how I was feeling. I didn't answer her. She asked me if I remembered what happened. The last thing I remembered was being bumped by the paparazzo. Lily took my hand and told me that my car hit a guardrail and flipped over twice. The car was completely totaled and in the process Gwendolyn and Bartholomew had been killed.

I won't go through all of what I thought or felt. Words can never adequately express what anyone feels toward losing those they have loved and lost, so I won't even try. I have, however, left the last page blank in memory of Gwendolyn Sangeeny and our son Bartholomew Gosnold, the two people who meant more to me than my own life.

Gwendolyn's parents, not knowing if I would recover from my injuries or whether or not I would come out of my coma went ahead with the funeral arrangements and buried Gwendolyn and Bartholomew side by side in her home town of Wellesley. Not being there for the funeral made everything even more mentally painful. Gwendolyn and Bartholomew were with me one minute and the next they were dead and I was in a coma. Since my car was totaled in the wreck, there was no way to prove I was hit or bumped by the paparazzo's car. No charges were ever filed against him. What was sick, even by paparazzi and tabloid standards, was the photos of the crash published in various magazines. No doubt these were taken by the same person who caused the crash that killed Gwendolyn and Bartholomew. To what circle in Hell would Dante assign paparazzi?

Although I could have probably used another week in the hospital, my insurance company wouldn't go for that, so after two days of recovering from my coma I was kicked out. I left the hospital in the care of my daughter, Lily. We went to the Vineyard. Lily did her best to take care of me, but after two weeks I asked her to go. I was too sad and depressed to have to face anyone. She realized this, felt it was very unhealthy for me to be alone, but I told her to leave anyway. I couldn't stop thinking I had killed my wife and child and I could barely face myself. I thought if I hadn't denounced Hollywood none of this would have happened. And then I thought it would have happened no matter what I said because once you're famous the press will not leave you alone. I hated the paparazzi but also realized they were only pawns in the game. They were paid to do what they did because the giant media companies had created a market for celebrity culture. The media companies say they are only giving people what they want, which is an obvious lie. Creating a demand that would not normally exist is what advertising is all about. Knowing that, I was glad to have said what I said about Hollywood—at least part of the time. I was also filled with self-doubt. Who did I think I was to tell everyone in Hollywood they were frauds? That all they cared about was money? Even creating formulaic drivel isn't easy, and many of the movies I hated had very talented people involved, people who I respected. Why did I feel so deeply that I couldn't hold my tongue? I could have been a wealthy man living a fabulous life of conspicuous consumption. Why did I ruin my life by speaking up?

On the Vineyard, I had a number of people call me but I wouldn't talk with them. The only person I let in the house was my young friend and driver, Leslie, because she was bringing me heroin. After a few weeks she said she would no longer get it for me because each time I was asking for larger and larger amounts, and she thought I was trying to kill myself. She was probably right. Kyle called a number of times but I wouldn't talk with him either. Finally, he flew up to the Vineyard to see me. He told me the president of the Cannes Film Festival wanted me to head the jury for the next festival. I thought about it but said no. Kyle tried to sweeten the deal by saying I could stay at his condo in Rapallo before and after the Festival. He said this would allow me to clear my head and get a fresh perspective about life. I told him I would think about it. A few days later George Clooney, who played Connor Gazelle, called. He said he heard about me heading the Cannes jury. He invited me to his house in Lake Como where he and Steven Soderbergh were spending a week prior to Cannes. I did know I had to get away from myself or I would end up dead, so I told George I would call him from Rapallo.

In Rapallo, instead of feeling better, I felt worse. I had stayed in the condo with Alexia and didn't want to think about being there with her when my mind was filled with thoughts of Gwendolyn and Bartholomew. I had a rental car so I drove up to Hotel Splendido, which is situated high above the picture postcard seaside village of Portofino, and is one of the most beautiful and luxurious hotels in the world. Even though I had made some money from *The Promised Land,* it was still too expensive for my budget, but I went anyway. I wasn't concerned with money or my future. Knowing it was the off-season, I knew it would be at least partially empty so I could eat and drink here in relative peace without, I hoped, the prying eyes of the press. I spent six days eating very little but drinking a good deal of wine as I gazed out at the Mediterranean Sea from the balcony of my suite or from the terrace restaurant. The air was cool and most of the few people who were there dined indoors, which was fine for me, as it left me alone. On my seventh day, I was sitting on the terrace when I heard a very sexy, accented voice say, "Blasket?" I turned to see Isabella Rossellini. I was embarrassed to see her because I had been thinking about Gwendolyn and there were tears in my eyes. I wiped them away and asked her to join me. We had met years earlier and would run into each other from time to time at various events in New York. I invited her to sit down. When the waiter came over I order another bottle of wine. She said she didn't want any wine, but I told the waiter to get the bottle anyway, I'd drink it myself. I think she could tell I was already rather inebriated, so after twenty minutes or so she left and went back to her room.

Isabella was surprised to find me the next afternoon back out on the terrace with another bottle of wine—I hadn't actually gone to bed. Again, I asked her to join me. This time she had a glass of wine. Before we knew it, a paparazzo had showed up and snapped a few photos of us together. These were the ones that made the papers and magazines and started the rumors that we were having an affair. There was absolutely nothing going on between us, but any time a famous man and woman have dinner or drinks together the press feels the need to say they are having an affair, as if two intelligent people cannot sit and talk without there being some sort of sexual element involved. Isabella knew what I had been through. She was just trying to help, and to get me to ease up on the booze. I had no desire to do so. I told her I was supposed to be in Lake Como two nights ago but just couldn't find the desire to go. I had to be in Cannes a day later, but had no desire to go there either. Unfortunately, in my drunkenness the previous evening, I had called Clooney and told him I would meet the following evening, that night, for dinner. My plan was to have dinner with George and Steven and get up early and drive to Cannes, about a five hour drive. I could have flown in a private jet with them, but I thought the driving would help me unwind and get my head together before I faced the onslaught of Cannes. With my gloom and depression, I told George I didn't want to stay at his house because I didn't want to face other people. I booked a room at Villa d'Este, the famous luxury resort hotel on Lake Como. This was okay with him as this is where he planned to have our dinner that night. He said he thought President Napolitano of Italy, another friend of his, would join us, but he wouldn't be sure until later in the day.

Isabella thought I was too drunk to drive up to Lake Como. She was right. I was drowning myself in drink and didn't care if I lived or died. I told her I was going to drive anyway. That's when she told me the dinner I was supposed to have with George and Steven wasn't just a casual meal with the three of us. She said Kyle and George had invited a number of friends who I had known over the years. Most of these people were going to Cannes as well. The dinner was supposed to be a surprise. Isabella said I was going to ruin the surprise if I drove drunk and killed myself or someone else. That was the reason she had come to Hotel Splendido. When Kyle couldn't contact me at his condo in Rapallo, he suspected, because of my depression, I might be on a suicidal bender. He began calling around to the various hotels and found out I was at the Splendido. He called George to see what he thought they should do. George called Isabella, because he knew we knew each other. Isabella, who was also going to Cannes, hired a driver to take her down to Portofino so she could talk with me, and hopefully, bring me back for the dinner at Villa d'Este. Since everyone had apparently put a great deal of effort into having the dinner, and because so many people had helped me with my film, I agreed to let Isabella drive my rental car to Lake Como.

I took two bottles of wine from the restaurant with us for the ride and was extremely intoxicated by the time we got there. Since many famous people stay at Villa d'Este, it wasn't a surprise to be greeted with the flash of a paparazzo's camera when we stepped out of our car. Normally, I would have been angry, but at that point I was too gone to care. When we went to the front desk to get our room keys, I was told a package had arrived for me. I had sent it myself. By watching "*Drugstore Cowboy,*" I learned about avoiding getting caught with drugs while traveling by having the drugs mailed to the addresses where I was going to be staying.

After showering and dressing for dinner, I sipped a Jameson and soda. As I sat there on the bed I fell into a deep depression. What was I going to dinner with a bunch of movie stars with Gwendolyn and Bartholomew dead? I realized I hated movie stars. I hated politicians. And, most of all I hated what I had become. I downed the drink and opened the package. I spilled some of the methadrine crystals on the top of the bureau and snorted two huge lines. My nostril stung but the quick rush the drug brought felt good. I told myself I just needed to get through the next few days and I would be all right. I said that to myself and a moment later I told myself I should just get on an airplane and fly back to New York. Before I could decide what to do there was a knock on the door. I didn't answer right away. I heard Isabella gently called my name. I opened the door and since I had burdened Isabella with my depression on our ride from Portofino, I told her I didn't think I should have dinner. I told her I was going to return to New York. She grabbed my hand and dragged me toward the dining area.

George had secured a private room, the double doors of which were closed. I felt that this was a sign that I shouldn't be dining with anyone. I turned to go. Isabella grabbed my hand again and pushed open the doors. Inside were many of the cast and crew from *The Promised Land,* along with their various girlfriends, boyfriends, or spouses. The President of Italy, Giorgio Napolitano, was also there. Everyone clapped and cheered when I came in. Although this was a generous gesture on everyone's part, it was the last thing I wanted. The methadrine had wired me and made me paranoid. I had done too much and now I was speeding my head off. After saying hello to George, Steven, and Kyle, and being introduced to President Napolitano, I needed a drink before I talked to anyone else. I grabbed Isabella's hand and walked toward the small bar to get us drinks. As soon as my back was turned I heard President Napolitano say, "It didn't take him long to find someone else, did it?" This made me snap. Isabella couldn't have been nicer to me. There was absolutely nothing untoward between us. I couldn't even think of another woman or sex. I spun around to the president and said "Who the fuck do you think you are?" Clooney quickly stepped between us. I punched him in his handsome jaw and he crashed into a dinner table breaking glasses and knocking over an open bottle of wine. Soderbergh came over and tried to hush me, but I wasn't having any of it. I used a karate kick to his chest to send him flying into Clooney who had just stood back up. A second later, two security men jumped in front of the President. A third security man grabbed me by the neck. I couldn't physically attack, but I still had my tongue. I called the President a stupid fascist pig! President Napolitano stared at me in disbelief, so I said "Your fascist father sucked the communist cock of Mussolini!" I spit at his feet. The security men grabbed and wrestled me to the floor, where they quickly handcuffed me.

As it was a private dinner thrown in my honor, President Napolitano decided not to have me arrested. Instead of being taken to jail, I was taken by the president's security men back to my hotel room where I was told to "get some sleep." Clearly, they understood it was because of the booze and because I was distraught about losing my wife and child. I did want to sleep but I couldn't because I had snorted too much methadrine. My mind was still quite addled so I attempted to leave my room, only to find two security men had been posted outside to make sure I remained. After getting in bed and trying to sleep didn't work, I redressed myself, packed my bags, dropped them quietly from my second-story window and climbed out the window, dropping to the soft grass below. It was so quick and easy I felt like 007, James Bond. I picked up my bags, walked around to the front of the hotel and surprised the paparazzo that was outside. He had heard about what I said to President Napolitano and asked me if it was true. I said, "Yes, Italy is filled with cocksuckers and whores, that's why they elected Napolitano." I guess he was a bit stunned at this because when I jumped into my car I wasn't followed.

Don't ask me why I said this. I was drunk and high. It wasn't really the President of Italy who I was insulting. I wanted to insult the world. At that point, I hated the world because of what had happened to my wife and child and I was looking for an excuse to let myself go. As I drove the dark streets along Lake Como I started to realize that President Napolitano might not have said anything. With the drugs inside my muddled mind, I might have just imagined him insulting me. I started screaming at myself: *What have I done! What have I done! What have I done!* I was really starting to lose my mind and tears were streaming down my face. I really didn't know what to do. I pulled over and thought about going back to Lake Como. I wanted to apologize to President Napolitano. I wanted to apologize to George and Steven, who had been so supportive of me since the beginning. I wanted to apologize to Kyle. I wanted to apologize to everyone at Villa d'Este, even the paparazzo. I wanted to apologize most to Isabella Rossellini. After all she did to try to help me I embarrassed her. I made a complete fool out of myself and I didn't even say goodbye. Not knowing what to do, I snorted some more methadrine. I knew this was wrong but it made me feel good. It made me feel great. I was soaring on the meth and knew everything would be all right once I got to Cannes. I got back on the road and started driving.

A few hours later, I was close to France. Not wanting to cross the border carrying the methadrine, I snorted four or five huge lines and threw the rest out the window. I wasn't worried about being out of methadrine because I had also sent a package to my hotel in Cannes. After my first trip, I had learned my lesson not to stay in the heart of Cannes during the festival. With my win the year before, I was deemed worthy of a suite at the Hotel Du Cap Eden Roc in Antibes, a short drive to the Croisette and the Palais des Festival. By the time I got there it was about 3 AM. I was so obliterated that they almost didn't let me in, but the general manager overruled the front desk staff. I was given the package that was awaiting me and showed to my suite. I wanted to sleep but couldn't because of my drug intake. I knew I needed to come down so I summoned my butler—in this hotel, all of the better suites were given private butlers—and told him to bring me a bottle of Napa Valley cabernet. I figured I shouldn't drink Jameson because it would give me a hangover and I had to meet with other members of the jury.

Horribly depressed and lonely, I started snorting line after line of methadrine and drinking my wine. Before I knew it, sunlight was bleeding through my hotel windows. I knew I needed to get some sleep before the evening's ceremony, so I tossed the empty bottle of wine away and threw some water on my face. I left my suite to go for a long walk to tire myself enough so that I would be able take a long snooze when I returned. But that didn't happen.

As I wrote in the beginning of this long justification of my life: "I only took a few steps outside the Hotel Du Cap's grounds when I knew it would be futile to try to go anywhere, as there were hundreds of bloodsucking paparazzi waiting for me like vultures after a slaughter."

As stated, I was out of my mind when I attacked President Napolitano and President Sarkozy. I freely admit that this was both foolish and wrong. But in no way should I have been deported to Bellevue Psychiatric Ward. The doctors in here are trying to tell me I am a danger to society. This is ludicrous. I realize now that our government is trying to censor me, censor my valuable work.

Governmental censorship is nothing new. Governments have been silencing, or trying to silence, great minds for decades, centuries, from the beginning of time, really. Look what happened to Socrates for telling the truth: he was forced to commit suicide by drinking Hemlock. Look at Galileo: it wasn't until 1992, 1992!, that the Vatican finally, begrudgingly, admitted that Pope Urban VIII was wrong, and that Galileo's defense of Copernicus was correct—that the Earth isn't the center of the universe. Look at the terrifying visions of Franz Kafka and George Orwell. For years, decades, they were both seen as paranoid crackpots. But the worlds of Joseph K and Big Brother are the worlds we are living in today.

The psychiatrist who is treating me wants me to sign a written document stating I never made *The Promised Land*. But if I didn't make it, who did? The psychiatrist is using all types of mind games to convince me no one made the film. That it does not exist. If I were free, I would return to my apartment and grab my copy of the film. If I were free to use the internet, I would find a copy online. If I couldn't find one, if you can't find one, it is only because the government has already confiscated all of the available copies. Isn't this what happened in Orwell's *1984?* The government simply erases history books and factual documents so their version of the "truth" becomes the official one. Only with me, it's not fiction. It's real.

About a month ago…or perhaps two, it is difficult to tell just how long it has been, how long I have been in here. Maybe it was a year ago, maybe longer. Anyway, I thought the doctors were finally going to let me go free. I thought they were finally going to make a public apology. Instead, they came up with another plan. They had a psychiatrist sent up from the Walter Reed Medical Center in Washington. Supposedly, this man is the top psychiatrist in the nation. If my life were a movie, this psychiatrist would be played by William Hurt because he's so good at playing characters with a smug, arrogant air. The smug, arrogant doctor came in holding a copy of William Styron's memoir on depression, *Darkness Visible*, telling me he had read it on the train ride up from Washington. He wanted to know if I had ever read it. I didn't even bother responding to this idiotic question. I told him I wasn't crazy and wasn't going to pretend to be just to please him. He asked me to what it meant to be crazy. Again, I told him I was not crazy. The psychiatrist asked me to envision a scenario with a crazy person. What would that be like, he said? I told him I didn't want to play his stupid mind games. The psychiatrist said if I ever wanted to go free I had to convince him I was sane. He said, go ahead, you have a vivid imagination, create a scenario that would not be possible, a scenario that illustrates insanity. This way he would be able to compare my visions of sanity and insanity.

I said, "Imagine a world where there are men and women who are willing to strap explosives to their bodies and walk into a crowded street to detonate the explosives in the hope of killing as many innocent people as possible simply because those people do not believe in the same god or hold the same religious or political convictions."

The psychiatrist said that would never happen.

I said, "Imagine that there are people in the most powerful and wealthiest nation in the world who advocate dropping atomic bombs on a Middle Eastern country so that the few survivors can be converted to Catholicism and capitalism."

The psychiatrist said that would never happen.

I said, "Imagine a world with more than a billion people who are starving or nearly starving, people who are living on a dollar or two a day. Imagine people who do not have indoor toilets or even electricity. Imagine people whose children are forced to play in refuse piles and streams of piss and excrement. Imagine these same people are forced to look for food for their families in garbage dumps. And imagine there are individuals with a billion dollars, or five, or ten, or twenty, or thirty, or forty, or fifty billion dollars. Imagine these billionaires, instead of helping the suffering and unfortunate, they strive to hoard more and more money so they can have their name moved to a higher spot in a magazine that celebrates the top 500 greediest individuals in the world instead of denouncing them."

The psychiatrist said that would never happen.

I said, "Imagine that after the incomprehensible genocide of World War II all the nations of the world uniting and creating a governing body whose purpose was to protect the innocent people of the world, and to make sure genocide never happened again. And imagine these united nations having security forces all around the world. And imagine the leaders of these united nations refusing to do anything to stop the genocide in Rwanda, Bosnia, Darfur, and other countries because those being slaughtered did not have white skin, or were poor, or because there was no money to be made by offering assistance to these countries."

The psychiatrist said that would never happen.

I said, "Imagine a nation created out of the horrors of World War II because their people had been singled out and persecuted because of their ethnicity, a people whose houses and land and valuables were stolen from them. Imagine before these people were exterminated in death camps they were walled inside crowded and filthy ghettoes, ghettoes where they could not work or travel freely, ghettoes where they would be shot on sight, if they dared to step outside its boundaries. And imagine the descendants and relatives of these people, in this new nation, singling out and persecuting another group of people because of *their* ethnicity. Imagine these descendants and relatives having the audacity to take the others' land and houses and have them walled inside filthy and crowded compounds where they could not work or travel freely, where they would be shot on sight if they dared to use the same roads as the other group of people. And imagine the most powerful nation in the world giving billions of dollars worth of weapons to those that enwalled the others, so that those weapons could be used against those inside the enclosed compounds, or anyone else who dared to help or support them."

The psychiatrist said that would never happen.

I said, "Imagine a world where a man can mastermind a plan where his followers fly planes into American buildings killing thousands and, directly after this, the leader of the attacked country saying it isn't

290

important to go after the man responsible for the death and destruction. Instead the leader of the country blames and then starts a war with another country because that country had oil and he wanted it. And imagine thousands of young Americans being sent to the oil-bearing country and killed, and tens of thousands of Americans wounded and maimed in battle, and hundreds of thousands of innocent foreign civilians killed and wounded because of this leader's blood-lust for oil."

The psychiatrist said that would never happen.

I said, "Imagine a country where the richest 1% own more than the bottom 90% combined, and imagine that country is ruled by politicians and lawmakers who have been put in power by the largest and wealthiest corporations in order to do the bidding of these mammoth corporations, and imagine that country believes itself to be a democracy."

The psychiatrist said that would never happen.

I said, "Imagine a country that spends more money locking up African Americans than it does on secondary education for African Americans, and imagine that country believes its justice system isn't racially motivated.

The psychiatrist said that would never happen.

I said, "Imagine that same country selling more weaponry and arms than any country in the world, selling weaponry and arms to almost any country willing to pay, and imagine those countries using the weaponry to slaughter their own citizens or the citizens in neighboring countries, or the citizens of the country who sold them the weapons, slaughtering millions around the world, and imagine the selling country saying it is a peaceful nation whose moral authority should never be questioned."

The psychiatrist said that would never happen.

I ask you, dear reader, am I insane? Or is the world from which I've been exiled insane?

The doctor said my scenarios show I do not understand how the world works. This makes me a danger to civil society and the general public. He said that if I do not admit I am not a filmmaker and have never made any films, including *The Promised Land,* he will be forced to give me a lobotomy.

I will never admit I am not a filmmaker! I beg of you, please, do not allow them to give me a lobotomy!

If you believe in me, and if you want to help me get out of this place, out of this madhouse, this insane asylum, I want you to make stickers, placards, banners and t-shirts that say Free Blasket McManus! I want you to tattoo your heads and arms and necks and chests with tattoos that say Free Blasket McManus! I want you to get together with

291

your families and friends and I want you to put the t-shirts on and I want you to come to Bellevue Hospital. I want you to march in front of the gates that they've used to lock me away, I want you outside the gates and I want you to make your right hand into a militant fist and I want you to raise your fist above your head like the Black Panthers used to do. I want you to pump that fist high into to the air, and I want you to shout at the top of your lungs, FREE BLASKET MCMANUS! FREE BLASKET MCMANUS! FREE BLASKET MCMANUS! I want you to continue shouting FREE BLASKET MCMANUS! FREE BLASKET MCMANUS! FREE BLASKET MCMANUS! until they let me out of here! Stand up now and say it! Shout it at the tops of your lungs: FREE BLASKET MCMANUS! FREE BLASKET MCMANUS! FREE BLASKET MCMANUS!

www.ingramcontent.com/pod-product-compliance
Lightning Source LLC
Chambersburg PA
CBHW021503240626
47154CB00002B/484